The Eighty-Five-Percenters

an FFSG novel

Bill Dughaille

Forethoughts

"'This time I'm going to get you, Frank Summers.'"

The thought fluttered into surprised existence, tested its new wings and found it rather enjoyed being around. It wasn't sure who this Frank Summers was, but that was going to be his problem. For the moment it would hang around with its creator and see what happened.

'You know, I don't think I have an enemy in the world,' Frank Summers told Eric Johns happily.

'No, but some of your friends make up for that,' Eric replied.

Contents

Week One: The Wave

Monday: A prophet speaks

Wellbury was not the sort of town that did traffic jams. Not naturally. They sounded rather vulgar. French and Italian restaurants, even bistros, yes, these obviously had some style. Swedish au-pairs, perfectly reasonable if you could afford them. Spanish flamenco dancing? Well, if you absolutely had to, but preferably in private and keep the wailing down.

But traffic jams? They sounded rather suspiciously American. Something they might consider amusement in Texas, Florida, or whatever they called that little state towards the bottom on the left.

It had, however, reached the point where it seemed every other town in Europe had the things, and, by what appeared to be a collective and unconscious agreement, traffic jams had appeared. But only twice a week. Monday morning and Friday afternoon. And for no more than fifteen minutes. You could have too much of a good thing.

Having decided to indulge themselves, they went the full hog and added the attraction of an inane local radio show they could fulminate against while they sat in their idling cars. Zack Kerouac – Zack the Man, as he called himself, just in case someone might mistakenly think they were listening to something like a penguin or porcupine called Zack – had restyled himself from disk jockey to news presenter. He was the type of person the worthies of Wellbury spent much time deliberately not inviting to prominent events.

'This morning we welcome Professor Jonathon Humphries,' Zack the Man was saying, 'the author of one of the most

1

controversial theories of our time, brought to you exclusively by Radio Pithead, straight after this short commercial break.'

'Five quid says it's something to do with butterflies,' Detective Sergeant Frank Summers said, sitting at the wheel of his car in the Monday morning fifteen minute traffic jam, listening to an advert extolling the joys of a new type of original Greek yoghurt.

'Why butterflies?' asked Acting Detective Constable Samantha Gregson, aka Giggling Gertie, drumming her fingers on the windowsill. Behind a pair of reflective sunglasses she had been trying to work out whether she was in a good or bad mood. On the negative side she had come home to her flat the previous afternoon to find that the flat above had sprung a leak, and hers was now effectively uninhabitable. On the positive side Frank, when she had called him, had been very sympathetic and had insisted that she stay with him until repairs could be made.

On the further negative side he had not made a single pass at her.

One of the good things about Frank was that he often acted like an old-fashioned gentleman who would never take advantage.

One of the bad things about Frank was exactly the same point. She had been praying for that pass.

Well, it was going to happen, even if she had to be the one who did it.

There was a time when she had decided that she definitely didn't want to go out with Frank Summers. She had since changed her mind. Seventeen times. That morning.

'Global warming,' Frank said, interrupting her thoughts.

'Everything's global warming these days. Even now, when it should be spring, the sun is shining merrily down on us and yet it's flipping freezing. And, due to some scientific magic which we mortal humans can never understand, it's all down to global warming. We're all going to freeze to death because of global warming. And it's all to do with butterflies and chaos theory.'

'I thought that was drowning.'

'Eh?'

'Drowning. The ice caps are going to melt, we're all going to drown, and the dolphins will swim through the Houses of Parliament.'

'Laughing themselves sick at the sight, no doubt. But there you go, you've done it again.'

'Done what?'

'See? I propose a bet, and the next thing you're talking about fish swimming through London. Come on, five quid, yes or no. Butterflies.'

'Dolphins aren't fish. They're mammals.'

Frank sighed and hit his head against the steering wheel in mock frustration, accidentally sounding the hooter. The driver stuck in front, a well dressed business-woman with two obnoxious children fighting in the back of a four wheel drive, showed him a finger.

The two children paused long enough to do the same.

'Toffee nosed bitch,' said Gertie angrily, 'who does she think she is? People like that should be locked up. They don't deserve to be allowed into civilised society. Tell you what, let's arrest her, making offensive gestures in public. What's that called again? Public disorder offence?'

'Normal, I think. These days, anyway.'

'Sod her. Thinks because she's rich enough to drive a four-wheel drive with extra large bull-bar and two snotty kids in the back she can be rude to the rest of us. I'm going to give her a piece of my mind.'

'Gertie, now – '

It was too late. Gertie was already out of the car and on her way. Frank watched as she showed the other woman her police ID, and took out her notebook to take down her details before giving her, presumably, a lecture on manners and the inadvisability of being rude to plain-clothes police officers. Only the fact that the traffic began to slowly move forced her to limit the lecture. She came back to the car with a smile on her face.

'Happy?' asked Frank

'Happier. It's so nice when you feel you're making a contribution to society. In future she'll think twice before showing total strangers any rude gestures.'

'Just shows you the advantages of having women policemen,' Frank mused, 'if I tried that she'd have shown me two fingers and told me to get lost.'

'That's a sexist remark. Even if it is true. Anyway, was it butterflies?'

'Butterflies?'

'Professor Higgins. On the radio.'

'Professor Humphries, wasn't it? I don't know, though. I must have missed it while watching you. You have no idea how sexy you look when giving another woman a bollocking.

Now the adverts are on again.'

'Really?'

'Yes, listen. Organic filing cabinets. Save the planet again.'

'No, silly. I meant, do you really think I'm sexy that way?'

'Well, let me, er, put it this way,' Frank said, coughing and concentrating on his driving as they inched forward. He was very aware that Gertie was an extremely attractive young woman. He was also very aware that he was her senior officer. He was saved by the radio.

'Welcome back after that short break,' Zack the Man was saying. 'And now, as promised, an exclusive interview with the man who is making the headlines in today's modern world, Professor Jonathon Humphries.'

'Bats,' remarked Gertie.

'Bats?'

'I think it's bats.'

'It's always bats,' Frank replied, 'the more daft the better, as far as these radio stations are concerned.'

'No, I meant the topic – bats, not butterflies. Something to do with bats becoming extinct, probably in South America.'

'Five quid?'

'Sshh! Listen.'

'Professor Humphries,' said the radio announcer, 'I understand that you wish to cull eighty-five percent of all humans, is that true?'

'No, that is the usual travesty of my theories,' said a calm, deep, urbane voice, suggestive of an academic man with a beard, 'a total distortion created by the media in order to dramatise something I never said.'

'So what is it that you never said?'

A voice sighed on air.

'Does it matter what I never said? I'm sure I have not said many things. I thought I was here to discuss my latest research.'

'Yeah, that's what I meant, your research. So what is this theory? It does have something to do with eighty-five percent, doesn't it?'

'Yes, it is carefully outlined in my book "The Coming Wave". Obviously it is difficult to condense such an important and ground-breaking work in only a few minutes, but I can give you a few of the essential facts and theories that underline and support my work. To start off with – and this is what the media normally ignore, the basis of the theory – you have to accept that our planet is vastly overpopulated.'

'By butterflies,' Frank said, 'go on prof, mention butterflies!'

'Shut up!' said Gertie. 'It's bats.'

'Overpopulated by humans, you mean?' asked the announcer.

'Obviously. I am hardly referring to any other species, many of which face extinction due to humankind's depredation of his environment.'

'Well, it could be cockroaches – they're hardly becoming extinct. Or rats. Rats are a big problem these days in some areas. Whitehall especially, so I'm told.'

'Bats,' said Gertie, 'mention the bats.'

'Shush,' said Frank. 'It's butterflies.'

'Quite so,' the professor continued. 'No doubt that is the humour I am told that you are well known for. However, the mention of cockroaches is entirely apposite.'

'Appo-what?'

'Apposite. Relevant.' Professor Humphries coughed, as if about to begin a lecture. 'Firstly, consider Darwin's theory of the survival of the fittest.'

'That's us, humans? Aren't we the best, eh?'

'Not at all. If we continue the way we are going we are likely to prove ourselves totally unfit to survive. In fact we're lucky not to have destroyed the planet with nuclear weapons so far. However, unless we do something, we will destroy ourselves and the planet by overpopulation and destruction of the environment, and the cockroaches could well be the only life forms to survive.'

'But that's pretty old stuff, isn't it, professor? Where does your famous eighty-five percent come in?'

'There are two points to be considered. Firstly, mother nature has so far done a good job of looking after the planet. So the first part is that we can expect her to continue to do so. If we do not control the population explosion, she will do it for us, as she has in the past.'

'You mean, disease, famine, that sort of thing? This bird flu stuff?'

'There are any number of examples, if you look at history. The plagues, yes, but especially wars. Both world wars were very efficient culls carried out by mother nature.'

'You're saying the world wars were a result of nature?'

'Precisely. We are all animals, we are driven by nature. When a species over-populates it destroys extraneous members.'

'What about the Germans, didn't they have something to do with it? I'm sure my history teacher mentioned something about that.'

'Very amusing, as I'm sure our tabloid press would agree. However, viewed from an academic perspective, who starts a war is not relevant. What is more important is what natural impulse causes such events.'

'So we can expect another war – another holocaust.'

'No, not at all. And that is precisely the point. I'm not saying it is entirely impossible, but it is extremely unlikely that even humans could be that stupid. So, no, not war. And not disease, either, since modern science is efficiently combating sufficient of that to mean that the population explosion continues.'

'So, how then?'

'Ah, before considering that question, we need to look at the second point. Who will be eliminated?'

'Well, who? The French? Ha ha ha, only joking, listeners, I love the French, really. Especially their cooking. Nothing like a pizza on a Friday night. Hold the garlic, though, they can keep that.'

Professor Humphries made a Humph sound before continuing.

'Historically we have been divided into various groups by class, religion, language, country and so on. These days, however, in the Western world – and that is where it is likely to start, since lesser developed countries have cruder methods of elimination – such factors are no longer sufficiently strong to be applicable. The coming killings – cull, if you really wish to use that word – will, I believe, be based more on individuals as individuals. Thus it will not matter whether you are a banker, a burglar or a beggar. If you are perceived to have qualities which are intrinsically worthy, you will survive. Otherwise you will not.'

'And eighty-five percent of us will not?'

'A rough figure. A maximum, you might say. Humankind can quite easily survive without eighty-five percent of the current population. Especially of those not wanted in the first place.'

'So we come back to the original question; if not war or plague, how will this cull happen?'

'Well, have you ever thought to yourself, or even said out loud, "I could kill that person"?'

'Of course. Who hasn't? Almost every day I drive home I could kill half the idiotic people I come across who shouldn't have been allowed out in the first place – and I'm sure all of my listeners would agree a hundred and fifty percent. You know, I'm not sexist, but some women should just never have been allowed to sit behind a steering wheel.'

'You snivelling little – ' Gertie began.

'Well, that aside, perhaps,' coughed the Professor on the radio. 'But I believe that that is exactly what is going to happen. Humans will simply start killing the unwanted. It will be an entirely natural and inevitable process.'

'Phew! Now there's a thought to start the day. Well, folks, you heard it first here, exclusively on Radio Pithead. Now we'll be having a short break, and after which we'll be taking calls, and I can see from my lovely assistant Julia – the one with the large bosom, you'll remember, and she's wearing an extra-tight t-shirt today, sexy stuff, Julia! – I can see the switchboard is already lighting up. Don't go away, folks, we'll be back shortly.'

The advert for new original Greek yoghurt began playing

again.

'Bit excessive,' Frank commented, 'I would have said twenty-five percent.'

'Twenty-five percent?'

'The number of people you could get rid of quite easily – and make the world a better place.'

'Oh, and who's going to decide who gets it?' asked Gertie snappishly. 'You by any chance?'

'Now, now, Detective Constable, calm down. I can think of two straight off you'd be happy to nominate.'

'Really? It must be wonderful to be a detective sergeant. You become psychic along with the stripes. Which two?'

'Not psychic at all. That woman in the four-wheel drive, and that radio announcer, Zack the Prat, or whatever it is he calls himself. How's that?'

'Well, that's only because she's a rude cow, and he's an obnoxious – '

The sound of a hooter drowned out the last word, but it sounded like it rhymed with "banker".

'I think I'll put some music on,' said Frank quickly, 'some nice, calming music. Vivaldi okay?'

'Wagner. I'm in the mood for Wagner.'

'That's what worries me.'

Frank had an eclectic music collection. His preference was for the pieces of music he liked, whether classical or modern, rather than the composers or singers. Gertie, on the other hand, had a distinct liking for the more stirring and aggressive approach of some of the classics.

Even with the fact that she was a little on the short side, and wasp-waisted, her attitude and impressive bosom would make her a disquietening Brunhilde.

Frank believed in an Epicurean enjoyment of life, not finding himself alongside a blonde-haired, axe-toting Valkyrian.

Then again, Gertie had some major coloured belt in Aikido. She probably wouldn't need the axe.

In the station Frank bumped into Detective Inspector Frieda Garold on his way to his office. She did not look happy. Technically she was his boss, so that should have made him unhappy too, but he rarely let other people's moods upset his own. He tended to view such things as an amused spectator.

It was thus surprising that he had managed to remain alive, let alone survive relatively unscathed.

'You didn't listen to Martin the Moron's broadcast this morning, did you?' Frieda asked angrily.

'Martin?'

'Martin the Moron. Zack the Prat, or whatever silly name he calls himself. That blasted idiot with an hour of drivel on the morning radio. Interviewed some professor who claimed that eighty-five percent of the population should be exterminated.'

'I'm surprised, Inspector,' Frank said, his eyebrows raised innocently 'I would never have thought that sort of show would appeal to an educated woman like yourself. Very sexist and populist, so I'm told.'

That earned him a baleful glare.

'As it happens I took my Mozart collection out of the car when I cleaned it over the weekend. I forgot to put them back. And there didn't seem to be much point in switching radio channels – until I got stuck in a traffic jam.'

'And then you changed to something more appropriate – Classic FM?'

She gave him a look to show that she knew he was baiting her, and his life was in imminent danger of ceasing to be.

'As it happens,' she said, almost haughtily, 'I decided to continue listening purely from an academic point of view.'

Frank's nose twitched as he tried to hide a grin. One "as it happens" from Frieda was an air-raid warning. A second was the sound of the bomb bay doors opening. Only the survivors heard the third. And normally wished they hadn't.

'And was it interesting? In an academic way?' he asked, pushing his well-known luck further than he should.

'That depends on your interpretation of the word interesting. I think the only difference between the people who phone in to that ridiculous programme and laboratory rats is that you think the rats deserve to live.'

Frank coughed gently.

'The callers would be in the eighty-five percent, then?' he enquired. She shot him a malevolent glance.

'So you did listen to it then, Detective Sergeant Summers?'

'Only the first bit. Where they interviewed the professor. Then we put some music on.'

'We?'

'I gave Gertie a lift in. Her flat was flooded on Sunday so I let her stay at my place.'

She paused and gave him a strange look.

'I see. Very cosy. I can't say I thought you were her type of man.'

'It wasn't like that. I was merely helping a colleague out. You wouldn't suggest things like that if it was a bloke.'

She arched her eyebrows.

'No, but I think rumours may arise. We wouldn't want the station thinking you were gay, now would we, Frank?'

He shrugged. Rumours and gossip blew through the station like litter in a tornado. Eric Johns, desk sergeant, was a world-beater when it came to inventing gossip out of nothing more than a paperclip and a piece of string. They should have made it an Olympic event just for him.

'So what sort of music did our Gertie choose this time?' Frieda asked.

'Wagner.'

'Wagner. Ride of the Valkyries, no doubt.'

'Spot on. And very loud. She isn't in a good mood.'

'Neither am I. Traffic jams, Zack the Prat, a weird sociologist – what a way to start a Monday.'

'He's a sociologist? That professor?'

'Yes, why?'

'Well, in the old days you needed a messiah to get people going around killing each other. Appears all you need these days is to be a sociologist.'

'Modern times, Frank, modern times. No respect for tradition. Everyone thinking they can do what they like, achieve anything, despite having no education, training or ability.'

'Didn't Prince Charlie say that once?'

'God, I hope not. I don't want people thinking I've sunk that low.'

She paused before turning towards her office.

'And don't even think of any cute comments to make in that regard, Frank. You might land up in the eighty-five percent yourself.'

Frank didn't. He was trying not to look at her legs showing in the slit of her navy-blue pencil-skirt as she walked away, her firm calves with feet encased in shining stiletto-heeled shoes, the way she held herself when angry, the way she swung her hips from side to side.

He was also trying not to think that Gertie had had much the same effect on him when she strode off to berate the cow in the four-wheel drive.

'Bookies,' said duty-sergeant Eric Johns as he shovelled a forkful of steak and kidney pie into his mouth in the canteen that lunchtime. Frank was inspecting a sandwich from the machine to see if it had any of the cheese filling promised on the label, and whether it was real cheese, or something reconstituted out of a cola can, a piece of cardboard, and the droppings of a Himalayan yak. He was trying to restrain his eating. Gertie was ploughing her way through egg, chips, peas and buttered bread, with a slice of apple pie and cream waiting as dessert.

'Bookies?' asked Frank giving up and taking a bite of the cheese-less sandwich. 'What about them?'

'I reckon they belong in the eighty-five percent. And good riddance to them.'

Frank swallowed and sighed.

'Don't tell me that that's the topic of conversation for the day. Football, yes, women, okay – '

'Eh, what do you mean, just "okay"?' asked Gertie indignantly. 'There's a lot more to women that just "okay".'

'Yes, yes,' said Frank hurriedly, 'I didn't mean it that way. What I meant was that, while the usual topics of discussion are hardly stimu – er, that is to say, well ... discussing what some plonker on Zack the Prat's show said? Some sociologist gabbering on about a theory he came up with while scratching himself in the wrong place? Surely we haven't descended to that level?'

'Our Frank, sorry, Detective Sergeant Summers,' commented Gertie, 'the intellectual of Wellbury police force.'

'Come on, now, Frank,' Eric said. 'You have to admit the bloke has a point. If you think about what he said – well, we could get rid of eighty-five percent of the idiots in this town and not notice. Actually you would notice. You'd notice how much better life seemed.'

'What, like all the petty crooks? We'd be out of a job.'

'No, no, you didn't listen to the programme, did you?'

'Yes, we did,' Gertie replied.

'We?' asked Eric, his eyes suddenly wide in the manner of a gossip who has just overheard a particularly tasty titbit.

'Don't even think of going there, Eric,' Frank said, 'I just gave Gertie a lift in this morning, that's all.'

'Of course, of course, I believe you. I would never dream of starting scurrilous rumours about you and Detective Constable Gregson here. No-one would believe them, anyway.'

'Why not?' demanded Gertie. 'Why shouldn't they?'

'Enough!' said Frank. 'Eric, get back to what you were saying about the eighty-five percent.'

'I thought you said you weren't interested.'

'I'm more interested in that than in you going on one of your missions to turn my normal life into a fantasy world,' Frank replied. 'Now, what about the programme?'

'Well, that bloke, the professor, what he said about the eighty-five percent not belonging to any class. He's right. I mean, you think about it. You can meet people from all different walks of life, teachers, plumbers – crooks even. Doesn't matter what they do, how much money they have, some of them are just a waste of space, get on your nerves, or worse. You can't really define it, but you know the feeling. You know a berk when you meet one.'

'Great,' commented Frank, 'Sergeant Eric Johns' method of population control. All berks up against the wall.'

'Sounds good to me,' commented Gertie.

'Okay, here's a different test,' said Eric. 'Divide the world into those you wouldn't mine having a pint with, get rid of the rest.'

'What if they don't drink pints?' asked Gertie. 'Maybe they don't drink at all.'

'That's not the point. They don't have to drink. It's the thought – the concept.'

'Blimey,' said Frank. 'Eric Johns, philosopher. And culler of the eighty-five percent. We live in esteemed times and company, Gertie.'

'I agree with him,' she said, reaching over for her apple-pie.

'You know what I hope?' asked Frank.

'No, what?'

'I hope Zack the Prat chooses a better topic tomorrow. Butterflies and global warming. I could live with that.'

'Bats,' said Gertie.

'Bats?' asked Eric.

'Gertie's got a thing about bats today,' Frank said.

'Ah, it's a well known phenomenon that,' Eric said, 'most women have this irrational phobia about bats getting into their hair.'

'That's not bats,' said Gertie, 'that's men. And it isn't irrational. And,' she added, 'the worst are the ones you want entangled in your hair but don't even try.'

Frank was just about to shut down his computer and close up for the day when he received a call to go to Frieda's office. Being unaware of any new reason he should have to worry about such a summons, and being relatively sure he had not that day committed some crime against Frieda's 1001 commandments, he hurried off to get the interview over and go home. Gertie had left fifteen minutes previously, planning to drop in to her own flat and pick up some things on her way home. She would be waiting for him when he got back.

He paused in his hurry. He rather liked the idea of Gertie waiting for him. He shouldn't, he was her superior officer, and had a duty of trust towards her. But he did like the idea.

He shook his head to clear it of any unacceptable thoughts and carried on hurrying.

'You can go straight in, Sergeant Summers,' Frieda's secretary Mary said as he walked in to the outer office of Frieda's eyrie. 'I'm just off home.'

'Me too, Mary,' he grinned. 'In five minutes, time me.'

Frieda was pulling on her summer overcoat as he walked in to her office.

'Sorry, Frank, work calls,' she said.

'Ah, you won't want me, then? I'll be off, shall I?'

'Very funny, Frank. I'm afraid you're going to have to tell Gorgeous Gertie she'll have to wait a little longer for you.'

'I told you she's just ... Oh, it doesn't matter. I'll have to tell her I'll be late, though, she promised to cook dinner.'

'Oh, how sweet. So soon and she's already cooking you dinner. It must be serious. You can use the phone on my desk.'

'It's just to say thank you for letting her stay at my place,' Frank said, picking up the phone and dialling. 'I did try to persuade her not to, but unfortunately she insisted.'

'Unfortunately?'

'You know what an appetite she has? I shudder to think what she considers a normal dinner – hello, Gertie? Frank here. Listen, about dinner, I'm going to be late so don't do any for me. What? Oh, okay.'

He put the telephone down, slowly and gently, as if it were an unexploded grenade with the pin loose.

'Not upset, was she?' asked Frieda.

'I think she heard the last bit – about a normal dinner. And possibly the bit about her appetite.'

'Oh, dear. And she didn't ask why you were going to be late. That's not a good sign. I'm sorry, Frank, I didn't mean to get you in trouble with her.'

'Look, Inspector, for the last time, and despite any rumours

18

that Eric Johns likes passing around, there is nothing between Gertie and myself.'

'Okay, Frank, okay, I won't mention it again,' Frieda placated him. 'You know, I can always tell when you get really mad. You start calling me Inspector. There's just one thing.'

'And what's that?'

'You know there's nothing between you and her, but does she?' She picked up her handbag. 'Now let's get moving. I like evening work as little as you do.'

'So why not leave it to the night shift? Hardly likely to be anything they can't handle.'

'That, my dear Frank, is where you are very, very wrong. The body of a dead woman has been discovered hidden in a clump of bushes in Trafalgar Park.'

'So? Night shift are used to bodies – admittedly most of them comatose rather than dead, but it isn't unheard of.'

'This one is. She had a note pinned to her coat. Apparently it says "Eighty-five percenter".'

Frank paused.

'It says what?' he asked slowly.

'My reactions exactly.'

'Eighty-five percenter?'

'Precisely.'

Frank looked at her in amazement.

'Oh ... sh ... ' he began, before ending, remembering her intense dislike of swearing, ' ... shugar.'

When they reached the park the area had been cordoned off

and a forensic team were already at work in the early evening sun, a white tent covering the spot where the body had been found. The blonde-haired figure in charge, wearing a white overall, turned at their approach.

'Detective Inspector Garold,' she said, smiling falsely, if enthusiastically, 'I'm so glad it's you. Someone suggested that you might send that useless sergeant of yours.'

'Good evening Doctor Pleadle,' Frieda replied. 'Sergeant Summers is here as you can see.'

'Is that Sergeant Summers?' Susan Pleadle said with mock surprise. 'I haven't seen him for so long I didn't recognise him. I thought he must have been posted away without saying goodbye. Though I could understand why you'd want to post him away. Timbuctoo would be a good destination. For us if not for them.'

'Sergeant Summers is one of my best officers, doctor,' Frieda said, like a protective mother hen.

Could I have that in writing? thought Frank.

'In that case I'd hate to see the others,' Susan replied with a lethal smile.

'Any chance of seeing the body?' asked Frank.

'Which one?'

'There's more than one?'

'Oh, sorry, I was getting ahead of myself,' Susan said. 'For a moment I had a vision of dissecting yours. Wishful thinking no doubt. But it would be interesting to find out what you have where most people have a heart.'

'I understand the body had a note pinned to it,' Frieda said.

'Yes. Come into the tent.' She turned and they followed. 'It's handwritten, "Eighty-five percent minus one". I'm told that refers to some discussion on Radio Pithead this morning. The special programme for those of a sub-standard or non-existent intellect.'

Frank suppressed a chuckle and carefully moved away to ensure he was as far out of range of the two women as possible. Things could get thrown.

'A sociology professor claimed that eighty-five percent of the human race were worthless and would be eliminated as a result of natural selection,' Frieda said. 'Some people might consider it a serious theory.'

'I wouldn't disagree with that. And I know one person who would immediately go into the eighty-five percent. Having said that, anyone who listens to that stupid radio channel would qualify.'

Frank tried to cover up another smile.

'It's very popular,' Frieda noted. 'Or so I'm told.'

'For some reason trash is very popular in our society today,' Susan said with a sigh. 'Well, there's your body. We've finished with it for the moment. And here's the note.' She handed over a torn scrap of paper in a sealed plastic envelope.

'Hit over the head?' asked Frank, crouching down next to the body of an thin woman in her late fifties or early sixties, lying face down.

'Blunt object, side of the head, an hour, maximum two hours ago.' replied Susan.

'Facing her attacker?'

'I don't think so. From the footprints I would say she had just turned away from him – or her.'

'The press aren't aware of this note are they?' Frieda asked, looking at the paper. "85% – 1" it read in scrawled handwriting.

'Not from us,' Susan replied. 'I don't know whether the person who found her saw it.'

'Who found the body?'

'A man who popped into the park for an emergency pee. He's at the station now, I believe. I thought you would have known that.'

'We came straight here,' Frieda said. 'If this business about the note gets out before we've had a chance to find some solid evidence, hopefully find the person that did this ... Well, you can imagine the field day the media will have. And god knows what will happen after that.'

'You've lost me,' admitted Susan. 'What do you think will happen?'

'Think about it,' said Frank from his squatting position. 'A professor gives the green light to kill people you don't like. He said that it's mother nature protecting the planet from over-population. In effect he's relieved people – the sort of people who would think that way – of responsibility. They've been told it's natural. They can't help themselves. There is a danger that, after the first, things could snowball.'

'What, so people are going to start running around killing others left, right and centre? I think your imagination is working overtime.'

Frank shrugged.

'Imagine a religious society where a priest announces that everyone with dark hair is a heretic and must be destroyed. What do you think will happen? What does happen when people think they're doing God's work?'

'We're hardly living in a religious society,' Susan pointed out with an irritated frown. 'This isn't the Dark Ages.'

'But in this case it's supposedly scientific – and it's a different kind of religion, rationalism, just as open to being used for pogroms. People can get caught up in frenzies. You don't have to go too far back in history to find examples. Think of mobs filled with righteous indignation. I've had to face them before. It isn't a pretty sight.'

'I think you're getting confused with football supporters, Frank,' Susan noted. 'This is Wellbury, not Dead Gulch, Wyoming.'

'That,' Frank noted, smiling wryly, 'is the only thing that gives me hope.'

Frieda's mobile phone rang. She took it from her bag, had a hurried conversation, muttered something under her breath and jammed it back in the bag.

'Our friend Phil Walthers from the Herald called the station. Wanted to know if it was true that someone had committed a murder and left behind a note claiming the victim was one of the eighty-five percent. I'll have to get back before things get out of hand. Frank, you finish up here. Get a lift back from uniform when you're done.'

He watched her leave with a nervous look on his face. He was alone in the tent with Susan. Suddenly baying mobs sounded like an attractive proposal. He could live with baying mobs.

At least it wouldn't be personal.

And it would be less painful.

'So, I hear the delectable Gertie with the large bosom has

moved in with you,' Susan said, busying herself with some equipment. 'I'm sure you'll both be happy together. Just don't bother sending me a wedding invitation.'

Frank gave a sigh.

'That will be our resident rumour monger Eric Johns spreading half-truths and gossip to a breathlessly awaiting nation, then,' he commented. 'No, Gertie hasn't moved in with me. There was a bad leak in the flat above hers which made it more or less uninhabitable, so I said she could stay over until the damage was repaired. Anyway I don't see it's any business of yours.'

'I see. I would have thought it was. But then I thought, after those dinners, a number of visits to the cinema together, theatre, that sort of thing, that we had some sort of relationship. It appears I was mistaken.'

'You said you wanted some time to yourself,' Frank pointed out, trying to work out how fast he could run relative to how fast Susan could throw.

'I meant an evening, not a bloody month, Frank. How do you think I felt, sitting indoors watching god-awful television, waiting for you to call? My mother said you couldn't be trusted. She was right.'

'Okay, okay,' said Frank hastily, with a sound of relief in his voice. 'Look, it was a misunderstanding. Let's go out for dinner then. Tonight. What about that?'

'I'll be working tonight. As you can see.'

'Well, tomorrow night then.'

'I'm busy tomorrow night.'

'When, then?'

'I'll give you a call sometime and let you know.'

Frank sighed again. He seemed to do a lot of that when Susan was around. He was going to be made to pay for his misunderstanding. As always. Sometimes he wondered whether the game was worth it.

'What else can you tell me about what happened here then?' he asked.

'I've told you all there is to tell at the moment. Elderly woman killed by a blow from a blunt object to her head. Can't say much more until I get back to the lab and run some tests. I don't know why Frieda left you here.'

'I think she hates me,' Frank muttered, walking out of the tent.

'I don't blame her,' Susan replied from within. 'You seem to have that effect on most women.'

Back at the station Frieda had already assembled an operations room and an investigations team, much to the chagrin of Detective Inspector Percy Hanson. Frank met Percy's loyal sidekick Sergeant Pete Phillips in the corridor.

'Your Frigid Frieda's making herself unpopular,' he commented. 'Percy reckons this should be his case. He's on duty and Frigid's supposed to be off.'

'I would gratefully hand it over if I could,' Frank replied.

'You'd gratefully hand over anything. I've never met a sergeant more cheerful to get rid of an investigation.'

'I have this strange approach to life,' Frank admitted. 'I like being able to walk out of the station and leave everything behind. For some reason I also prefer not working very strange hours, while all sensible people are down the pub with a pint, or tucked up in their beds.'

'Got the wrong job for that, then.'

'True. But I suppose if I had a nine-to-five desk job I'd dream of being a copper. Might as well enjoy what you've got, I suppose.'

He turned into the operations room, leaving Pete shaking his head in disbelief.

'Ah, Frank, just in time,' Frieda said. 'We're just about to start. Close the door.'

Frank did as he was bidden and took a seat at the back of the room. There were four others, two plain-clothes detectives and two uniformed men.

'Right, Constable Edgars, what have you found out about the victim?' Frieda asked. She picked up a pen and turned to a whiteboard, making notes as young Kenneth Edgars spoke.

'One Mrs Agnes Whitehead. Age, sixty-two. Lived on her own, no pets. Husband died ten years ago or so, heart attack. According to one neighbour he was happy to go. Her nickname is Nagness. Pokes her nose – poked her nose – into everyone else's business, continually complained about everything from neighbours' noise to fouling of the pavement by other people's dogs. No close friends – no friends, really – believed to have a niece as the closest relative, address unknown, but thought to be Portsmouth.'

'Not very well liked, then,' observed Frieda, writing "Nagness" on the whiteboard.

'Did she ever complain to us? About the noise and whatever,' asked Frank.

'I don't know,' admitted Ken.

'Why do you ask?' asked Frieda.

'I just wondered whether there was a real reason, or whether she just liked putting people's backs up. Maybe complaining to her neighbours was the only way she knew of communicating. Doctor Pleadle said she might have been turning away from the killer when he struck. Maybe one of the neighbours decided they'd had enough and lost it.'

'I'll check it up,' Ken said, making a note.

'Any of the neighbours strike you as the murderous kind?' Frieda asked the two uniformed constables. They shrugged in unison.

'Old bloke on the left of her place, didn't like her very much,' said Ken, 'but I can't see him having the strength. Young family on the right, mother's got three young kids, husband wasn't back from work – works late sometimes, or goes to the pub first. Don't blame him, those kids were making a hell of a racket.'

'Maybe if he was there they wouldn't be making one hell of a racket,' observed Frieda caustically. 'What about the others?'

'Middle-aged couple a door away,' Ken replied, 'seemed a little afraid of her – well, not afraid as such, more like they were afraid they would bump into her and have to listen to her moaning for half an hour. But they did seem quite shocked by the news. Couple of houses on the other side occupied by university students. They had their run-ins with her. Seems it was their noise she complained about. You know what students are like – messy bunch, don't bother with what other people think.'

'Yes, I know,' said Frieda looking him in the eyes, 'I was one once.' Ken went red and there were muffled grins from the others. 'Apart from their bad manners, did they have anything to say which might help us?'

'Not really. I think most of them were sleeping the afternoon away before going out for the night.'

'Spending our tax money on debauchery?' enquired Frieda.

'I don't know, Inspector. However, there was one who seemed a little strange. A small girl, about eighteen, little plump, but with weird eyes. Could have been on drugs. She was wearing black, black dress, stockings, shoes, black and white makeup. She looked real weird.'

'Ah, a Goth. Not many of them around these days.'

'A Goth?' asked Ken.

'Before your time, young Constable Edgars,' replied Frieda, 'for which you may thank any god you believe in. Anything else?'

Both uniformed constables shook their heads.

'Okay, you two are supposed to be off duty now, so go home before you break the overtime budget. And if anyone asks, you don't know anything, understand? If I find anyone leaking information, no matter how unintentional, they will be singing falsetto before they can say "altar boy". Understood?'

The two nodded their heads and began to leave. On their way out Ken leant over Frank.

'What's that mean, Sarge, that singing fals – whatever it was?' he whispered.

'It means she'll have your balls off,' Frank translated in a low voice.

'Right,' said Ken, and left rapidly. Frank smiled innocently at

Frieda watching him.

'Okay,' she said, turning to the plain-clothes detectives, 'I want you two to re-interview the neighbours – everyone in the street, including the missing husband, the one supposedly in the pub – especially him, I don't like the sound of him. Ten to one whoever did this lives locally and was known to our friend Nagness. You know the drill; cover story is that you're just carrying out routine enquiries, uniform lost their notes in the tumble-dryer, the search dogs ate them, whatever. What you're looking for are alibis that don't match up with their earlier stories. Times are crucial. I want minutes. I know you won't get them exactly, but "about ten to" or "roughly quarter past" isn't good enough. The body was discovered shortly after it happened. If we act fast enough we'll get whoever did it before the night's out. Any questions?'

There were no questions.

'Off you go then. Frank, a word.'

Frank strolled up to the front of the room as the two others left.

'So why are you so insistent on taking on this case?' he asked.

'It's likely to be an important case.'

'High profile, you mean?'

She shot him a look telling him to watch his step. There was a race between herself and Detective Inspector Percy Hanson for the prize of promotion to Chief Inspector. It had started when the current incumbent had announced his decision to take early retirement in the near future. Neither of the two inspectors were likely to achieve the post – someone from outside would probably be brought in – but solving high-profile cases would help in future climbing of the greasy pole.

Frank did not understand it. Climbing the greasy pole only meant getting your suit dirty. And dry-cleaning was expensive.

Percy could have appealed to the Chief Inspector for control of the case, but shortly after his announcement of impending retirement the Chief Inspector had gone fishing, and had hardly been seen since. All Percy could do was try to remonstrate with Frieda, and he wasn't about to do that. He was like a rabbit in the beam of Frieda's eyes. He wasn't equipped to deal with the smart-looking, attractive and intelligent woman. He didn't know how to. At least with blokes he could threaten to kick their balls in. As far as he was concerned Frieda had too many, and he wasn't sure where she kept them.

'I've issued a statement giving the name of the dead woman,' Frieda told Frank. 'Plus a bit about saying that it is uncertain whether or not it was an accident.'

'She slipped, hit her head, and then wrote a note before passing on?'

'Don't be silly, Frank, I didn't mention the note. I'm playing for time. I'm going to carry on here until about ten o'clock. I don't suppose there's any chance you'll want to stay?'

There was just the slightest element of pleading in her voice, one that flew way over Frank's head.

'No sense in sitting around spending the overtime budget, is there?' he asked reasonably. Frieda shot him a glance.

'I thought you might say that. No, there isn't. It would be nice to have company, but not at the price of the overtime budget. You get off. Eight o'clock start tomorrow, okay?'

'If you say so, boss,' Frank grinned.

'Remember what I said I'd do the last time you called me

boss?'

'No.'

'Luckily for you, neither do I. But I suggest you get out before I do remember. See you tomorrow.'

'Night, ma'am,' Frank said racing to the door. A marker pen hit the wall alongside as he made it through the door.

'You're the strangest policeman I've ever known,' commented Susan as she leaned over the mortal remains of Agnes Whitehead on one of the steel examination tables in the university pathology laboratory, a small, whirring, circular-saw in her hand. Frank sat on the other, casually tossing a scalpel from one hand to the other.

'In what way?' he asked.

'Would you mind not playing with that?' she asked. 'Apart from the likelihood of doing yourself an injury, which I'll have to explain – and clean up the mess – I'll have to sterilise that scalpel again.'

'Sorry.' He put the sharpened instrument down next to him. 'You don't have a tennis ball by any chance, do you?'

'No. Why?'

'It helps me relax. A squash ball would do at a pinch.'

'Sorry, no balls. And don't even think of a clever remark.'

'I wasn't about to. Not while you're holding that nasty gadget. So, how did you mean, the strangest policeman you'd ever known?'

'Oh, that. Well, in my experience police officers, including women, fall into one of two categories as far as corpses go. Either they're fascinated by them, or they're repelled. Most

31

can't wait to get out of here. You don't seem affected either way.'

'I'm lucky. My imagination switches off when it sees a dead body. The first corpse I saw, when we were doing training – well, there were seven of us. Two fainted, four threw up. I just looked. It was as if there was a glass wall between myself and the body. Probably a mental self-defence thing.'

'Hmmm,' Susan murmured, a disbelieving tone in the Hmmm.

'What about you?' he asked.

'Me? And corpses? You get used to them. Sometimes I can relate better to the dead than the living. Anyway, why are you here? Running an errand for hot-legs?'

'Inspector Garold? Yes, she does have rather nice legs, doesn't she? But no,' he said, as if not noticing that the saw had suddenly increased revolutions at his agreement in regard to Frieda's underpinning, 'I just thought I'd drop in on my way home to see if there was anything new.'

'Really? You voluntarily dropped in? Need the overtime? That doesn't sound like the Sergeant Frank Summers we all know and ... well, know, anyway.'

'I'm not on overtime. If anyone asks, I'm not even here. Anyway, what's the verdict? Anything new on Nagness's demise?'

'Acute angina, I suspect,' Susan said, lifting what had been a beating heart a few hours before. Frank's nose twitched and his jaw tightened.

'Nothing to do with her death, though?' he asked.

'Oh, no. Could have killed her at any time, but something like a brick got her first.'

'A brick?'

'The indentation in the skull is remarkably suggestive of the corner of a brick. Or something with a corner edge. If I were you I'd arrest all bricks within a two-metre radius. Threaten them with cementation or the crusher until one of them confesses.'

'Very funny,' remarked Frank, rubbing his jaw thoughtfully. 'You going to tell Frieda this?'

'Of course. It will be in my report.'

'I meant soon, not tomorrow. Might help the search team at the site.'

'Why don't you tell her yourself? You'd get a little gold star from her. Or maybe even something more. Poodles get petted when they're good little doggies.'

'No thanks. Frieda might get the idea I can be conned into doing overtime. Anyway, you're the specialist. I'd probably muck things up in translation.'

He slid off the table.

'Leaving so soon? Before we've got to the good bit?' asked Susan.

'I'm obviously not welcome here,' he replied, making for the door. 'Unless I lie down on that table and let you take a saw to me. Besides, Gertie's waiting for me.'

As the door closed behind him he heard the sound of something wet and flabby hitting it.

Susan looked at the door in fury.

'Bastard,' she said softly. She took off a surgical glove and pulled a phone from a pocket.

'Inspector Garold?' she said. 'Sergeant Summers suggested I contact you as soon as possible. Hmm? Yes, he popped in on his way home. Anyway, it appears, on primary investigation, that your victim might have been killed from a blow struck with a brick, or half-brick. I'll be able to be more specific later, but if you find any rectangular objects in the vicinity you could send them over for analysis. He asked me to inform you as soon as possible.'

She paused as Frieda said something.

'Sergeant Summers?' Susan asked. 'Oh, he seemed eager to make sure that Constable Gregson was comfortable, Gertie, as I believe she's called. The one with the large ... yes.'

She put the phone back with a smile on her face. Had Frank seen it he would have become very, very worried.

Had he seen the look on Frieda's face he would have left town.

Back at his flat Frank opened the door and called cheerfully, 'Hello, darling, I'm home.'

Gertie looked up over her glasses as he walked into the lounge. She was barefooted, wearing an old shirt, comfortable skirt, tucked up in an armchair, legs underneath her, textbook in her hands, half-full glass of wine alongside. She looked at him inquiringly as he dropped his jacket onto the couch and went into the kitchen, returning with a bottle of beer.

'What's that all about?' she asked as he threw himself onto the couch.

'Oh, I don't know.' He unscrewed the cap of the bottle and tossed it at a waste-paper basket. It missed. 'I've always had the urge to say that.'

He took a deep drink.

'Know what I like about you Gertie?' he asked.

'Do tell,' she said, closing her book.

'You're straightforward. I can talk about things without wondering whether you're trying to tell me something in Greek. Everyone else thinks we're having an affair or something, but the great thing is I can come home, you're sitting there quite happily doing your own thing, uncomplicated – oh, and those glasses make you look very sexy, by the way. What is it you're studying this time?'

'Law. It's an Open University course. You really think these glasses ...?'

'Absolutely. What was it they used to say? "Men don't make passes at girls wearing glasses"? Load of nonsense.'

'You haven't been drinking, have you?'

'Not yet. But I'm starting.' He sighed and rubbed a hand over his eyes. 'Why is it women can't just say what they mean?' he asked. 'Susan's having a go at me because I took her at her word about wanting to be alone, Frieda – well, I'm never certain about what Frieda wants – as a woman, that is. Thank god you're normal.'

'For a woman you mean?'

Frank looked at her and took another long pull from the beer bottle.

'Let me guess. I've upset you as well, now.'

'I think you're tired. You need a good meal and then some sleep.' She stood up. 'I'll make you something.'

'Gertie, I am more than capable of getting my own dinner,' he said as she moved off to the kitchen.

'A few more beers and then a call to the local pizzeria?' she called back. 'I think I can do better than that. Oh, and you shouldn't be drinking out of a bottle. It isn't hygienic.'

Frank sighed. He had been looking forward to the call to the pizzeria. The female receptionist had a very sultry Italian accent. And the pizzas were filled with all the terrible things he avoided during the day, and so loved at night. With lots of garlic. He liked garlic. And onions. And peppers. And salami. And ...

The telephone rang. He dragged himself up to answer it.

'Still awake, Frank?' asked a sultry voice. Not the woman from the pizzeria. Frieda's voice. Laced with one or two gin and tonics. 'We've got the murder weapon – thanks to you. I mean it. Doctor Pleadle contacted me after you'd spoken to her. It's saved us a lot of time.'

'Glad to hear it,' he replied.

'You sound tired.'

'I'm exhausted. It's been a strange day.'

'I understand, Frank. Listen, first thing tomorrow?'

'First thing tomorrow,' he agreed.

'And no fooling around with Gertie.'

Frank sighed.

'Your word is my command, I shall obey absolutely,' he said.

He could have sworn he heard Frieda giggle as she put her phone down.

As he put his phone down he turned to find Gertie in the doorway, bottle and glass in her hands.

'Another beer, Frank?' she asked.

Frank told himself that the top couple of buttons on her shirt had already been undone when he walked in.

Any other explanation would end with the word "trouble". Preceded by "big".

Trouble gave him a seductive smile and poured his beer for him.

Tuesday: The three meet

'Of course the police are refusing to confirm it,' Zack Kerouac was saying as Frank and Gertie drove to work the following morning, 'but I have it from reliable sources that a young woman found murdered last night had a sign printed on her forehead saying "Eighty-five percenter". Now, at great expense we have convinced Professor Humphries to give up some of his precious time to give my listeners the benefit of his extensive experience. Join us after this short commercial break, folks!'

'Ten quid and a free cup of coffee,' Frank noted.

'Mmm?' asked Gertie, her mind in a world of its own.

'The "great expense" Zack the Prat mentioned. I'll bet the Herr professor was gagging to get on the radio again. Probably never thought he'd get a second chance to expound on this ridiculous theory of his.'

'If you say so, Sarge,' Gertie replied, as if she weren't listening. Frank gave her a glance. He wondered what she was thinking about behind her sunglasses. Her mind obviously wasn't on the case.

Gertie was thinking about a dream she had had the night before. In it she was lying in Frank Summer's arms. They were in a meadow, lying on a blanket after a picnic she had prepared, blue summer skies overhead, just the slightest of breezes so that it wasn't too warm, a tinkling river flowing a few feet away, giving its soft approval to the two lovers.

Somewhere in the background an orchestra had been playing. Violins. Lots of violins.

When she had woken up to realise that it had only been a dream, she wasn't sure whether she was glad to have had it, or upset that it was merely a dream. She had really, really liked that dream.

There were two problems with Frank. Firstly he had this rule about not having a relationship with anyone in his own station. Secondly, the way he took his duty as Sergeant too strictly. She, as an acting Detective Constable, and his responsibility, was off limits. There were the further added obstacles of Doctor Susan Pleadle, Frank's would-be girlfriend, and Inspector Frieda Garold, who was also obviously taking more than a professional interest in Frank Summers. She, Gertie, could handle those two obstacles. They were merely battles in the war to be won. The first two problems appeared insurmountable.

Gertie was used to being plied with drink by men who wished to take advantage of her. The previous night was the first time she had tried it on a man.

It hadn't worked.

Bastard.

What she truly hated about Frank Summers was the way she invariably lost her hard-earned professional approach in his presence, ending up in girlie-mode. It had taken her years to get out of that sort of thing.

Damn you, Frank Summers, she thought, get out of my life. Either that or I will have to kill you.

The unwitting target of this death-threat turned up the volume on the radio slightly as the adverts finally ended.

'Welcome back, listeners,' Zack said, as if it were they that had gone away. 'With me, as promised, is the world-famous Professor Jonathon Humphries. This is truly an exclusive interview, folks, brought to you by the makers of Zitblast acne cream and radio Pithead. Now, Professor Humphries, are you surprised at the news that this woman was murdered because someone considered her one of the eighty-five percent?'

'Not at all,' the urbane voice came over the airwaves. 'I knew it would happen sooner or later. I predicted this very thing in my book, "The Coming Wave". Similar to a wave, it is unstoppable.'

'What would you say to those who might suggest that you were the cause of this? That if you hadn't mentioned your theory this would not have happened?'

'I can hardly be held responsible for the actions of others,' Humphries said reasonably. 'After all, when a meteorologist forecasts a storm you do not blame the storm on the meteorologist. And ultimately I cannot decide on what people do, that is for each individual to take responsibility for.'

'Stormy stuff, Professor!' Zack said enthusiastically. 'Now, listeners, you might be surprised to hear that Professor Humphries' book, which is now on the best-seller list, was ignored by publishers when he first wrote it. You actually ended up in selling it door to door, didn't you, Professor?'

'That was unfortunately the case, but it was crucial that people should be aware of the coming wave. Not a very pleasant experience, but, as you say, now a best seller. Available in the better bookshops for a very reasonable amount. Eminently reasonable, since it is likely to forestall a cataclysm of the most unimaginable dimensions.'

'And we have a real treat in store for one of our lucky listeners. We will be giving away free a signed copy of "The Coming Wave", signed by the author himself! All you have to do is answer a simple question which I will be asking right after this short break. Don't go away now, folks!'

'Oh good,' said Frank, 'a signed copy of a book, signed by the author himself. Instead of being signed by the cleaning lady or a passing humpbacked whale, I suppose.'

He turned the volume down as an advert for a local supermarket came on.

'In a strange way I wouldn't mind reading that book,' he said. 'In the same way you might read Mein Kampf. Not because you believe in any of it, just to try to understand the minds of those who do believe that sort of nonsense. But I wouldn't want to part with any of my hard-earned salary to actually pay for it.'

'Hard-earned?' Gertie asked. He smiled.

'Well, earned, anyway, in a manner of speaking,' he said.

Gertie smiled as well. She thought he looked ever so appealing when he smiled. If this book didn't cost too much she might buy him a copy.

She wondered when his birthday was.

Frank stopped in reception when they arrived at the police station, sending Gertie on to the office they shared. His first order of the day was to report to Frieda, but he paused to have a word with desk Sergeant Eric Johns, the man who had been gleefully spreading gossip about Gertie's current place of abode, and his relationship with her.

'Any news, Eric?' he asked.

'Not that I'm aware of,' Eric replied, taking a gulp from an overlarge mug of tea. 'According to the logs we nicked twelve people for being drunk and disorderly – on a Monday night? Very unusual. Probably decided to cure their weekend hangovers and took the cure too far. Three domestics, one resulting in the arrest of a woman who tried to attack a young constable with a potato-peeler – nasty weapon, that. Thirteen commercial alarms going off for no good reason, complaints about three or four car alarms. No murders, though, apart from the one last night. But it's been a strange time. Way too many people doing things they wouldn't normally do on a Monday night.'

'Is that the report on the potato-peeler maniac behind you?' asked Frank innocently. 'I seem to recall a similar incident a few months back.'

His hand hovered briefly over Eric's mug as the desk-sergeant turned around to look.

'Nah, all filed already,' Eric said, turning back. 'You know I like to clear the paperwork.'

'Oh, well, never mind. Time I checked the lie of the land with the Inspector.'

Eric leaned over confidentially.

'Listen, what about these stories I've been hearing? That this woman who was murdered last night had a note pinned to her coat?'

Frank smiled. Frieda's injunction not to leak had obviously been taken to heart. No-one would dare confide such news in Eric. He normally managed to bowdlerise any information he received, but even he could not get this one too far wrong.

'You've been reading those nasty newspapers again, Eric,' he said, moving off. 'Not even Phil Walthers believes anything you say these days, and he'll print anything.'

He hummed to himself as he took the stairs up towards Frieda's eyrie. Half-way up he thought he heard the sudden emission of a mouthful of tea, followed by a "bloody hell!".

'Morning, Mary,' he said to Frieda's secretary. 'Am I permitted to pass?'

'The Inspector's waiting for you, Sergeant,' Mary replied with a smile. 'Go straight in.'

'You're looking cheerful,' Frieda commented as he walked in. She was sitting at her desk, perusing a number of files with little enthusiasm in her peruse.

'Sometimes it happens that way,' Frank said, sitting down. 'Some days you just wake up with the joy of spring. And it is a rather nice day, after all. A lovely, warm early summer's day. Not at all like yesterday.'

'Hmmmm,' Frieda noted slowly. 'Gertie wouldn't be sharing this feeling by any chance?'

'Gertie? She seemed to be in a world of her own this morning. A little more cheerful than yesterday. But then she phoned the decorators on the way – they always start early, seems like a habit in the building trade – and they reckon they'll be finished by Thursday. She's probably looking forward to moving back into her own place.'

'Is she?' asked Frieda, rhetorically. 'Tell me, Frank, if my house suffered a devastating leak, would you be willing to accommodate me? As a colleague?'

'Of course,' Frank said, surprised. 'Though surely ... '

'Surely?'

'Well, I don't know. I suppose I just presumed that far better offers would come flooding in. After all, it's just a little flat, my place. You'd have to sleep on the sofa-bed in the lounge, that sort of a thing. A bit plebeian, if you like.'

There was a pause as Frieda took this in.

'Let's hope it never comes to that, then, mmm?'

Frank knew better than to reply to a Frieda "mmm?". He never knew just quite what they might mean.

Frieda sleeping on his sofa-bed. Now there was a thought. He could imagine ... Hastily he slapped his imagination down. It had been measuring the distance from the lounge sofa-bed to his bedroom.

'Right, down to business,' sofa-bed image Frieda said. 'About this case last night.' She patted the folders gently as if she really wanted to slap them. 'Despite what I told those two they never managed to nail things down precisely. Understandable, I suppose, but it means we don't have an opportunity to complete this one quickly.'

'I thought we had the murder weapon?' asked Frank.

'We do. Standard half-brick, comes from the crumbling walls around the park. Anyone could have picked it up. No fingerprints to speak of, no DNA, apart from Agnes's – nothing. Suggestions of glove marks – but it was a cold day yesterday, plenty of people wearing gloves.'

'Students wouldn't wear gloves,' suggested Frank. 'Far too bourgeois.'

'I wish I could agree. Unfortunately students never conform to their non-conformism. And most of them these days wouldn't know what "bourgeois" meant.'

'So, it's the long haul, then?' Frank asked.

'With a difference. I have a media briefing session at nine.

Apparently the national media are sniffing around as well. Maybe Phil Walthers couldn't keep his mouth shut long enough to get an exclusive this time.'

'Not like Phil Walthers,' Frank commented thoughtfully. 'But I presume we're going to say "investigations are continuing, I'm afraid I can't comment on the suggestion of a note being found", etc?'

Frieda looked at him for a while before speaking.

'Did you listen to Zack the Prat this morning?' she asked.

'Part of it.'

'The bit where he asked how many people might die? Who would be next, and why?'

'No, Gertie wanted to play some music. "The Summer of Love", I think it was.'

'Gertie isn't interested in the case? Very unusual for such an ambitious young woman.'

'Her mind does seem to be elsewhere at the moment. Maybe she's found herself a boyfriend. I thought it best not to enquire.'

Frieda's fingers drummed on her desk. Frank tried to avoid looking at the red-painted nails.

'"The Summer of Love"?' she asked finally.

'It's a CD I was given once. Not bad. Some of the tracks are quite – '

'Yes, thank you, Frank, I'm sure they are. As it so happens I have the CD myself. However the taxpayer isn't paying us to discuss our tastes in music.'

Frank fell silent. Frieda was having one of her moods, he decided.

'We have to catch this person as soon as possible,' she said. 'Before any other idiot gets similar notions. This could easily spiral out of control. I am not going to let that happen, Frank, understand? There will be no "next" person. We are not going to have a free-for-all of people being killed simply because their neighbours think they have no option but to rid the earth of useless mouths. It won't do our reputation any good, and it will make the streets look untidy.'

'Right,' said Frank, deciding that Frieda had made a Frieda joke. 'I'll start going through the statements then, shall I? Get up to speed, as it were?'

'You do that, Frank.'

He left the office with some relief.

Frieda stood up and walked to the window, looking out on the good citizens of Wellbury going about their lawful business. She had once told Percy Hanson that she liked having Frank on her team because he was, in Napoleon's dictum, "lucky". And he was. Lucky to be alive, anyway. He had three women after his blood. Doctor Susan Pleadle, acting Detective Constable Gregson, known as Gertie, and his own Inspector, namely herself. Worst of all he seemed oblivious to the fact that she was a woman.

Why, oh why did you have to come to my station, Frank? she asked.

After divorcing a wife-beater of a husband, also a police officer, she had sunk all her efforts in her career. Extremely ambitious, she was also extremely successful. She had sworn never to get involved with another policeman again.

Until Frank had turned up.

He was only a little younger than herself. She knew she was

an attractive woman. There were the twin barriers of her being his superior officer, and his declared promise not to get involved with a colleague, but these could be overcome, surely?

She went back to her desk and sat down. She slammed a file in front of her angrily. On impulse she pressed the button connecting her with her secretary.

'Mary? Get me Detective Sergeant Summers' personnel file. Now.'

Mary didn't get a chance to reply.

If Frank's luck didn't hold up he was going to find himself posted somewhere else.

She stopped suddenly at the thought.

If Frank were posted somewhere – say to one of the neighbouring towns, who were always complaining of being short-staffed – she would no longer be his boss, and, technically, they would no longer be colleagues. Or, at least, not immediate colleagues. That dispensed with both objections.

And if he were posted to a nearby town he would undoubtedly keep his current flat and commute. He wouldn't want to leave Wellbury.

And there were bound to be reasons to pop in to see him occasionally.

On a purely social basis.

Now, what should she wear for a purely social visit to an ex-colleague's flat? Something that showed a bit of shoulder and cleavage. Men liked that. Frank would like it.

Mary knocked, entered, and laid Frank's personnel file on

Frieda's desk.

'He's not in any trouble, is he?' asked Mary nervously. Frieda mentally noted the nervousness. Mary was in her late fifties, happily married with four grown-up children, and even she was concerned about Frank.

Blast the man.

'A very lucky man, our Frank,' Frieda noted. She looked up at Mary. 'But I think his luck is about to change. Such a pity.'

Mary looked at Frieda with alarmed eyes, and backed out, closing the door behind her. She was rather proud to be the secretary of such a young female Detective Inspector. But she hadn't liked the look in Frieda's eyes.

Frieda opened the file.

'Interesting,' she thought to himself.

So, Frank's birthday was in just over a week.

It wouldn't be nice to post him just before then, now would it?

Still, one sometimes needs to be cruel in order to be kind. And it would hurt her more than it would hurt him.

Wouldn't it?

The object of her kindness walked into his office unaware that he was faced with an approaching storm brewing above him, about which, even had he known, he could do little. In the office another figure of kindness awaited him.

'I've printed all the statements out for you, Sarge,' said Gertie. 'I know you prefer paper to screen.'

'Very kind, Gertie,' said Frank. 'Have you read them?'

'Just browsed through, Sarge.'

He sighed.

'I suppose I'll have to pretend to be professional and actually read them,' he said.

Gertie giggled.

Instead he turned and placed his feet on the windowsill and looked out the window.

'Let us adopt the approach of the Enlightenment, Gertie,' he said.

She sat down in the chair in front of his desk, placed her elbows on the desk, her chin in her hands, and listened in fascination.

'Logic,' he said, 'let us apply logic. What do we know? A professor, probably of dubious academic origin – note that down, Gertie, we need to check on Professor Humphries' credentials.'

'Right, Sarge,' said Gertie automatically, not moving for pen nor paper.

'I meant, Acting Constable Gregson, write it down. As in apply pen to paper. We'll never remember otherwise. I sure as hell won't. You check up on that.'

'Right, Sarge,' said Gertie, grabbing Frank's own pad and pen. How he had known that she hadn't done anything was a mystery, as he had his back to her.

'So Professor Humphries comes up with this half-baked notion that we're all going to suddenly fall on our neighbours and associates and murder eighty-five percent of them. Later that day a woman is murdered. An old nosy-parker and general complainer. Not the sort, to use Sergeant John's analogy, that you'd have first on your list for going down the pub to have a pint with.'

'No, Sarge, she sounds like a real cow,' agreed Gertie, having put pad and pen down and re-assumed her position of fascinated audience.

'So, has the cull begun? Or is there something more to this?' Frank asked in a soft voice, as if his thoughts had moved on to some other plane.

They sat in silence for some moments as Frank sat staring, unfocused, out of the window.

'I don't buy it,' he said finally, forcefully, lifting his heels and swinging around to face her. The sight of Susan Pleadle in the doorway watching them surprised him, and his elegant swing went wrong, his legs catching the side of his desk.

'Aaargh!' he cried out, rubbing his shin. 'Bloody hell!'

'I'm sorry, I really didn't mean to disturb you,' said Susan, a certain malicious enjoyment in her voice. 'Though I wouldn't use language like that in Frieda's station, you know how much she disapproves of it.'

Gertie sprang up and moved around to Frank's side of the desk.

'You okay, Sarge?' she asked, kneeling down to massage Frank's legs. 'You took a right crack there. It must hurt like hell.'

'Gertie, Gertie, please don't,' he pleaded, lifting her by her arm. He patted her on her shoulder. 'I pressed these trousers only the other day. You might get them creased. Go on, sit down.'

Gertie did as she was bid, unwillingly.

'I was passing by, so I thought I would drop off my initial written report,' said Susan. 'I didn't expect to find the high priest of theory expounding his thoughts to an admiring acolyte.'

Frank waited for several moments before replying. He had understood the words. The meaning totally lost him.

For Frank it wasn't an unusual experience when there were women around.

'Anything new?' he asked.

'As far as Mrs Agnes Whitehead goes, no. But on entering this sanctuary of humming police work I discovered an entirely new species.'

Frank waited for her to continue. Gertie wasn't listening.

'Ever heard of the Chinese Flying Frog, Frank?' asked Susan.

Frank covered his mouth with his hand, pretending to stroke his jaw.

'No, can't say I have. Not my field, really, biology.'

'Sometimes I wonder if your field isn't too wide, Sergeant Summers. If you know what I mean.'

Frank didn't. Not a clue. But he knew about the frog. And it was totally deniable.

'Go on,' he said, 'it sounds fascinating.'

'When I entered reception Sergeant Johns asked me to have a look at a frog he had discovered in his mug of tea, a frog which he subsequently carefully put in an old coffee jar to keep safe and alive. He had heard about rainstorms of frogs. He was convinced that the frog had somehow flown in and chosen his mug of tea as a resting place. Thinking that, as a doctor, I would know about such things, he asked me to look at it and tell him the exact species.'

'Still alive, was it?' asked Frank, his mouth twitching.

Susan gave him a look which indicated that she thought he belonged to a species best not mentioned.

'I had to point out the "Made In China" stamp on its underside before he would believe that it was a rubber toy. Very convincing, but not quite a flying frog. I wonder how it came to be in his tea.'

Frank shrugged and smiled innocently.

'The constables are always playing tricks on him,' he said.

Susan looked at him through disbelieving eyes.

'No doubt they'll be pleased that he proudly displayed this Flying Frog to several of them before I had the chance of disabusing him of its origin, then,' she noted.

'No doubt,' Frank echoed. 'Is that the report?' he asked, pointing towards the folder she was carrying. 'I'll have a look at it,' he continued, holding out his hand. 'Constable Gregson will show you out. Can't have civilians wandering around the station unescorted. Inspector Garold sent out a strict memo about the subject only a week ago.'

He took the report, opened it, and was apparently soon immersed in it.

Susan gave his bowed head one last dirty look before accepting the inevitable and allowing Gertie to escort her to the front door. They walked in silence until she opened the front door.

'It doesn't matter what you do,' she said, turning to Gertie. 'Frank will never go out with a colleague in his own station. You can forget about him.'

Gertie returned Susan's look with one of implacability.

'I'm prepared to resign if I can get Frank,' she said. 'I'm prepared to give up my career for him. You aren't. We'll see who wins, shall we?'

Susan's jaw tautened. She gave Gertie a glare, and stalked off.

In her car she tried to control her tears. She didn't have to give up her career for Frank, that was one of the bloody points in their relationship. On paper she was the front runner, way ahead of Gertie with the big boobs or Frieda with the – well, that was another problem. Frieda had class and style. Frieda had control. Frieda had been through a lot, and come out still surviving.

Bitch! thought Susan, without meaning it.

Bastard! she echoed, meaning it.

It might not be Frank's fault, but boy was he going to pay for it.

The way he had dismissed her! As if she were a mere nothing. Oh, yes, he would pay for it.

Frank sat in his office reading Susan's report. At first he had enjoyed throwing her out, for that was effectively what it was. Up until then it was Susan who had done the dismissals. The score was about three hundred to one, but, boy, had he enjoyed that one. It was time he gave up on her anyway. He had tried his best. Time to move on.

Without realising it he forgot about everything else as he became slowly engrossed in the pages he was reading.

Sergeant Eric Johns watched Gertie return towards Frank's

office with a heavy feeling in his heart. He knew it was Frank who had slipped the frog into his tea. He, Eric Johns, would be the joke of the station for the next few days, but he didn't blame Frank. Fair play. He had gossiped about Gertie and Frank, and had received his come-uppance. Frank was the only person he had met to whom he would have deferred in such a manner.

Funny that, because he had a good twenty years on Frank. Frank had received his stripes because of his degree, whereas Sergeant Eric Johns had slaved for years to achieve his. But at the same time, Frank was a good bloke. One of those, to use his own analogy, who he would be glad to have a pint with. Even if he did get brain-ache after fifteen minutes of listening to Frank's mind changing directions like the pinball in a pinball-machine.

Eric Johns sighed and pushed the day's log book around the reception desk, trying to make it look neater. He had seen the signs in Frank's eyes. An officer getting personally involved in a case. Frank would deny it, but Eric knew better. He didn't know what Gertie had said to Doctor Pleadle, but he recognised the body movements. At a time when Frank's concentration should have been on the threats from those nearby, he was concentrating on the case. When the wotsits hit the fan he wouldn't know what had hit him.

In his office Frank was looking out of the window.

I don't buy it, he said to himself. People do not suddenly murder each other because some so-called sociologist suggests that they will.

But that is what you yourself suggested, replied a voice within.

Yes, but not in Wellbury. Wellburians just aren't like that. Not here, not now. Another time, another place, yes. In the States, no doubt. Spain during the Mistral. A little town in France after eating the wrong sort of mushrooms. Corsica, after an insult including the mention of a goat.

But not here. This is all wrong.

I bloody well hope it's all wrong.

In her own office Frieda closed her eyes, leaned back and stretched her neck muscles.

She needed a massage.

The image of Frank giving her a massage caused her to reopen her eyes, quickly. It was too appealing.

She had made notes about the frog affair. At first she had thoroughly enjoyed the incident. Frank teaching Eric Johns a lesson in his school-boyish way.

She had been quite proud of Frank.

But it did add to her quiver of reasons why Frank needed to be posted.

To somewhere nearby. Somewhere where he would retain his flat in Wellbury. A flat she could visit on the odd occasion. A sofa-bed she had once fallen asleep on.

Happy memories.

The next time she might kick off her shoes and accidentally show a little leg.

If Frank Summers liked leg, she was prepared to give him an eyeful. More than an eyeful. She had been ruthless in her pursuit of her career, especially after realising what her ex-husband had done to her mind. She was prepared to be ruthless in her pursuit of her man.

But that was the problem. Frank didn't like ruthless. She would have to be far more subtle. She had to come up with a plan. A plan that would neutralise Susan and Gertie.

Frank was studying the map of Wellbury on his office wall when Gertie returned.

'What now, Sarge,' she asked, taking comfort from the fact that she was now alone with Frank, and Susan somewhere on the outside.

Frank tapped a finger on the map.

'Trafalgar Park, where Nagness met her Waterloo,' he said. 'If I remember correctly there's a bank close to the main entrance.'

'It's a branch of Collings Bank,' agreed Gertie. 'They've been talking about closing it for years, but each time their customers close their accounts and only re-open them when the bank agrees not to close.'

'People power, eh? Nice to know it still works from time to time.'

'Why are you interested in the bank, though?'

'CCTV, Gertie, my sweet. I know Wellbury is old-fashioned, but I'm pretty sure the bank will have external cameras. There's just the slightest chance we might find something. And cameras are far more reliable than the witnesses we don't have at the moment. Come on, let's see what they have. You can drive. I want to carry on with these witness statements on the way.'

Gertie grinned. She enjoyed driving, and she especially

enjoyed driving Frank. It was the one time she knew she was doing something useful for him.

She wasn't too sure she liked the way he read in silence as she drove this time. Normally he liked to chat about anything and everything, so long as it wasn't police work or something depressing, such as goings-on in the rest of the world outside Wellbury.

She hoped he wasn't coming down with anything.

But then, if he was, he would need someone to look after him. And who better than her?

Her thoughts were interrupted by their arrival at Collings bank, a solid edifice constructed in the Victorian style, possibly the last throw of the period, flanked by shops and other businesses which, fortunately, had escaped the onslaught of modernity. The bank manager was a relatively young man happy to assist the police – or happy to show them where the CCTV tapes were stored, and leave them to get on with it. Frank and Gertie sat down after he had inserted the first tape from the previous evening and he pressed the Play button on the remote.

'Sixteen hundred hours,' he noted. 'Or four p.m. in old money. Susan estimates time of death between three-thirty and five-thirty. But two of our witnesses saw Nagness alive just before four o'clock, so I think it's safe to narrow it down to between four and half-five.'

'Not the best of times,' noted Gertie. 'The street's empty at the moment, but come five o'clock everyone's going to be heading home after work, or popping in to the pub for a quick pint before going home.'

'Yes,' agreed Frank. 'And our killer could have entered the

park from almost anywhere, so, in terms of long shots, it's one of the longer. Hello, what do we have here?'

'A vicar and his wife, looks like.'

The screen showed a fuzzy image of an elderly looking man wearing a black jacket and a dog-collar. He was accompanied by a stern-faced woman in tweeds in her early-fifties.

'Doesn't look like his wife,' Frank noted.

'No,' agreed Gertie, 'more like his minder. Unless they don't have a very happy marriage.'

'Do me a favour, Gertie. We need to put names to faces. Pop out and ask the manager if he could lend us one of his staff most likely to recognise these people.'

'Will do, Sarge,' she said happily, and left to carry out her mission. Frank continued to watch the figures on the screen in silence.

Gertie's countenance had lost some of its cheer when she returned, with a young woman in tow.

'This is Clarissa Hunter,' she said. 'She works on the counter.'

Frank stood up and shook hands with the attractive young woman wearing the bank's smart uniform.

'Unusual name, Clarissa,' he noted. He also noted her smile, and the twinkle in her eyes.

'My parents are very artistic,' she said. 'They thought an unusual name might bring out the artist in me. Most people just call me Jo. I don't know where it came from, but I like it.'

'Jo? Very nice name,' Frank said, his hand still holding Jo's. 'So you never became an artist then?'

'Not quite. Though I really would like to be, one day. Unfortunately my work tends to be old-fashioned. When I paint a person they look like a person. I wish I could paint a single stroke on a wide canvas, title it "The Crowd" or something, and sell it for a small fortune, but I'm afraid I would just feel somewhat of a fraud.'

'I like old-fashioned myself,' Frank replied, finally letting go of her hand. 'You must show me some of your work sometime.'

Jo blushed slightly.

'It's not very good, I'm afraid,' she admitted.

'I'm sure it's better than that. Let me be the judge.'

'If you want.'

Gertie coughed meaningfully. Jo started, and looked around.

'What is it you want me to do?' she asked.

Please do not ask me questions like that, thought Frank, I might have indecent thoughts.

Bugger off, thought Gertie. Like now, you little cow.

'We need to put names to faces on these tapes,' Frank said. 'If you sit here, next to me, and I'll freeze the shot when someone comes up.'

They sat down and Frank rewound the first tape. Gertie stood behind them, glowering.

'This is about the murder of that poor old woman, isn't it?' asked Jo.

'I'm afraid so,' Frank admitted.

'Poor, poor thing. And it's all the fault of that horrid little man on the radio. Talking about killing people just because you don't like them. It makes you afraid to go out.'

She shivered. Frank felt a shiver go through himself. He had never heard a young woman using a word like "horrid". There was something attractive about that.

'We'll do our best to protect you,' he said, hoping he wasn't sounding as big a twerp as he thought he was. A noise from Gertie behind him suggested that she thought he was.

'That's very kind of you, Sergeant,' Jo said, giving him the full effect of her large eyes and long eyelashes.

'Call me Frank,' Frank said. Another noise from Gertie made him turn quickly to the television set. 'Here we go, first couple. Recognise them?'

'Ooh, yes, it's the vicar and Mrs Blower. He's such a sweetie! Why he never got married I don't know. Too shy, I suppose. He's the gentlest, kindest man I think I've ever met. He gives the services at my church, Saint Mary's.'

'But Mrs Blower isn't? Kind and gentle, that is.' suggested Frank.

'Oh, no, it's not that. She's a nice woman, very efficient. Her husband died a few years back, quite a wealthy man by all accounts. Mrs Blower more or less runs the church now, spends a lot of her own money on getting things right. She does all the things that Mr Parsons – the vicar – shouldn't have to worry about. The flowers, accounts, produces the weekly newsletter, that sort of thing.'

'Mr Parsons? A vicar? Rather apt, I suppose.'

Jo smiled.

'It is, rather.' She paused. 'Do you attend church, Frank?' she asked.

'I try to,' he said, to the accompaniment of Gertie holding in hysterical laughter. 'More often than not duty gets in the way.'

'You should,' Jo replied, missing Gertie's reaction. 'It's important to nourish the soul at least once a week.'

'I'm sure you're right,' Frank said, and hastily pressed fast-forward. 'Now, our next candidate.'

'Oh dear, Mr Bagley,' said Jo in a sad, disapproving voice.

'Mr Bagley?'

'Mr Robert Bagley. He's a councillor. He also runs a night club beyond Lords Acres. The Blue Bliss, I think it's called. I've heard terrible stories about it. Topless dancers. People getting drunk. Terrible stories. Terrible. Sodom and Gomorrah.'

'I've, ah, heard about it,' said Frank, who had spent a few hours there one evening some weeks before when he couldn't face the idea of spending another night alone in his flat. The topless dancers had all worn mechanical expressions of desire under the haze of blue lights. The drinks had been incredibly expensive. He had declined the offer of annual membership which would admit him to the "inner sanctum". Had they known he was a police officer he would never have received the offer.

And their choice of music was the ultimate sin in his book: both loud and brash. Bare nipples he could excuse. Bad music was a totally different matter.

'Next,' he said, fast-forwarding again. He stopped when the screen showed the street with dozens of people on their way home, or to a night out. 'This is just after five o'clock. Recognise anyone?'

Jo leaned forward and concentrated on the screen with her eyes screwed up.

'There's Mr Sampson. You might know him, he's a retired

policeman.'

'Can't say I've heard of him. Any idea of his first name?'

'Thomas, I think. And there's Mr Walthers,' she said, pointing to a man wearing a loud waistcoat under his jacket, and even louder bowtie. 'He runs the Herald.'

'Ah, indeed, I recognise him now. Dear Mr Walthers, eh?'

'I like him. He pretends to be cynical, but I thinks he has a kind heart inside. I feel quite sorry for him at times.'

Apart from the bit about feeling sorry for Walthers, Frank had much the same appreciation of the man.

He forwarded the tape a few frames.

'What about that chap on the right?' he asked. 'The one with a beard?'

'No, I recognise most of them, but I don't think I've ever seen him before.'

The man with the beard stood out from all the rest. Apart from the beard, where all the other men were clean-shaven, he wore a pork-pie hat and tinted glasses. It would be a good disguise had it been a disguise, but Frank had the feeling that it wasn't. He suspected that the man was the sort you might invite to a party when you wanted the guests to leave early.

'Anyone else,' he asked, as he slowly forwarded the tape, screen by screen.

Gertie took notes as Jo pointed out the shop and office-workers she recognised, but Frank wasn't really interested in them. They were in places you would expect them to be. They would be unlikely pop out of the office for fifteen minutes to do Nagness in, or take a stroll through the park after work for the same purpose. If the worst came to the worst he could ask uniform to get statements from all of them, and then he would whittle down the list to those who definitely did not have unbreakable alibis.

The most likely scenario was that Nagness had nagged one of her neighbours a nag too far. The second option was that she had been a specific target, known by the killer. The third option, that it was a mugging gone wrong, he doubted. A mugger was unlikely to have left the note. Not even Wellbury's muggers were that sophisticated.

They got to five-thirty on the tape and Frank pressed the rewind button.

'You've been a great help, Jo,' he said, standing up. She stood up and faced him, a little smile on her face.

'Let me know if there's anything else I can do to help,' she said. 'We have to stop whoever did this before they do it again, don't we?'

They shook hands, and this time it was Jo who held on to his.

'Give me a call when you want to see my paintings,' she said. 'And maybe we could have a drink sometime – possibly at the Blue Bliss. I'd love to see what the fuss is all about.' She gave him a wink. 'You know I'm not as prissy as some people think.'

Frank watched her leave the room, his mind in a whirl. He had heard stories of what convent girls got up to. Maybe innocent little Jo's artistic side held a rather wicked secret.

'Poor little thing,' said Gertie, 'being flat-chested like that. Still, she's very young, maybe she'll fill out a bit when she grows up.'

'I, er, didn't notice. How old do you think she is?'

'Oh, can't be much more than seventeen, I would imagine,' Gertie replied offhandedly. 'Can't have been working for the bank for very long. Probably just out of school.'

Seventeen, thought Frank. Just a little bit too young.

Though she had seemed to him to be much older.

'Isn't it about lunch-time?' asked Gertie with absolutely zero subtlety. Frank laughed.

'Okay, Gertie, time to fill your tum-tum.'

Gertie smiled at him.

'After that I want to revisit the crime scene,' Frank continued, 'and see if we can't have a few words with her neighbours. According to their statements they all had pretty unbreakable alibis for the two hours in question. I know they've already been interviewed, but I like to get a personal feeling for these things.'

'I wouldn't mind a personal feeling myself, Sarge,' said Gertie.

Frank smiled. Wherever her mind had been earlier, Gertie was obviously back on the case. Gertie was an ambitious police woman. If she agreed that the personal touch was essential then he had to be doing something right.

'Nothing,' said Frank that evening in Frieda's office. 'Zilch, nowt, not a sausage. All their alibis stand up. In some cases rather too much. The Goth student gave me a blow-by-blow account of her activities during the two hours. She was making love to another student. It was a little too graphic for my taste.'

The afternoon had been a busy one, with no results apart from the elimination of the top suspects. Gertie had been told she could finish for the day while Frank was required to report the latest proceedings to Frieda.

'I'll make sure the beers are cold for when you get home,' Gertie had promised.

There were some decided advantages to having Gertie as a house-mate, Frank had decided.

'Two hours?' asked Frieda, breaking into his reflections. 'A bit impressive, wouldn't you say, Frank?'

Impressive wasn't the word. Gertie had listened with open-mouthed astonishment. Frank had considered sending her out. It was bad enough that he had had to endure the detailed descriptions, he didn't see why Gertie should have to. At the same time he had rather suspected that Gertie had been enjoying herself. At one point she had stood up against the back of the chair he was sitting on, presumably to make sure she didn't miss a word.

And now Frieda was looking at him, playing with her top button. He wished she wouldn't do that.

'What would you say your best time was for that sort of thing, Frank?' she asked. 'In terms of staying power, that is.'

The question hit his mind like a tornado of mayonnaise. Just in time he noticed a twitch around her lips, and the look of amusement in her eyes.

Frieda was teasing him?

She must be in a good mood.

He cleared his throat.

'It's not something I think I could really comment on, not objectively,' he said weakly.

She smiled and shook her head.

'You are far too easy to tease, Frank,' she said. 'Maybe that's what makes you so attractive as a man.' She sighed. 'Go on Frank, go home. I have some unfortunate business to tidy up.'

Frank left her office with some relief. His worst nightmare was that he would find himself locked in a room with a passionate Frieda.

Actually it was a dream he had had once or twice, and very enjoyable it had been. Until he woke up.

It made looking her in the eyes very difficult when he went to work.

He paused suddenly as he descended the staircase towards his own office.

Frieda had not asked the magic question, the one she always asked when a meeting was concluded.

"What's our next step, Frank?"

Why had she not asked it, he wondered. Had she somehow gained such trust in him that it was no longer needed?

Not a chance. If, in the middle of the coldest winter on record, with snowdrifts twenty feet deep and howling gales, blizzards, thunder, lightning and the minor interruption of half a dozen earthquakes, he had gone out, wearing only a loin-cloth, to capture the hundred most-wanted criminals of all time, struggling back wounded and exhausted with the hundred neatly tied up with signed confessions around their necks, she would still have asked that question: what's our next step?

He shrugged his shoulders and carried on. There were many things he did not understand. Quantum physics, for a start. Double-entry bookkeeping. How to construct a nuclear weapon, which, according to the news these days, any child of ten could log on to the Internet and successfully build. Not understanding something never fazed him. He just ignored it, and eventually whatever it was would give up in disgust and go away to plague someone else.

In his office he found a hand-delivered letter awaiting him. He hesitated before opening it. He was surprised to find himself filled with joy when he recognised the little bunnies on pink scented writing paper that Susan loved using. The contents made him want to sing.

"My dearest, darling Frank

Okay, I surrender. I know I haven't treated you fairly, and I deserved to be thrown out of your office this morning. In fact you looked quite sexy when you did it. So I'm pleading with you to allow me to get back in to your good books again. I will trust you with Gertie. I promise not to say a word about her staying with you, I know your determination not to get involved romantically with anyone at work, and I promise to trust you explicitly. You can quote my words here should I ever go against them: I promise I will never criticise you unfairly, or suspect your motives without undue cause or reason, or ever, ever again listen to anything that might have come from the mouth of Eric Johns.

So please, please allow me to buy you drinks tomorrow evening. The Hangman in Heading Square at six? Maybe dinner as well?

Please, Frank?

All my love

xxxx

Susan"

His heart began to sing its own song. There were just two little flies in the ointment. Firstly, the qualifications. Susan promised never to criticise him "unfairly", or suspect his motives "without due cause or reason". Unfortunately he was well aware that he could be criticised extremely fairly on any given day. But he put that to one side.

The second was the dreams he was beginning to have. He dreamed of being with Susan. Fair enough. But he dreamed of Frieda, too. And last night he dreamed that he and Gertie were lying in a meadow, her in his arms, next to a twinkling stream, violins playing softly, and very nice it had been.

Sod it, he thought. Dreams were one thing, reality another. He was back on track with Susan. Drinks and dinner tomorrow night. Things were looking up.

He left the station, waving goodnight to the desk Sergeant, whistling to the tune of a Chubby Checker song, "There'll be a place for us".

Had he been a fly on the wall of Frieda's office he could have added to the others in the ointment.

'Susan?' asked Frieda on the phone, 'it's Frieda Garold here.'

'Yes, Inspector, and what can I do for you?'

Susan's voice dripped ice and blood.

'Call me Frieda, please. Look, we have a certain shared interest. But just because we are, effectively, competitors in that shared interest, I'd hate us to fall out because of that. I think we can approach this with in a much more logical manner.'

'Go on.'

'There's something you need to know about our shared

interest. And I think it's in his best interest that you should know. It's something we need to do something about, if I can put it that way. And we need to ensure that we don't find ourselves losing out to other competition, of which there are too many.'

'I'm listening.'

And listen Susan did. Towards the end of the conversation she called Frieda "Frieda".

'I'll ask Gertie to come in early tomorrow and we can hammer out the details,' Frieda said.

She put the phone down with a smile on her face.

The plan was in place.

It wouldn't be long before Frank Summers was also in his place.

Wednesday: A prophetess speaks; the traffic warden

Frank drove in to work on his own. Gertie had left early, claiming she had things to do before getting to work. The previous evening she had received a telephone call which, after a few exchanges, she had gone into the kitchen to take. Frank presumed that it was her new boyfriend, whoever that might be. She had not mentioned it afterwards, and he had respected her privacy. But she had seemed changed. They had just settled down on the couch to watch a film on the television, and she had tucked herself up next to him. Too close, possibly, but after a couple of beers and a good meal which she had prepared he could hardly see any danger if they cuddled up and watched a film together.

Sort of, like, brother and sister. The younger sister he had never had.

After all, he was having drinks and dinner with Susan the following evening. It wasn't as if he was being disloyal or anything.

Though he felt a bit guilty about not mentioning that to Gertie.

Why, he wasn't sure.

But after the telephone call it seemed that Gertie was keeping her distance from him. He couldn't understand it.

In the morning he had woken early, as he heard Gertie moving about, and had decided he might as well leave fifteen minutes early himself. As he drove in to work, he was listening to Queen's Greatest Hits. Gertie, he thought, would have wanted to listen to Zack the Prat, and, in his own way, Frank thought he should be doing the same. Zack and the professor were a link, however tenuous, with this "eighty-five percent" murder. He decided he would have to interview Professor Humphries. He didn't think it would bear any fruit, but he couldn't afford not to do it. It was one of those boxes that had to be ticked. Sooner or later someone, probably from the newspapers, would ask the question, and he had to be able to reply, yes, we have spoken to Professor Humphries, but he had no information relevant to the case.

The representatives of the media would understand the coded reply: we wasted our time just for you, now please get lost. What they printed might well be another story. "Desperate Police Seek Help From Academic Specialist".

Total rubbish.

'Morning, Frank,' said a tired looking Eric Johns as he entered reception. 'I would say Good Morning, but I would be lying.'

'Morning, Eric, you don't look your usual cheerful self. What's wrong?'

'Oh, nothing much as far as myself goes. Just had to come in to cover for Keith. He had to leave early because his wife's having another baby. Would have thought they had enough as it is, but there you go.'

Keith Bute invariably did the very early shift on desk duty. He and his wife had four children, and were expecting their fifth. After the third he had requested permanent early shift, hoping it might halt the flow. It hadn't.

'And you won't believe the aggro that's being going on overnight,' Eric continued. 'Punch-ups, domestics, pub fights, traffic accidents. Almost all of them claiming that they were innocent because the other party belonged in the eighty-five percent.'

'You're joking.'

'Wish I was, Frank, I wish I was. We've got the entire Wellbury Rugby Club locked up in the cells at the moment. One of their lot was getting married, so they threw a party in the Nag's Head in the Old Village. From what I hear it'll take a few months to repair the damage. The only good thing is that they were fighting each other – front row against back row. I'd hate to think what would have happened had the local gay club or whatever being having an outing at the same time.'

'You mean they would have had a problem choosing which side to support?'

'Very funny, Frank,' Eric said as if he found it not in the least amusing. 'But as far as you go, there's something I think you should know.'

'Kylie Minogue's called and wants to have my babies?' suggested Frank.

'Not yet. But it is a question of women.' He leaned forward and spoke in a soft voice. 'Your Doctor Pleadle came in about ten minutes ago. She's currently in Frigid's office. And Gertie's there as well. It doesn't look good, Frank.'

Frigid was Frieda's original nickname. It was in the process of undergoing a metamorphosis.

'Sorry, you've lost me, Eric. How do you mean, it doesn't look good?'

'Think about it, Frank,' urged Eric.

Frank thought about it. He shrugged.

'Nope, I still don't understand. Susan probably popped in to drop off a report. Frieda wants to speak to Gertie about something. Seems perfectly normal to me.'

'Frigid and Doctor Pleadle spoke to each other as if they were bosom buddies, Frank. All "Susan, how delightful to see you", and "Frieda, what a pleasure".'

'Eric,' replied Frank, laughing, 'you don't understand women-talk. We would say "sod off you wotsits" when we don't like someone. They say "Oh how delightful to see you". It's a question of razorblades. You can hear them in their tones. Now, anything else I should not be worrying about?'

Eric sighed. He had tried his best to warn Frank.

'There's someone waiting to speak to you in interview room two,' he said. 'Professor Humphries.'

'Professor Humphries? Excellent! Saves me a wasted journey. Has he been there long?'

'About ten minutes. But he seems quite happy to wait. Last I saw he was sitting there making notes in a pad. I think he might be coming up with ideas on how to improve this place. He's a sociologist, isn't he?'

'Something like that. It gives me time to have a coffee first, though. Wouldn't want to interrupt his note-taking, now would we?'

'If you say so, Frank,' Eric replied sadly.

Frank made his way towards his office, whistling. If Eric wanted to feel depressed that was his choice and right. Frank had never understood the notion. There were plenty of things to be depressed about, and sooner or later one of them would get him. He had no intention of inventing things to worry about.

One of the reasons to be cheerful now appeared in front of him in the corridor.

'Susan!' he exclaimed. 'I heard you were about. My morning just gets better and better.'

'Frank,' she replied, looking surprised. 'You're in a bit early aren't you?'

'Only ten minutes or so. Come to drop of your report on Nagness?'

'Er, yes,' she said nervously. 'Only you weren't in, so I left it with Frieda.' She looked at her watch. 'Sorry, I must rush.'

'See you this evening then. At the Hangman's.'

'What? Oh yes, of course. This evening then.'

She scurried down the corridor. That wasn't the Susan he knew. His Susan normally had a way of walking half way between a skip and a dance. As she was about to turn a corner she looked back. It was a look he recognised, the sort of look others had given him just before he began reciting the words "You have the right to remain silent ... ".

Guilt.

He scratched his head. His main problem with Susan had always been the way she had always been so confident, especially as it was confidence in the idea that he, Frank, had been up to no good. She had been invariably wrong, but that had never made a difference to her. He had never even thought of the possibility that she might one day seem unsure of herself.

She hadn't expected him to be in, yet she had popped in to drop off her report.

He shook his head and carried on towards his office. If you ignored worries they eventually gave up and went away. "We are the champions of the world" Freddie Mercury had once sung. Now he was dead. Frank wasn't quite aiming to be champion of the world, but he intended to have a good laugh and a good time while he was able to.

Inside his office he found Gertie with a cloth and can in her hand. She was polishing his desk. She looked up with a start as he came in.

'What on earth are you doing, Gertie?' he asked in astonishment.

'I didn't expect you in this early. I was just doing a bit of cleaning,' she said defensively. 'I know how you like everything looking smart.'

Well, that was true enough. His professed feeling was that you could make all sorts of cockups and get away with them, so long as you were wearing a smart suit and bright tie, your shoes brightly polished, and your desk looking like a model of efficiency. It was an absolute requirement if you were, like him, prone to periods of incompetence, such as when someone foolishly gave him some work to do.

There was another argument which a little voice in his head came up with, one he tried hard to suppress. It suggested that, just perhaps, just maybe, there was a little, tiny element of vanity involved.

'I thought we had cleaners to do that sort of thing,' he said, dropping into his chair as Gertie put her polishing materials away in her own desk.

'They never do a proper job,' she said.

'I shall have to have a word with them then,' he replied, trying to conceal a smile. Any suggestion that the cleaners were slacking would have them in revolt. They might pretend otherwise, but they were, to a woman, quietly proud of their work. Any person criticising them would have to endure not only their wrath, but that of the rest of the office. There were two types of people you did not get on the wrong side of: the cleaners and the canteen staff. Agnetha in the canteen especially.

'It's okay,' Gertie said hastily, 'I don't mind doing it. You can't really blame them, they just have too much to do. Er, would you like a coffee, Sarge? I was just about to get one.'

'Just what I was thinking of, thanks Gertie.'

He watched her scurry out of the office and shook his head in perplexity once more. Gertie was somewhat of an enigma. One minute she would be the career-obsessed young woman he had first met, a proto-feminist ready to take offence to the sisterhood at the slightest remark, the next she was a domestic incarnate, polishing his desk for him, almost like a little girl hoping to please. He presumed that it was one of her ways of thanking him for letting her stay at his place while hers was being repaired. He had already noticed that she was overly scrupulous about keeping his flat tidy, in the manner of one who is more used to a sink full of three-day old dishes, and clothes dumped anywhere and everywhere in their own home.

For some reason that made him think of Frieda. She gave the appearance of being a perfectly turned-out martinet. He had never been to her house. He wondered if she got back from work and threw everything down in a jumble, kicked her stiletto heels off, and sank into a couch littered with clothes she had discarded as she took them off.

He shook his head to get rid of the image. It was the types of clothing that he had been thinking of that worried him. A Detective Sergeant should not have those sort of thoughts about his Detective Inspector.

'You okay, Sarge?' asked Gertie, walking in with two mugs of coffee. 'You looked as if someone had just walked over your grave.'

'Just trying to clear my head and concentrate on work,' he replied, thinking that, if he wasn't careful, someone would be walking over his grave, and it would be Frieda. In high-heeled shoes.

'Concentrate on work?' she asked, teasing. 'That's not like you, Sarge.'

'Careful, now, acting Detective Constable Gregson,' he said in a mock-serious tone. 'Impertinence does not lead to promotion, you know.'

'I've been thinking about that, Sarge,' she said, sitting in the chair in front of his desk, tucking her legs underneath her. 'Promotion isn't everything. There's happiness as well.'

'Happiness?' he asked, his eyebrows raised in surprise. 'I think you've been around me too long, Gertie my sweet. Everyone has their own personal karma to follow. Mine is to enjoy life as much as possible. Yours is to become the youngest head of police in history, and the first woman to hold the post. I look forward to sitting in a pub enjoying a pint, and seeing you on television announcing that you have just nicked the prime minister and the entire cabinet for fraud, or for being total prats, or something.'

Gertie smiled.

'You'd enjoy doing that yourself, wouldn't you, Sarge?'

He smiled back at her.

'It's one of my better dreams,' he said, 'trouble is I always cock it up somehow. You'd have a watertight case. Anyway,' he continued, putting his mug down, 'enough idle banter. We have a case to solve. Nagness might not have been the best example of human nature, but we can't allow people to go about topping nosy neighbours just because they feel like it. Have you found out anything about Professor Humphries?'

'Sorry, Sarge,' said Gertie, looking embarrassed, 'haven't had a chance to do anything yet.'

Frank was tempted to suggest that following his instructions might take precedence over polishing his desk, but there would be too much of the element of pots calling kettles black. He doubted whether he would ever resort to polishing desks, but it wasn't unknown for him to get side-tracked onto something more interesting when he should be doing police work.

'Pity,' he said to Gertie, 'the dear Professor is currently awaiting our presence in interview room two. It would be nice to have known something about his background.'

'I could start now,' she offered. 'Should be able to get some details within an hour or so.'

'No, don't worry, Gertie. Apparently he's been waiting for half an hour or so already. Normally I'd leave him to stew, just to put him on the back foot, but from what Eric said the Professor is happily composing new theories about policing in the modern age. Come on, let's go hear what the whacky wonder has to say. Once we've finished with him I want to go through our witness statements again. There has to be something we've missed. Nagness's murder was a chance thing, I'm sure of it. I can't believe someone could do that in broad daylight and get away without someone seeing something.'

Gertie followed Frank to the interview room. He was in a

jaunty mood. One of his pleasures in life was to subtly ridicule those he thought were a little too pompous for their own good, and he had no doubt that Professor Jonathon Humphries belonged firmly in that category. He didn't know how, but he was going to have fun with the Professor.

The two of them stopped abruptly as they entered the interview room. Professor Humphries was sitting at the table engrossed in some notes he was making, a cup of tea long gone cold at his elbow. It wasn't the tea that they noticed. It was the beard, pork-pie hat and tinted glasses they had last seen on a CCTV tape.

'Professor Humphries,' Frank said, recovering his poise, 'how do you do. I'm Detective Sergeant Summers and this Detective Constable Gregson. How may we help you?'

Humphries looked up in surprise.

'Sergeant?' he asked mildly. 'I have no wish to give offence, but I had expected someone of a little higher rank.'

'Detective Sergeant is a relatively high rank in the police force,' Frank noted, sitting down. He crossed an elegant leg over a knee and leaned back. 'So how may we be of assistance?'

'Ah, of course,' Humphries replied, as if involved in his own thoughts. 'Due to my military experience I always think of a sergeant as somewhat of the lower ranks.'

I'd love to see you say that to an army sergeant, Frank thought. I'd be taking bets on which parts of you would land where.

'You were in the army?' he asked instead.

'I was of assistance to them once,' Humphries replied in a tone of self-importance, 'and in reply to your earlier question, it is not that of how you might be of assistance to me, but rather the converse.'

'And how may that be, sir?'

Humphries wasn't aware of it, but the "sir" was not a sign of politeness. Rather the converse.

'You may be aware of my work, Sergeant,' Humphries continued. 'I have been interviewed several times by the media. I have a book which is currently considered very highly, not only in the academic world, but also commercially. I say this not out of self-importance. The sales figures speak for themselves.'

'I'm afraid I haven't come across your work, Professor. Is it to do with sex?'

Gertie hid a smile behind her hand.

'Sex?' asked Humphries in astonishment. 'Why should it be about sex?'

'The media seem fixated by sex these days,' Frank said. 'It seems a good probability that your work would lie in the same field.'

'Most certainly not. I have more important issues to consider.'

'You don't consider sex important, Professor? Do you not enjoy it?'

Humphries' eyes boggled.

'How dare you ask me such an impertinent question, Sergeant?' he demanded.

'I meant in the professional sense, Professor,' Frank said soothingly. 'In terms of academic study.'

'Ah, yes, I see. Well, as far as that goes, I am of course experienced in that area. But,' he continued as Gertie took out a handkerchief to stifle a giggle, 'I currently concern myself with something of crucial import to our future. You have, no doubt, heard of my theory of the eighty-five percent?'

'No, sir, can't say I have. Is it something to do with farming?'

A slow look of understanding came over Humphries' face.

'I think you do know who I am, Sergeant. I think you are, what is the common phrase? Taking the Mickey?'

'I wouldn't know what you mean, sir.'

Humphries leaned forward.

'Sergeant, a woman has been murdered. She was murdered because someone considered her to be in the eighty-five percent who deserve to be eliminated. I predicted that. I know what is about to happen. I am the most important source you will have in the coming days. Now I think I would like to speak to someone more senior. Someone who has enough intelligence to understand the reality of what my theories mean.'

'Sorry, sir, you're stuck with us plods,' Frank replied, wondering whether he should send Frieda in.

No, Humphries was a berk, but he hadn't done enough to merit that. Maybe in the future, not yet.

Humphries stood up.

'There will come a time when you will beg for my help, Sergeant,' he said. 'Once the bodies begin to pile up, which will happen in the days to come. In the meantime I will let the media know that the police have declined my assistance. It is a decision I think you will come to regret, Sergeant. But possibly it will be for the better of all that you are not promoted beyond the level of your own incompetence.'

Humphries' threat struck a nerve. Frank often thought that he had indeed reached the level of his own personal incompetence. That made his dislike for him grow into something approaching hatred, an emotion he had rarely felt, and considered a waste of precious energy best spent on something more enjoyable.

'Before you go, there is one question I would like you to answer,' he said offhandedly. Humphries paused.

'Ah, so you do want my help, then?' he asked.

'Not quite as you think. I'd like to know what you were doing close to Trafalgar Park at the very time that Agnes Whitehead was murdered.'

The self-satisfied smirk left Humphries' face, to be replaced by one of fury.

'Are you trying to suggest something, Sergeant?' he almost bellowed. 'I'll have you know – '

'Answer the question,' Frank said quietly, inspecting his fingernails, ignoring the bellow.

'I refuse to be treated in this manner! I demand – '

'You can either answer the question now, or we can make it more official,' offered Frank. 'Detain you until we can get the tapes set up. Ask your lawyer in if you wish. Of course, our incompetence might mean your being stuck here for a few hours more. Naturally we'd have to take your pen and notebook away, plus anything that you might be of danger to you – belt, tie, shoelaces, pork-pie hat, glasses, that sort of thing. We can't afford to take chances, now can we? Don't want you having any accidents while in our custody, do we?'

This was all said with the broad and pleasant smile of a simple police officer determined to do his utmost to be helpful.

Humphries hesitated. No one could doubt that Frank meant what he said. Humphries might be able to force an apology out of him afterwards, which he undoubtedly wouldn't mean, but it would mean being incarcerated in this building for most of the rest of the day.

Holding his trousers up.

'If you must know, Sergeant,' he said finally, capitulating, 'I had been for a stroll in the park. I find such light exercise not only good for the digestion, but also beneficial to thinking, an activity you might try some day.'

'You were on your own?'

'I am frequently on my own, Sergeant. There are few other people of my intellect who I consider worthy company.'

You mean nobody wants to talk to you, thought Frank. At least, not more than once.

'You don't, in other words, have an alibi then,' he said. 'You, the man who predicted a sudden spate of murders, are in the vicinity of just such a murder as you claimed would happen. Some people might consider that somewhat of a strange coincidence.'

'Some people – fortunately the majority of those with at least some intelligence – would consider your ill-thought suggestions ridiculous. There would also be the question of evidence. I would watch what you say, if I were you, Sergeant.'

'Fortunately that isn't the case,' Frank said, standing up. 'Detective Gregson will show you out,' he said, opening the door and walking out. 'Let's just hope you don't find yourself in the eighty-five percent,' he added as a parting shot.

'He was brilliant,' Frank overheard Gertie enthusing as he neared his office door after lunch. He walked in to find a surprising tableau. Gertie was sitting in her swivel chair, leaning on the armrest, one leg tucked underneath her, the other pushing on the floor, making her chair swing from side to side. Frieda was half-sitting on the end of Frank's desk, hands resting either side, relaxed as she listened to Gertie. They could have been two girlfriends having a natter, rather than being Inspector and Constable.

'Hello, Sarge,' Gertie said happily as Frank walked in. 'I was just saying how brilliantly you handled that Professor Humbug. You should have seen his face when you told him to be careful about ending up in the eighty-five percent.'

'Perhaps not that clever in hindsight,' Frank noted, perching on the other end of his desk. It was not a position he would normally adopt, but if it was good enough for Frieda then who was he to complain?

And it kept Frieda's lovely legs in view. He rather liked those legs.

'It gives him a stick to beat us with if we go after him,' he continued, trying not to look as if he was thinking of legs.

'You intend to go after him?' asked Frieda. Frank shrugged.

'I don't like the coincidence of his being so close to where Nagness was murdered. Maybe he was worried that his prophecy wasn't sufficiently self-fulfilling. Maybe he thought it needed a kick-start.'

'What was your impression of him?' Frieda asked. 'Do you think he would have been cold-blooded enough to murder someone just to support this idiotic theory of his?'

'I don't think it's a question of being cold-blooded. I think he's a bit warped between the earlobes. There's something in his eyes suggestive of a Messianic complex. People like that are quite capable of deluding themselves into thinking that what they are doing is right. If it was him, he's probably already convinced himself that it was someone else who did it.'

'It's a possibility, I suppose,' said Frieda dubiously. 'The question is, if it was him, what does he do when no other murders follow on? Go out and kill someone else?'

'I doubt it. He might, in some demented way, be able to justify one. Having to do it a second time would be tantamount to admitting his theory is a failure. Anyway, he knows we have our suspicions. He'd need a watertight alibi for a second, and from the sounds of it he hasn't got any close friends foolish enough to give him one.'

'I wouldn't worry about him too much, Sarge,' said Gertie, swinging from side to side, a smile on her face. 'I did some checking up on him. He's a fraud.'

Frank raised his eyebrows.

'That was quick. How did you find that out?'

'Well, you know these law courses I'm doing with the Open University? When I started off a couple of years ago I began with a sociology course, to see if I could do it, as it were. Anyway, I've stayed in touch with my tutor from that course. So I gave her a call to see if she knew anything about Professor Humbug. Apparently he's quite well known in sociology circles, and not well liked. His qualifications come from some place in America. Send them a hundred dollars and they'll send you a piece of paper stating that you have a degree from them. My tutor thinks a professorship would go for about a thousand dollars.'

'Well, well,' Frank said, nodding his head. 'Excellent stuff, Gertie. I am most impressed.'

Gertie blushed happily at the praise.

'I agree,' said Frieda, 'very good work.' She stood up in preparation for leaving. 'You had better be careful, Frank, Gertie will outrank you before very long if you're not careful.'

'Doesn't worry me,' Frank said, smiling. 'I'm quite happy where I am now. Who was it who said that we should strive for perfection, but also be content with what we could achieve? Goethe? Mills? Or am I thinking of someone quite different? Charlie Brown, perhaps.'

'I thought Epicurus was your personal hero, Frank,' suggested Frieda.

'Oh, I'll nick ideas off anyone if I think it worth it,' Frank grinned. 'St Augustine, for example – "give me chastity and continence, but not yet".'

Frieda smiled and patted Frank on the shoulder as she walked towards the door.

'I have one for you,' she said, pausing in the doorway. 'Who was it who said "go find me a murderer or your job is on the line"?'

'I don't recall the name, but I remember she was a beautiful woman,' Frank replied, sucking in his cheeks. Frieda gave him a warning look.

'Watch your step, Frank Summers,' she said, and left. She had been unable to keep a note of pleasure out of her voice.

A bemused Eric Johns appeared in the doorway.

'Was that Fabulous I just passed?' he asked. 'Smiling?'

'Just an effect I have on women,' Frank assured him.

'Oh, good. Because I have someone in interview room three who wishes to speak to you. It's a woman. One who could do with trying to smile every few months or so. Maybe just a one-off for Christmas. Ever heard of Clementine Ziggurat?'

'Clementine Ziggurat? Strange sort of name.'

'Oh, she used to be known as Molly Smith until her voices told her to change it.'

'Voices?'

'She's a psychic,' Eric said, smiling evilly. 'She wants to speak to you about these murders. Asked for you specially. Said your name came up in a séance.'

Frank groaned.

'Tell her I'm out, Eric,' he said. 'Tell her I might be gone some time. Months, probably.'

'Ah, but she knows you're in, Frank. She must do, she's a psychic,' Eric said, laughing as he walked away.

'Right, let's get it out of the way,' Frank said, standing up. 'This case seems to have most of the less mentally balanced people popping out of the woodwork, a few minutes with a psychic would be par for the course.'

To his surprise Clementine Ziggurat was a small, mousy-looking woman wearing plain clothes and no jewellery apart from a wedding ring. He had expected something a little more Oriental and exuberant.

'There will be ten,' she said after introductions were concluded. 'The list has been made and cannot be unmade.'

'I see,' said Frank. 'Make a note of that Gertie.' He leaned forward. 'Now, I don't want to sound a little dense, Mrs

Ziggurat, but could you perhaps expand on that? Possibly tell us what it means?'

'I don't know. That's all the voices said. They didn't tell me what it means. They never do.'

'Ah,' said Frank, leaning back. 'Not a whole lot of use, then.'

Clementine Ziggurat shrugged.

'Mebbe not now. But in time it will come clear.'

'Nothing else? A name or two? Couple of addresses?'

She looked at him with eyes that said she knew he was taking the Mick, and it was something she was used to.

'I know you're an intelligent man, Sergeant Summers,' she said. 'You don't have to believe me now, but you will.'

'I'm sure you're right,' Frank said, standing up. 'Many thanks for your time, Mrs Ziggurat. Constable Gregson will show you out.'

Clementine Ziggurat waited until he had left before turning to Gertie.

'It's true what the voices said,' she told her. 'But I really came to see what your Sergeant looked like. He is in great danger.'

'Oh?' asked Gertie, with the strange mixture of boredom and tingling excitement people have when visiting a fortune-teller at a fair, knowing intellectually that it's just a bit of harmless fun, but wondering if it wasn't.

'"Beware the demon angels three

Beware the twin cycles of the devil machine

Beware the two eyes of green

Beware the fate that sets you free,"' Clementine Ziggurat intoned.

'Um, right,' said Gertie. She paused. 'Twin cycles of the devil machine?' she asked. 'As in washing machine? The one in the flat above me flooded me out a week ago.'

'I don't know,' admitted Clementine, standing up. 'I'm just telling you what the voices said. Doesn't make any sense to me. Oh, and he mustn't wear leather. He must never wear leather.'

'That's bad luck, is it?'

'No, I'm a vegan. I don't believe in wearing the skins of murdered animals. And no black. He mustn't wear black.'

'Because ...'

'It wouldn't go with his hair colour.'

'Right,' said Gertie, standing aside to allow the strange, perfectly-normal looking woman out of the room. She escorted her to reception, running the warning through her head. Most of it didn't make any sense.

Apart from the "demon angels three". That made perfect sense.

'You took your time,' Frank said when she returned to their office.

'Oh, Mrs Ziggurat just wanted someone to talk to,' she said offhandedly. 'She seems like a dear old thing, just a bit scrambled in the head.'

'You're probably right,' he said, 'but we aren't paid to be social workers. Come on, Gertie, let's go pay our retired policeman Mr Sampson a visit. And, as a reward for hard work, you can drive.'

'Thanks, Sarge. Hey, do you know what "the eyes of green and the devil's twin cycles of the machine" means?'

'Haven't a clue. Sounds like a mixture of Agatha Christie and a soap powder advert. Where did you read it?'

'Oh, can't remember, Sarge. Probably doesn't mean anything.'

'Actually it could come from a Pink Floyd album,' Frank said thoughtfully. 'Remind me to check sometime.'

'Surely he would have come to the station if he had anything to tell us,' suggested Gertie as they drove through Wellbury's quiet afternoon streets later that day. 'As an ex-copper, I mean.'

'Any number of reasons why not. Maybe he hasn't heard. Maybe he never listens to the news. Maybe he did it himself. According to Eric, Tom Sampson was the epitome of a gentle giant. Retired two years ago. His only problem was a sudden temper, very rare, but it got him into trouble on a few occasions over the years. And it looks like whoever did Nagness in did it on the spur of the moment.'

Gertie shivered.

'I hope it isn't him,' she said. 'The newspapers would tear him apart, him being an ex-copper. Doesn't seem fair, somehow. Nice old bloke like that.'

Frank found himself once again in the mystified position of trying to work out how women could automatically decide a person was one of the good guys, without even meeting them, and even if they were suspected, or had done, something which would normally be considered abhorrent.

Still, he thought, at the moment he was in the good books of three women who were more than prepared to consider him the lowest form of life possible. Susan, Frieda and Gertie. For over twenty-four hours not one of them had had a go at him.

He crossed his fingers, touched wood, and said a prayer to the god of chaos.

There was no answer when they rang the bell of the neat little house where Thomas Sampson was supposedly enjoying his retirement.

'Should have called ahead first, I suppose,' noted Frank.

'Maybe he's around the back,' suggested Gertie.

'Can I help you?' asked an aggressive voice. They turned to find a tall, grey-haired man looking over the neighbour's hedge.

'Detective Sergeant Summers,' said Frank, showing his warrant card. 'This is Detective Constable Gregson. We were hoping to find Mr Sampson in.'

Suddenly the man's suspicious face dissolved into a smile. He looked Gertie up and down.

'Good thing you weren't around when I was in the force, love,' he said with a chuckle. 'I would never have retired. I would have come in every day just to get a glimpse of you.'

'You're Thomas Sampson?' asked Frank as Gertie blushed.

'Aye, lad. Call me Tom. I was just doing a spot of tidying up for the neighbour. She's got arthritis. Finds weeding too painful these days. Hang on a tick, I'll come round.'

As he came around to the front Frank saw why he had been called a giant. He was at least six foot six, and built like an overweight rugby player.

'Come in,' he said, opening his front door. 'About time for a cuppa anyway.'

They followed him into a neat little kitchen. Everything about the house spoke of a bachelor existence, the sort where everything was kept in its place, everything neat and tidy the way he thought his mother, or wife, if he had ever had one, would have liked it.

'No Mrs Sampson?' asked Frank out of curiosity.

'Nay, lad,' answered Sampson with a deep northern accent, 'never did get around to marrying. Had high hopes once, mind, but it never came to nothing. Job got in the way, I suppose.'

He laid out three teacups and saucers with his massive hands, the tea service delicately floral patterned.

'So, to what do I owe this honour,' he asked. 'Have I committed a crime, or are you here to pick my brains? Can't say you'll get much out of them, mind.'

'Have you ever heard of an Agnes Whitehead?' asked Frank.

'Agnes Whitehead? Oh, aye, I remember dear Agnes.'

'Dear Agnes?'

'I was what you might call being polite. She were a right pain in the posterior, about – let me see – ten years ago? No, mebbe less. Come, sit yourselves down.'

They sat at the little kitchen table as he poured tea and continued.

'She had a nickname, Nagness, which is what she was. Kept phoning the station to complain about something. At first they sent me out – I had a reputation of being a bit of a softy, thought my pleasant manner would keep her quiet. But after about, let me see, ten times? Mebbe more. Even I was growing a little impatient, as you could say. She had a right whiny little voice, enough to drive the sanest man mad. I can't deny there were a time I was tempted to take her by her shrivelled little shoulders and shake some sense into her, I can tell you.'

He paused, looked at Frank, and then passed each a delicate cup of tea.

'What happened?' asked Frank.

'Percy the Pouffe – Percy Hanson, new Inspector at the time, he settled it. Went round to Nagness's place and read her the riot act. Wasting police time, that sort of thing. He still around, by any chance?'

'Oh, yes, Inspector Hanson's still around,' said Frank. And probably as miserable as he was in your day, he wanted to add.

'Good bloke, Percy,' said Sampson, 'always one for a laugh, in those days, anyway. When I retired, couple of years ago, seemed like he'd lost his spark. Old before his time, he was. Too ambitious, see? Always trying too hard. Thinking about being Chief Constable in ten years instead of enjoying himself with what he had at the time. Any road, hasn't changed much, I would guess?'

'No, he hasn't changed much,' replied Frank, trying to reconcile the baggy-eyed, Beagle-faced Percy he knew with someone much younger who was "always one for a laugh".

'Pity you didn't let me know you were coming,' observed Sampson, looking down at his teacup, 'I could have made some scones. Maybe some Danish pastries, I found a recipe for them the other day.' He looked up with a weak smile. 'Still, you lot haven't come around to gossip and eat scones, have you? Nagness has reared her ugly little head again, I take it.'

'Not exactly,' said Frank. 'I take it you don't follow the news?'

'Nay, lad, can't abide the stuff. They do it deliberately, you know.'

'Do they? Who does what?'

'Oh, the government, the newspapers, the lot on the telly. Try to scare you into being too afraid to walk out of your own door. If it's not cancer or dying alone of old age on a hospital trolley it's terrorism and muggers. I tell you lad, I were in London when the IRA were doing their worst, and it was never as bad as it is today. Then they would just give you news. Unemotional, like. These days everything is a tragedy, a catastrophe. I haven't heard anyone as say the end of the world is nigh, but not far off it.'

Frank had to smile.

'Yes, I must admit I also get irritated with the news these days myself.'

'Irritated? I once almost put my fist through my television set. That's when I gave up on telly news, the newspapers, radio news, the lot. Even the local newspaper I skips to page five before reading, when I bother to buy it, that is.'

'You don't have a television set?'

'Oh, I still have the set. Wouldn't be able to watch Coronation Street without it, now would I?' said Sampson, smiling.

'I have some bad news about Agnes Whitehead,' Frank said, deciding that they had had enough polite conversation. 'She was murdered on Monday afternoon, in Trafalgar Park.'

Sampson paused with his cup halfway to his mouth.

'Murdered?' he asked incredulously. 'I can understand why

someone would think of it, but who would actually do such a thing? After all, this is Wellbury, not Arizona or Kansas or New York.'

'You haven't heard about a theory concerning eighty-five percent?'

Sampson waved his hand as if to ward Frank off.

'Nay, lad, I know you modern coppers love statistics, but if you start on that you can leave right now. Gives me a right brain-ache, does that. Politicians love that sort of thing. Adverts are full of it. Ninety percent of people who fed their bow-wows with canned woof-meat felt better within themselves in two days. Load of rubbish, it is. You start believing it, then it turns out they've diddled the figures, one way or another. But it's like the news. Seems like they attacking you from every direction, until you just feel like hitting back. Still,' he added, giving Frank another grin, 'what the Lord giveth he also taketh away, or whatever the saying is. Whoever invented the remote control deserves the Nobel Peace Prize. I bet I can switch channels faster than anyone else.'

Some married couple might disagree about the Peace Prize for the remote control, Frank thought. But the suggestion told him a lot about Sampson's life.

If Sampson were telling the truth, of course.

'It probably isn't relevant in this case,' he said. 'The thing is, we reviewed some CCTV footage from close to where Agnes Whitehead was murdered, and you appeared in it. We were hoping you might have spotted something.'

Sampson looked at him. It was a far from friendly look. Suddenly the temperature in the kitchen seemed to have plummeted.

'You mean you think I might have done it. That's about the size of it, isn't it?'

Frank looked him in the eyes.

'Maybe,' he said calmly. 'You have form for losing your temper. On the other hand, if it wasn't you, you still have a copper's eyes and ears. You could well have seen or heard something that could help us.'

Sampson looked back with glowering eyes.

'Get out!' he said with some vehemence.

Frank did not respond. He sat waiting for Sampson to repeat his injunction, or collapse and apologise for losing his temper.

Sampson stood up, and Frank and Gertie found themselves looking up at a furious giant.

'Did you hear me?' shouted Sampson. 'I told you to get out! Now!'

Frank stood up calmly. Gertie was almost shivering.

'I mean you no harm, lass,' Sampson told her. 'I wouldn't touch a hair of your pretty head. This one, on the other hand … mebbe I'll just rip his head off and not worry about the hairs.'

Frank looked at him dispassionately.

'I'm a copper, Tom,' he said calmly. 'You're still a copper, even if you've retired. When you feel ready to apologise you know where to find me. Thank you for the tea. It was very nice. Come on Gertie.'

He led a shaken Gertie out of the neat little house. Behind them they heard the front door slam violently.

'Would you mind driving, Sarge?' she asked. 'I feel a little shaky.'

He smiled and gave her a hug. He kissed her forehead. She leaned into him, showing, he presumed, how shaken she was.

'You'll be fine, Gertie, my sweet. It's the shock of the unexpected. Nobody expects a copper to come across like that, especially not a retired copper. Come on, once you feel that accelerator under your foot you'll forget everything. Trust me.'

His prediction came true far sooner than he expected, and in a way he should, from experience, have expected. Crossing his fingers and touching wood had not deterred his own personal hex.

'That was bloody unfair,' she said, ramming through several gears in seconds, making him fear that she might accidentally slam the car into reverse at fifty miles an hour.

'Gertie, calm down. What on earth are you talking about?'

'What am I talking about? That poor old bloke, in retirement, goes out of his way to help his neighbour, gives us tea, even wishes he had baked us some scones, and you dig right into him. A right sweet old bloke, but no, Sergeant Frank Summers likes to put the knife in, doesn't he? Sergeant Frank Summers, original bastard and total son of a bitch.'

Frank held on to his safety belt as they took a corner at speed, narrowly missing a four-wheel drive with extra-large bull-bar being driven by a woman with two children in the back. He could have sworn the woman was about to make a rude gesture, until she seemed to think better about it.

'Gertie, you're being unreasonable,' he said, with far more fear in him from Gertie's driving than Tom Sampson's standing above him, which had been sufficiently terrifying.

'Fuck you,' was the astounding reply.

Normally he would have come back with a witty repartee, such as "I'm busy right now, what about in five minutes' time?", but this was definitely not the time. Enough was enough. He slapped his hand on the dashboard.

'Pull over. Now,' he said.

'No,' she said.

He held his hand over the handbrake.

'You will obey orders, Constable Gregson,' he said, stressing the word "will". Reluctantly she pulled in towards the pavement, put the car in neutral, and folded her arms.

'Keys,' he said, holding his hand out. She stayed sitting with folded arms.

'Sorry about this, Gertie,' he said, reaching across her and switching the engine off, taking the keys.

He had been caught out before the same way. Only then it had been an ex-girlfriend he had watched drive off into the midnight darkness, leaving him standing watching his own car disappear.

'Out,' he said, 'passenger seat time.'

'I'd rather walk,' she said, climbing out of the driver's seat.

'I'm not given you the option, Gertie, you will bloody well do as you are told, got it?'

He had never, ever said that sort of thing to anyone. Not as a beat bobby, not as a detective constable arresting the lowest of the low. He had always got his way by charm and a joke. To his surprise Gertie obeyed his instructions. She wasn't happy, but she did as she was told.

'Okay, Gertie, what have I done wrong this time?' he asked as he slipped into the driver's seat and switched on the ignition.

Constable Gregson remained silent. Her pursed lips needed no comment.

'Gertie, Tom Sampson might be an ex-copper, but he's also a prime suspect. Notice how clean and neat his house was? Those pretty little teacups? Talking of baking scones? Boy, talk of repressed urges. If we had a psychologist doing a profile our Tom would be in the front line-up.'

'And you, of course, being such a macho man, would never dream of baking scones. In fact you never cook at all. I've seen it. If you haven't a little woman to look after you, you order a takeaway from that greasy little Italian place.'

Frank took a deep breath as he drove. Gertie was being totally and unreasonably unfair.

There was nothing greasy about the Italian place. It was always spick and span.

'As it happens,' he said, 'I have a very good recipe for scones. Best in the world, if I say so myself. I'll make some tonight, if you want. Or tomorrow night, rather,' he added, remembering his date with Susan.

'I wouldn't want to get in the way of you and Doctor Death.'

Frank knew when he was beaten. He decided to give up.

'Your mum's recipe, is it?' asked Gertie suddenly, with a great deal of scorn.

'As it happens, yes,' replied Frank with some surprise. 'They say nothing compares with mother's cooking. In my case they're right. My Mum could out-cook anyone she cared to.'

'You are a total, total shit, Frank Summers,' said Gertie, leaning in to the window, sobbing. 'I hate you, I really, really hate you.'

Frank was a good driver. He managed to avoid running over three lampposts, four post-boxes and untold pedestrians on the way back to the office. Which, considering his state of mind, was a miracle. He wondered vaguely if there was something more than Tom Sampson's outburst behind Gertie's reaction.

But experience told him that once one of them blew, the others followed shortly after. He didn't know why Gertie had lost it. Tom Sampson was an obvious suspect. Gertie was experienced enough to know that.

He did, however, know that he was about to end up in deep trouble with Frieda and Susan. It didn't make sense. But he had long given up on life making sense.

The ancients had realised after long experimentation that you could make fire by rubbing two sticks of wood together. No one had ever worked out the result of rubbing two women together.

Probably none of them had survived to tell the tale.

Back at the station Gertie disappeared into the ladies'. Frank wasn't unhappy to see her do so. He was trying to solve a murder. He didn't need the added hassle of Gertie throwing a wobbly.

In his office he found Frieda standing looking out of the window. Of all the things he really did not need at that moment was Frieda's statuesque back.

'Anything I can help you with, Inspector?' he asked savagely as he threw himself into his chair. 'Or have you already been through my drawers and filing cabinets?'

She turned and paused before replying.

'That is very unworthy of you, Frank,' she said softly.

He wished he still smoked. He would give anything for a good cigarette right then. He knew he was being unfair.

Frieda was glad he had his back to her. Otherwise he might have caught the guilty look in her face. She had been through his desk and filing cabinets while he was away. It was almost an automatic response. She had always gone through her ex-husband's clothes when she had first suspected that he was having an affair. While he was not using his fists on her.

'I apologise,' Frank said, finally.

'Are you going to tell me about it?' asked Frieda softly, putting a hand on his shoulder.

He might well have, had not Gertie walked in, red-eyed, and gone straight to her desk, putting her head down to read some report, ignoring both of them.

Frieda sighed.

'I'm sorry, children,' she said, 'but you're both going to have to pretend to be playing happily for another hour or so. There's been another one.'

Gertie turned around. Frank looked up at Frieda, but, with her hand on his shoulder, all he caught was an eyeful of her bosom. He stood up.

'Another what?' he asked.

Frieda took a step back.

'A body was found half an hour ago,' she said. 'It had a note pinned to it. Eighty five percent. Minus two.'

Frank stood looking at her in silence for a while.

'You are joking, aren't you?' he suggested. Her look denied

the suggestion. 'Where?' he asked.

'Old Merrick. A traffic warden.'

'Right,' said Frank, 'let's be off then.' He turned to Gertie. 'You get along,' he said, 'your shift was over a while ago.'

'Gertie's coming with us,' Frieda said quietly. Frank turned towards her.

'Are you telling me how to run my own case, Inspector?' he asked looking her in the eyes.

To his surprise she took his hand in hers, squeezed, returned his look and said one word.

'Please?' she asked softly.

He looked down at her hand. He turned to look at Gertie. She was hunched over her desk, like someone awaiting the final blade of execution.

'Very well,' he said, taking a deep breath. 'Against my better judgement. But I don't want to hear a peep out of you, understand?' Gertie didn't answer. 'Let's go then,' said Frank.

They left, Frank leading, the other two trailing silently. They got into his car, Frank in the driver's seat, Gertie and Frieda in the back seats. Had he been observant, Frank might have noticed Frieda taking Gertie's hand and squeezing it in comfort. Instead he relied on Frieda's instructions to arrive at their destination.

I'm responsible for her, Frieda thought. I'm her senior officer. She's in a bad way.

At the same time she's the competition.

What the hell am I supposed to do?

Blast you, Frank Summers. As soon as this case is over you

get posted.

There was a small gap between a restaurant and a clothes shop, one which would have been an alley before the front end was bricked up. Now it was used only for deliveries and waste bins. The open end at the back was cordoned off and guarded by a uniformed constable. He saluted as Frieda approached, and lifted the police tape to let them through. In the alley a white forensic tent had been squashed between the walls. Susan, standing outside in white overalls and sterile over-boots spotted them and came towards them.

'We've only just begun,' she said. 'Better not come any further until we've finished.'

'I understand there was another note attached to the victim,' Frieda said.

'Tracey,' Susan called to someone in the tent. 'Could you bring that note here for a second.'

A young girl wearing spectacles and white overall came out of the tent with a plastic holder in her hand. She gave Frank a smile and an appraising look. She and Frank had spoken on the telephone a few times. He had been fascinated by her voice. Then he had invited her out for drinks as an excuse to avoid a multiple date with Susan, Frieda and Gertie, believing Tracey to be gay and his motives thus above suspicion. She had turned out to be more attractive than he had hoped.

And not gay.

Susan, Frieda and Gertie had not been impressed. Despite his protestations that he liked Tracey, but not in that way, he had ended up in the doghouse. He didn't see why either Gertie or Frieda should have anything to do with his social life, but he had been far too experienced to point that fact out to either of them.

'Thank you, Tracey, now get back to work,' Susan said, having caught the looks that passed between them. 'I don't want to spend all night here.'

Frank took the folder from Susan, apparently immediately forgetting about Tracey. It contained an A4 piece of paper which had at some stage been folded in three. On it were pasted cuttings from a newspaper or magazine. The first was two numbers "8" and "5", followed by a percentage sign, a dash, and the figure "2".

'Now that changes things,' he said softly. 'Oh, yes, that really does change things.'

'In what way?' asked Susan.

'Nagness was killed on the spur of the moment – or that's my guess, anyway. This was obviously planned. Someone took the time and trouble to put this together beforehand.'

'Do we have any details on the victim?' asked Frieda.

'Female, about fifty. Dressed in a traffic warden's uniform. Name of Chiffon Brady, according to the warden's identity card she had. Height about five foot four. Rather badly overweight, though I don't suppose that will bother her anymore.'

'Cause of death?' asked Frank, handing back the folder.

'She was hit on the back of the head with a blunt object. There's an iron bar we've tagged up which could be the murder weapon. Time of death – at a first guess, quite a few hours ago. Maybe six or seven, possibly longer. A couple of your constables are making enquiries of the people who work in the restaurant. They might be able to narrow it down – I would imagine they have fixed delivery times, rubbish collection, that sort of thing. No-one who came into this alley this far could have missed seeing the body.'

She looked at Frank.

'I'd better get back to work. Looks like we'll have to reschedule those drinks,' she said with a bitter smile, and walked back to the tent.

'That's a nuisance,' Frieda commented.

Frank presumed she wasn't talking about having his evening's social activity curtailed.

'In what way?' he asked.

'If the body's been lying here for six hours or more there's not much we can do here. I'll get a couple of the night shift to start interviewing anyone who works around here, but they'll be at home or out doing whatever it is they do on a Tuesday evening. It will probably take all evening, if not longer. Come on, you can give me a lift back to the station, then get on home. I want you both in bright, early and fresh tomorrow. Hopefully Susan will have come up with something for us to work on by then.'

'Pretty unlikely,' Frank noted as they walked back to his car. This time Gertie got in the back and Frieda took the front passenger seat.

'Yes,' agreed Frieda as she slipped her safety-belt on. 'Whoever it was took the trouble to prepare for it. We'd be incredibly lucky if they slipped up enough to leave fingerprints or other damaging evidence lying around.'

'Who found her?'

'A young waitress working in the restaurant. Took some

rubbish out and found the body. She's now under sedation, apparently.'

'Interesting choice of victim,' Gertie noted hesitantly.

'How so?' asked Frank, concentrating on driving.

'A traffic warden. Nobody likes traffic wardens.'

'Good point,' commented Frieda. 'And nobody liked Nagness either. If you had to choose two victims whom most people would agree belonged in the so-called eighty-five percent, those two would qualify quite easily.'

'We don't know if there is a direct link between them,' Frank noted as they drove into the station forecourt and stopped before the entrance.

'First thing tomorrow we're going to start finding out,' Frieda replied, opening her car door. You two get off home.' She paused before getting out. 'And, Frank, before we start tomorrow I think you and I should have a chat about the correct way to address your senior officer.'

Gertie skipped around to the seat Frieda had just vacated. Frank watched Frieda's back disappear into the police station.

'Great,' he said miserably, 'now I'm back in the doghouse with Frieda.' He looked at Gertie. 'You still mad at me?' he asked. 'Pity I didn't manage to get Susan's back up, I could have done the triple.'

'No, Sarge,' said Gertie humbly. 'I'm sorry I lost it, it was my fault.'

'Can't blame you, really, our Tom Sampson is quite a terrifying sight when he loses his rag. I suppose I shall have to go back and apologise. I could have been a little more tactful.'

'I don't think you did anything wrong, Sarge.'

'Oh, well, sod it. The day's over. What say we have a drink on the way home?'

'Er, it's not really my night,' Gertie said, and suddenly stopped.

'How do you mean, not your night?'

'I meant it hasn't been my day,' she replied quickly.

'Oh, I don't know, it hasn't been that bad. I've known worse.'

'But wouldn't Susan be a little upset if we did that? You were supposed to be having drinks and dinner with her tonight.'

'I'm sure she'll understand,' Frank said confidently.

If she actually found out in the first place, he thought. And there was no reason for that to happen.

Thursday: Mrs Blower and motorbikes

Frank had hoped to get in before Frieda. It would have given him a slight but crucial psychological edge, and he rather suspected he would need any advantage he could get during the "chat about the correct way to address your senior officer" that Frieda had decided upon the previous evening. It would be one-way, and not much of a chat. If it looked as if he were already hard at work when she arrived to take him to task she would be slightly on the back foot by interrupting. Not much, but sinners especially needed all the moral high ground they could find or steal.

Keith Bute on early desk duty disabused him. Frieda was in her office, war paint on, and wanted to see him immediately he got in.

'From her mood I don't think she's planning on giving you a sweetie for being a good little boy,' Keith commented.

'Great,' said Frank. 'Round one to Frieda. Oh, by the way, congratulations on the new baby.'

'Cheers, Frank,' Keith said morosely. 'You know, the missus and I talked about kids before we got married. I said three were more than enough, and she agreed. Sometimes I wonder if that was just to make me feel good. I think she meant to have as many as possible right from the start.'

'Taking paternity leave?' asked Frank.

Keith paused in contemplation.

'I was going to,' he said, 'in a week or two when Marie's out of hospital. But – well, there's strange things happening.'

'Strange? In what way?'

'Last night's Wednesday, right,' Keith said, leaning his elbows on the reception desk. 'Normally it's a quiet night, but not this one. Drunk and disorderlies all over the place. This eighty-five percent business, it's getting out of hand. And then, you'll never guess what.'

'In that case I won't try. What?'

'Know the Albany home for old folk? Six o'clock this morning we get a call about a disturbance there. Patrol car goes to investigate. Turns out one of the residents called another an eighty-five percenter. One's a retired headmaster, the other's a retired headmistress, respectable as the day's long, you'd think. You won't believe this, but they were chasing each other around a couch in the day room, or whatever they call it – both on Zimmer frames. Going about a mile an hour and threatening to kill each other. Trouble is, most of them have walking sticks hooked on to those Zimmer frames. Ed Watts tried to calm them down. He's now in hospital having his head looked at.'

'You're joking.'

'Not a word of a lie, Frank. I mean, who gets up at six o'clock in an old-age home?' He shook his head slowly. 'Now we've got Ed in hospital and two old folk sitting in the cells with their Zimmer frames. And we had to find them wheelchairs. We also had to put them into different cells, and those were already almost full from last night.' He gave Frank a direct look. 'Bobby Stang was down there to check on everything at one point. Comes back up holding the side of his face. Says one of the old folk almost poked a walking stick into it when he opened the grill to do a fifteen-minute check. So I go down to have a look, and he's right. At the back of one cell there's a group of drunks – perfectly respectable, normally that is, businessmen, that sort of thing – sharing a bottle of vodka and egging this old boy on. He's sitting in a wheelchair waiting at the cell door with his walking stick, ready to have a go at anyone who comes too close. At the other cell, exactly the same, only there it's an old woman and her supporters – who look like they come from the Women's Institute – have a bottle of whisky they're passing around. I don't even want to think of how we're going to explain how the bottles got in. If we ever find out.'

'Still, look on the bright side, Keith,' Frank said. 'You'll be handing over to Eric soon. I'm off to see the wicked Witch of Wellbury.'

Keith Bute perked up at the thought.

'I wouldn't stop for coffee or anything if I were you, Frank,' he said with the cheerfulness of someone who knows that, however bad their day had been, someone else was going to have a worse one.

'The Inspector ready for me now?' Frank asked Frieda's secretary.

'I'm afraid so, Sergeant Summers,' Mary replied unhappily.

'Cheer up, Mary, it's always darkest before the dawn.'

'Following that analogy, Sergeant Summers, it is currently about two in the morning, I'm afraid.'

Great, thought Frank, opening the door to hell.

Frieda was sitting at her desk with her reading glasses on. It was a bad sign. She had a trick of looking over them in the manner of a stern school-teacher dealing with a truculent and obtuse pupil.

'Morning, Inspector,' Frank said with a cheerfulness he didn't feel.

'You have that correctly, at least, Sergeant. It is morning. I note you did not use the prefix "good".'

She waited for him to respond.

'Okay, I was wrong to have snapped at you yesterday. I apologise. Can I have my bollocking and get on with some work?'

She drummed painted nails on her desk.

'I prefer the phrase "dressing down",' she noted. 'What was the cause of your little tantrum? You don't often lose your temper, Frank.'

Noting that he had been promoted from Sergeant back to Frank, he explained what had happened at Tom Sampson's house, and Gertie's reaction.

'Interesting,' she said when he had finished. 'This Sampson sounds like a dangerous man. I'll have a word with Percy about him.' She took her glasses off and stood up. 'However I am your senior officer, and I have decided that your lack of respect deserves a suitable punishment.' She smiled. 'You can take me out for drinks after work tonight. I don't see why I should have to pay every time.'

He blinked. Several thoughts raced through his head. He was planning on asking Susan out that evening. If she found out he had taken Frieda out instead he might as well leave town – if he got the chance.

On the other hand he had no objection to going out for drinks with Frieda, she was the best of company, and their professional relationship prevented any accidental misunderstanding.

And his career, such as it was, was likely to be on the line if he said no.

Possibly not just his career.

'That is, if you haven't anything better to do, of course,' added Frieda in the sort of tone of voice that someone holding several guns to your head might earnestly assure you that you did, indeed, have a choice in the matter.

'Not at all,' Frank replied, smiling. 'Sounds like an excellent idea. Best punishment I've ever been given. Trouble is it might even encourage me to – '

'Don't even think of going there, Frank,' Frieda warned. 'I can cope with the occasional outburst. But if you deliberately try to wind me up at work you will suffer a slow and agonising death. Capisch?'

'Capisch,' agreed Frank, still grinning.

'Go on then, bugger off you useless sod. Get yourself some coffee. I'll meet you and Gertie in the ops room in fifteen minutes.'

Frank left the office humming "Blue skies" to himself. He blew a kiss at Mary as he passed her, leaving her with an incredulous look on her face. People did not leave Frieda's office that way after a bollocking. Not normally. Not ever, until now.

Frank felt like a man who had faced the gallows only to find he had won the lottery instead. He didn't know what it was about Frieda, but he really liked her.

He paused in mid-walk. Had Frieda actually used the word "bugger"? And "sod"?

He shook his head in amazement. If he told anyone else that

they wouldn't believe him.

'Blue skies, nothing but blue skies,' he sang in a deep voice as he walked into his office and sat down.

'Blimey, Sarge, I thought you were going in for a bollocking,' said Gertie.

'The correct phrase, my dear Gertie, is "dressing down".' He looked at her. 'You won't believe this, but Frieda actually used the words "bugger" and "sod".'

'I think I'd better get you some coffee, Sarge,' Gertie said, standing up. 'You seem to be hallucinating.'

'Morning, Susan,' Gertie sang out as Susan appeared in the doorway. 'I'm just off to get Frank some coffee. Like some?'

'Morning, Gertie,' Susan replied. 'I won't have time, just popped in to drop my initial report off. But thanks, anyway.'

'Okay, see you later,' Gertie said happily, leaving to get Frank's coffee.

Frank had watched the scene with eyes that had grown progressively wider.

'You okay, Frank?' asked Susan.

'Gertie said I was hallucinating. I think she was right.'

'In what way?'

Because I've never seen you two being such pals before, Frank wanted to say. Not so much as being at daggers drawn, more like daggers, knives, boots, nails and anything short of nuclear weapons.

'Oh, nothing,' he said instead. 'Listen, sorry about last night.'

'Hardly your fault, Frank. Comes with the job.'

Now he knew he was hallucinating. Susan being reasonable?

And happy with it?

'Look, I'll make it up to you,' he said. 'How about, um, when are you free next?'

Please don't say tonight, he thought. Please, please don't say tonight.

'Let's see,' Susan replied, her lips moving as if counting. 'Today's Thursday ... How about Saturday evening?'

'Great, great, Saturday evening sounds perfect.'

'One thing left over from last night which I still want,' Susan said, leaning over his desk and pulling him towards her with his tie. 'A goodnight kiss.'

To his surprise he found himself receiving the sort of kiss normally preceded by several gin and tonics.

'That was nice,' she said, finally letting him down in his chair. 'See you Saturday,' she sang, and turned to go.

Frieda and Gertie stood in the doorway.

'Not against the rules, is it?' Susan asked gaily as she walked out between them. 'After all, it's just delayed from last night.'

'I shall have to check the rules,' Frieda muttered, frowning. Gertie put a mug of coffee in front of Frank, and Frieda came around to his side of his desk.

'Your tie's all skew, Frank Summers,' she noted, straightening it and dusting his jacket. 'There, we can't have our best-dressed officer looking all rumpled, now can we?'

For some reason Frank experienced the same feelings he normally did in a dentist's chair. Susan, Frieda and Gertie were being very, very nice to him, and it made him very, very nervous.

There was something very, very wrong here.

'Time we got on with a little work, isn't it?' he suggested, almost coughing.

'I suppose so,' sighed Frieda. 'Come on, bring Susan's report with you. The others will be waiting in the ops room.'

Frank spent most of his time avoiding work. It was only when something interesting came along that he found himself unable to let go. Now he had an added reason for losing himself in the case.

Three added reasons.

'Chiffon Brady,' Constable Ken Edgars said, reading from his notebook. Constables Sidney Feeler and Steve Right sat alongside. The three had been working overnight, and looked ready for some sleep. 'Pronounced "Shivonne", apparently,' Edgars continued. 'Lived on her own in a small flat in the Grovelands. Divorced, no children. No close friends or near relatives. Managed to rub along with her neighbours, but only just. Apparently she could be rather abrasive. Her colleagues at work regarded her in much the same light. She tended to work on her own. According to her boss she did just sufficient work to stay in the job. Not a slacker, as such, but unlikely to win the employee of the month award.'

'For which many motorists would have given thanks,' noted Frieda standing at the whiteboard. 'But none of the people you interviewed disliked her enough to murder her, would you say?'

'No, Inspector. She doesn't appear to have been liked a great deal. At the same time she wasn't the type to inspire any great emotions in anyone, not enough to physically attack her.'

'What do we have from that Path report, Frank?'

Frank flipped through the pages.

'Weapon used was the iron bar Susan mentioned last night. Victim was facing away from her killer. Evidence suggests she heading out of the alley when she was struck, and the body rolled behind a rubbish skip. No fingerprints or any other helpful evidence. A large number of partial footprints, mainly from the type of boots refuse collectors and builders might wear, but also some from children and a few from the sort of heels made by women's shoes. No details yet on the paper the note was made of, or anything to indicate where the clippings were taken from.' He looked up. 'It's only a preliminary report. Hopefully we'll get more later.'

'That alley used to be what you might call something of a lovers' lane,' Sid Feeler commented. 'I expect it still is on Friday nights.'

'When you say "lovers' lane", is that a polite reference to what might be called a commercial trade in sex?' asked Frieda.

'On the odd occasion, probably. But more a favourite place for youngsters whose parents are at home. Somewhere to pop in on the way home from a night out, to get to know each other better, if I can put it that way..'

'What about the girl who found the body?' asked Frank.

'One Kerri Heeler,' Sid replied. 'Works at the restaurant. Seventeen, all of about five feet tall, probably wouldn't have been able to lift an iron bar, let alone hit anyone over the head with one. Had hysterics at the sight. I don't think there's much she'll be able to tell us.'

'Times of deliveries,' Frieda said. 'Did you manage to get those?'

Steve Right flipped open his notebook.

'Rubbish is collected first thing every morning,' he noted. 'The restaurant started employing a private firm rather than rely on the council ever since they discovered rat droppings in the kitchen. The other shop, the ladies' clothes shop – La Maison Chic – that's French for The House of Chic, isn't it?'

'It's English for very expensive,' noted Frieda. 'I wouldn't shop there, you couldn't afford it and they probably don't have your size.'

Sid coloured a little as the others hid smiles.

'They had two deliveries yesterday morning,' he continued quickly. 'Last one was just after eleven. There were two men and a girl involved with that, driver, loader and a designer. They all agree that the alley was empty when they left. I certainly didn't get any impression that they might be hiding anything. The girl was your arty sort, too involved with her own dresses to consider anything else to be of importance. I think the other two thought she was a bit off her head.'

'I'm pretty sure we can scratch any idea of this being a plot of more than two people,' Frank said. 'In fact I'd put money on it being a single person.' The others nodded.

'I'd bet good money on it being an escaped loony,' Sid said, yawning.

'Okay, you lot go home and get some beauty sleep,' Frieda said, taking the hint. 'Leave your notebooks here in case we need to check anything. You can write up your reports when you come back on shift. And don't forget, not a word to anyone about the note.'

They uttered various degrees of grateful thanks and left before Frieda could change her mind.

'So, Frank, what does your crystal ball tell you about this

one?' Frieda asked, snapping the cap back on the marker pen she had been using, and throwing it onto the table in irritation.

'Approaching this logically, we have two possibilities,' he said after some thought. 'Firstly that the two murders are unrelated, committed by different people. In a way that's the best case scenario for us because they would be one-offs, though it would make it twice as difficult for us. The worst case scenario is that the same person committed both murders. It would make our lives easier, but it would also mean that further murders are almost guaranteed if we don't catch the person in time.'

'That's precisely what worries me. I have this horrible feeling that that's exactly what is going to happen.'

'I think we need to pick one of the possibilities and approach it on that basis,' Frank continued. 'We don't have the resources to handle both at the same time. We can always change tack if it seems we're wrong.'

'And which would you go for?'

Frank stood up.

'I think they were done by the same person. The modus operandi is too similar. Crude, but effective. We have a list of people who were in the area when Nagness got hers, now we need a list of those around when Chiffon was killed. If we're lucky we'll be able to narrow it down to one or two names. Someone must have seen something. The restaurant is no good, they wouldn't have opened until late in the day.' He turned to Gertie. 'How do you fancy a shopping trip, Gertie? Let's find out how observant the people are in La Maison de l'argent.'

'La maison de what?' asked Gertie.

'The house of money,' Frieda translated. 'Frank's just trying to show he knows three words of French.'

'Ah, mais je parle la francais tout bien,' Frank said, smiling. And hoping they didn't test this assertion.

Gertie looked at him in admiration. Frieda had a different look. She pursed her lips.

'In that case, Frank, I suggest you allez, and be vite about it, before you get le kick up votre derriere.'

'I think that should be "la" kick,' Frank said, before exiting a la rapide.

Le marking pen de l'Inspector hit la porte shortly afterwards.

Unlike the bank the clothes shop did not have external CCTV, but it did have internal cameras watching over the various departments. Ms Healey, the manageress, was more than willing to go through the relevant tapes with Frank and Gertie. She was also more than willing to share the trials and tribulations of her trade.

'Unfortunately it's difficult to get decent staff these days,' she was saying as she slotted in the first tape, starting at ten o'clock the previous morning. 'You have to have a good memory for names and faces, to make customers feel welcome. And then you have to have a thick skin to handle some of them. Add to that the fact that it isn't the best paid job in the world, and you end up with youngsters who just aren't interested. Now, let's see,' she said, pressing the Play button. The screen showed an empty lingerie department. 'Bad time for business, Tuesday morning,' she commented, and pressed Fast-Forward. She stopped when a figure appeared in the frame.

'Well, well,' said Frank, 'if it isn't our friend from the media, Phil Walthers. What's he doing wandering around ladies' underwear early on a Tuesday morning? Shop here often, does he?'

'No, he was here about an article on the latest fashion in Wellbury,' Ms Healey said. 'I thought we'd agreed on Wednesday morning, but he turned up yesterday instead. It was a little irritating because I'd arranged for one of our young assistants to show off some of our latest lines. Clothes look much better on a body. If you photograph them on a mannequin or hanger, or lying flat, they just appear lifeless.'

'Why would he be in lingerie, though? Isn't that at the back of your shop?'

'He was looking for my office, or so he claimed.'

'Well, that's one on the list to have a word with.'

'You don't think he could have – not Mr Walthers, surely? He might be a little strange, but I never thought ... '

'It would be very fortuitous for us if the murderer popped in for a pair of sling backs and a cross your heart girdle before committing the crime, Ms Healey,' Frank said, 'but pretty unlikely. What we're looking for are people in the area at the time who might have seen someone who didn't want to be noticed or someone acting in a strange manner.'

'I see. In that case Mr Walthers could be useful, then, Sergeant? As a journalist he probably keeps his eyes open more than most.'

'Quite so, Ms Healey,' lied Frank. Of course Walthers would be a suspect. Frank just didn't want him to find that out via Ms Healey.

Fast-forwarding of the tape revealed only one other customer in lingerie: Mrs Blower.

'That would mean the vicar was in the bookshop up the road,' noted Ms Healey. 'He finds it embarrassing to enter a ladies' clothing shop. He really is a dear.'

'So I'm told,' replied Frank, adding the vicar and Mrs Blower to his list.

Ms Healey changed the tape to that from Nightwear. Only one customer, a thin, middle-aged unshaven man wearing a gold earring.

'Mr Kerouac,' Ms Healey said with some distaste. 'Apparently he has a programme on the radio. He offered to mention our name if we gave him a discount. I declined as politely as I could.'

'Zack the Prat,' said Frank thoughtfully. 'Very interesting.'

The Daily Wear department revealed only two elderly women looking suspiciously at the garments on display. They looked the type who could be dangerous on the first day of a sale, but unlikely to be serial killers.

The final tape, of Evening Wear, showed a bearded man wearing tinted glasses and a pork-pie hat studying an evening gown.

'Hello, Christmas has come early,' Frank noted.

'That isn't Christmas,' Ms Healey said, 'the Christmas sale won't begin until September at the earliest.'

'Ah, yes, my mistake,' replied Frank. 'Let's finish off this tape. See what other delights we have in store.'

But there were none. As Ms Healey had noted, Tuesday morning was not the best time for fashion. Frank and Gertie left, assuring Ms Healey that she had been most helpful, and she had no reason to worry, the previous day's murder undoubtedly the result of a mugging that went wrong, or, more probably, seeing the look of concern on her face, an argument with an enraged ex-husband which had ended tragically.

'Enraged ex-husband?' asked Gertie in disbelief as she pulled out from their parking space on their way back to the station. Frank had been amused to find a parking ticket stuck to the windscreen.

'No good in getting the general populace worried about their personal safety, is there, Gertie?'

'I suppose not, Sarge. But if this eighty-five percent killer is targeting those he thinks surplus to requirements, well ... a lot of people think the fashion world – how can I put this?'

'I know, Gertie. Wealthy women wearing expensive clothes and contributing not a jot to society's well-being. But what about hair-dressers? Ticket collectors? Bus inspectors? Tax inspectors? Where do you stop?'

Gertie made a grimace. Frank was right. She could have made her own list. The question was, if the murderer was what they thought possible, whom might he have in his own top ten?

And it could be a she. She might well have a totally different list.

'You going out with Frieda tonight?' she asked, to change the subject.

Frank felt like he had been hit with two damp squids at the same time. Firstly, how could Gertie have known, and secondly, what was this "Frieda" business?

'You're being a bit familiar, aren't you Constable Gregson?'

'I apologise, Sergeant,' she replied angrily, 'I didn't realise a simple question was intruding into your private affairs.'

Here we go again, he thought.

'I was referring to your use of Frieda's name,' he said agreeably. 'You usually call her Inspector.'

'You call her Frieda,' she pointed out.

'True. I was just surprised to hear you do so, that's all.'

'Well, if you insist on me calling her Inspector, your wish is my command, Sergeant.'

'Now, now, Gertie, let's not have another tiff. Tell me, do you mind being called Gertie, or do you prefer your given name, Samantha.'

Gertie smiled.

'I like Gertie. I didn't at first, but after a while, well it makes you feel as you belong when people use a nickname they've given you.'

'Very true, Gertie, very true. Though I tend to prefer it when people don't use mine.'

Phew, he thought, that averted World War III. Gertie was like old nitro-glycerine. She didn't need much careless treatment to explode.

'I think Frank's a lovely name,' she said. 'Much better than your nickname. And anyway, yours doesn't suit you.'

'So, what do you reckon, Psycho?' asked Eric Johns as they sat in the canteen having lunch. 'Topping traffic wardens. It's almost like doing good, I reckon.'

'Eric,' said Frank, investigating an alleged chicken sandwich he had obtained from the machine, 'you call me Psycho once more and I shall do something both of us will regret. Me purely because I will have to put on clean clothes afterwards.'

'Sorry, Frank,' Eric said, grinning. 'It's just that it feels, I dunno, a bit like one of those weird movies, Michael Caine playing a transvestite murderer bringing justice to the world, something like that. First Nagness, then a traffic warden. Not the sort of people anyone will shed many tears over.'

'Perhaps that would contribute to the definition of a civilised society,' Frank remarked. 'One where even the lesser-liked of people can feel safe.'

Eric sighed and looked at Gertie who was tucking into a hamburger and chips.

'I feel sorry for you, love, having to spend all that time with Frank here. I reckon his book-learning turned his mind.'

'Having a university degree hardly makes me the intellectual of the year, Eric.'

'Does around this place, Frank.'

'What about Frieda, then? She has a Masters.'

'Ah, Fabulous is special, Frank, you have to admit that yourself. You know,' he said as a thought hit his mind like a comet encountering a passing spaceship, 'it would be great if you and Frieda could get together. I mean, you're both single, you're both ... '

He paused as he realised that four baleful eyes were aimed in his direction.

'I hope you haven't been talking to anyone about the second murder, especially not Phil Walthers,' Frank said, changing the subject.

'Course not, Frank. My lips are sealed, you know that.' He

looked morosely down at the remains of his pie, gravy and chips. 'And after a word from the Inspector they are now triple-sealed. She doesn't half make her meaning clear.'

Frank laughed. He could easily imagine the scene. Eric wouldn't have understood most of the words Frieda might use. He definitely wouldn't have liked the ones he did.

'A word of warning, though Frank,' Eric continued. 'You'd better watch your step. I reckon you might have women trouble brewing.'

Brewing? thought Frank. If that was the word his life would have been a distillery.

'Anything specific you have in mind?' he asked, chewing at a lifeless sandwich.

Eric nodded towards the canteen counter.

'Our Agnetha isn't too happy with you,' he noted.

Frank turned slightly to have a look. It wasn't promising. Agnetha was standing behind the counter, her normal dour look vibrating with a sense of deep grievance. She wasn't officially in charge of the canteen. In reality, however, you crossed Agnetha at your peril. Percy Hanson had tried it once. It had been two months before he dared enter the canteen again, and ever after was only permitted in on sufferance.

'You'll be okay, Sarge,' Gertie said reassuringly, 'she likes you.'

'If that look on her face is liking someone,' Eric said, 'I'd hate to see what she looked like when she didn't like someone.' He turned to Frank. 'Listen, Frank, it's because you're getting your lunch from the machine. She thinks you don't like her cooking.'

Making sure that her boys and girls were properly fed had,

over the years, become Agnetha's very reason for existing. For one of them to reject her food was intolerable.

'The problem is I like her cooking too much,' replied Frank. 'I dream of her cooking. But if I indulged every day I would soon end up looking like – looking like the Michelin man,' he ended lamely, since he had been about to say "like you" to Eric.

He sighed and dropped a half-eaten sandwich into its plastic container.

'Some choice, eh?' he asked rhetorically. 'Pig out on what I like, or suffer the rubbish from the machine. You finished, Gertie?'

Gertie finished her last bit of apple-pie and fresh cream with a smile and nodded happily.

'That was yummee,' she said.

'Come on, then, duty calls.'

Gertie trailed after him. They were almost out of the canteen when a voice called.

'A word with you, young lady.'

Agnetha's voice was soft, with a faint Scottish burr. It didn't need to be loud. It was the type of voice that could carve its way through icebergs. It was the type of voice you might hear in the densest of fog, and be either very grateful, or very, very afraid.

'Something the problem, Agnetha?' asked Frank in his bestest, most charmingest, schoolboy voice, hoping his terror didn't show through.

'It was the young lady I wished to speak to, sir,' Agnetha said, directing her gaze upon him. 'Women's business.'

'Come on, Frank,' said Eric coming alongside, 'I need to speak to you about something.'

Frank let himself be led away reluctantly. Leaving Gertie in Agnetha's clutch seemed rather cowardly.

He wasn't afraid of being called a coward. He just would have preferred that both himself and Gertie could have made a run for it at the same time.

'Never get involved with women's business, Frank,' Eric said, guiding him away. 'You just end up finding yourself being hated by both of them. Leave them to sort their own problems out.'

Frank presumed that Eric was right. He knew Eric was right. It didn't make him feel any better.

He made his way back to his office. Concentrate on the case, he told himself. Why was Phil Walthers in that shop? Professor Humphries? What possible excuse could he have?

His stomach rumbled.

Those hamburgers Agnetha made. They were the real thing. She had taken a concept and turned it into her own idea of what a hamburger should be. Half a minced cow with spices and peppers, topped off with real cheese, a dash of home-made tomato sauce made with onions, and enveloped in a large toasted bun, freshly made that morning.

Walthers. He was supposed to be in Maison Chic on the Wednesday. Why had he turned up on the Tuesday?

To his surprise Gertie walked in with a covered plate in her hands and a broad smile on her face. She put the plate in front of Frank and came round to his side of the desk.

'Compliments of the canteen,' she said, taking off the

covering plate. 'Agnetha says that, if you really must eat sandwiches, at least eat decent ones. She's made sure everything is low fat. And she says it's my responsibility to see that you eat properly, and I don't intend to get into trouble with her.'

'Toasted chicken mayonnaise,' Frank whispered, looking at Agnetha's creation. It was one of his all-time favourites. Along with toasted cheese and mushroom, toasted ham and cheese, mushrooms in garlic ... well, better not waste time thinking about it. Agnetha did not do small. She did tasty and filling. And large. And all-round yummy-I-wish-my-stomach-was-bigger-so-I-could-carry-on-eating.

To his surprise Gertie dropped herself in his lap and picked up a half-sandwich.

'Gertie,' he began protesting, before finding his mouth attacked by a toasted chicken mayonnaise sandwich.

'Watch the birdy,' Gertie said, teasing him with the sandwich.

Which is when Frieda walked in.

'I think I'd like a word with you about the rules, young lady,' she said. 'In my office. Now.'

A chastened Gertie put the sandwich back on the plate, got off Frank's lap and headed for the door. Frieda looked at Frank as Gertie passed her. 'And I'll speak to you later, Sergeant,' she added before leaving.

There were some days he seemed to lead a charmed life, Frank reflected, listening to Frieda's departing heels clicking like the members of a firing squad cocking their rifles one by one. The sort of day when he would get away with almost anything, even if only by the skin of his teeth. And then there were days like this, when Frieda seemed to drop in just at the wrong moments. He was going to get the bollocking of all bollockings. This time Frieda would not let it go. A Detective Sergeant in his office with a WPC on his lap? People had been fired for less.

And it wasn't even his fault.

He looked at the toasted sandwich.

Sod it, he thought. Present pleasures. Last meal of the condemned man and all that. He tucked in.

He was licking his fingers and burping gently when Gertie returned. He looked behind her for his executioner. There was no one there.

'Frieda wishes to see me in her office, I presume?' he asked. 'As of now, along with chopping block and axe for her personal use? On my neck?'

'She didn't say anything about that, Sarge,' Gertie said, surprisingly cheerfully.

'Ah, it's the let-them-sweat treatment,' noted Frank. 'It will come in due course, no doubt. Anyway, you're very happy for someone who's just had the riot act read out to them. What happened?'

'Oh, nothing much. Frieda just gave me a bollocking, that's all. It was worth it.'

Frank was rarely surprised. Baffled, yes, perplexed, often, confused, regularly, but rarely surprised. He had never seen anyone walk away from a Frieda-bollocking with anything less than a severe attack of the shakes. Mostly they didn't walk away at all. Crawl would be a polite description. Yet here stood Gertie as if all Frieda had said was "don't do that again, please Gertie. At least not in the office."

Though his own, earlier "dressing down" hadn't turned out the way he quite expected either.

And what did Gertie mean "it was worth it"?

Some questions a sane man does not go looking for answers to.

'Phil Walthers,' Frank said, standing up, deciding it was time to be elsewhere. 'Let's go have a word with him. Find out whether he's been making his own news headlines. We can walk, the Herald office is only a few blocks away.'

'You don't think he murdered the two women?' she asked as they headed out of reception.

'I don't know him very well – in fact I doubt anyone does. He's somewhat of an eccentric, or that's the way he likes to portray himself. On the one hand he has airs of refinement, so he's unlikely to murder someone with a brick over the back of the head. On the other he's quite intelligent, so maybe that's exactly what he'd do.'

'But what motive would he have?'

'That is the question Gertie, my sweet. Nagness, yes, maybe someone just lost their temper and lashed out. But even that's stretching things a bit far. Lashing out with your fist, yes, but picking up a half-brick to attack an old woman with is hardly spontaneous combustion, you'd have to go through the mental process of having the thought, looking for a weapon, and then physically picking up the brick, by which time most people would have thought better about it and thrown the brick away. And the people who would be first in the frame – neighbours, etc – all have alibis. And the second murder was definitely planned. So we have to ask ourselves, what motive could one person have had to commit both murders?'

'Maybe Professor Humbug is right,' suggested Gertie. 'Or, at least, that someone has decided that they have a god-given mission to carry out Humbug's prophecy.'

'Which is where we come to the land of the mad, or the land of the eccentric.'

'Phil Walthers?'

'That's what worries me. Phil Walthers is a plausible fit. But if we're looking for a nutter ... I reckon eighty-five percent of people would qualify. At least fifty percent of the time, that is. And fifteen percent would qualify a hundred percent of the time. As Abraham Lincoln would have said had he thought of it.'

The front of the Herald's office in the Old Town looked as if it would have when it first opened back in the nineteenth century, back in the days of wealth and Empire. Or, possibly more accurately, how someone thought it would have looked like back in the nineteenth century, quite possibly confused by something they had once seen in a movie. It had a large window front, with "The Herald" scripted on it in an arch in golden Gothic lettering. Behind the glass was a reception, with deep, worn leather chairs. On white-painted walls hung some of what were presumably the more famous of the Herald's front pages, held in surprisingly modern, bright, aluminium frames.

Frank opened the door and they stepped inside. The office was empty. If it wasn't for the bright, white walls and the fact that the room was almost surgically clean, they might have entered a deserted museum. A shining brass call bell of the sort old hotels would have had stood on the reception counter. Gertie's eyes lit up. She hit the bell hard with the flat of her hand and shouted "Shop!" She looked at Frank mischievously.

'I've always wanted to do that,' she confessed.

Frank smiled.

'Nice to achieve an ambition,' he noted. 'But it would appear that we are all alone. Phil Walthers must be out somewhere, no doubt digging for his latest scoop.'

'Just the two of us,' Gertie agreed, her nose twitching.

'My goodness, this is a surprise,' said a tinny voice, disabusing them of the notion that they were alone. 'The good officers of Wellbury Police Force coming to speak to me instead of my having to go to them to plead – vainly, in most cases – for just a soupçon of something approaching facts with which I can earn my humble living. A moment, a mere moment and I shall be with you. Don't run away, now.'

Frank and Gertie looked at the little speaker on the receptionist's counter where the voice had come from. Frank's gaze wandered to the top of the internal door.

'We're being watched,' he observed, nodding at an inconspicuous little CCTV camera just above the door frame. Gertie shivered.

'Ugh! Nasty little man. What if we were doing something – um, well, something we didn't want others to see.'

'We'd hardly be doing something we didn't want others to see with anyone walking past able to look through the window, now would we?' Frank asked rhetorically. 'Anyway, what odious activity were you thinking about? Going through the drawers behind the reception desk while no-one was here?'

'Um, something like that, Sarge,' Gertie said, without much conviction. 'Anyway, it's just the feeling that you're being spied on without your knowledge. It's creepy.'

'It is, a bit, I suppose,' Frank agreed. 'Silly, really. We have cameras watching us all the time. And Phil Walthers has every right to have one in here, we'd probably encourage him to do so if it's going to be empty from time to time. Never know when some lager lout might pop in to nick one of those frames. Very artistic, some of these lager louts, these days, so I'm told.'

He was interrupted by the opening of the internal door and the appearance of Phil Walthers. Walthers was jacketless, white sleeves rolled up, loud bow-tie firmly in position, his gaudy waistcoat hidden by a frilly kitchen apron. He was taking rubber gloves off as he entered.

'Sorry about there being no-one to receive you,' he said. 'I think young Sheila must have gone on her lunch break. I'm afraid I was engrossed in developing. I tend to leave the world outside when I indulge.'

'Developing?' asked Frank. 'You do your own?'

'I like to keep my hand in. Most of it's done by machines these days, but I find that there's nothing more satisfying than developing and printing a good black-and-white photograph the old-fashioned way. I could show you?' he offered hopefully.

'Perhaps some other time. At the moment we need to ask you a few questions.'

'Ah, so you have indeed come seeking information from a poor pressman,' Phil Walthers said jocularly, in a voice that failed to hide a certain nervousness. 'Come, let us go through to my office.'

They followed him through the door, down a passage, and into his office. Unlike the pristine reception, the passage was packed with piles of boxes, old issues of the Herald, and other assorted gifts from the past which probably should have been thrown out, but had been kept just in case. Phil Walthers' office was only slightly tidier. A kettle and other coffee-making accoutrements on a side-board suggested that Phil Walthers' pedantically pristine public image did not follow him into his workplace.

'Take a seat. Shall I make some coffee?' he offered. 'Or perhaps tea. I have some Earl Grey teabags somewhere. Or some of those modern fruit-things. I'm sure they're around here somewhere.'

'No, thanks,' Frank replied, eyeing the mugs on the sideboard. They had the look of mugs for which "washing" was a perfunctory rinse under the tap.

'Ah, well, yes, they could really do with a good bleaching, couldn't they?' Walthers said, noticing the glance and looking at the mugs as if for the first time. 'Perhaps when young Jane gets back. I could get her to make a pot of tea and bring in the good china.'

'Jane?'

'My latest receptionist cum reporter cum maker of tea and general odd-job girl. No, wait a minute, it isn't Jane, this one is called Sheila. I lose track, they keep changing so often. Eager young journalism graduates, learning the ropes at a provincial newspaper before going on to become famous names working for the Guardian or the BBC, just like their tutors told them to. I try not to disabuse the poor things by being too cynical.'

Frank hid a smile. Any aspiring reporter working for Walthers would be likely to end up being thoroughly confused about what life as a newshound was supposed to be.

'Mr Walthers, you were at La Maison Chic yesterday,' he said, getting back to official business.

'Ah, this is about that poor traffic warden,' Walthers replied, a note of relief in his voice. Frank had mentally marked his earlier nervousness. Now the man sounded relieved. It didn't make sense.

'It is indeed, Mr Walthers. Could you tell us what you were doing in the area at the time?'

'My goodness, am I a suspect? Of course, I suppose I must be. Dear me, dear me.' He gave Frank a sad smile. 'Not a very good journalist, am I? Twice in three days I am within shouting distance of a murder and I did not notice a single thing, not the slightest thing.' He paused, leaned forward and lowered his voice. 'Is it true that this latest victim had a note left in her pocket claiming that she was one of the eighty-five percent?' he asked conspiratorially.

'If you could answer my question, Mr Walthers?' Frank suggested. Walthers sighed and leaned back.

'The official response of the police was "No comment",' he noted to himself. 'Well, yes, I shall answer your question, Sergeant, on the understanding that it remains confidential. For the time being, of course.'

'I will decide that, Mr Walthers. Now, your answer to my question?'

'Ooh,' Walthers said in a camp voice. He looked at Gertie. 'He looks very sexy when he's being stern, doesn't he, my dear? I'm surprised you can keep your hands off him.'

It's my bloody fists you'd better worry about, Frank felt like replying. He knew Gertie was covering her mouth with her notebook. He settled for eyeballing Walthers in silence.

Walthers held up a hand in surrender.

'I do apologise, Sergeant. I shouldn't have said that. I'm afraid receiving a visit from the police – as a suspect, too – has quite undone my nerves.' He coughed delicately. 'I shall tell you everything, Sergeant. I was in La Maison Chic because I needed an excuse.'

'An excuse?'

'Yes, an excuse. You see, I had an appointment for the following day, but I slipped in and pretended to have got the day wrong. I'm afraid Ms Healey was most put out.'

'Why did you need an excuse?'

Walthers paused before replying.

'I suppose I shall have to tell you. I shall have to trust you to remember where you got this information from, and that I do have a newspaper to run.' He linked his fingers together and gave Frank a straight look. 'You know of Councillor Robert Bagley, I presume?'

'I've come across his name once or twice.'

'He has a number of interests in Wellbury. Runs the Blue Bliss club. Rumoured to have a finger in a number of dubious pies. Property, that sort of thing. Yet at the same time he is a lay preacher in his local church. Quite the evangelical sort, as I found out when I attended a service a few weeks ago. Not at all your typical Wellburian. I decided that it was my duty both as a journalist and as a citizen of Wellbury to do a little investigating to find out exactly what he is, and whether he isn't involved in any illegal or disreputable practices.' He sighed sadly. 'Unfortunately, apart from the fact that he turned up anonymously about five years ago, I haven't managed to uncover anything useful at this stage. Nothing I could print without finding lawyers on the doorstep the next day.'

'What has that got to do with La Maison Chic?'

'Ah, well, you see I was trailing Councillor Bagley at the time. You know, journalist working undercover, blending in with the local populace, invisible to his prey.'

The idea of Walthers being invisible with his gaudy waistcoat and bow-tie made Frank smile. He himself wore bright ties for the same reason. The difference was that you could change ties in seconds.

'Unfortunately he spotted me,' Walthers said sadly. 'Demanded to know why I had only attended one of his services, and when I was going to return to hear the word of the Lord. I don't think he's essentially a stupid man. If I kept on popping up around him he'd soon realise that something was up. So I apologised and said that the church wasn't really for me, and that I had an appointment with Ms Healey for which I was late. I'm not overly sure he believed me. In fact I think he might have guessed my purpose several weeks ago.'

Frank was only mildly interested at that point in whether or not Councillor Bagley was involved in any non-legal acts. What he was interested in was that Councillor Bagley was now placed at the scenes of both murders.

Cancel that, he thought. If Councillor Bagley had something to hide, something the two women either knew about, or suspected, it would give him a motive for removing them. Suddenly he was very interested in Councillor Bagley's activities. He made a mental note to ask around at the station. If that failed he could ask Walthers what he had dug up. At the moment he didn't want the journalist guessing right about his interest.

'Did you notice anyone else around at the time?' he asked.

Walthers began ticking off a list on his fingers.

'Our dear parish vicar, a man far too nice for his own good. He makes me want to retch sometimes. And, where the vicar is, so shall Mrs Blower be. A dangerous woman, that.'

'Dangerous? How so?'

'When Mrs Blower's husband passed on – a heart attack while in the bed of a young woman not his wife – she inherited his fortune. Unfortunately she also found religion, though I rather suspect she had it all the time, but her dearly departed husband had managed to reign in that foolishness. Now a man who loses himself to religious mania is to be avoided, but a woman who does so – well, they are the deadlier of the species. Far more cunning. And far more persistent. Sergeant, if you have to interview her – and I presume you will – if she mentions the phrase "the Lord's work" it is time to leave.'

'In what way?' asked Frank

'I had to do an article on the church fete last year, as I do every year. Unfortunately Mrs Blower had taken charge of the organising. She was tolerable enough while discussing the merits of home-made jam and pickles, but once she got onto the subject of belief, well, all I can say is that she'd out-zeal the zealous. Brimstone and fire, Sergeant, brimstone and fire. I can't repeat what she said about homosexuals.'

Frank grinned to himself. Phil Walthers liked playing the camp eccentric. He rather suspected Walthers had deliberately wound Mrs Blower up.

'I'll bear that in mind. Anyone else? That you noticed?'

'An ex-colleague of yours, Tom Sampson. A lovely man, normally I would have stopped to pass the time of day, but I was trying to be undercover. I had to slip into a shop doorway to avoid him seeing me.'

Damn, thought Frank. The last person he wanted on his list.

'And then, finally, there was Professor Humphries,' Phil Walthers continued. 'Wandering around La Maison Chic as if he didn't know where he was.'

'No-one else?'

'No-one that I recognised, Sergeant. A few people that I didn't. I would be quite happy to come to the station if you have any photographs you wish me to look over.'

I'm sure you would, thought Frank, but you aren't going to if I can avoid it.

'That's very kind of you to offer, Mr Walthers,' he said, standing up. 'If the need arises we'll let you know straight away.'

'Before you go, Sergeant,' Walthers said in an almost pleading voice, 'you can tell me whether the latest victim is an eighty-five percenter? I promise it will remain entirely confidential until you say otherwise.'

'I'm afraid not,' Frank replied. 'However, there is something I could suggest that might interest you.'

'I am all ears, Sergeant. Even my bow-tie has turned into a little pair of ears.'

'You might want to do a little digging into Professor Humphries' background. You might find something useful.'

Phil Walthers' eager face dropped. He sighed.

'I've already done that, I'm afraid. As soon as I heard about his ridiculous interview on that ghastly radio channel. The man's an absolute charlatan. I spoke to him on the phone that very day. Do you know, he actually threatened me?'

'Threatened you? In what way?'

'He claimed I would regret it if I published any lies about him. Nothing specific, but his voice was extremely unpleasant, and he seemed to be suggesting I might be in physical danger, if you see what I mean.'

'Oh, well,' said Frank, 'at least it gives you something to print.'

'That is unfortunately true, Sergeant. But very distasteful. Very distasteful.'

Humphries threatening people physically, thought Frank. Now that was interesting. Very out of character.

'Walthers seemed a little nervous at first,' Gertie commented as they walked back to the station.

'Yes,' agreed Frank, 'and then somewhat relieved when he found out why we were there. As if he knew he had nothing to worry about concerning the murder of Chiffon Brady. But there was something he was worried about.'

'Nagness? He could have done that one. Hit her in a fit of temper.'

'Possible,' Frank said in a doubtful tone. 'He's the type who likes to present a controlled image. Anything could happen when that control slips.'

'But then we're back to two murderers. Which is not our main hypothesis at the moment.'

'Correct, Gertie. I think we stick to the one-murderer idea for the moment. After lunch we'll go have a chat with the vicar and Mrs Blower. I'd like to meet this vicar who makes Phil Walthers want to retch.'

'But not Mrs Blower?'

'No,' admitted Frank, 'I can't say I'm overly looking forward to meeting her.'

'What would you like for lunch, Sarge?' Gertie asked, a thought having struck her. 'After all, I have to look after you, Agnetha said so, and I don't want to risk upsetting her.'

Gertie did not sound like she found the idea onerous at all.

'I'll have some scrambled eggs on toast in the canteen, I think. Agnetha's toasted sandwiches are delicious, but there's a little too much of them.'

'I'll get it for you, Sarge. How many slices of toast?'

'Gertie, I am quite capable of getting my own lunch,' he said irritably.

Gertie did not reply, a pout on her face.

'Gertie,' Frank said gently, 'imagine what the others would say if you ran around like my skivvy. Apart from that, it wouldn't do your career any good. Frieda wouldn't be inclined to recommend you for promotion, you know.'

Gertie stayed silent. She knew exactly what Frieda would think, and until they'd resolved the problem of Frank Summers, she, Gertie, wouldn't stand a snow flake's chance in hell of Frieda recommending her for promotion.

And she didn't mind being Frank's skivvy to start off with. Once she had bought the furniture she would then decide how to arrange it.

Eric Johns was in the canteen when they got back to the station. He was reading a morning tabloid someone had left behind, while pleasurably finishing off a fruit tart with whipped cream.

'You must have a doppelganger, Eric,' Frank said as he and Gertie sat down.

'A doppel-whatter?'

'A doppelganger. Someone who looks exactly like you, a twin almost. Because, even though I know one of you works in reception at times, every time I walk into the canteen, there you are, eating, and reading a newspaper.'

'Have to keep my energy up,' Eric replied, eyeing Frank's scrambled egg on toast. 'Food for the body and food for the mind. That looks nice. I could do with a little snack like that.'

'A little snack?' asked Frank in amazement, looking at the empty plate in front of Eric Johns which contained minute traces of what must have been pie, gravy, mash and peas, quite possibly twice.

Eric finished his tart with cream and sighed with enjoyment.

'If food be the music of love, play on,' he said. 'Or something like that. By the way, Frank, I have a message for you from Tom Sampson.'

'What, "If I ever see you again I'll rip your arms off and beat you to death with the bloody ends"? I think he's already given us that message.'

'Now, now, Frank, you don't know Tom. He's a gentle soul, at heart.'

'It's not his heart that worries me, it's his fists. I could handle being hit with his gentle soul.'

'Your problem is that you've only met him once, and that was an unfortunate occasion. If you really want to know, he came in to the station to apologise. Even brought some flowers for Gertie. They're in your office.'

'Flowers? For me?' Gertie asked in happy wonder, astonished enough to pause in her steady demolition of steak-and-kidney pie, chips, gravy, and, as a sop to healthy eating, sweetcorn in butter.

'He asked me to say how very sorry he was to have frightened you, Gertie, love,' Eric said. 'I think you might have a new admirer.'

'It's been years since anyone bought me flowers,' Gertie said dreamily. 'And last time it was my dad, so that doesn't count.'

'You sure this Tom Sampson is right in the head?' asked Frank. 'First he loses his rag and would have gone berserk if we hadn't left, and now he comes bearing flowers? Sounds a bit soft to me.'

Eric smiled as he stood and picked up his tray prior to taking it to the disposal point.

'He said he'd be at home most of the week, or could come in if you gave him a time. But just one thing, Frank.'

'What's that? Don't mention the word "murder"?'

'Oh, no, nothing to do with Tom. I just thought I'd mention that jealousy doesn't become you.'

He laughed as he left. Frank's face was filled with puzzlement.

'What the hell did he mean by that?'

'I like getting flowers,' Gertie said, continuing her attack on her lunch as if in a hurry to see the flowers, but determined not to miss a good feed.

If anyone was going to buy Gertie flowers, thought Frank to himself, it was going to be him, not some weird retired bachelor policeman who kept his house unhealthily neat.

Inside his head some voices were stirring.

'Silly bugger's doing it again,' said one.

'Oi! Frank! Leave it out,' said another.

'Yeah,' said a third, 'you'll only get us all into trouble again if you start buying Gertie flowers.'

Gertie and I have a purely professional and platonic relationship, Frank's mind replied, before closing the lid firmly on the voices and getting on with his scrambled egg and toast.

He noted that Gertie looked very happy. He wished he could make her look that happy.

Vicar Parsons met them at the front door of the old vicarage and took them to his study. He was a slightly stooped man of average height with very closely cropped grey hair and a lined face which matched Frank's idea of the convict Magwitch from Great Expectations. Frank disliked him from the start. Or to be more accurate, as soon as the old fool had complimented Gertie on the beautiful pink carnation in her buttonhole. Frank had wanted to order her not to wear it, but he realised that that would end in a blazing row, and one of his voices had told him that Frieda would probably approve of the idea. The pleasant face of policing, Wellbury style. He had listened to that voice. He had a strange feeling that, though getting on the wrong side of Frieda was not a good idea at any time, this was a particularly bad time to do it. Why, he didn't know, but he did know from experience that bad premonitions tended to come true. It was the good premonitions that usually failed him.

Gertie, he could see, had taken an instant liking to the old fool.

What was so special about carnations, anyway?

'Please, take a seat,' said Vicar Parsons. 'Something to drink? Tea or coffee? A light sherry, perhaps?'

'No, thank you vicar, we've just finished lunch,' replied Frank, sitting down. Gertie took her normal post of note-taking sentry, standing slightly out of view.

'Ah, somewhat of a relief for me, I must admit,' the vicar said in a slightly embarrassed tone. He sat down and motioned towards what looked like a hanging drape next to an old fireplace. 'I'm not allowed to undertake such mundane tasks as making tea or coffee. I have to ring the bell if I want anything. Then Mrs Sharples shuffles out of the kitchen and eventually makes it through to here. Then, if it's tea or coffee or some such, she shuffles back to the kitchen. If I'm really lucky, and she doesn't forget what it was I wanted in the first place, she gets back about half an hour later. I've never got used to the idea. Unfortunately trying to change the way things are done here has so far proved impossible.'

'You've been here long?'

'About four years,' Parsons replied, smiling a sad sort of smile. 'I worked in an inner-city part of London before that, for fifteen years. A very tough posting, with few rewards. In the end I wore a leather jacket and rode around on a motorcycle to show how modern I was. Thoroughly enjoyed it, too, though it resulted in little. And then they sent me here for a rest.'

He gave Frank a thin smile.

'Some rest. The first thing that went was the leather jacket. And the motorcycle, once delivered from London, has lain in the garage ever since. I'm afraid Wellbury expects its vicars to be staid, elderly academics.' He sighed. 'The academia I rather enjoy. The vicarage has, as you can see, an extremely well-stocked library, not only on Christian history. And I have a discreetly hidden laptop on which I can access the Internet, as well as having electronic exchanges with religious scholars throughout the world. My only lack, really, is that Wellbury also expects vicars to be bachelors. I intend, should that be my only contribution to modern Wellbury, to break the mould as far as that idea goes.'

He noticed a surprised look on Frank's face.

'Oh, I understand, Sergeant, you think I'm an elderly duffer set in his ways. I'm afraid that's also part of the Wellbury process. Perhaps built on those long years in London. Conditioning, I believe it is called. But I'm really not that old, you know.' He smiled impishly. 'One of these days I might even strip the motorbike, oil it and get it going again, and roar through the town, quite possibly getting arrested and thoroughly scandalising my parishioners. It's a day-dream I often have.'

'What type of motorbike?' Frank asked.

'A Moto Guzzi 750. Lovely machine. I managed to get it for a very affordable price from someone who was leaving the country for a few years.'

Frank revised his estimate of Parsons. Anyone who owned a Moto Guzzi 750 couldn't be all that bad.

'Let me know if you need a hand,' he said. 'It's been ages since I rode a motorbike.'

'You never quite lose the thrill, do you?' agreed the vicar, guiltily.

'No,' agreed Frank. 'I was looking at a shop in the Old Town the other day – I think it was called Rorders. Some lovely machines they had. I just wish I could afford one.'

'Oh, Pete Rorder's shop. Now that is one good thing about Wellbury. You still find shops run by people who have devoted their lives to their interests, real enthusiasts. I'm sure he could give you a good discount. Possibly even find you something second-hand at an affordable price.'

A not very discreet cough from Gertie reminded Frank that they were not here to discuss motorcycles. Reluctantly Frank dragged himself back to the case.

'Ah, yes, I might give you a call about that some time, if you don't mind. However, I need to ask you some questions about two incidents that have taken place recently.'

'The eighty-five-percent murders? Yes, I suppose I should have expected that. I was in the very vicinity at both times, if what the media have reported is accurate.'

'Could you tell us if you saw anything out of the ordinary at the times? Anyone you recognised who seemed out of place? Anyone behaving suspiciously?'

Parsons considered this for a few moments.

'No, I can't say that I did. However I probably wouldn't

notice if a tribe of rampaging elephants crossed my path. I tend to keep my head down and act the absent-minded pastor. One meets too many parishioners wishing to pass on minor scandals. They expect me to be shocked, I'm afraid. It's another temptation I have, to counter their little tales with real stories from London. But,' he sighed, 'even if I did they would ignore them as tales from some foreign land where the natives have always been restless and uncivilised.' He smiled. 'And if they meant some of the local politicians, I would thoroughly agree with them.'

'You believe that these were some sort of natural act?' asked Frank, picking up on Parsons' easy use of "the eighty-five-percenters". 'Members of society culling the unneeded?'

'Oh, but of course, Sergeant,' Parsons replied. 'But not the way you mean, nor the way the supposedly eminent Professor Humphries thinks of it. You see, one area of study I have always found fascinating is that of religious mania. It doesn't have to be organised religion, such as Christianity, it could be something such as fascism, the Nazis, or even football hooliganism. People become tied up with strange thoughts and feelings, they think, believe deeply, that what they are doing is right. What you or I would regard as perfectly normal people do things totally out of character.'

He gave Frank an earnest stare which suggested his own beliefs on the matter were quite passionate.

'Sergeant, I have studied this question to some length. I have discussed it with friends and colleagues, of different religions. They all agree that it is some form of mental or psychological virus. I am afraid Wellbury is quite possibly the perfect place for such a virus to take hold, somewhere struggling to retain a hold on a way of life, a norm, a perfection that never was, a simulacrum, I believe the word is. I feel sorry for you, Sergeant, indeed I do. I think your days ahead will seem almost impossible. I will pray for you, if that is of any comfort.'

I've always needed all the prayers I could get, Frank felt like replying.

What worried him was that Parsons was right. The conditions were in place. Everything suggested that this was exactly what was happening.

Except that he didn't believe it. He couldn't believe it. Not in his Wellbury.

He was rarely passionate about anything. It went against his Epicurean ideal. The original Epicurean ideal, not the modern one. No passions. Good friends, good food, a good life. Wellbury was his epitome of that philosophy.

And if it turned out to be true, that Wellburians were in the grip of some delusion, he would hunt down every bastard involved and see that they were given a fair trial. After he had kicked their guts into the next century. Personally.

'Getting back to Monday,' he said, trying to keep his thoughts at bay, 'you went to the bank.'

'Yes, some papers to sign. Mrs Blower does the accounting. She just needed me to sign some official document. Very trivial. I could have done it here and posted it, but Mrs Blower is very conscientious about doing things properly. Propriety, Sergeant, propriety. I believe Shakespeare or someone had something to say about that. I don't quite remember the quotation. Polonius, quite possibly.'

'And yesterday you went to the bookshop?'

'Yes, I'd ordered a copy of a new book on the Knights

Templar. I suppose I could have waited until they posted it, but I'm afraid I have a secret passion for bookshops. Using the Internet is all very well, and extremely handy for out of print editions, but I can't resist the smell and feeling a good old-fashioned bookshop gives.'

'And Mrs Blower went to La Maison Chic?'

'Yes. She isn't interested in books, fortunately, and she had apparently seen a dress in their window which she rather admired. She is a rather wealthy lady. She can afford their prices. I am afraid I find it somewhat of a moral dilemma. The money she spends on a dress could well be better spent on the poor and needy, but at the same time, it is hers to choose, and she does a lot of good work for the parish.'

'Fortunately?' asked Frank.

'I'm sorry, I don't understand.'

'You said it was fortunate Mrs Blower isn't interested in books.'

'Ah, a little Freudian slip, I suppose,' confessed Parsons.

He looked at Frank as if deciding how much and what to say.

'Mrs Blower, as I have mentioned, does a lot of good work for the parish. It was something she began to take an interest in, if I understand correctly, when her husband died, shortly before I took up the post here. But I'm afraid she rather overdoes it. She tries to take control of everything. At the moment, for example, she is at the printers, apparently they made a couple of spelling errors in last week's parish newsletter. Now I quite agree with the idea of a weekly newsletter. It keeps you in touch with those who feel that attending weekly services is not a necessary component of their beliefs. But my idea of a newsletter is something like an ordinary, chatty kind of letter, photocopied – badly, normally on an old machine – and delivered by smiling volunteers, or posted, if you can afford the postage. Mrs Blower, however, thinks of it more as an edition of a newspaper. She would have made a very good journalist, or possibly more of an editor.'

'You haven't thought of stepping in and, how shall I put this, reigning her in somewhat?'

Parsons smiled another sad smile.

'One of Christianity's principle tenets is compassion and understanding, Sergeant. I believed, when I began here, that it was a safety valve for the emotion she felt on the loss of her husband. We must have Christian forbearance and tolerance, Sergeant.'

'But what do you do when tolerance for one means that others get hurt?' asked Frank. 'I get the feeling that Mrs Blower has ruffled quite a few feathers.'

Parsons sighed.

'Yes, Sergeant, you have reached the same conclusion that I reached only a few weeks ago. It has taken far longer than it should, but it is human nature not to argue against comfort. Mrs Blower took on all the sort of tasks I didn't want to do, or was unsure of – what flowers to have in church at Easter, if any, that sort of thing. It made my life much easier, much simpler. But I am afraid I am going to have to do something about Mrs Blower. What, I am as yet unsure of, but, yes, something must be done. Before she takes over entirely.'

'They're very dangerous,' Gertie said as they drove away.

'Who? The vicar and Mrs Blower?' asked Frank in surprise.

Parsons was a man with wide-ranging interests, and he had been more than willing to share them with Frank and Gertie. Frank felt a little guilty about what was technically a waste of time, but he had enjoyed Parsons' enthusiasm. But Parsons had come across merely as a harmless academic, unlikely to have anything to do with the murders, your typical absent-minded vicar in what was not far off from being a rural retreat.

'No,' said Gertie. 'Motorbikes. And the vicar's one sounds old and even more dangerous. I don't think you should get involved.'

Frank pondered this in silence. Gertie had a right to her opinions, he supposed, but this was dangerously close to mothering him, something she tried on every so often, which she did not have a right to do.

And he had a right to ride a motorbike if he so wished.

He would visit Pete Rorder's motorbike shop that Saturday, he decided.

'I wouldn't worry too much, Gertie, I don't think the vicar's going to be fixing up his bike any day soon. I think he just likes saying he's going to do something.'

'Like the bit about doing something about Mrs Blower.'

'Exactly. I think he's too scared of her to do anything. Wouldn't say boo to a goose, let alone Mrs Blower. Time to have a word with the dear woman, I think.'

Mrs Blower lived in Lords Acres in a large house that was probably only one bedroom short of being a mansion. To their surprise, rather than a maid or butler, it was Mrs Blower who answered the door. She was wearing a similar set of tweeds to those she had been wearing in the CCTV video, along with a pearl necklace and a mauve brooch on her jacket embossed with a dove of peace.

'Mrs Blower? I'm Detective Sergeant Summers and this is Detective Constable Gregson,' Frank said, holding up his warrant card. 'I wonder if we could have a word?'

'From the Salvation Army?' asked Mrs Blower, a confused look in her eyes.

'No, Mrs Blower, we're the police.'

'The police? Why would that be?'

Frank paused, trying to understand the question.

'Why would what be, Mrs Blower?'

'Why would you be from the police?' She checked her watch. 'Anyway, I'm afraid I haven't time at the moment. If you're looking for a donation you'll have to speak to me at the church. I'll be there tomorrow afternoon.'

'Mrs Blower,' Frank said firmly, putting a hand against the closing door. 'We're here on official police business, this is nothing to do with donations of any kind.'

'Oh.' Mrs Blower seemed at a loss. 'Well, you'd better come in then, I suppose.'

Frank and Gertie followed her down a passage and into a living room scattered with clothing of all descriptions.

'I'm trying to get things ready for the fete in two weeks time,' she said. 'So you're not from the Salvation Army? I thought it was strange, someone coming to the door for a donation. Which police force did you say you were from? I really don't think that red and maroon jumper is going to sell. I'm sure we had it on the second-hand clothes stand last year, you know.'

Frank blinked at this strange stream of consciousness.

'Mrs Blower, you were at Collings Bank last Monday, were you not?' he said, deciding that the best way of handling Mrs Blower was to ignore half of what she said.

'Collings Bank? Monday? No, that was Tuesday. Shoes are the problem. People don't seem to like buying second-hand shoes for some strange reason. Definitely. I had to take the vicar to sign some papers. We shall probably give them to a second-hand charity, you know. He really is a very forgetful man. Dead man's shoes, I suppose. I have to look after everything. He would only forget, very forgetful. Come to think of it, it was Monday. Yes, definitely. Very forgetful. Would you buy this shirt, Superintendent?'

'Sergeant,' Frank corrected, looking at an extremely loud Hawaiian shirt. 'I'd have to think about that. Can you remember seeing anything suspicious while you were there? It's a bit on the loud side, isn't it?'

Gertie blinked. She knew Frank had an ability to drop into the same manner of speaking as the person he was speaking to, but this was a bit much.

'No. Yes, you're right. Perhaps. The vicar mentioned something about that. Apparently there was – what do they call them? A mugging? I suppose someone might want it. Close by. Perhaps for a party. While we were there. Imagine that!'

'Er, rather worse than a mugging, Mrs Blower. You're probably right.'

'Oh, well, the ways of the world,' Mrs Blower said, dropping the shirt and picking up a pair of purple flared velvet trousers which had probably last been worn back in the Seventies. 'It might go with this, do you think? Are you sure it was Monday? I have a very good memory, and I could have sworn it was Tuesday. We could sell both as an outfit.'

Frank decided that Mrs Blower was one of those fortunate people whose memory was so bad that she couldn't even remember how bad it was. Her attention span was also lacking in longevity.

'Quite sure, Mrs Blower. It is a possibility. However, we mustn't take up any more of your time. We'll see ourselves out.'

They left Mrs Blower standing in the sitting room holding the flared trousers in a puzzled way.

'I should have offered them tea, don't you think?' she asked the trousers. 'They might have volunteered to help with the Tombola stand if I'd asked them. They didn't look like Salvation Army.'

Outside Frank breathed a sigh of relief.

'I think I know why everyone is afraid of Mrs Blower,' he said, getting into the car.

'Why's that, Sarge? She seemed harmless enough.'

'Can you imagine having to listen to her on a regular basis? I was getting brain-ache in there. If I was the vicar or one of the parishioners I'd probably dive for cover at the very sight of her. Phil Walthers totally misunderstood her, strangely.'

'Still, it means we can cross her off the list,' Gertie said, switching on the ignition. 'I can't see her murdering anyone. She'd probably forget what it was she been planning to do by the time she got there.'

'Unless it's a front. I had a great-aunt once who was much the same. Went around talking to pot-plants, looked permanently confused, kept misplacing things. At the time I thought she was a little doolally. It was only when I overheard my parents discussing her that I realised that my great-aunt had an amazing knack of getting her own way, and despite her apparent nuttiness managed to cope very well on her own. I'll bet you Mrs Blower manages to flog that shirt and those flared trousers to someone. No, I think we keep an eye on Mrs Blower.'

'What now, Sarge?' Gertie asked as they reached the end of the driveway.

Frank checked his watch.

'Time to give Frieda the latest, I suppose. Not much of the afternoon left for anything else. Let's hope someone else has had a more fruitful day.'

Frank had just finished his report to Frieda in her office when there was a knock at the door. Gertie, standing by the door, raised her eyebrows. Frieda nodded. Gertie opened the door and Susan walked in, a folder in one hand.

'Susan,' Frieda said warmly, 'you bring good news from afar, I hope.'

Frank blinked. He should have felt relieved that Frieda and Susan had ended their usual antagonism. Instead it worried him. It was unnatural. And when two people who like fighting each other stop, it's normally only because they intend to spend their energy on some other poor victim. And there was only one obvious victim he could think of.

'Not that far, just from the Path lab,' Susan said, coming up to Frieda's desk, brushing against the victim's chair. 'And it's news in more than one sense, though how good it is is another question.'

She opened the folder, took out a copy of the Herald and placed in on Frieda's desk.

'Last week's edition, page eleven,' she said.

Frank leaned forward as Frieda flipped through the pages. Susan perched on the edge of Frieda's desk. Gertie came and stood behind Frank to get a better view.

'Wellbury's Top Ten Dislikes?' asked Frieda irritably.

'Yes. Recognise those numbers from anywhere?'

Each paragraph was numbered, from one to ten. The numerals were large, the size of a paragraph.

'That note we found on the traffic warden,' Frank said.

'Yes. The numbers are a perfect match. Type of paper also a perfect match. And the number eight which was cut out wasn't quite cleanly done, it included a small amount of the paragraph alongside, about a third of a character, but it lines up exactly. My guess is that whoever it was chose the numbers for a number of reasons, but also for a very specific one.'

'Which is?'

'The size. It's very unusual to find numbers printed that large, and a note boasting of killing one of the eighty-five percent would look a little pathetic if they had to cut out something like page numbers – they'd be far too small.'

'That would make sense,' Frieda agreed, looking at the article in some distaste. '"A recent survey of the good citizens of Wellbury has revealed the top ten things they most dislike",' she quoted. She pushed the newspaper away in disgust. 'If there's anything I dislike, it's lists. Top ten best reads. Top ten best films. It's intellectually vacuous, dishonest and pretentious at the same time. I'm sure most people would vote Dickens in as one of the best authors even when they've never actually read one of his books. Like sheep all going baa because they've been told to.'

'I agree,' Susan said, as Frank picked up the newspaper to scan the article, resisting the urge to say "baa". 'It's a bit of a giveaway sign that they haven't anything original to print.'

Frank chuckled suddenly.

Both Frieda and Susan gave him looks that suggested they suspected he might be about to disagree with them, and they didn't think that would be a good idea.

'If you wish to read any of that nonsense kindly do it some other time, Frank,' Frieda advised.

'Oh, I think you'll be interested in this,' Frank said, smiling as he looked at her. 'Guess who's at number ten.'

'The prime minister?' suggested Frieda sarcastically. 'Frank, we really have no wish to know.'

'Okay, I won't tell you then,' he replied.

He folded the newspaper, slipped it into his jacket pocket, folded his arms and sat there smiling at them.

'Gertie,' Susan said, standing up straight, 'you hold him down while I throttle him.'

'I think it's my turn to throttle him,' Frieda said. She held out her hand and snapped her fingers. 'Give,' she said, much as one might say "Sit" to a dog.

Frank took the newspaper from his pocket and handed it over. Frieda looked at number ten on the list.

'That little – ' she began. Susan leaned over to look, and burst into a peal of laughter.

'I never bothered reading the list,' she said, 'but I wish I had. The police make it into Wellbury's most disliked top ten, at number ten. I presume they were thinking of one specific Detective Sergeant.'

'Very funny,' Frank said. 'However I think it explains one thing. Gertie and I went to have a word with Phil Walthers this morning. He seemed nervous about something, but relaxed when he realised we were there about the traffic warden. I think he was worried he might be receiving some retribution for including us in the list. Anything from checking up on his television licence to inspecting his car for road-worthiness, measuring the treads on the tyres, that sort of thing.'

Frieda folded the newspaper with a look that suggested she wished she could endorse the idea.

'Do you need this?' she asked Susan. Susan shook her head.

'It's told us where the clippings came from,' she said. 'Apart from that – well, I presume the Herald print run goes into the thousands, if not more. If you find any with those numbers cut out, let me know and we'll see if the cuts match up.'

'We can always hope,' Frieda said. 'Gertie, take this so-called newspaper and add it to the file. After that you can finish up for the day.'

'I'd better be off as well,' Susan said. She ruffled Frank's hair as she passed him. 'Remember to be a good little boy and get a decent night's rest,' she added.

Frank watched the two leave, a puzzled expression on his face. He turned back to find that Frieda was slipping her coat and scarf on.

'Your turn to buy me drinkies, Frank, I hope you hadn't forgotten.'

'Of course not,' he replied, standing up. He was tempted to add, "I could hardly think of anything else the whole day", but that would only prove he was lying, and the evening promised to be dangerous enough as it was.

Frieda hadn't lost her preference for wine-bars over pubs, but she had found one which went in for the cosy low-lit, low-couch and coffee-table approach rather than the more sanitised brightly-lit, tall-circular-table and stools effect they had previously shared drinks in. Frank found himself sitting alongside Frieda on a couch which encouraged intimacy.

'Long life and happiness,' proposed Frieda, raising her glass.

'Amen to that,' Frank agreed, clinking his glass against hers. He looked up into her eyes.

At the back of his head he could hear the slamming of manhole covers as all his voices took cover.

Frieda's normal severe stare had been replaced with the deep pools of the sirens. They had a softness that tugged at his heart strings.

Oh, shit! said the last voice to make an exit.

Frieda looked down and took a sip of wine, her face colouring slightly. Frank took a gulp of his and coughed. He leaned forward, put the glass down on the coffee table and took out a handkerchief.

'Oh, dear,' he said, 'some of that went down the wrong way.'

'You okay, Frank?' Frieda asked, patting his back gently.

'Yes, yes, fine.'

So long as I face front, he thought, so long as I face front. He took another gulp to calm his nerves, a large one.

'I see someone sent Gertie flowers,' Frieda noted, slipping her shoes off, tucking her legs underneath her, facing Frank, her arm along the back of the low couch.

'Tom Sampson,' replied Frank, desperately trying to ignore the navy-blue covered limbs next to him. It would have been the most natural thing in the world to put out a hand and ... 'Apparently he came in to apologise for losing his temper.'

'That was sweet. He seems a bit of a contradiction, our Tom.'

'Yes, and we'll have to go back and have another word with him. Hopefully this time I'll somehow manage to be a bit more diplomatic.'

'Well, at least that's one thing you're normally good at. Any ideas or hunches yet? About the case?'

Frank played with his wine glass, finished what was left and refilled it. Frieda covered hers to show that she wasn't ready for a refill. He put the bottle back in its bucket.

'I don't know,' he said slowly, rubbing his jaw. 'I can't help but feel that this eighty-five percent business is something of a smokescreen. But, after listening to the vicar's views, well, intellectually, or perhaps more accurately, academically, there is an argument for it.'

He chuckled.

'I didn't tell you about the vicar's motorbike,' he said.

'The vicar has a motorbike?'

'A Moto Guzzi, it's been idle since he got here. I got the feeling it was his pride and joy, but he felt that a motor-bike riding vicar would not be appreciated by the good citizens of his new parish. He said he was trying to resist the temptation to restore it and go roaring around the countryside on it.'

'I could live with that idea. Ages since I rode a motorbike.'

He looked at her in surprise.

'You? Ride a motorbike?' he asked.

She smiled and squeezed his shoulder.

'I used to have a Suzuki 1100. That was my pride and joy. I had to give it up when … ' Her voice trailed off. 'Let's just say the time came to give it up. A police inspector might get away with it if he's a man, I decided it wasn't quite appropriate for myself.'

'Oh, I don't know,' Frank replied, picking up on the point as if he hadn't realised that the real reason she had to give it up was because of her wife-beating ex-husband. 'I think turning up to work in leathers and crash helmet on the odd occasion would do even more for your image. I reckon the Chief Constable's eyes would pop out if he saw you like that. You certainly wouldn't be forgotten.' He chuckled. 'And please let me know when you're first going to walk into reception like that. I want to see the look on Eric Johns' face. He'd be gobsmacked for at least five seconds, which is five seconds longer than I've ever known.'

Frieda giggled at the thought, disturbingly for Frank, just like Gertie might have done.

Except Gertie didn't like motorbikes.

But Frieda did.

'And you, Frank,' Frieda asked, taking a sip of wine and holding her glass so as to hide her mouth, 'how would you react when you see me in leathers with crash-helmet in hand?'

Frank coughed and held up the wine bottle.

'We seem to have polished this off rather quickly,' he noted. 'I'll get another.'

While he was waiting at the counter to be served he realised that he was a lot less nervous than he had expected. After all, there was a major difference between having a drink with your boss and chatting about motorbikes with a fellow enthusiast, wasn't there?

The difference between getting into deep trouble, and getting into trouble deeply? asked a voice sarcastically, from somewhere deep within the recesses of his mind.

Go away, said Frank, I'm enjoying myself.

When he returned to their couch he noticed vaguely that Frieda had done something to her hair. It was much looser than normal. He gave a mental shrug and sat down next to her. In his experience women were always doing something to their hair, or makeup, or whatever.

'Ever heard of a bike-shop called Rorders?' he asked, filling their glasses.

'I've walked past it a few times.'

'Me too. I've managed to resist the temptation to have a serious look, I don't think I could afford one. But the vicar said he thinks Pete Rorder might be able to find a good second-hand one at a reasonable price. I was thinking of popping in on Saturday. Fancy coming along?'

'Oh, yes, please,' Frieda replied enthusiastically, and totally unlike her normal dispassionate self. 'Just a second, though, Saturday ... ' she added, as if a thought had struck her.

Frank could have sworn she was counting to herself.

'Saturday might be a problem,' she said slowly. 'Unless it's just for an hour in the morning. We're going to have to put in a morning's work at least. So long as it's classified as work we might get away with it.'

'Excellent,' Frank replied, raising his glass in salute, 'it's a date then.'

Frieda suggesting skiving off work for an hour, Frank? asked a voice from somewhere safely far away.

'It certainly is,' Frieda replied, clinking her glass against his, and giving him an enigmatic smile.

She took a sip of wine and looked at him over the rim of her glass.

'There's a new Italian restaurant opened a few streets away called Gino's,' she said. 'What say we try it out after we've finished this bottle? I'm famished, and it'll save you going back to make something and disturbing Gertie while she's studying.'

Frank raised his eyebrows at the thought.

'Excellent idea,' he said, smiling.

Suddenly the world seemed a very nice place. Dinner with Frieda, whose company he thoroughly enjoyed – when she wasn't in one of her Inspector Schoolmarm moods. And Frieda being so thoughtful about Gertie. Maybe the three women who seemed to figure so largely in his life really had reached a rapprochement which meant that he no longer needed to go in fear of his own life.

He could live with that.

He didn't notice that, in his state of happiness, he had

unconsciously and automatically squeezed Frieda's knee next to him.

Friday: The estate agent

Frank sang softly to himself as they drove to the station.

'And I-ee-ee-aye will always lurve yoo-ooo-oo, I will always lurve yoo-oo-ooo …'

Gertie gave him a funny look and turned up the volume on the car radio. Classic FM. Beethoven beat Frank by several decibels.

Frank shrugged and smiled. He was in a good mood. Dinner the previous evening had been wonderful. Frieda had given him a goodnight kiss which was probably a little more intimate than he would have expected, but women used kissing differently to men. You couldn't read too much into it. The most it meant was that he wasn't in her bad books, and that was sufficient to hope for. She had remarked on how nice it was to be able to just relax with someone for a change. Having to play all the political games an inspector would find herself in must be pretty exhausting, he had thought. At least she'd be in a good mood this morning.

Gertie had cooked him breakfast, a meal he normally consumed as coffee. She hadn't asked him a single question about the previous evening, which showed something. He wasn't too sure what, but it had to be a good omen. Even the news that the builders and decorators, despite their earlier promises, would apparently not be finished in her flat for a good few days more hadn't upset her too much. Or, rather, she wasn't in a bad mood over it, despite how much he knew she wanted to move back to her own place. No doubt she had taken it out on the builders the previous evening when she received the call.

Tomorrow he had a date with Susan. Tonight, he decided, he

would cook dinner for himself and Gertie, just to show he could.

'The sun has got his hat on,' he wurbled to himself, 'hip-hip-hip hooray the sun has got his hat on and he's coming out to play.'

Gertie shook her head sadly. There was nothing more depressing than being with a cheerful person. Especially one who didn't seem to realise you existed.

'Cheer up, Gertie,' he said. 'It's a wonderful summer's day, it's good to be alive – tell you what, let's go for drinks after work, and then I'll cook dinner. What say you to that?'

Gertie smiled.

'I'd say, yes please, very much,' she replied. 'After all, it's my day today.'

'Eh?'

'I meant it feels like it's going to be my day today,' Gertie said quickly.

'Yes, it does feel a bit like that.'

Maybe he should buy Frieda some flowers. And Gertie. And, of course, Susan. That way he would appear as a thoughtful, friendly person, purely platonic of course. It sounded like an excellent idea. What harm could there be in making people happy? Especially on such a gorgeous summer's day?

'Morning, Keith,' Frank said as they walked into reception. 'What's the score this morning?'

Keith Bute looked back at him with baggy, blood-shot eyes.

'Know what post-modern relativism is, Frank?'

'You haven't taken up sociology, have you Keith? I'd keep

away from post-modern relativism if I were you. Dangerous stuff if you don't handle it properly. Could explode just when you don't expect it.'

'You're telling me,' Keith sighed. 'We've got a dozen assorted professors, doctors, lecturers, what have you, in the cells at the moment. We had to split them into two groups on account of how they were trying to kill each other. I spent most of the last few hours listening to one lot calling the other eighty-five percenters because of this post-modern relativism thing, and the other lot accusing the first bunch of being neo-Conservative fascists and educational dinosaurs. Apparently it started off as a quiet dinner at the University. Didn't end that way. We got a report of students rioting. Only it wasn't the students, it was the bloody teachers.'

Frank chuckled.

'Students, eh? Just can't get decent ones these days. The professors have to do their rioting for them.'

'Glad you find it amusing, Frank'

'Ah, well, it'll give Fabulous something to smile about when I tell her.'

Contrary to his expectations Frieda was not in a happy mood. Frank and Gertie had hardly stepped into their office when she came blazing in.

'Don't bother taking your coats off,' she said grimly, 'there's been another one. Come on, we'll go in my car.'

They followed her to the car park at the back of the station.

'Another eighty-five percenter?' asked Frank in dismay as he climbed into the front passenger seat of Frieda's black Range Rover, Gertie taking cover in the back.

'I would hardly be talking about anything else when I use the phrase "another one", now would I?' Frieda snapped, gunning the engine and leaving some tyre tracks on the tarmac. 'If I'd being paying more attention to my duty we might have found him earlier.'

She didn't say "instead of gallivanting around with a useless Sergeant last night", but she didn't need to.

'When was he found?' asked Frank.

'Seven o'clock this morning, apparently. A house in Lords Acres, which is all we need. The wealthy don't like it when someone starts knocking them off, and they make sure we get to feel their pain. No doubt the Chief Constable is on the phone as we speak.'

'Good job the Chief Inspector is still away fishing, then,' remarked Frank.

That earned him a filthy look from Frieda.

'Do we know who he is?' asked Frank, pretending not to have noticed. How on earth their having dinner the previous evening could have made any difference to someone found early this morning was a mystery to him. Did Frieda think she would have been patrolling the wealthy mansions of Lords Acres instead? All night?

'No, I only heard that there had been another one when I got in this morning. I was in late.'

Ah, thought Frank, so that's what she means. Instead of starting at eight, or seven, or midnight, Frieda had had an extra hour's lie-in, and he was to blame.

Oh well, he thought, back to normal. At least he had had about twelve hours of life during which nobody had been wishing his instant and nasty demise.

'Interesting, though,' he said thoughtfully.

'In what way?' asked Frieda, taking a corner almost on two wheels.

'You wouldn't want to consider putting the light and the siren on, by any chance, would you?' Frank suggested. 'Just in case some innocent pedestrian steps out from the pavement not expecting an unmarked police Range Rover to come down a suburban road at ninety miles an hour.'

That earned him his second filthy look of the morning. No-one had ever earned three and lived to tell the tale.

'Sort out the light, Gertie,' Frieda said, leaning forward to activate the siren, 'it's under Sergeant Summer's seat. Try not to hit him with it. I'll probably do that afterwards.'

Gertie grinned happily as she opened her window and placed the flashing blue light on the car roof. She enjoyed fast driving, preferably with herself in the driver's seat, but being a passenger would also do. She also found herself quite perversely happy that Frieda was angry with Frank.

If there's one sin you should never commit, Frank thought to himself, it's the one of being right when your Inspector is in the wrong. He would pay for that, he knew. Oh, well.

'So what is this interesting insight you've had, Sergeant? Care to share it with your lesser mortals?'

'You said it was a "he". That means a man.'

'I believe that's the accepted use of the terminology, Sergeant, unless you know differently.'

'The first two were women. If the third was also a woman we might be looking for someone with a grudge against women. If this one is related to the other two – and that's an important if – then that isn't likely to be the case.'

Frieda thought about this for a few seconds.

'Point taken, Frank. It's a small step on the way.'

Now it was back to "Frank". He had a nasty feeling it was going to be a see-saw kind of a day.

Frieda hauled the Range Rover into a wide driveway, passing a "For Sale" sign, missing it and a hedge by a few inches.

'That was quick,' Frank noted, 'an hour and a half after the body was found and they've already got the place on the market.'

'I presume that was your attempt at humour, Sergeant,' Frieda noted.

Frank looked at the car ceiling and rolled his eyes.

'And don't roll your eyes at me, Sergeant, not unless you fancy walking the beat for the next five years.'

Frank was tempted to say that walking the beat for the rest of his life sounded like the ultimate luxury at that moment. He chose to remain silent as the Range Rover stopped abruptly at steps leading to the double-front doors of a large house set in extensive gardens. As they stepped out of the car one of the front doors opened and two men appeared, wheeling out a stretcher covered with a blanket. They were followed by Susan in her white overalls, taking plastic gloves off and breathing in the fresh morning air.

'Hello, Frieda,' she said, giving a thin smile. 'Morning Gertie, morning Frank. If you've had breakfast, I hope you had it a while ago. They're taking the body away now, but it's not a pretty sight inside.'

'In what way?' asked Frank.

Susan sat down on the low balustrade lining the sides of the steps and stretched her fingers slowly.

'The initial attack was much the same as the other two – a blunt object over the back of the head. The victim fell forward, probably lying face down. Then the killer turned him over and hammered a stake into his stomach. At the moment I can't say for sure whether he was technically dead when that happened, but, considering the amount of blood, I would imagine he was close to it.'

'There wasn't a lot of blood?' Frank asked. Susan looked at him with a pale face.

'Quite sufficient, Frank, quite sufficient even for me.'

'You look like you could do with a shot of something,' Frank said.

'A cup of hot, sweet tea,' Frieda said. 'I could do with one myself. Gertie, there's a transport caff about a mile and a half down the road. Turn left at the T-junction, then right when you come to the second roundabout.' She tossed her keys over.

'Oh, wow!' said Gertie happily. She ran down to the Range Rover and pulled off with a squeal of tyres. Before she got to the end of the driveway she had the siren on and the light flashing.

This time it was Frieda who rolled her eyes in exasperation.

Frank sat down next to Susan and massaged her neck.

'Mmm, that feels better,' she said appreciatively, closing her eyes. 'I think it was just the shock so early in the morning. I was still half asleep when I got here.'

'Where are the uniforms?' asked Frieda. 'There should have been at least one on guard at the gates.'

'They're out knocking on doors. I told them Tracey and I could handle things inside. They seemed happy enough to get outside. I've got Tracey checking for fingerprints upstairs at the moment, gives her something to keep herself occupied. She was even less prepared for the sight than I was. She's not feeling too well.'

'Two and a half hours,' Frieda muttered. 'They should be doing something better than just knocking on doors. Any idea who was in charge when the body was reported? Which detective?'

'No, I got a call from the desk Sergeant, I think it was Keith. I came straight over here with Tracey.'

Frank knew, but he wasn't going to say. It was Pete Phillips, Inspector Percy Hanson's Detective Sergeant. By rights he should have called Percy in immediately, and no doubt he had. When Frieda found out that her rival was sniffing around her own case she would hit the roof. Frank had no intention of being around when that happened. Parts of the roof could well hit him. And he had already taken more than sufficient abuse off her so far that morning.

'What can you tell us?' Frieda asked.

'Male, Caucasian, about thirty. Made an attempt to be smartly dressed, suit, tie – cheap stuff, though. Name of Kegley or something, according to his wallet. I gave the name and address to one of your constables, the wallet's inside, bagged, along with his mobile phone and other effects. I'd better get going. There's going to be a lot of work to do at the lab.'

'Might as well hang around for your tea,' Frank said, as

Frieda's Range Rover appeared at the bottom of the driveway, lights flashing and siren going. Gertie switched both off as she came to a stop and jumped from the driver's seat with a slotted cardboard tray containing six teas.

'Thought I might as well make it a round number,' she said. 'Just in case there was anyone else inside.'

'Tracey is,' said Susan. 'Could you tell her to come out and have a breather and a cup of tea?'

'Will do,' Gertie said, putting the teas down and going inside.

'Any time-scale?' asked Frieda as Susan took the top off a polystyrene cup and sipped the hot liquid carefully.

'Somewhere between six and midnight, I would say. More likely to be between eight and ten, at a guess.'

'What are the chances of recovering anything useful?' asked Frank.

'Pretty minimal, I'm afraid. The place is empty, not a stick of furniture in it. If it's been on the market for any length of time I would imagine we'll be picking up plenty of fingerprints, most of them useless.'

'Dozens of them,' a pale-faced Tracey said, appearing at the door with Gertie. She gave Frank a shy smile. 'Hello, Sergeant, I thought I heard your voice.'

'Hello, Tracey, grab yourself a cup of tea,' Frank said, smiling. 'And please call me Frank.'

'Leave the socialising until later, Sergeant,' Frieda said. She turned to Susan. 'This stake – you did say a stake, didn't you?'

Susan nodded.

'Much the same as the one holding up the For Sale sign at the end of the driveway,' she said. 'The body was next to the stairs. Whoever did it must have stood on the stairs and hammered it in from there. Which would explain why there aren't any bloodied footprints.'

'And the blow to the head? Any sign of what did that?'

'No. Something round and hard, could be anything from a piece of lead piping to a cosh. Whatever it was, it doesn't appear to have been left behind.'

'Is the note still here?' asked Frank. Susan nodded.

'Be a dear and get the note for Frank, Tracey,' she said.

'Large house, large grounds, all deserted,' Frank noted, looking around. 'If it is the same person they had time and space to do more than just a whack to the head and then run like hell. But it gives us something.'

'Do tell, Sherlock,' Frieda said acerbically.

'Firstly a stake through the stomach. There's more symbolism in that than you'd find in a barrelful of French art films. Why the stomach? Why not the heart? Secondly, whoever it was knew the property was empty – that should narrow down our suspects. Thirdly, the victim must have known his killer, otherwise why would he have agreed to meet him here? Or her, if it turns out that way.'

'Her?' asked Susan. 'Not the sort of thing I could imagine a woman doing.'

Frank was faced with three women who had probably thought of doing something of the ilk to him on a number of occasions, but he was saved from mentioning it by the re-appearance of Tracey with a plastic folder. She handed it to Frank.

'Well, well, things get better and better. Our friend has made a bad mistake this time.'

Frieda and Gertie crowded around him. The numbers "8", "5", followed by a percentage sign, a dash, and the figure "3" were almost exactly the same as in the previous note.

'The same as last time?' he asked Tracey. She nodded.

'I'll need to do some tests, but I'm ninety-nine percent sure.' She shivered. 'I think I'll give up using statistics, they're starting to make me feel queasy.'

'Why do you say it's a mistake?' asked Susan.

'Firstly, no-one but the killer could know what the last note looked like, we haven't released the details yet. Secondly, if it is from exactly the same issue of the Herald, it means our murderer has had, or had access to, at least two copies. There can't be too many people who would have two copies of the same edition.'

'Such as Phil Walthers,' suggested Gertie.

'The name does kind of jump out at you, doesn't it?' mused Frank.

'All very well,' said Frieda angrily, 'but we can't jump to conclusions until we know who this man was. And I want to know what excuse for a detective has been handling this since seven this morning, and why I haven't been called. Someone is going to discover parts of their anatomy missing that they didn't realise they had in the first place. Come on.'

She strode off to the Range Rover, Gertie following.

'I'll get a uniform or two over as soon as possible,' Frank told Susan. 'The least they can do is keep the curious sightseers away. I'll give you a call later.'

'Bye, Frank,' she said as he walked away.

'Bye, Frank,' called Tracey. He waved at her.

'My radio's in the dashboard,' Frieda said as he got into the car. 'Give the station a call and ask them what the hell is happening and which irresponsible idiot is supposed to be in charge of this. I am not happy about this. Someone is going to answer for it.'

Frank opened the cubby-hole and took Frieda's radio out. He looked at it, and pursed his lips.

'Well, get on with it Sergeant Summers,' Frieda said angrily, picking up speed as she drove down the driveway.

'Um, there's something you should know, Inspector,' he said, almost apologetically.

'There's a lot I need to know, so get on with it.'

Frank held up the radio.

'It's not switched on,' he said softy.

'It's not switched on?' asked Frieda disbelievingly. 'I never switch it off. I – Oh, no.'

Frank understood her reaction. She was known for being contactable at all times. She always had her radio switched on, unlike himself, who almost always had his switched off. Or broken. It broke down on a remarkably regular basis.

'I switched it off last night before … well, just before leaving work. I can't believe I forgot to switch it back on.'

'And your mobile?'

She paused before replying.

'Likewise,' she said.

Frank was trying very hard not to hear the muffled noises Gertie was making in the back.

He was also trying hard not to say anything with the words "irresponsible" or "idiot" in it.

'Actually, it wouldn't have made a difference,' he remarked instead, opening the battery compartment. 'It's broken, see?' he said, removing the battery, twisting a wire slightly, replacing the battery and closing the case. 'Happens quite often with these models.'

They continued towards the station in comparative silence. Frieda had just seen the Frank Summers' technique of being non-contactable. Next time he complained of a faulty radio she would know exactly what had happened. But she wouldn't be able to do anything about it. Because she was about to use exactly the same excuse herself.

Pete Phillips stood up as they entered the operations room Frieda had set up on the Monday.

'Inspector!' he greeted her nervously, 'I've been trying to contact you for hours.'

'Yes, I know, Sergeant Johns told me.' She had deliberately parked in front of the station so that they had to go through reception, and she could quiz Eric Johns on who was supposedly looking after the case.

'I tried your radio every fifteen minutes,' Pete Phillips insisted.

'The radio chose the worst moment in its soon to be terminated life to go wrong. I think it must have been out of action since last night.'

'And your mobile – '

'I switched that off. There was someone I didn't want a call from. I thought the radio would be sufficient.'

'And your landline kept going straight to voicemail.'

'It does that if I haven't used it for a while.'

'I left messages, Inspector, honest I did.'

Frank found it hard to resist a smile. Pete Phillips, despite having done everything and more than he should, was obviously still in trepidation of the worst bollocking he would get in his career. And he wasn't getting it, which made him more nervous.

'I forgot to check my voicemail this morning. These things happen, Sergeant, unfortunately. I'm sure you did everything you should have. We've wasted enough time, though. Take me through it, from the start.'

'Well, um, I received a call from Sergeant Bute on the desk just after seven,' he said, consulting his notebook. 'He said a body had been found which suggested that it might have something to do with the eighty-five percent case. I called Inspector Hanson, and he told me to get in touch with you immediately. I attempted to get hold of you by radio at twenty-three minutes past seven. Finding that that did not work I – '

Frieda held up a hand.

'Sergeant, forget how many times you attempted to get in touch. Forget the radio, the telephone, and especially pigeon post, in case you tried that. Just tell me the facts about the case. Who discovered the victim, who he is, that sort of thing.'

Pete Phillips looked as if he was sorry he had not thought of using pigeon post. He went back to his notebook.

'Well, the body was found by a Miss Sharon Nally, an estate agent from the firm handling the property. She had an appointment for someone to view the property at seven-thirty, and wanted to get there early. She used her mobile phone to call the station at approximately seven-oh-five, and Sergeant Bute dispatched a patrol car. When they reported in he informed me and I immediately called Dr Pleadle and tried to contact you, Inspector.'

'Yes, yes, Sergeant. Do we know who he is?'

'One Wayne Kegglon. Miss Nally confirmed his identity. He works – worked with her at the estate agency.'

'An estate-agent? Ah, well, no loss there, then,' Frieda said.

Frank's eyebrows raised. Obviously Frieda had had problems with estate agents at some stage.

'Where is Miss Nally now?' he asked Pete.

'Back at her office,' Pete Phillips replied, relieved at being able to speak to someone other than Frieda. 'Apparently she cancelled the seven-thirty appointment while she was at the house, and then left to deal with others later in the day.'

'The patrol uniforms didn't detain her?' asked Frieda in astonishment.

'From what I can gather she sort of slipped away while they weren't looking,' Pete Phillips said apologetically.

'I'll be having a word with them later,' Frieda said in a voice of controlled fury.

'Did you visit the scene of crime?' Frank asked.

'No, I was too busy here trying to get things organised. I did my best, Inspector, honest.'

'No-one is saying you didn't, Sergeant Phillips. It obviously wasn't your fault that things went wrong for a while, but they're back on track now, so don't get yourself hot and bothered about something you couldn't do anything about.'

'But you heard the description of what happened, didn't you?' Frank persisted.

'Yes. And I'm glad I didn't see it. Probably would have thrown up. It sounds ... really bad.'

'Yet Miss Nally returns to the office and gets on with the day job. Rather suspicious, I would say. She did actually see the body, didn't she?'

'From all accounts, yes. Now you mention it, it does sound rather funny.'

'I think the sooner we pay Miss Nally a visit the better,' Frank said to Frieda.

'Good thinking, Frank. First on the scene, she knew this Wayne Kegglon, she doesn't react in a normal way. You and Gertie get onto it straight away. Sergeant Phillips and I will continue to go through the detail here.'

'Come on, Gertie, let's be a-moving.'

'Oh, and Frank? Do make sure your radio is working. I will probably want to contact you shortly.'

'It always is, Inspector, it always is,' he re-assured her with a wink.

He and Gertie made it out of the door just before the whiteboard pen hit the frame.

'Do you mind if we talk out the back?' Miss Sharon Nally said in a voice that suggested it was merely a not-so polite gesture. 'I could do with a fag. The phone's being going all morning. Tricia, look after things for a while. If you can.'

They followed her out to the back of the office, to a yard of cracking concrete and weeds used as a car-park and general disposal area. The front office itself had been everything a smart, sophisticated estate-agents should be. Everything beyond the connecting door spoke of lack of care and temporary usage.

Miss Nally lit a cigarette and blew the smoke out in an irritated fashion. She was about thirty-five, with a thin, pinched face which suggested a concern with her weight enforced by diet and drugs rather than exercise, and an overly aggressive use of make-up. She had been dealing with a client when they had turned up, her voice filled with empathy and concern. When the client had gone, and Frank had introduced themselves as police officers and not potential purchasers, the empathy and concern had quickly changed into irritation.

'You were due to meet a client at the house? At seven-thirty?' Frank asked.

A nod. A puff of irritated smoke.

'And then you found Mr Kegglon?'

Another nod. More smoke.

'Did you see Mr Kegglon's body?'

'Course I did. How do you think I recognised him?'

'It didn't put you off? You didn't think of, maybe taking the rest of the day off?'

'I work in a dog-eat-dog business. There's no place in it for anyone wanting to take time off just because they don't feel well. Besides, I've seen worse at the movies.'

Sensitivity, Frank decided, was not Miss Nally's strong point.

'Bad news if you're a dog,' he commented. 'Did you know of anyone who might want to kill Mr Kegglon?'

A shrug.

'Plenty, if they knew what he had done. Quite a few husbands out there who weren't aware of their wives having private viewings.'

'He was something of a ladies' man?'

A short, scornful laugh.

'He liked shagging 'em, if that's what you mean. And they weren't that slow at spreading their legs.'

'No-one complained about his behaviour?' Frank asked, feeling that Gertie beside him was beginning to boil.

'Goes with the territory. You have to earn your sales, get your commission. You do what you have to. No-one asks how a sale was made. Afterwards it's on to the next one. If you can't keep up, you're out. End of story.'

Which meant, Frank deduced, that Miss Nally was quite ready to wave her skinny little backside in front of any male purchasers should the need arise.

'You didn't like Mr Kegglon?' he asked.

Another shrug.

'We're in competition, ain't we? He gets a sale, that's one I've missed. We've been trying to flog that place for months now. It would be a really good commission, but people are becoming stingy these days, what with the cost of living and all.'

Thank god for the cost of living, Frank thought.

'Can you think of anyone, a client perhaps, who might specifically have a grudge against Mr Kegglon?'

Another shrug. Had it been anyone else Frank might have taken the shrugs as a sign of some mental activity. As it was he was trying to suppress the urge to give her a good slap.

'We'll need a list of everyone who viewed the property,' he continued.

'There'll be hundreds,' she protested. 'All sorts wanted to look at it. Most just wanted a look, nosy buggers, but you couldn't take a chance on a sale. There was even one old codger, obvious he couldn't afford it, he was just there to look at the gardens. Here, he was a retired copper, I'm sure of it. Big bugger, grey hair.'

Frank's face showed no sign that he recognised the description of Tom Sampson.

'How about Phil Walthers?'

'Oo?'

'Phil Walthers, editor of the Herald.'

'Oh, him. Course he was there. Took a load of photos. Good publicity.'

'We will need a full list. And today, I'm afraid.'

She looked at him as if he were mad.

'Do you know how much work I have on?' she asked in disbelief. 'I've had to cancel five viewings this morning already. That's five sales. And I have to take on Wayne's work as well. I don't have time to go searching through records and notes and what have you.'

'I'm afraid it has to be done, Miss Nally,' Frank said firmly. 'If you won't co-operate we will come in and do the job ourselves. You won't have to cancel five viewings, you will have to cancel all viewings, closing the office while we're doing it. You will get the publicity you talk of, only it might not be the kind you desire. Your choice.'

Miss Nally looked at him with a tinge of newly found respect.

Someone who lives in a dog-eat-dog world respects a man wielding a whip.

'I'll get Tricia to do it,' she said. 'Only she's a bit dim, see? Good with filing, but not too bright, if you know what I mean.'

Frank knew exactly what she meant. Tricia had at least one brain cell where Miss Nally had a void.

'Why do I feel I need a shower to clean myself off?' asked Gertie as they drove back to the station.

'I know what you mean,' replied Frank.

Tricia, a thickly bespectacled, plain and dowdily dressed young girl with listless long blonde hair in a pony tail, had been only too eager to help. It was as if she had been an orphaned soul in a heartless world, and Frank and Gertie had appeared as the parents she had once hoped would turn up to rescue her from her blighted bondage. She had not only promised to get the details one hundred percent right – Frank now understood Tracey's loathing for the word "percent" – but had also promised faithfully to deliver the information to the police station before five o'clock that evening.

While she was speaking to them they could overhear Miss Sharon Nally speaking to two middle-age prospective purchasers about the importance of buying a home rather than a house, how she understood that they were about to spend their hard-earned savings on the first home they could call their own, and how important it was to her, personally, that their dream came true. She only wished that one day she would find someone as caring as Mr Smith, since they were obviously such a happily married couple, and she had yet to meet the man of her dreams.

Frank had felt like throwing up. All over Miss Nally.

Gertie had been more practical. She had picked up a piece of paper, walked over to Miss Nally's desk, introduced herself to the couple as a police officer, apologised for the intrusion, and sweetly asked Miss Nally to confirm that this record had indeed been properly signed off according to standard agency procedures.

Just in case questions arose later.

Since they had to do a thorough audit, considering they were investigating a murder case.

Mr and Mrs Smith, or whatever their names might be, had suddenly decided they needed to have another think about the property they had been looking at. Or possibly through which estate agency they were looking at it.

When they left Frank had wished Miss Nally, "Oh, and break a leg, as they say in the theatre".

He had meant it literally. He could have added all the limbs skinny Miss Nally was composed of.

'If there was anyone you would include in whatever percentage of the human race this world would be better off without,' he said, 'Miss Nally would be included, even if it were zero percent.'

'I wonder if there's anything we could nick her for,' pondered Gertie.

'No, we'd have to have the station fumigated afterwards. Unfortunately I don't think we can even include her on the list of suspects. She wouldn't have the imagination to make those notes, even if she could read and write. Come on, let's go have a word with Tom Sampson.'

Irritation was an emotion alien to Frank most of the time. He could accept a world populated by all sorts of characters, accepting their foibles and eccentricities as part of a rich tapestry of life. He was beginning to wonder whether that was a practical reaction to something he could do nothing about, and now that the possibility of a different world arose, the irritation was beginning to leak through.

And if he was able to think of such a thing purely on an academic level, how far might others let themselves go in the physical sense?

Tom Sampson was extremely contrite and apologetic when he found Gertie and Frank on his doorstep. He invited them in. Frank declined the offer of tea or coffee.

'There's a house for sale in Lords Acres,' he said as they sat in Sampson's neat kitchen. 'Glenborough Road. Would you ever have gone to view it?'

'Glenborough Road? Yes, if it's the one you mean, I was there last week.'

'You were thinking of buying it?'

'Oh, no,' Sampson answered with a surprised look. 'I doubt I could afford it even if I won the lottery. No, I was there purely to see the garden. I'd heard it was quite something to see. In the end it turned out to be a disappointment. Large, yes, but that was it. No special features, not even landscaped in any way. Pleasant enough, and I can't say I wouldn't mind owning it, it would be lovely to sit out there on a summer's evening, but otherwise? Not quite a wasted journey, but close to it. Why do you ask?'

Frank paused before replying.

'An estate agent was found there this morning. Murdered.'

Sampson's eyebrows raised. His mouth twitched, almost in a smile.

'I hope you are going to tell me it was that woman, what's her name? Wally? She was the one who took me around.'

'You didn't like her?'

'One shouldn't speak ill of the dead, but I thought she was a truly revolting creature. Pretended to be all charm and helpfulness, but I've met all types in my life. I could see that all she was interested in was getting a sale. I think she guessed I couldn't afford the house. She carried on pretending, just in case I really was a wealthy old man who she could diddle, but she didn't put too much effort into it.'

'Did you meet her colleague? Wayne Kegglon?'

'No, can't say I remember anyone of that name. And I tend to be good with names.'

'I don't suppose you have an alibi for yesterday evening by any chance?'

Sampson smiled sadly.

'I'm afraid not. Most evenings I spend on my own, watching a little television, or reading a book. I'm afraid I had enough of human company while I was in the force. Much of it I would have preferred to forego.'

'On Tuesday you were in the shopping area in the Old Village?'

'Every Tuesday. There's a cake shop there, a patisserie I believe they call it. It's my weekly treat. This week I bought a selection of cream cakes.' He looked embarrassed. 'I'd offer you one, but I seem to have finished them.'

'Tell me, do you buy the Herald?'

'I used to, at one stage. Haven't bothered for a long time now – too full of adverts for my liking.' His face took on a puzzled look. 'Why do you ask?'

Frank stood up.

'I know it's a strange question, but there are reasons for asking strange questions, as I'm sure you've discovered in the past.'

'True, true,' said Sampson standing up. 'I'd hoped I'd left that all behind, if I were to be perfectly honest. You sure you won't stay for a tea or coffee?'

'No, thanks. Oh, by the way, I'm afraid I have some disappointing news. The estate agent who was murdered wasn't Miss Nally, it was a Mr Wayne Kegglon.'

Sampson looked at him with a wry grimace.

'I suppose I shouldn't have said that about her,' he said. 'After all, we're supposed to love our fellow human beings, aren't we, despite all their faults.'

'I wouldn't worry about it. I don't think Miss Nally qualifies as a fellow human being,' Frank replied.

'I'm beginning to thoroughly dislike this case,' Frank said as Gertie drove them back to the station. 'It's almost as if I feel I'm gradually been drawn to agree that the world would be better off without some people.'

'But it's true, Sarge, isn't it? When you really think about it?'

'You can't think that way if you're a police officer, Gertie. It's the slippery slope. It's the first step to fudging evidence because you think someone's guilty but you can't prove it. Once you do something like that, the next step seems logical – framing people, turning a blind eye when someone you like does something they shouldn't, whatever. Each time you justify your actions to yourself, until, in the end, you no longer even think that what you're doing might be wrong.'

'But sometimes you have to turn a blind eye, Sarge,' protested Gertie.

'I know, Gertie, but there are degrees. I think our murderer, whoever it is, no longer understands that.'

'It can't be Tom Sampson. He's a sweet old dear.'

'Yes, and Hitler liked dogs. No doubt Machiavelli was fond of kittens. I'm sure Ghengis Kahn had a soft spot for something. Yaks, quite possibly.'

'I don't believe that you can suspect Tom Sampson for even a second,' Gertie said in a voice that Frank recognised, one that suggested that he had done something unforgivable, and he was now due for an extended period of unforgiving.

'Logically he has to stay on the list,' he pointed out.

'Your problem is that you have too much logic and too little emotion,' she said angrily. 'I've never met anyone as cold-hearted as you.'

He was tempted to remind her of Miss Nally. Instead he decided to let it go, and hope that Gertie would get over it.

Frank spent his lunch hour in his office with a mug of coffee and witness statements taken during the past few days. The last thing he felt like facing at that moment was food. Agnetha only got upset if she saw him eating a machine-produced sandwich in the canteen. If she couldn't see him, she couldn't get upset.

The notes the uniformed constables had made of that morning were useless. Nobody had seen anything or heard anything. Some claimed they had seen Kegglon turn up in his car, others thought they had seen lights on in the house, but that could have been the day before, or even last week. They were so used to one or other of the estate agents turning up at odd hours they no longer noticed, and the gardens were so large, and the houses so far set back, you could probably drive a red double-decker bus with fairy-lights down the road without anyone seeing it.

The only thing they agreed on was that it was not done for a house in Lords Acres to have a For Sale sign at the front. People who lived in Lords Acres did not advertise such things in such a way. They certainly did not employ a tatty two-bit little estate agency to carry out the transfer of ownership, either. It was just not the done thing. Not in Lords Acres.

Normally Frank would have dismissed such views as the pomposity of the upper middle-classes, but in this case he was prepared to make an exception. He made a note to find out who the current owner was, and why they were selling.

Someone had slipped into, or been in, Trafalgar Park and had killed Nagness. Someone – the same someone, he had to assume – had known about the alley where Chiffon Brady had been killed. That someone had also known about the house for sale in Lords Acres.

It didn't help very much. Trafalgar Park was hardly a secret. The alley was apparently well known to many as a trysting spot, to put it politely. And from what he had heard the house in Lords Acres was visited by any number of people wishing to see how the other half lived, apart from serious house-seekers.

A knock at the open door interrupted his thoughts.

'Frank?' asked Eric Johns. 'You have a visitor in reception, a Miss Leigh.'

'Miss Leigh? Can't say I know anyone of that name.'

'You probably remember me as Tricia,' said Miss Tricia Leigh, appearing in the doorway with a smile on her face.

'Hey! How did you get in here?' asked Eric Johns in surprise.

'I followed you,' Tricia Leigh said.

'You can't do that. Civilians wandering around the station, I –'

'Don't worry, Eric, Miss Leigh is here to help us with an investigation. Come in, Miss Leigh. Oh, and Eric, shut the door on your way out, would you?'

The door closed on Eric Johns' puzzled face as Tricia Leigh took the seat opposite Frank. She placed a folder on his desk.

'Was that naughty of me?' she asked, grinning.

'Very naughty,' Frank agreed, smiling. 'I might have to arrest you for it.'

'Oh, please do,' she said, her eyes flirting.

Frank coughed.

'Um, yes, well, yes. Um, that wouldn't be a list of people who viewed the house in Lords Acres, would it?'

'Yes, Sergeant,' she said with a small sigh as if regretting the change of subject but accepting it as something she expected. 'I knew you'd want it as soon as possible. I was supposed to be reconciling the accounts, but I thought that this was more important. And more interesting. And I wanted to see you again.'

Frank blinked. He had known forthright and straightforward women before, but Tricia Leigh had not struck him as such.

'I suppose you think I'm a right little tart.'

'Er, no, of course not.'

'Liar. I can see you do. I'm not, really, not normally. But I've worked in that office for almost six months now, and I'm desperate to meet normal people.'

Frank smiled.

'I'm not sure you've come to the right place, then. A police station is hardly the place to look for normal people.'

She thought about this.

'Maybe you're right. Maybe it's abnormal people I'm looking for. If it's abnormal for people to have a heart, to care about others. You don't have any jobs going here, do you?'

'Jobs?'

'Work. Employment. Jobs. I can type. I'm quite good with computers. I'm really good with filing and that sort of stuff. I don't mind if you take me on for a month or so, just to see whether I'd fit in. I promise you I will.'

'Well, that isn't my field, really. I'll ask around, but I can't promise anything.'

She sighed.

'Okay, I'll have to live with that. Only I'm so desperate to get out of that place I'd do almost anything.'

The straight look in her eyes when she said "almost anything" made him wonder what exactly she was thinking of. He knew what he was thinking of, and as a responsible Detective Sergeant he shouldn't be.

'Could I have a look at your list?' he asked, hoping that it might distract him from the look in Miss Tricia Leigh's eyes. She had changed from the plain looking young girl to someone with a rather attractively winsome look on her face.

She handed him the file and he opened it.

'Name, address, telephone number, date of viewing,' she said. 'The last column is a guess of mine as to whether or not they were seriously interested, on a scale of one to ten. But I'm afraid that it's only those who made an appointment which I knew about.'

'How do you mean?'

'Those two back in the office hate each others' guts. Or hated, I should say. They were continually trying to steal each others' clients. Quite often they'd keep an appointment to themselves so that the other wouldn't find out. The cow is already nicking every client Kegglon had that she can find.'

'A charming couple. Sounds like they were made for each other.'

'Yes. A pity the rest of the world has to put up with them, though. Here, you know this eighty-five percent theory?'

'I have heard about it, yes.'

'You don't think that's why he was done in, do you? Both of them would be ideal candidates.'

'I'll bear that in mind,' he replied, scanning the list of names.

'I thought it was a lot of rubbish at first, something dreamed up by that moron on the radio. But since then I've been thinking, well, it makes sense, doesn't it? In a way.'

'Not in my world, Miss Leigh.'

'Call me Tricia.'

It was something he had feared. Perfectly sensible people, charming and appealing people like Tricia Leigh, reacting to the murders of those they looked down on, and shrugging their shoulders. Frieda's reaction to the news that an estate agent had been murdered had shocked him. Or, to be more accurate, he was shocked at how little he was shocked. Even now he would have to admit that he was finding it hard to keep his feelings purely professional. There was a murderer or murderers out there and it was his job to stop them.

Sooner or later someone not in everybody's eighty-five percent was going to get killed, and, similar to Pastor Niemoller's realisation when the Nazis came to power, they would find that everyone was a potential victim and there was nobody left to help them. But that would have to wait. It would come in time if he didn't do something now.

'Tell me,' he asked, 'do any of these names mean anything to you? As people?'

Tricia stood up and came round to his side of the desk. She leaned over him, looking at the names.

Which is when Gertie walked in. She froze at the sight of Tricia Leigh leaning over Frank's shoulder in a pose that she herself had so often attempted to achieve.

'Hello, Gertie,' Frank said, totally missing the look on her face. 'Miss Leigh has brought in that list we were promised. We were about to go through it.'

'Really? Is that what it is?' asked Gertie with heavy sarcasm, sitting down in front of Frank's desk. She noticed how Tricia Leigh's blonde pony-tail was just dragging against the back of Frank's shoulder. He didn't appear to notice.

'Mr Sampson,' Tricia said, pointing at a name. 'I really liked him. It was obvious he wasn't interested in buying, just in seeing the gardens. I would have been happy to take him along in my lunch hour just so that he could wander around, but that would have got me fired. Trying to steal one of their sales. As if they didn't do the same, and it wasn't going to be a sale anyway.'

'How about this Robert Bagley?'

'Councillor Bagley,' Tricia corrected him. 'He was ever so insistent on being called councillor, puffed up old fart. He wanted to convert the house into some sort of church. He would never have got planning permission, even if he is a councillor.'

'A church? What sort?'

'I don't know. Latter Day Church of the Screaming Heeby Dweebies, I would imagine. I didn't like the look in his eyes. Sort of mad, but as if he knew it and didn't care, if you know what I mean.'

'Interesting. Anyone else?'

Tricia went through the other names, some she couldn't remember, others apparently harmless sight-seers.

There were two names missing, though, two names he could now cross off his list. The vicar and Mrs Blower. It was a matter of elimination, if that were the right word to use under the circumstances. Whittle down the list until only one possible suspect remained.

And the slight problem of proof.

'Tell me, do you know who the current owners are?' he asked when they had run out of names.

'He's an Australian. He inherited it when his great-aunt, or something, died. Didn't even bother coming over to look at it, just wanted it sold. Pity, really, apparently the old woman had meant to leave it to the local parish, but she never got around to changing her will.'

'The local parish?' Frank asked, having a sinking feeling that he knew only too well what he was about to discover.

'Yes, she was ill for a long time, so they say. The vicar, or whatever he is, used to visit her every Sunday. He was almost the only contact she had with the outside world, apart from nurses who used to change every other week.'

She sighed.

'I wouldn't mind a job like that,' she said, 'caring for some old woman, all alone. So long as it's the same woman. I couldn't face having to look after a different person each time, never getting to know them. You know, like you walk into a strange place, just do things automatically, as if you were a machine, and the other person – well, just some old nobody. If you know what I mean.'

'I think I do, Miss Leigh, I think I do. Thank you for your help, it's been very useful.'

'Tricia,' she replied, holding her hand out. 'If you need anything else, just give me a call. And you won't forget?'

He smiled as they shook hands.

'No, Tricia, I won't forget. Gertie, would you see Miss Leigh out?'

He turned to look out of the window as they left.

Councillor Bagley, he thought. A man obsessed by religion. If you were looking for someone likely to go around killing the unworthy, then Bagley sounded like an ideal candidate.

The trouble was that, unless they caught him in the act, at this stage they had absolutely no evidence apart from the circumstantial fact that he had been in the right place at the right time for two of the killings, and was known to have visited the site of the third.

Somewhere there were two copies of the Wellbury Herald with damning clippings taken from them. That sort of evidence no killer could get away from.

But would the killer have disposed of them? Burnt them? Put them through a shredder?

Not if they weren't aware they were under suspicion. Quite possibly they were still lying in someone's study or kitchen, just waiting to be found.

But as soon as they went to have a word with Bagley, which they had to do, and soon, and he were the killer, those newspapers would disappear faster than you could shout "read". You'd never get to "all about it".

'Pretty little thing,' Gertie said, coming back into the office, a note of disapproval in her voice.

'Hum? Sorry, Gertie, I was a little lost there. What did you say?'

'I said Tricia Leigh is a pretty little thing. Was it her you were thinking about?'

'Hmm? No, I was thinking about a certain Councillor. Gertie, you hang around here for a few minutes, I want to have a quick word with Eric.'

Gertie watched him walk out with a concerned look on her face. When Frank Summers failed to notice a pretty young woman, it was time to get the doctor in.

Admittedly by the time the doctor arrived it was time to call the undertakers in.

Tricia Leigh had all but rubbed herself up against Frank, and he hadn't even noticed. Ironically that worried Gertie. It meant that Frank was in a world of his own, and nobody could reach him, including her.

But she'd give it a damned good try, though.

'Sorry, Frank, the answer's no,' Eric Johns said, unhappily, but firmly.

'Come on, Eric, we have to go around to speak to him. All you have to do is radio us that someone's reported a suspected burglar in his house, and could we investigate, seeing as we're already in the area? I need an excuse to get inside and have a look around while he's not there.'

'Frank, there are more holes in it than a colander. Firstly, you say you're going around to speak to him, except you're pretty sure he won't be at home. Why not go around to his office, or wherever he works? You wouldn't need to be a lawyer to work out it was deliberate. And secondly, if anyone checks the logs they'll know there was no call. It's such an old trick a judge would spot it in his sleep. Both our heads will be on the chopping block, only I'll be the one to get the chop, and you'll probably get away with a telling-off.'

Frank sighed.

'Okay, Eric, I suppose you're right. Oh, well, might as well pop around to have a word with him at his office. You never know, maybe we'll get lucky.'

'Just be careful, Frank.'

'Where to, Sarge?' asked Gertie as they drove out of the station car park.

'Council offices. See if we can have a word with Bagley. It'll probably be a wasted effort, or worse, but it has to be done.'

'Or worse?'

'If Bagley is the killer, all we'll be doing is alerting him to the fact we have our eyes on him. If he isn't, I rather suspect we're in for an hour or so of pontificating. He sounds the sort of person too sure of himself to ever bother listening to anyone else.'

Gertie's radio crackled.

'Control to Constable Gregson, come in Constable.'

Gertie managed to answer while still holding the steering wheel. It was one of the drawbacks of working with Frank. Control had given up trying to contact him first, knowing that it would be much easier just to radio Gertie.

'Gertie here, Control. Over.'

'We've had a report of a prowler, possible burglar, in your area. Property is owned by one Mr Robert Bagley. His neighbour called in. Can you investigate?'

'We sure can,' sang Frank happily.

'Gertie to Control, we're on our way.'

'Be careful, Gertie, there could be more than one,' Control said.

'Will do, Control, out.' She looked at Frank. 'Lights and siren, Sarge?'

'Oh, no, Gertie, not this time,' he replied happily. 'We don't want anyone to know we're coming. About turn and let's get ourselves to chez Bagley. I wonder what happened to change

Eric's mind.'

'Eric? Sergeant Johns?'

'Yes, Gertie, dear old Eric Johns. I asked him to send us a message about a burglar being spotted at Bagley's place, something to give us an excuse to give the place the once over while he wasn't there.'

'You mean there isn't a burglar?'

'Not so much as a whiff. But don't spread that around.'

'I won't, Sarge,' Gertie replied, smiling. She liked breaking into the places of the baddies lawfully. It was part of the fun of the job.

Gertie brought the car to a quiet halt opposite Bagley's house. Frank had expected an imposing residence, but, while hardly small, it was not the stuff millionaires dream of. A tall, old tree in the front garden screened off much of the front. The garden itself looked as if someone tended it on an irregular basis, without enthusiasm. A low wall in the front had seen better days. A young girl of about six sat on the wall, watching them. She stood up as they got out and walked over.

'Are you the police?' she asked.

'Er, yes, we are,' Frank replied, puzzled. How could a young girl recognise them as police officers? They were both in civilian clothes. Was it the way they walked?

'You've come to rescue my kitten!' she exclaimed, clapping her hands. 'The man I spoke to said you'd be here soon! But you're even quicker than that.'

'Kitten?' asked Frank, with the feeling that the world was slipping from his grasp.

'In the tree. She ran up, but she can't get down again. You will get her for me, won't you?'

He looked at Gertie. She grinned back at him.

'Of course the nice Sergeant will get your kitten down, love,' she said. 'He likes doing that sort of thing.'

Frank looked at the old tree, and something larger than a normal kitten clinging to one of the upper branches. Typical Eric Johns, manages to translate a kitten up a tree into a prowler on the loose. No use to man nor beast. He could hardly break into Bagley's house because a child's kitten had got itself stuck.

What he should do was call the fire brigade, they had ladders for this type of situation. But, since it would take no more than five minutes, and he was here anyway ... He took off his jacket, handed it to Gertie, and began to scale the tree.

It was when the first branch broke that he began to have misgivings.

'It's awfully old,' the child said, not very helpfully.

Frank gritted his teeth and continued upwards. Apart from the danger of the tree breaking underneath him, he was also beginning to see that the little kitten was far closer to being a fully grown adult cat, and the flick of its frightened tail suggested that Frank was not a welcome visitor.

'Here, kitty, kitty, kitty,' he said as he finally managed to get within finger-touching distance.

Kitty pulled back, snarled, hissed, and a pawful of razor-sharp claws just missed Frank's grasping hand.

'Look, kitty, I'm here to help you. Now just let me pick you up and we can both go down. Nice little kitty, good kitty.'

A mouthful of small but sharp teeth suggested that kitty did not buy that story.

Frank sighed.

'Okay, you little shit,' he said under his breath, 'I'm taking you in the hard way.'

He gently inched forward, keeping his hands away from the kitten, until he was close enough.

'Gotcha!' he cried, bringing a hand behind the kitten, and grabbing it by the scruff of the neck. For a few seconds he hung perilously by one hand and two desperate feet. Then he inched his way back until he was sitting on one of the stronger branches, holding a bundle of fire, spit and claws by its neck, and took a deep breath.

He looked down to find that, in addition to a rapt audience of Gertie and the little girl, Frieda was also looking up at his precarious performance, a very, very strange look in her eyes.

'A kitten up a tree, Frank?' she asked in an amused voice. 'Are you going to arrest it?'

I might do just that, Frank thought to himself, as he continued his downward journey. A vicious assault on a police officer.

When he finally found himself with two feet on the ground the little girl came rushing up.

'Oh, thank you, thank you, come here Lucy, Lucy, you naughty little girl.'

She held up her hands for the ball of fury. Lucy was spitting threats that fortunately couldn't be translated into English.

'Um, I'm afraid Lucy's a little upset now,' Frank said. 'Maybe you should wait until she's calmed down. She might scratch you without meaning to.'

'She's just scared, aren't you, Lucy?' the child said, firmly taking the cat from Frank. 'She wouldn't hurt me, would you, Lucy?'

Lucy did indeed settle down in the child's arms, having taken a last swipe at Frank's hand, and almost caught it. It continued looking at Frank with venomous eyes.

The child leaned forward.

'Can I tell you a secret?' she whispered.

Only so long as you keep the kitty from hell away from me, thought Frank. He knelt down so that his face was level with hers.

'What is it?' he asked softly.

'There's a nasty burglar in Mr Bagley's front bedroom window,' the girl said in a loud whisper. 'He's looking at us now.'

Three pairs of police eyes turned upwards towards the window. In it stood a man who had become transfixed with Frank's errand of mercy, and who had apparently forgotten that he was supposed to be staying out of sight. The eyes stood fixed for a few seconds, until the man turned suddenly and disappeared as if he had just fallen over something.

'Frank, you take the front door,' called Frieda. 'Gertie, come with me.'

'Oh, great, you always take the fun jobs,' Frank said as they disappeared around the back.

He walked up to the front door and tried the handle. To his surprise the door opened.

'You stay back by the wall back there, my sweet,' he told the little girl, and entered the house softly.

There was a staircase about fifteen feet in front of him. He moved quickly to the bottom. At the top was a man desperately fighting to get a sheet off of his face. He had just managed to do so when he discovered the stairs.

'Oh, shit, no!' he cried as he fell.

Frank's head nodded with each bounce, until the man lay at his feet, groaning. Frank folded his arms and leant against the wall.

'Don't move, or I shoot,' he said conversationally.

'No, please don't shoot me, please,' the man cried, covering his head. 'I'm just an honest criminal, honest, officer, please don't shoot!'

'An honest criminal,' mused Frank. 'An interesting concept.'

The man paused, opened an eye and looked up at Frank.

'You haven't got a gun,' he pointed out.

'No, but I am a police officer, and you are under arrest. Now I hope you aren't going to be difficult, or these two will handle you,' Frank said as Frieda and Gertie came rushing in from the back. 'They look like they could do with some fun.'

The man looked at them. Frieda had a thin, extendible truncheon in her hand. It was swinging slightly, viciously. Gertie was cracking her knuckles. She did indeed look like someone looking forward to a little fun, only the other person wasn't about to enjoy it.

'No, please, constable, you've nicked me, I'll come quietly, honest. Only don't let them two get at me.'

'Sergeant,' corrected Frank. 'Now stand up and let me get the cuffs on you like a good little burglar.'

The man stood up slowly, groaning. He turned around and put his hands behind his back as if used to the procedure.

Frank patted his pockets. He looked at Gertie and Frieda.

'Um, anyone got any cuffs on them?' he asked.

Frieda looked at Gertie. She shrugged and showed her empty hands.

'They're in the car,' Gertie said apologetically. The man turned around.

'No guns, no cuffs?' he asked. 'What sort of police force are you?'

'The caring kind,' replied Frank. 'You sit down there on the bottom step and behave yourself. Gertie, watch him. Inspector, I think we need to check if anything has been stolen.'

'I haven't stolen anything, honest, guv.'

'Shush now, there's a good criminal. Inspector?'

'But, Frank – '

'We'll start with the kitchen,' he said, pulling her by her arm.

'Frank, what are you playing at?' she asked, once inside the kitchen.

'It's a game called hunt the newspapers. The ones with little bits cut out of them.'

Her eyes widened and she smiled as she realised what he meant.

'I'll take upstairs,' she whispered. 'We'd better hurry, we might not have long.'

'Nothing,' said Frank half an hour later as they stood once

more at the bottom of the stairs. The burglar, one Victor Brown, had been taken to the station by a patrol car, to sit in the cells, awaiting the taking of a statement. Frieda, Gertie and Frank had searched the house as thoroughly as they could, but had found nothing to suggest Bagley was anything but an upright and honest citizen with little interest in literature apart from the Bible, and a fondness for naughty films which would have been illegal at one stage.

'What the hell's going on here?' asked an indignant voice from the doorway. It was filled with a large man with a surprised face.

'Mr Robert Bagley?' asked Frieda.

'Yes, I'm Councillor Bagley, who are you?'

'Inspector Garold,' Frieda said, producing her warrant card. 'This is Detective Sergeant Summers and Constable Gregson. Your neighbour reported a burglar in your house. We believe we apprehended him before he could steal anything, but we'd like you to check to make sure.'

'A burglar? Well, I doubt he'd find much to steal. Nothing of value in the house.'

'You have a television and video recorder, Mr Bagley,' Frank noted. 'They should be worth a bob or two.'

'Not likely, son, the telly's ancient, and so is the recorder. People want DVD machines these days, a computer at least. You wouldn't get a fiver for those.'

'Your door appeared to be unlocked when we got here,' Frank said.

'Never lock it,' Bagley said, walking past them towards the kitchen. 'Fancy a cup of tea or coffee? I normally have tea, but I think I've got some coffee somewhere.'

Frank raised his eyebrows in surprise. He looked at Frieda, then at Gertie. They shrugged their shoulders.

'You finish up here, Frank,' Frieda said. 'I'd best be getting back.'

They went into the kitchen as Frieda left.

'We'll pass on the tea, thanks all the same, Mr Bagley. May I ask why you never lock your door?'

'I believe we must put our trust in the Lord, not in locks, Sergeant. Apart from which, it will cost more to repair the doors than anything they could steal, so financially it's worth it. Sure you won't have any tea? I think I've got some coffee somewhere, if it hasn't congealed.'

'No, thank you, Mr Bagley. While we're here, there are one or two questions we need to ask you.'

'Ask away, Sergeant, I have nothing to hide.'

'I presume you are aware that a women was murdered a few days ago, and another more recently.'

'Eighty-five percenters? Yes, quite aware, Sergeant. I was in the area they took place on both occasions. I'm surprised you haven't paid me a visit yet.'

'It's on our list of things to do. Since we're here we can kill two birds with one stone. You didn't spot anything suspicious while you were in those locations?'

'Depends what you mean by suspicious, Sergeant. The second one, the traffic warden – do you know a man called Phil Walthers? Editor of the Herald?'

'Yes, sir, we know him.'

'He was acting suspiciously. I think he was trying to trail me. Stood out like a sore thumb.'

'Why would he want to trail you?'

'He's a journalist, so-called. I'm a Councillor, I have a nightclub which offers such delights as lap-dancers and strip-tease, I am also a committed Christian. No doubt he thinks he might find a story in that. Apart from which, I wouldn't be surprised if the ex-wife has fed him some nonsense.'

'Ex-wife?'

'Technically we're still married. She ran off with some gigolo. Thought she could get hold of half my money. Not if I avoid giving her a divorce, she won't. And I'm spending it as fast I can, so there won't be anything left for her by the time she does. Anyway, it matters little, her time is coming, just as for all of us, to face the final judgement day.'

'Do you have a date for that, Mr Bagley?'

Bagley gave him a look which showed that he knew Frank was taking the Mickey.

'Scoff if you want, Sergeant, the proof of the pudding, and all that. If I'm wrong I will look foolish, perhaps. If you're wrong you'll lose your immortal soul. I think I know which way the bookies would lean.' He held up a stern finger. 'These killings are a sign of the truth, Sergeant, a sign that chaos is coming. We will have many more to come. Many more.'

'You believe they are a sign of God's wrath?'

'That's a simplistic notion. God does not create murderers. It is our own indulgence and decadence which has caught up with us.'

'Could you tell us where you were last night, between about eight o'clock and midnight?'

Bagley smiled.

'Let me guess, Sergeant, there's been another one. I told you it would happen. As for me, I was sitting in my lounge reading the bible until midnight, at which time I went to bed. No alibi, I'm afraid, but that worries me little. You can frame me and lock me up if you wish, my path is the way of the just, and I trust in the Creator, that He will guide me and look after me. I now follow a much higher law than yours, Sergeant.'

'Phew,' said Gertie when they were back in the car, 'any longer and he might have me believing as well.'

'Actually, I was thinking of shoving a bible in his gob. Trouble is, I had to let him carry on, to see if he really believes it, or whether it's all a show.'

'And did you? Work out whether he was for real?'

'I think that either his wife leaving pushed him over the edge, or maybe she left him because he was already over it.'

'He certainly qualifies under the psychological heading.'

'I can't argue with that assessment, Gertie. "A much higher law than yours"? That's normally a justification for some very nasty business. Come on, Gertie, back to the station. We should have just about enough time left to sort out Victor Brown.'

'Are you going to charge him, Sarge? Vic Brown?'

'What with? About the only thing we've got is trespass and attempted burglary. Bagley doesn't give a damn. Even if it went to court the judge would give him a rap over the knuckles at most. Let's give him the rap ourselves and kick him out.'

'Aren't you supposed to record this?' Victor Brown asked nervously as they sat in the interview room.

'Why would we want to do that, Mr Brown? We just want a quiet little chat. Avoid the paperwork, that sort of thing.'

'I know the sort of quiet chats you lot do. I want a lawyer.'

'Now, Mr Brown, we will get you a lawyer if you really want, but one or two questions first. Let's start with where you come from, you obviously aren't a Wellburian.'

'London,' Victor Brown said, after a small hesitation. 'Things were getting well out of hand there, it was dangerous just trying to make a living. I come here, and almost in the first few days you lot almost kill me.'

'Be fair, Mr Brown, we didn't push you down the staircase.'

'No, but you threatened to shoot me.'

'Since I wasn't carrying a gun, I think a jury might come to the conclusion that I was joking.'

'Might be a joke to you,' Victor Brown said plaintively, 'but it wasn't so funny from my side. Them London coppers are right dangerous these days.'

'Well, sorry about that. I'll try to bear it in mind in future.'

'Look, guvnor,' Victor Brown said suddenly, leaning forward and pleading, 'okay, you got me bang to rights, I admit that. But, look, I'm a married man, I have a wife to look after. And if she finds out I was on a job she won't half kill me. I promised I was going to go straight. Can't you just give me a caution and let me go? I promise I won't do nuffin again. Straight up, guv, not a word of a lie.'

'Victor, I might consider the possibility, but there's at least one condition.'

'Anything for you, guv, honest.'

'Drop the Cockney bullshit. It makes me feel ill.'

Victor Brown looked hurt.

'I worked very hard on that, I'll have you know. I could have been an actor. Anyway, there's been more than one time it's saved my life. These young coppers, they think they're Cagney and Lacey, or whatever it's called. Come out with a little bit of the Cockney, if you're lucky they'll remember they're in Brixton, not the Bronx.'

Frank stood up.

'Just you remember that you're in Wellbury now, Victor. Over-worked Cockney accents are punishable around here. Especially if I'm around. Come on, time for you to go home.'

'You're not charging me?' Victor Brown asked happily as he jumped up.

'Not worth the paperwork, is it?'

'Gawd bless you guv, you're a real gentleman, a diamond geezer, a – '

Frank held up a warning finger.

'Okay, okay, I'm going, I'm going.'

'Show him out, Gertie.'

Frank walked back to his office, whistling.

'You're in a happy mood,' Frieda noted, standing in the doorway as he dropped into his chair.

'You meet some nasty people in this job,' he said. 'And then sometimes you come across someone like our Victor Brown. What did he call himself? "An honest criminal". He's so full of made-up Cockney blarney you can't help but smile.'

Frieda smiled herself.

'Sounds a bit like a certain Detective Sergeant I know,' she said. 'Without the Cockney, of course.'

Frank wasn't so sure he agreed with the description. He did wonder, however, what Frieda wanted. He hoped she wouldn't suggest after-work drinks. He had already promised those to Gertie.

'Why don't you get along home, Frank. I want an early start tomorrow. We've got to get somewhere with these killings. First thing tomorrow, clear-headed and bushy-tailed, we are going to start throwing everything we have into the case. Even if I have to ask Percy to come in with us.'

Blimey, thought Frank as she walked away, she must be serious if she's willing to let Percy have some of the action.

'I like our Victor,' Gertie said as she came into the office. 'The original cheeky chappie.'

'Based on an original myth by someone who's seen Mary Poppins too often and who'd never seen London in his life, I expect,' Frank remarked. 'Come on, Gertie, get your coat. A couple of drinks and I'll show you the Summers' approach to haute cuisine.'

'Can't wait, Sarge,' she said happily.

'What I find interesting,' Frank said as they sat on a couch in the Sergeant's Arms, 'is the choice of victims.'

Gertie had chosen the Sergeants Arms pub as a good place for a post-work drink. She didn't like the Hangman, which was Susan's preferred venue, or the wine bars that Frieda went in for. Frank was rather relieved. He didn't want the added danger of absentmindedly thinking he was with Susan in the Hangman, and putting an arm around her only to find that he was sitting next to Gertie. It could be extremely embarrassing for both of them.

'In what way, Sarge?' She looked at him. 'Is it okay to call you Frank when we're off duty? Only calling you Sarge all the time, well, I'll never get to know the real Frank Summers, and I'd really like to.'

Frank pondered this, taking a swig of his pint. He had to admit that being called Sarge every waking minute was a bit too much for him. You had to leave the job back in the office.

'Sounds reasonable to me, Gertie. Only I think you'll be disappointed if you try to get to know the real Frank Summers. It'll take about five minutes and you'll wonder if it was worth it afterwards.'

'Frank.' She mouthed the name. 'I like it. I think I'll call my baby boy Frank.'

Frank rubbed his forehead. Gertie had long ago decided that she was going to have a husband, a son, a daughter, another one of either gender, and a career. It was a dangerous conversation to get into.

'Why not name him after your father?'

'My dad's name is Frank, strangely enough.'

Right, thought Frank. When you find yourself slipping into a hole, stop digging and throw the spade away.

'Anyway, as I was saying. It was in one of the Hitchhiker's Guide To The Galaxy books where Arthur Dent comes across these crash-landed spaceships. The survivors had all been told that they had been chosen to start the nucleus of a new civilisation, as their own planet was doomed.'

'A bit old-fashioned.'

'Old-fashioned? Science fiction?'

'No, the name Arthur. Makes me think of a great-uncle or something.'

'Gertie, you aren't paying attention, are you?'

'Sorry, Sarge – Frank.' She snuggled closer to him. 'There, now I can hear you better, Frank. You were saying? About these space-ships?'

'Yes, well,' he said, feeling Gertie pressed up close next to him. 'They had been told that they had been chosen especially to start a new civilisation.'

'That would be fun. Can you imagine the two of us being set out to some foreign planet to start a new civilisation? I'd have to have a lot more than three little babies.'

'Ah, but the point is that these people had been lied to. They had jobs such as telephone receiver cleaners, if I recall correctly. They had been chosen especially, but not because they were to start a new civilisation, but rather to get rid of spare mouths from the old.'

'Ugh! That's a nasty trick. If they ask us to volunteer we're not going to go. We'll stay here.'

Frank sighed. Normally he was the one to insist on no shop-talk, and here he was talking shop while the ambitious Gertie had left it so far behind it was no longer in calling distance.

'It's the same thing as our victims so far,' he said, ploughing on regardless. 'A nagging old women, an unloved traffic warden and an estate agent. In a utopian society you wouldn't have any of them. I wonder if that's the key.'

'Why did you leave your last girlfriend?' asked Gertie

suddenly, looking into his eyes. 'Was she too demanding? Too clingy? Or maybe too weepy?'

Frank blinked. He tried to remember when he last had a permanent girlfriend, what her name was, and why they broke up. Since coming to Wellbury everything before seemed to have happened to someone else.

'I can't remember,' he admitted.

She leaned back from him as if he were Satan.

'You can't remember? Frank, you can be a real shit at times. How can you say you can't remember your last girlfriend? Use them and lose them, is that your approach to women?'

'Okay, okay, Gertie. Let's just say I prefer to forget. To forget and look to the future.'

'Oh, in that case it's different,' she said, snuggling into him once more. 'I can understand wanting to forget a grand passion.'

Jean, he thought. Her name was Jean. Bugger! He had managed to avoid remembering that name for months, and now it was back.

And she had dumped him, rather than the other way around. Typical mistaken idea that he was seeing other women in his spare time.

No. He was not going to let Jean re-appear. That was over.

The past is a foreign country.

'It makes you wonder, though,' Gertie said softly. 'Nagness, for instance. Do you think she ever had a grand passion? Or was she a right cow right from the start?'

Epicurus, Frank's wavering lodestar, would have been dead-set against grand passions. Good company, nice food and wine, but grand passions? Nope, probably bad for the indigestion. Nowt wrong with a good old bonk, but you wouldn't want to get carried away with things. That was the mistake he had made before. Never again.

'Maybe that's what turned her sour,' he suggested, blotting out certain thoughts. 'Fell deeply in love, it all went wrong, and she was left a bitter and twisted old woman at a young age.'

'I suppose you're right,' Gertie said reluctantly. 'I never did like the end to Gone With The Wind. I prefer it where the woman gets her man.'

'I wonder if the vicar had anyone in mind when he said he intended to marry.'

'Now there's a thought,' Gertie said, gripping his arm. 'Do you think we could help him along? Help him find romance?'

'Gertie, I rather doubt whether that's included in the official specification of police work. I have this tiny, tiny feeling that Frieda might disapprove.'

'No, no, that's against the rules,' she said, holding a finger to his lips. 'You aren't allowed to mention Frieda or Susan, or anyone else from work while we're having drinks. Promise?'

She took her finger from his lips.

'Well, er, I – '

The finger was re-applied.

'Promise?'

'Okay, Gertie, okay, I promise to try not to mention anything about work.'

'Oh, good,' she said, hugging his arm against her breast and giving him a peck on the cheek.

'Right, er, well, right,' he said, confused.

What really confused him was that he was quite enjoying Gertie holding his arm and snuggling up tight.

Still, they were off duty, right?

'No, it bloody well isn't right, Frank Summers,' said one of his voices. 'You'll be back in trouble before the night's out.'

'Nonsense,' he said, closing off the voice.

'What did you say?' asked Gertie.

'Uh? Oh, the notion crossed my mind that Mrs Blower might be attracted to the vicar. I just thought it nonsense.'

'Oh, I don't know,' said Gertie, leaning her head on his shoulder. 'Maybe that's what she's really after. All this stuff about helping out in the church could be a blind. Once she's got him she'll leave the flower-arranging and that stuff to someone else.'

'A long shot, if ever I heard one,' he said, draining his pint. 'Drink up, Gertie, we've time for another.'

'Ooh, goodie, I could do with another,' she said, downing her gin-and-tonic. 'Same again please.'

'Another double?'

'Another double. I feel like having fun tonight.'

Saturday: Mobilisation

'This is the third eighty-five percent murder,' Zack Kerouac said on the radio, 'and the list can only grow longer and longer with local police at a loss to understand the dynamics behind the outbreak of violence. Things are going to get much, much worse as people respond to their natural instincts. While I can't condone what's happening, I'm sure we all fully understand it.'

'Moron!' exclaimed Gertie mildly. 'Don't we have some music to put on?'

'Vivaldi?'

'Mmm. Vivaldi sounds nice.'

'And other reports confirm that a riot erupted last night when a group of young men in a pub in Old Merrick accused an older group of being in the eighty-five percent. Many honest and innocent citizens of Wellbury are calling for a vigilante force to be set up to maintain law and order, and it's time to – '

Kerouac's voice was terminated by Frank's finger.

'Last thing we need in the morning, that idiot trying to wind everyone up.'

Gertie hummed happily along to Vivaldi. Frank felt pretty cheerful himself. Possibly Gertie had been a little carried away from mixing gin at the pub and wine at home, but they had had a good meal, Gertie had complimented him on his cooking skills, and afterwards they had curled up on the sofa to watch a film on the telly, where she had gone to sleep in his arms.

Just like brother and sister.

At the back of his mind a voice groaned.

Frank ignored it. It was drowned out by another voice saying that Kerouac had said something significant.

Kerouac saying something significant? Now there would be a first.

'You okay, Frank?' Gertie asked solicitously. He realised he had been drumming his fingers on the windowsill, irritably. 'If it's the music we can change it if you want. I don't mind.'

'Hmm? No, I like Vivaldi,' he said. 'Tell me, what did the prat say just now? On the radio?'

'Oh, I don't know. Something about the third victim and a fight in a pub.'

'No, there was something else. Damn, it's almost there. On the tip of my tongue.'

'Shall I have a lick and see?' offered Gertie.

'Don't be silly, Gertie, it's important.'

Gertie went into sulk mode.

'You don't like me anymore, that's what you're trying to say, isn't it?' she said.

'Shush, Gertie, my love. I'm trying to think.'

Gertie was only slightly mollified by the "my love". She knew he didn't mean it literally, not at that moment. But he would, eventually.

The previous evening hadn't quite gone according to plan – if it could be said that she had a plan – but if she had, falling asleep next to Frank while watching telly wasn't quite part of it. She had been exhausted by a long day, the drinks, and then a gorgeous dinner. But then, if you thought about it, that was even better than the other. Anyone could have a quick affair, one which ended as soon as it started. Being able to fall asleep in each others' arms on a sofa showed commitment.

'Morning, Keith,' Frank said as they entered reception.

He and Gertie stopped suddenly at the sight of a group of toddlers sitting on the floor playing with paper and crayons, being looked after by two WPCs.

'We've opened a crèche?' Frank asked in astonishment. Keith Bute looked back at him morosely.

'I came to work to get away from my kids,' he said, 'not to find myself surrounded by other people's.'

'What happened?'

'The Sunshine Happy Play Nursery, or something like that. Some of the parents and staff had a little disagreement. I believe it started off with what might be politely termed a debate over the ownership of a piece of Lego. By the time the patrol car got there it was a full-on battle, with most of the older kids joining in. Ed Watts reckons two of the mothers were on the ground wrestling each other while their kids were hitting them with those small plastic chairs they have.' He sighed. 'The parents of this little lot are in the cells, along with all the staff.'

'A bit early for that sort of thing on a Saturday morning,' Frank observed. 'The phrase eighty-five percent wasn't used by any chance?'

'Oh, no more than a dozen or so times.'

'Cheer up, Keith. It's good practice for you.'

'I've had all the bloody practice I need,' moaned Keith, closing his eyes and putting his hands over his face. 'I'm going to resign and become a hermit far, far away.'

Frank looked at the toddlers, and shook his head slowly in disbelief.

'At this rate we're going to have to post a riot vehicle on every street corner. Time we did something about this. Gertie, you get us a couple of coffees, I'm going to grab something from the office. I'll meet you in the ops room.'

'Good morning, Gertie,' Frieda said as Gertie entered the ops room. Gertie was amazed to see that more than a full team were arranged. The room was full, including Inspector Percy Hanson, looking tired as ever, sucking on an unlit pipe, and his sidekick, Detective Sergeant Pete Phillips. 'I hope our Sergeant Summers has had a good rest?' continued Frieda.

'Whey-hey,' said a couple of anonymous voices at the back of the room.

'Probably shagged himself shitless,' commented Pete Phillips to himself. Or rather, he thought it was to himself. He found Gertie standing over him.

'You said something, Detective Sergeant?' she asked sweetly.

He found himself confronted with two imposing breasts, two mugs of hot tea, and a woman who was rumoured to have once thrown a man ten feet before he landed.

'Er, no, no, Gertie, I never said a thing.'

Gertie smiled and moved to the back, where she knew Frank would gravitate to.

'That will be one pound for the words you didn't say, Sergeant,' Frieda said, tapping a charity box. 'Fifty pence a swearword, ladies and gentleman. There will be no foul language while I am running things.'

Pete Phillips looked at the swear box. He had two choices, refusal – which meant he'd be off the case – or surrender.

'I thought you said it was only fifty pence,' he said, raising the surrender flag.

'If you count the words you recall you didn't say, Sergeant Phillips, I think you will find two of them unacceptable.'

Grudgingly he stood up, took a pound coin from his pocket, dropped it in the box and sat down again, to cheers from the others present.

'I'm glad to see you all cheerful and enthusiastic,' Frieda noted. 'I hope you will feel the same way by the end of your shifts, but I rather doubt it.'

That quieted them. Frieda was in Boadicea mode. She might regret how many dead and wounded she had at the end of the day, but she would still use them up, however much it might pain her.

'Constable Gregson, I presume Sergeant Summers is going to grace us with his presence at some time in the near future?' she asked.

'Yes, ma'am, he should be – '

She was saved by the entrance of Frank, folder clutched in his hand. He went straight up to Frieda.

'Something I want to pass by you before we begin,' he said.

Frieda saw the look in his eyes and nodded. They discussed what he had to say in low murmuring.

'Alright, Frank, sit down, we'll get to that in due course,' she said at the end.

'Now, ladies and gentlemen, some of you know what the

situation is, but for the benefit of all of us I am going to start at the beginning and take it through to where we now are. You all know how easy it is to miss or overlook something, so don't try to be a clever Richard – something you wish to say, Sergeant Phillips? I thought not. So, as I say, don't presume you know everything.'

She took the room through everything, right from the original broadcast of Humphries' theory, to the discovery and investigation of the killing of Wayne Kegglon.

Frank was impressed. He always was when Frieda spoke to a group. He would have thrown in the occasional joke. Quite a few occasional jokes. Frieda merely paused at crucial points to ask if anyone had a question. And she knew when someone did. They could either ask it or wait until she forced them into asking it. Whenever that happened she would rap out words to the accompaniment of a slow drum roll using a marker pen: "The- only- stupid- question- is- the- one- that- is- not- asked. Understood?"

After an hour she had finished outlining what they knew to date.

'Now, we have to nip this one in the bud – if it isn't already too late to use that phrase,' she said in conclusion. 'All the resources we can spare are going into this investigation. We will work in two teams. I will lead one, and Inspector Hanson the other. Inspector Hanson's team will work this weekend and nights next week. My team will take the days next week, and, if we haven't achieved a result by the end of next week the two teams change shifts.'

Frank was impressed. Percy Hanson obviously wanted a piece of the action. Either he was desperate or Frieda had been very convincing. In political terms he would be invisible during the first week, and come the second week the Chief Constable would be demanding to know why there had been no results, and Percy was the one who would have to give the answer, being the one visible.

'Now,' said Frieda, 'Sergeant Summers has come up with a theory which I think could do with further attention. Frank? The floor is yours.'

Frank coughed at the back, and made his way tentatively to the front.

'It's the pussy man,' someone joked, and laughter spread around the room.

'I hope you enjoyed that,' said Frank, standing by the whiteboard. 'I hope you'll still be laughing when I've run your derrieres into the ground. As I intend to do, if we're to solve this case without any further murders. I've had enough of this eighty-five percent nonsense.'

There were a few smiles. Nervous ones. They all knew Frank as an easy-going person. This image of him as a man on a mission boded ill. Especially as the lieutenant of Boadicea.

'I think he's quite sexy,' whispered a WPC in front of Gertie to her colleague. 'Rescuing a little girl's kitten from a tree? The rest of this bunch would have called the fire brigade, and left the poor little child in tears.'

Gertie only just managed to resist the urge to accidentally dump the remainder of her tea over the unsuspecting woman's head.

'Now, we know the clippings came from the Herald,' said Frank, 'and we know the article, but there's something I want to show you.'

He clipped the offending page to the whiteboard.

'Wellbury's ten top dislikes,' he quoted. 'Number one: nosy neighbours. That's Nagness. Number two: traffic wardens. Chiffon Brady. Number three: estate agents. Wayne Kegglon.'

He paused for effect.

'I think you'll be glad to know that the police only made number ten. So we have a little time in hand before one of us gets it.'

The room was silent. If Frank was right they were no longer chasing an ephemera. They actually knew the identity of the next victim.

Or his or her description.

And their being on the list made it personal.

'Number four is White Van Man,' Frank continued. 'I won't bore you with my own thoughts about the matter – I used to think it was a largely media-invented concept until one of the buggers almost killed me while doing an illegal left turn against a traffic signal. But however it was invented it is no longer relevant, because we have a little problem. At least one. Firstly, is the surmise correct? Is our killer following a list? It would certainly fit the psychological profile of someone obsessed, perhaps religiously so. All faith systems have lists. Secondly, at the moment we're running this investigation on the theory that we're looking for a single person, but even that might be wrong. Now we can't issue a statement warning all people who fit the White Van Man stereotype to be on their guard, at this stage we just don't have the proof, and we might precipitate attacks on people regarded as the stereotype by someone not involved in the killings. Zack the Prat would love winding things up.'

He noticed that Gertie had her hand up.

'Yes, Gertie?'

'If we did announce that we thought the killer was following a list – well, is it possible the murderer would change the order anyway? Do someone from number six, rather than number four? Come back to number four afterwards, as it were.'

Frank considered the idea.

'It's a possibility,' he admitted. 'My gut feeling is that we're looking for someone who has lost touch with reality, so I think they'll follow the list order. But that's the point. I don't want anyone presuming that my gut feeling is unquestionable. It's a possibility. We have to consider other possibilities at the same time.'

'Well put, Frank,' Frieda said, taking control again. 'Right, you all know as much of the situation as anyone else. Inspector Hanson is now in charge, he will direct things over the weekend. Percy?'

Percy Hanson stood up and moved to the front.

'You all know the score, we've all been here before,' he said to an audience who had never in their lives seen the rival inspectors co-operating and wondered what score he was talking about. 'If we throw everything into this murder investigation the media will complain that we're neglecting other duties. If we don't throw everything into it they'll complain that we aren't pursuing the case properly. Add to that the fact that the victims so far won't have many flowers at the funerals, and it pretty much doesn't matter how we balance things, we're going to have something smelly thrown at us. So we're walking a tightrope. Let me make a couple of things quite clear, though. One, we're going to catch this person. The sooner the better. Secondly, Inspector Garold is in overall command. We will have clear lines of communication. We're going to need them. Does anyone have any questions?'

They might have had questions, but no-one voiced them. Percy Hanson, old-style inspector, abdicating to the heir-apparent, Frieda Garold.

'Any questions, Inspector?' Percy asked Frieda.

She shook her head.

'Gertie, you get off and enjoy your weekend,' she said. 'We'll have a debrief first thing on Monday, and take it from there. Frank, I'd like to see you in my office for half an hour.'

The officers in the room stood automatically as she left the room, followed by Frank who had an urge to hold his tie out as if he were being pulled along on a lead, and Gertie, whose face was lowering with suspicion. She left them and made her way to the office she shared with Frank. She had a feeling that Frieda was up to something.

Inside her office Frieda closed the door behind herself and Frank and smiled at him guiltily.

'Percy's thorough,' she said. 'I think we can leave him with it and go interview a suspect ourselves.'

'A suspect?'

'Pete Rorder. You never know. He might have something interesting to tell us.'

'He might well indeed,' said Frank, smiling.

'I think we might slip out the back unseen, though, inquiries are a little confidential at the moment. It's only a short walk away.'

'Very confidential,' agreed Frank.

They slipped out the back, unseen.

Almost unseen.

Gertie was very good at trailing people.

'A perfect evening,' Frank said as he drove himself and Susan back towards her cottage, forgetting firstly to touch wood, and secondly that, when life is being is perfect, it's best not to interrupt it by pointing out the fact.

It had started off with a glass of wine in the Hangman. Then on to a film, a tragic romance which had most of the women, Frank noticed, surreptitiously holding handkerchiefs, Susan included. Not strictly his usual cup of tea, but it had been well made and convincing, and with his arm around a tearful Susan he was prepared to put up with a lot. Afterwards dinner at an Italian restaurant, where the owner – a large, grand-mother type figure – had taken one look at them and put them into a quiet alcove ideal for young lovers. The food had been superb, the service as good, the music perfect. Frank could never remember such an enjoyable evening.

Even better than yesterday with Gertie and the day before with Frieda? one of his voices had enquired sarcastically at one point. He shut it out. That was different.

After the meal, back to the Hangman for a final glass of wine, and now, here they were, wafting along a quiet road on their way to Susan's country cottage, a full moon lighting the countryside, Susan humming happily to herself along to one of Beethoven's piano concertos. No doubt when they reached her cottage he would be invited in for a coffee, and what gentleman could refuse?

'It was a good evening, wasn't it?' Susan agreed. 'Best time

I've had in years.'

'All in all, not a bad day, overall,' he carried on while a voice at the back of his head tried to get him to shut up. 'Even started off well this morning. Earned myself some serious brownie points with Frieda this morning. I think I might be in danger of being considered competent for once in my life.'

'Really? And how did you do that?' she asked in a tone that should have alerted him to the fact that Susan did not wish to hear Frieda's name mentioned, not even thought about.

'Well, it was when I was driving in to the station this morning with Gertie,' Frank continued like a blind man waltzing through a minefield. 'Zack the Prat said something on the radio that stuck in my mind. It took me a little while to work out what it was, but I got there in the end. It was all about lists.'

'Oh, Frank, this isn't about this eighty-five percent case, is it?'

'Well, yes, but it's quite interesting, you see – '

'Darling, please, no shop talk tonight.'

'But it is rather an interesting – '

'No! No, Frank, no! Not tonight. Okay?'

'Well, okay, then,' he mumbled. Sometimes Susan made him think of a schizophrenic cat – or tiger, perhaps. One moment she would be purring away happily, the next the claws were out and he was tiger food.

They continued in silence for a while.

'Hey!' he said, remembering that morning. 'There's this shop called Rorders in town. They've have a brilliant collection of motorbikes. I popped in there for an hour this morning.'

Mentioning the fact that Frieda had accompanied him wasn't

necessary. It would probably only upset Susan, and he had no intention of doing that.

Too late.

'Motorbikes?' she asked disapprovingly. 'I hope you aren't thinking of getting a motorbike.'

He blinked. She had said it in much the same manner as his mother had once talked to him as a ten year old.

'Why not? There's nothing like the feel of – '

'You are not getting a motorbike, Frank. If you do I will never speak to you again.'

He paused. She was being entirely irrational. Plus he didn't like the way she thought she could boss him about. Sometimes a man has to put his foot down.

At the same time a man should watch exactly where he was putting it.

'Susan,' he said as they drove up to her little cottage, 'I hardly think you're being fair. And if I want to get myself a motorbike – '

'Fine,' she snapped, throwing her door open as he brought the car to a stop. 'Get yourself a death machine if you want. But you can forget about ever seeing me again if you do.'

She slammed the door shut and almost ran to the door, fumbled for her keys, got the front door open, and then slammed that one too, closing out Frank and the rest of the world.

Frank sat watching this with a face that spoke one word: "What?"

As in: "What was that all about?"

As in: "What the hell happened there, then?"

As in: "What, no coffee?"

In her cottage Susan flung her handbag down on the couch, sat down in an armchair and held her face in her hands, crying miserably. It had been the perfect evening. Until Frank mentioned Frieda. And then followed it up by reminding her that Gertie was staying at his flat. But she should never have let that upset her. She really shouldn't. After all, once she had got him, he would still see them on a regular basis. She couldn't spend her life erupting into jealous fury every time he mentioned their names.

But it was the talk of a motorbike that had caused her to lose her temper.

What she should have done was tell him the truth. When she was twenty her boyfriend of the time had telephoned to say that he was going to ask her a very special question the next time they went out. She had known what the special question would have been, and her answer would have been yes.

Only the boyfriend never got to ask the question. He was killed on his motorbike the very next day. She had loathed the things with a passion ever since.

But she didn't want to ruin a wonderful evening by mentioning ex-boyfriends, especially not one she was likely to have married.

Stupid! Frank would have understood her feelings had he known. He would have been sympathetic. Instead she had tried ordering him around, telling him what he could and couldn't do. She had put him in an impossible position. She would never have respected him had he meekly agreed, nor could she have allowed him to get away with not meekly agreeing..

So instead she had lost her temper.

What an idiot. What an absolute, total, bloody stupid idiot.

Tomorrow was Sunday. Sunday was a free-for-all. Frank's choice, if it could be said that he had one. The rota continued on Monday depending on who got him Sunday. She would phone him first thing, apologise profusely, and ask to be let into his good books again. It was an infuriating thought, but, she had to admit to herself, were she being honest, she had mucked up and deserved it.

She would suggest a walk in the countryside, followed by lunch at a pub. Or something different, if he preferred. The one thing she was not going to do was blow it again.

In his car Frank shook his head in bewilderment and drove off slowly. He had been planning to suggest they went for a walk in the country the next day. A nice relaxing stroll through summer fields, along the river Wellbury, pausing for a smallish lunch in a pub along the way, followed by another slow saunter, and then having tea around about four in the afternoon: scones, jam, cream, the works.

Well, sod that, he thought. He still wanted a walk in the countryside. He would ask Gertie if she fancied the idea. At least he wouldn't have to worry about upsetting her because he was thinking of getting a motorbike. She might lose it occasionally when they were at work, but outside of work she never did.

Outside of work she was a lovely girl.

And it would be purely platonic, he re-assured himself, to the accompaniment of several voices laughing uproariously at the back of his mind.

Sunday: White van man

Frank stood in his kitchen, whistling softly, whisking eggs for scrambled-egg-on-toast. The onions were diced, ready for braising, as were the mushrooms, a dash of garlic and a hint of parsley. Fresh tomatoes awaited consumption, from a greengrocers which obtained its produce from a local, council-owned, allotment, the commercial sale of which produce was probably totally illegal, but much more tasty than that from any supermarket he had found. A little bacon from a local farm, because, whether it went with scrambled eggs or not, he liked his bacon. The music, from the CD A Summer of Love, played softly. Normally an early riser, he had slept late after a turbulently sleepless night, but Gertie was an even later riser. Once she was up he would suggest going for a walk; they would have breakfast, and then languidly begin an exploration of the finest countryside Wellbury could offer, far from the madding crowd.

'Goodbye, Ruby Tuesday, still gonna miss you,' he sang to himself. Somewhere out there Percy's lot were probably battling in the streets. Well, today was his day away from the trenches and he intended to enjoy it to the full. He had no desire to find out the score from Saturday night and Sunday morning.

Gertie appeared in the doorway, rubbing her tousled hair. She was wearing some diaphanous night-wear garment. When she had first moved in she had worn a tatty old dressing gown over a long t-shirt. He presumed that she had moved to the night-dress because she now felt at home. She had two brothers and a sister; no doubt appearing in minimal night-garments first thing in the morning was something she was used to. He, as an only child, wasn't – not on a platonic basis, anyway – but he was prepared to live and let live.

'There's a message on your voice-machine,' Gertie said, yawning, covering her mouth with one hand while stretching with the other, pulling the night-dress up rather more than his eyes could cope with.

'Sorry, Gertie, I should have pulled the plug on it. I didn't want to disturb you.'

'You can disturb me whenever you want,' she said, giving him an enigmatic smile from one eye, the other covered by her hair. 'I need some coffee,' she continued, turning to the cupboard holding the bottle of instant. He hastily turned back to concentrate on the task of breakfast, chopping parsley with more enthusiasm than attention.

'Who was it?' he asked.

'Don't know. I was fast asleep at the time, didn't hear a thing.'

'Probably a double glazing salesman, or someone offering time-share, I expect. I get at least one recorded message a week for some holiday in America or somewhere. Ironic, really, their machine talking to my machine.'

She smiled as she leant against the sink work-surface, sipping her coffee, watching him adding a touch of salt and pepper to the bowl of eggs.

'Doing anything today?' he asked casually.

'I haven't anything planned. Were you thinking of something?'

'Oh, I don't know. I rather fancy a walk in the countryside, lunch at some pub on the way, a slow stroll back, and then tea at Ethel's in the Old Village. How does that grab you?'

'Very nicely,' she said, putting her mug down and walking

over to hug him from behind. By standing on tiptoe she managed to stretch high enough to give him a kiss on the back of the neck. 'I'd better have a shower to wake up.'

She skipped back to the lounge to get her showering accoutrements. Frank stood in a state of bemused shock.

The last person who had kissed him on the neck like that had been Jean.

Gertie skipped back past him on her way to the shower.

The last person who had done that, night-dress flapping, had been Jean.

He shook his mind to clear it of the association, and went through to the lounge to listen to the message. Apart from it being something that had to be done, he enjoyed the pleasure of pressing the delete button after having heard the latest inane offer of cheap time-share holidays in California from someone with an unbelievable American accent. He sat on the edge of the couch and pressed Play on the machine.

'Frank? This is Susan. Listen, I'm sorry I lost my temper last night, I really am. There's a reason for it, though, and I hope you'll give me a chance to explain. I really want to make it up to you. Can we go for a walk today? Along the river path into the countryside? There's a pub there that does great lunches. My treat. Please, Frank? Give me a call when you wake up. Even if the answer's no. I'll understand.'

That ended the message.

Right, not exactly time-share, then.

That wasn't bloody fair, he thought. Her voice had been pleading. That was definitely unfair, taking advantage of his better nature.

She deserved a lesson. A cooling off period. Time in the cooler department. A lesson in what happened when a woman tried to tell Frank Summers what to do.

But yesterday he had been looking forward to exactly that walk with Susan on this bright summer's day.

And, if he treated her too coldly, maybe she would turn to someone else. After all, she had sounded rather cut-up.

But maybe that was part of her plan. He knew well that women could be very, very devious.

And he had already asked Gertie. She had been extremely enthusiastic. Probably saw it as a rare but very welcome escape from the solitude of her studies.

He couldn't face the thought of Gertie's face if he had to tell her that the walk had been cancelled so that he could do exactly the same with Susan.

With Susan, who seemed to lose her temper with him on about the same number of times they went out together.

'So?' asked Gertie's voice as she came into the lounge carrying her night-dress, dressed only in a towel, 'What was it? Double glazing?'

'Time-share,' he replied, leaning forward and pressing the delete button.

There would be a way to resolve this.

He would think of one during breakfast.

So long as Susan didn't call in the meantime.

He crouched down and pulled out the telephone lead.

'Time you were getting dressed, Miss Gregson,' he said gaily, and meaning it. 'Can't have you prancing around almost in the altogether in front of one of your colleagues. It might give me ideas.'

'What if I were in the altogether? Would that give you even more ideas?' she asked coquettishly, pretending to begin unwrapping the towel.

'Get dressed, Gertie,' he said, edging past her, 'I don't think you realise the effect you have on a poor weak-willed bloke like me. I'll get brekkie started.'

She pouted at his back as he closed the door behind him. She took the towel off and flung it on the couch.

There were one or two incidents in her past she preferred to forget; they involved nights out with the girls when the alcohol had flowed a little too freely. She would see a bloke she thought was Mr Right, and flaunt herself a little. Unfortunately that had invariably ended with her trying to remove Mr Right's hands from all parts of her anatomy, in one case having to break an arm to bring home the point that "Stop it" meant just that.

Now she had met Mr Right, and had done all but throw him to the floor and ravish him to point out her interest. That night-dress had cost a small fortune.

Life could be a bloody sod at times.

She began dressing with a mixture of frustration and hope. After all, he had asked her out, hadn't he? That meant something, didn't it?

Maybe she was pushing too hard.

Maybe she wasn't pushing hard enough.

Frank was strangely quiet during breakfast, as if he had something on his mind. Gertie decided that the best course to follow was to look after her own best interests, and enjoy a good breakfast. Frank knew a lot more about creating a good meal than she did. It was something she would have to correct. At a later stage. Maybe.

They had just finished the washing up when the doorbell rang. Gertie had tidied up the lounge and was about to sit down on the couch and go through a large book of local walks, fully illustrated with many pictures of open countryside, river paths, canal walks, forested glades, old cobbled streets, almost any preferred perambulatory scenery possible. Frank had hunted out his pocket camera and placed it in his jacket before joining Gertie. He stood up and went to answer the door.

Frieda stood there.

'Good morning, Frank,' she said, swinging her car keys in her hand, 'how do you fancy a drive in the countryside this morning?'

Frank looked at her, trying not to show his dismay on his face.

This was all he needed. He had more or less made up his mind that he would have a pleasant Sunday with Gertie, and worry about Susan later – possibly tell her that he hadn't noticed the message on his answering machine until afterwards. Having resolved that one by effectively bypassing it, he was now faced with something he couldn't avoid.

'Come in,' he said, standing aside, the thought passing through his mind that, if he moved quickly enough, he could close the door from the outside and be gone within seconds, leaving Gertie and Frieda to sort themselves out while he found a dark, anonymous pub to spend the day hiding in.

'I tried to telephone you,' Frieda said, stepping inside as

Frank's vision of escape to freedom faded out, 'but I think your phone's disconnected.'

'Ah, the plug's probably fallen out of the socket. It does that every so often.'

'Really, Frank?' she asked with a smile, plainly disbelieving him, 'you must get it fixed, you never know when I might need you, urgently.'

The ambiguity of that flew over Frank's head. His mind crouched down to make sure that it did.

'Ah, Gertie,' Frieda said as they entered the lounge, 'studying hard on such a beautiful summer's morning? You should take time off now and again, you know.' She noticed the coffee-table style book Gertie had been looking at. 'Walks of Wellbury. I see, possibly you were intending to. Well, unfortunately Frank and I are going for a drive into the country – you're quite welcome to come if you want.'

'Now just a second,' Frank began.

Frieda held up a hand.

'Just for an hour or two, Frank. It's business, I'm afraid. They've found our White Van Man.'

It took Frank a few seconds to realise what Frieda was saying, dragging his mind from a relaxing Sunday back to the realities of work.

'Dead, I presume?'

'I'm afraid so.'

'With a note attached?'

'Apparently so.'

'I suppose we'd better be going then,' he said slowly.

'No great rush, Frank, Percy's been looking after things. He gave me a call in case we wanted to have a look at the scene and get an update today rather than waiting until tomorrow. I think it's best we spend an hour or so today seeing things properly rather than half an hour tomorrow getting everything garbled in translation. What do you think?'

'I can't see we have any choice,' Frank replied.

It wasn't the first time he had welcomed the intrusion of work to solve a social difficulty. But the previous times had been made-up excuses.

And the previous times there had been only one woman involved.

'Coming, Gertie?'

'Bloody sure I am,' Gertie replied. 'Sometimes you have to protect your own interests.'

'Oh, I'm sure we can trust Percy on this one,' Frank said, going to get his jacket, missing the look Gertie was giving Frieda.

'I'm sure we can, Frank,' Frieda replied, speaking to Gertie. 'This is strictly business.'

The thought crossed Frank's mind that Gertie had sworn in Frieda's presence, and had received neither bollocking nor an invitation to contribute to the swear box.

Well, fair enough, he thought, they weren't strictly on duty.

'What do we know so far?' Frank asked as Frieda drove them in her Range Rover.

'Not much. A farmer was out early doing his rounds when he noticed a body lying on one of his farm roads. He called the station, the duty officer called in Percy, and he's been there since the early hours. He very kindly waited until a more civilised hour on a Sunday morning to give me a call.'

'So how do we know he's our White Van Man?'

'I think Percy's guessing. As soon as they found the note on the body he jumped to that conclusion. You might be able to hold an idea while considering the possibility that it could be wrong, I'm afraid Percy is rather more dogmatic.'

'Somehow I have this feeling he might be right,' Frank mused as they turned off the tarmacked road. A police constable undid a tape stretched across open farm gates and waved them through. They drove along a track bordered with growing maize stalks.

'That wasn't the main entrance, I take it?' Frank asked.

'No, apparently there are a number of entrances.'

'And consequently a number of exits.'

'Precisely. Add to that footpaths and stiles, and Percy's got quite a bit of work on his hands. Ah, there they are.'

A small group of cars sat parked at the edge of a clearing. Various figures walked around or lounged about. Frank spotted Susan leaning against the bonnet of her MG, arms folded, wearing ankle-length hiking boots, jeans and a polo-shirt. It was the first time he had arrived at a crime scene to find her not wearing the regulation white overalls.

Pete Phillips was chatting to her. Frank felt an unusual emotion stir.

Jealousy.

He stomped on it very hard, and it scuttled away in terror.

Percy spotted them and came ambling over as Frieda parked behind the group of vehicles.

'Morning,' he said as they got out. 'Sorry to have disturbed your Sunday socials. Good day for a walk, I would imagine,' he said, looking up at a blue sky dotted with occasional, unthreatening wispy clouds to give it a little added interest. 'Probably be too warm for fishing, mind.'

Percy had taken up fishing some years before when he discovered that it was the Chief-Inspector's hobby. For a couple of months the Chief Inspector had spent his fishing hours nervously trying to avoid the then over-enthusiastic Inspector Hanson. Then Percy had discovered that he rather enjoyed sitting quietly looking at a placid river with absolutely no thought in his mind. For the next two months both men had spent their fishing hours both nervously trying to avoid each other. Finally an unspoken agreement had been reached. If they encountered each other they would politely nod, and sit a good distance apart, if not hidden from view, watching a placid river flow slowly past, their only concern that they might actually catch something.

'Not your fault our murderer is uncivilised enough not to take weekends off, Percy,' Frieda reassured him. 'Anything definite you can tell us so far?'

'Quite a lot, actually,' Percy said, smiling and rubbing his hands. 'We might not have the brilliance of our young Frank here, but there's a lot to be said for good old fact-finding, door-to-door stuff.'

The sight was a shock to Frank. It was the first time he had ever seen the morose Inspector smile, or at least smile genuinely. Normally he and Pete Phillips slouched around like two bloodhounds with bad hangovers.

And he would have preferred Percy not to jocularly tease him like that. Once people got the mistaken notion that you had some of the answers, which was a bad enough mistake, they soon thought you had them all.

'The victim's name is one Damien Hellman,' Percy continued, 'and he does – or did – drive a white van as an occupation. Not the most savoury of characters. Two charges of drunken driving, one upheld, one dismissed. One charge of negligent driving, though apparently, if we had a more thorough and objective method of measuring such things, he could have been done at least a dozen times a week. Five cases in which he was suspected of fencing stolen goods, only two of which came to court, the first he got off scot free, the second on a technicality. And, according to one of the constables, there were a number of incidents where we were called to his house to resolve domestic situations, though whether he was the aggressor or victim seems uncertain. His live-in girlfriend sounds as bad as he is – or was.'

'How was he killed?'

'Ah, now that is interesting. Maybe Doctor Wood can explain that better than I can. Doctor Wood?'

A smallish, elderly man wearing a forensic white overall, a pipe in his mouth looked up absent-mindedly. Frank knew him only as Susan's boss, Doctor Henry Wood, a vague, elusive character he had not previously met. Doctor Wood took the pipe from his mouth and ambled over to them.

'Inspector Garold was asking how the murder was committed, Doctor Wood,' Percy prompted.

Henry Wood looked around the group.

'You must be Frank Summers,' he said, peering at Frank from underneath bushy eyebrows. 'And you must be Gertie,' he noted. 'I've heard a lot about you.'

He paused, smiled, scratched his head, and looked at the pipe in his hands as if wondering how it had got there.

'From what I have seen,' he said, frowning, 'my interpretation is that the victim was somehow inveigled into standing in front of a vehicle which subsequently drove over him. It then reversed and repeated the process backwards. All in all, I would say the driver carried this out five times. What you might call over-kill. He was probably dead, or at least fatally injured, by the third time. My guess is that it was done more to obliterate footprints.'

'Footprints?' asked Frieda.

'We recovered a note from his jacket pocket – 85% minus 4. Susan tells me that it's almost identical to the previous two. However, an initial inspection suggests that the note was only in the pocket during one, at most two, of the times he was run over.'

'Suggesting that the person responsible got out of the car, or whatever it was, after the third time, walked over to the body, placed the note in the jacket, and then gave him two more shots to muddy the evidence?' asked Frank.

'Precisely,' Henry Wood said, smiling at him. 'However they didn't quite manage to do the job properly. There are some interesting footprints which are almost undoubtedly from a lady's shoe. Quite recent, too.' He scratched his head again, as if suddenly remembering something. 'However, speaking of ladies, I've told Susan that I'll handle this case for the moment. You young people really should be out enjoying yourself, not working on a glorious day like today. Go for a walk in the woods, stroll along the river, take the day off.'

'I'll bear that in mind, Doctor,' Frank said, thinking that the next person who suggested the idea of a country stroll might end up being thumped.

'We've got the vehicle used, a Ford Transit,' Percy said, interrupting Henry Wood's paternal moment. 'At least we're pretty sure it's the one. It's this Hellman character's own van. Once we got the registration from his girlfriend we put out a bulletin. One of the patrol cars spotted it parked in the Old Town. According to them there's some damage on the front, plus what looks like dried blood.'

'Any ideas on time, Doctor Wood?' asked Frieda.

Henry Wood shrugged.

'I wouldn't be prepared to speculate on anything less than between six o'clock yesterday evening and four o'clock this morning. I think Susan would opt for sometime between eight and midnight, but I tend to be a little more cautious in my guesses.'

He looked from Frieda to Percy and back again.

'Anything more, or can I get on with things?' he asked mildly.

'No, thanks, Doctor, you've been a great help,' Frieda said.

Henry Woods acknowledged this with a gentle nod of his head and ambled away.

'I don't suppose we're going to be lucky in the choice of this clearing, are we, Percy?' Frieda asked. 'To my eyes it looks like the sort of spot unlikely to be known to very many people, but I have this feeling you're going to disabuse me of such a fortunate notion.'

'I'm afraid so. Firstly it's on a public right of way, you can see the path coming in there, and leaving on the other side, very popular with schools doing a day out, and of course with ramblers, dog-walkers, you name it – so I think Doctor Woods is being a little optimistic about the footprints. Secondly, a few years ago, before you came to Wellbury, there was a very widely reported case of suicide here, so most people would be well aware of this spot. A young couple, boy and girl of about fifteen and sixteen. The boy borrowed his parent's car without telling them. The young couple came here, attached a pipe from the exhaust into the car, started the engine, and fell asleep in each other's arms in the back. Never woke up again.'

He paused.

'It was my case. They looked like two angels asleep when I got here,' he said sadly. 'Poor things. Everything to live for. I wished – I wished I could have had the chance to speak to them before they did it. Told them to bugger off and live in sin and poverty somewhere rather than do what they did. Anything. Anything rather than that.'

'Come on, Percy,' Frieda said softly. 'You can show us where and how things happened last night.'

'I'm going to wander up that footpath,' Frank said. 'If we're lucky someone might have been passing around the time Mr Hellman was getting a taste of his own driving.'

'The others have already checked the path out,' Percy said. 'But have a look if you want, lad, they might have missed something.'

Frank didn't expect to find anything, but he rather hoped he might pass Susan, bid her good morning, and find out whether he was still in the dog house. To his disappointment she seemed to have disappeared, and it was Pete Phillips who joined him on the well-cared for path, wide enough to accommodate three people walking abreast. Gertie had wandered off with the others, intrigued to see the scene where two young lovers had committed suicide. She was pragmatic, ambitious, and had a romantic streak running through her as tall as Nelson's column.

'Anyone ever tell you what a right shit you are?' asked Pete in an offhanded way. Frank's eyebrows rose.

'Quite a few women,' he admitted. 'Anything specific you have in mind, or are you just trying to wind me up out of a general sense of bloody-mindedness?'

Pete laughed.

'Oh, I wouldn't do that to you, Sergeant Summers, everyone knows how dangerous you can be. If you must know, I was thinking about Doctor Pleadle.'

'Doctor Pleadle?'

'Look, Frank, let's be honest about it. She's crazy about you, everyone can see that. But you treat her like – like a toy to be played with. She wasn't in a good mood to start off this morning, but as soon as you turned up she became as miserable as sin. That isn't fair.'

'Sounds like you fancy her yourself.'

Pete kicked at a clump of grass.

'If I was single I would,' he said.

'Marriage a bit rocky, is it?'

Pete looked at him.

'I suppose there's been gossip about that. People gloating, no doubt. I know not everyone likes me.'

'I haven't heard any gossip, Pete, not my sort of thing. But it doesn't take a fortune teller to work out you aren't happy at home. If you were you'd be moaning about having to be out here when you could be with the missus. Oh, and you have very large bags under your eyes, and you look like you haven't slept for a week.'

Pete considered this.

'I look a bit of a mess, don't I?' he asked rhetorically. 'I suppose you heard about last night on the radio – the demonstration against eighty-five percenters?'

'Nope, Pete, today's my day off, today I ignore the world. Or at least that was the plan.'

'You're a lucky bastard. Wish I could go home and forget about it all.' He sighed. 'But you're right about the wife. Bloody woman. She knew I'd have to work funny hours as a copper. Said she'd marry me when I got my stripes. I worked bloody hard to get them, and when I finally did we got married. Now she complains the whole time about how I'm never home. Bloody whinge, whinge, whinge. Enough to drive a man crazy.'

'Nothing here,' Frank said, looking at the path. He turned around and Pete followed. Frank just wanted to get back to the others and escape Pete's moaning.

'You're lucky,' Pete said. 'Doctor Pleadle wouldn't be like that. I don't know why you don't just take her and get married instead of mucking around.'

The thought was most unwelcome to Frank. He tended to live for the day. He had never considered what life might be like settled down and married. Or rather he had always avoided the concept. It sounded too much like a death knell.

And since most of his encounters with Susan tended to end with either a phone being slammed down or a door being slammed shut on him, it did not augur well for a long term relationship.

'I wouldn't bet on that, Pete,' he said. 'You know why the grass is always greener on the other side?'

'No, why?'

'Because there's more shit there, that's why.'

Pete chuckled.

'I like that one,' he said.

'If I were you, Pete, I'd take a couple of weeks holiday. Take the missus away somewhere. Tell her it's a second honeymoon. Promise her you'll take a holiday at least once a year, give her something to look forward to. You work too hard as it is.'

'Easy for you to say.' He glanced at Frank. 'You reckon that'll do the trick, though?'

'Worth a try. You aren't likely to lose your job just for taking a holiday; you don't want to lose your marriage.'

Pete smiled

'Sod it, you're right,' he said. 'Soon as this case is sorted I'll take two weeks off, I'm owed a lot more than that. Percy will just have to cope without me.'

'Why wait until then?' Frank asked as they came back to the clearing. Frieda and Gertie appeared to have disappeared.

'I wouldn't want to miss the chance of working with the Wellbury Wonder, now would I?'

Frank smiled. He had never heard Frieda called that before, but he had to admit it was apt.

'I must admit I quite like working with the Wellbury Wonder myself, Pete. Frieda really is quite something, isn't she?'

Pete looked at him and shook his head in disbelief.

Frank went in search of Frieda and Gertie. He noticed they were the other side of her Range Rover, chatting to Susan in quite an animated way.

'No motorbikes!' Susan was saying emphatically as he came around the bonnet.

'I agree,' Gertie said, 'no motorbikes, or none of us will end up with anything.'

'Now look, you two, I – '

'What's this about motorbikes?' Frank asked cheerfully. They turned guiltily, as if surprised to see him.

'Frieda thought she saw some motorbike tracks,' said Susan in an angry tone. 'But she was wrong, weren't you Frieda?'

'I suppose so,' sighed Frieda.

'Just as well, really,' said Frank. 'I hate it when you're strolling along a quiet country path and some idiot comes along over-revving his engine and turning the path to mud. They should have separate tracks for themselves where they could go to town and not bother anyone else. That would be fun.'

'Yes, I'd like that,' Frieda said, getting a filthy look from Susan.

'Are we finished here?' asked Gertie, checking her watch. Frieda looked at hers.

'Half-twelve already. I don't think there's anything else we can do here, apart from get under Percy's feet. I tell you what, why don't we all go for lunch? If we're lucky we might be able to find a table at the Grove.'

'The Grove?' asked Frank.

'It's a pub-cum-restaurant on University Hill. They do the

best Sunday lunch I've had anywhere, and you get a lovely view of the Old Town – on a good day you can just see the Old Village too. Tell you what, Susan, you've got your car here?' Susan nodded. 'I'll take Frank and you and Gertie can follow. Come on, Frank, I'm famished.'

Frank got into the Range Rover. Susan and Gertie gave Frieda looks which didn't suggest she was their favourite person just at that moment. They walked off to Susan's MG.

'I'm beginning to wonder if this rota is such a good idea,' Susan said grimly as she revved the car's engine loudly, causing Percy and the others to look up in surprise.

'I think the rota is a good idea,' Gertie said as they followed Frieda's Range Rover up the farm road. 'Like Frieda said, it saves us spending our energy fighting over him. And he'll have to choose one of us in the end. And like Frieda also said, we don't want to be fighting each other only to find some other dolly bird has slipped in and stolen him from underneath our noses.'

'True,' said Susan, 'at least this way, should any dolly bird and Frank get ideas, she'll be facing the three of us.'

'I hope we catch this eighty-five percent bastard soon,' Gertie said. 'I had a date with Frank today. We were supposed to be having a quiet walk in the woods.' She looked at Susan. 'I was surprised to see he'd come back last night. I thought you'd have him all bagged up for today.'

'Let's just say we had a small disagreement about motorbikes,' Susan said grimly. 'If he thinks he's going to get one he is very, very mistaken. And if Frieda doesn't play ball, I'm taking myself out of the rota.'

'I agree,' said Gertie forcefully. 'The very first call I got as a beat bobby, the very first, was to a traffic accident. A truck had hit a motorcyclist. I still have nightmares about it. I'd rather lose Frank to you or Frieda than have him risking his life like that.'

Susan drove in silent agreement for a while. She was wondering how on earth she had let herself be conned into this nonsense of sharing Frank on a rota system. She liked Frieda and Gertie, and she hated being on bad terms with them. Frieda's proposal had seemed so reasonable at the time. Susan knew of Frank's determination not to get involved with a work colleague, so the idea had formed that a rota was simply a way to have two Frank-minders, baby-sitters keeping an eye on him while she wasn't there.

Now she was not so sure.

'Don't you think we should continue the rota on a Sunday?' she asked. 'I'm not sure I go for this idea that Frank should have one day where he gets to choose.'

'I think it makes it a little more exciting,' Gertie replied. 'Plus it means we don't end up having him the same day of the week.'

'Ah, but that's only true if one of us does get him on a Sunday. Fine, the rota shifts according to whoever gets him, and then the one after that gets him on the Monday. But what about today? We seem to be sharing him.'

'He's in Frieda's Range Rover, so I say this is her day. That means tomorrow he's mine.'

'Much as I'd like to agree, Gertie, I doubt we could really make that argument stick.'

Gertie sighed.

'That means it's Frieda's day tomorrow,' she said.

'Cow,' said Susan.

'Cow,' agreed Gertie.

'Maybe we could do something to nobble her,' suggested Susan.

'I agree,' said Gertie. 'They slipped off to a motorbike shop yesterday morning. That's cheating. We owe her one.'

'I don't understand,' Frank said in the Range Rover, 'I thought you really liked the idea of having a motorbike.'

'Oh, I love the idea, Frank,' Frieda replied, her mouth twitching uncomfortably, 'but let's face it, they take over your life, don't they? Look at today, for example, a lovely day for a stroll in the countryside. If we had motorbikes, what would we be doing? Oiling them, checking the engines, is the chain taut enough, that sort of thing. Taking half an hour to get dressed, then spending the day roaring around on the roads. Yes, it would be fun, but you find you have no time for other things, like going to a concert, the theatre, taking in a movie. You wouldn't have the money, anyway.'

'I suppose you're right,' sighed Frank. 'A motorbike engine might sound like music, but it can't take the place of the real thing. Pity.'

'The National Orchestra are putting on a presentation at the University this week,' Frieda said. 'I've been given a couple of tickets. Fancy going along tomorrow evening? It's a selection of American music, from Civil War to the Twentieth century. Jazz, the big bands, swing, that sort of thing.'

'Oh, wow!' said Frank enthusiastically. 'That sounds like heaven. Count me in.'

Frieda smiled.

'It's a date, then. We'll just have to pray our eighty-five percent friend takes the evening off.'

'I'm beginning to get a little pi – brassed off with whoever it is,' Frank said. 'Gertie and I were planning to go for a walk today.'

'I was surprised to find you at home,' Frieda said without thinking, 'I thought you'd be at Susan's place.'

'Susan's place? Why should I be there?'

'Oh, er, something I overheard, partly overheard,' Frieda said, thinking rapidly. 'I got the impression that you'd be, um, helping her with something. Just goes to show you shouldn't jump to conclusions when you don't know the full story.'

'No, can't imagine what it could have been,' Frank said, thinking that, in a way, he was lucky he didn't get an invitation to coffee the previous evening. Had it progressed further he might have ended up opening the front door to Susan's cottage this morning only to find Frieda standing there.

And for some reason he rather thought he wouldn't like that to have happened.

Though he wasn't sure why.

'I'm surprised Gertie agreed to a walk,' Frieda said. 'I thought she'd have her head buried in her books.'

'That's one of the reasons I suggested it,' said Frank. 'She spends all her spare time studying. Every time I get back, there she is on the couch with a book on her lap. She gets a little absent-minded from time to time.'

'In what way?'

'Oh, er, forgets where she's left stuff, that sort of thing,' Frank replied, deciding that mentioning Gertie's occasional lapses in doing her blouse up was something probably not spread around.

'I know you mean well, Frank,' Frieda said as they turned into the car park of the Grove, 'but you mustn't get in the way of Gertie's studies. We don't want her to work so hard and fail, do we?'

'Of course not,' said Frank as Susan's MG pulled into the parking space next to them. 'But an occasional day off can't hurt.'

Frieda led them around the side of the Grove to a pub garden. Beyond the garden the land dropped down to the houses in the Old Town.

'This is gorgeous,' Frank said, taking in the view.

'It is, isn't it?' said Susan, standing next to him. 'I haven't been here for ages. I used to love coming up here for Sunday lunch. Silly, really, you get involved with work too much, and one day you look back and realise that you haven't done any of your favourite things for years.'

'Wellbury's full of little secrets like this,' Frieda said, sitting down at a table. 'Though for some strange reason most people prefer to sit indoors on a lovely sunny Sunday while they have Sunday lunch. I've never been able to fathom it out.'

Susan and Gertie were still standing taking in the view, Frank noticed.

Tricky.

If he sat next to Frieda, Susan would be upset.

If he didn't sit next to Frieda, she might not be too happy. And if Gertie sat next to him both Susan and Frieda might take it askance.

'I'll get the first round in,' he said, taking the dishonourable but wisest course of running away and leaving them to sort it out. 'Who's having what?'

'Sit down, Frank,' Frieda said, patting the bench she was sitting on. 'They have waitresses here.'

Well, thought Frank sitting down next to Frieda, orders are orders, I can hardly refuse my boss. Gertie and Susan sat opposite, disapproving looks on their faces.

'Waitresses, eh?' said Frank. 'Unusual for a pub.'

'It's only when they do meals,' Frieda said. 'Ah, here we go.'

'Hello, Inspector, nice to see you again,' said an attractive-looking young girl walking up to their table, notepad in hand. She was wearing a white blouse, black skirt, and a small white apron.

'Hello, Melanie,' Frieda said. 'It seemed just the day to drop in and over-feed ourselves. Let me introduce the others; Detective Sergeant Frank Summers, Doctor Susan Pleadle and Detective Constable Gertie Gregson.'

'Hello all,' Melanie said. 'What can I get everyone?'

'A drink first, I think,' Frieda said. 'I'll have my usual glass of wine.'

'One large glass of Dry Riesling, South African or Australian preferred,' noted Melanie. 'Doctor Pleadle?'

'I think I'll have the same.'

'Two glasses. Constable Gregson?'

'Dry Riesling sounds good. Why don't we have a bottle?'

'One bottle of Dry Riesling,' agreed Melanie. 'Sergeant Summers?'

'Please, call me Frank,' Frank said, giving her the most charming smile he could. 'I think I'll be a complete philistine and go for a pint of ale, if you have something decent.'

'I'm sure we have, Frank,' Melanie said, smiling back at him. 'I'll be back with it in two ticks.'

They watched her walk back to the pub, hips swinging.

'Those heels look a bit high to be walking around on grass with,' Frank noted.

'Frank, could you for once not let your imagination carry you away when you see a pretty pair of legs,' Frieda said.

'Did I say anything about her legs?' asked Frank, giving her a surprised and innocent look. He turned to the others for support. 'Did I?'

'You were thinking it,' Susan accused.

'Precisely,' said Gertie.

He looked around the table. He almost always managed to upset one of them at some stage or other. But that was normally compensated by being in one of their good books. Now he seemed to have done the triple without even trying.

'Let's not be too hard on poor Frank,' Frieda said, squeezing his shoulder. 'It's his day, after all.'

'My day?'

'Er, I thought you said you thought this was going to be your day,' Frieda said, unconvincingly. 'I must have been thinking of someone else.'

Now where have I heard that recently? Frank wondered to himself. He had a suspicion the smell of something fishy wasn't only coming from the pub kitchen.

'Why is it that men have only one thing on their mind most of the time when you aren't interested, and start talking about football or work when you are?' asked Gertie morosely.

'You have to remember that men are just little boys, Gertie,' Frieda said. 'They might look from the outside as if they've grown up, but inside they're still eleven years old, wanting to splash in puddles and kick tin cans along the street.'

'That's okay, you lot carry on, pretend I'm not here,' said Frank.

They laughed and Frieda ruffled his hair.

'Sorry Frank, sometimes it's just too easy to tease you. We can't resist it.'

'Nice to find a man with a sense of humour,' Susan noted. 'Most of them are like Pete Phillips. I think the only thing he would find funny is someone slipping on a banana skin.'

'Pete isn't all bad,' Frank said, surprised to find himself defending the man. 'He's having marital problems. I think he's made the mistake of letting the job take over his life. I told him to take two weeks off and go away on holiday with his wife. He said he would, as soon as this case is solved.'

'That was thoughtful of you, Frank,' Frieda said. 'I'll have a word with Percy, make sure that Pete does take time off.'

'Frank's always a thoughtful man,' Gertie said, looking at him, 'apart from the times when he's been an uncaring little shit.'

'Swear box,' said Frank. 'That will be fifty pence in the kitty, please.'

'It doesn't count when we're not on duty,' Frieda said mildly, 'and we definitely aren't on duty now.'

'What's this about a swear box?' asked Susan.

Frank grinned.

'Frieda's set up a swear box in the ops room at the station. Fifty pence fine for any swearword.'

'I think that's an excellent idea,' Susan said to Frieda, who blushed slightly. 'I might do that at the lab.'

'I wouldn't have thought you would have a problem at the lab.'

Susan laughed.

'No, not really. It would probably end up being just myself and Tracey contributing. I must admit to the occasional "bugger", and Tracey's quite fond of the word "tosser".'

'Tracey uses language like that?' asked Frank. 'I'm surprised, she seems like quite a sweet young girl.'

'No shop talk,' Frieda said as Melanie returned with their drinks and menus. 'Melanie, I will have the five course special, as usual.'

'Five course special?' asked Frank. 'What's that?'

'Whatever Mrs Goodall – the landlord's wife and kitchen maestro – has decided. It's the least expensive option, because everything's prepared in advance, and she hates her concentration being interrupted by piffling details such as whether someone likes their steak slightly underdone or slightly overdone. I've yet to have a five course special I didn't like.'

'Sounds a bit like Agnetha – "I know what you like".'

'That isn't too far off the mark, if you think of Agnetha as a roly-poly type.'

They decided they would all have the five course special. Nobody argued with Agnetha. Nobody could argue with a roly-poly version of Agnetha.

Frank found himself in an unusual position as the food came. Frieda, Susan and Gertie chatted happily amongst themselves, a sight he would never have believed had he not been there himself. He felt a bit like a little boy at the table, to be patted on the head occasionally, or have his mouth wiped, while the others got on with the serious business of the day. Still, he couldn't complain about the food: soup, an entree of breaded mushrooms on toast with garlic-mushroom sauce, followed by fillet steak with roast potatoes and vegetables, a dessert of sticky toffee pudding with ice cream, and finally a tray of cheese and biscuits, with a pot of strong coffee.

'Mmmm,' said Gertie, leaning on the table watching Frank cut a thick slice of Edam, 'I'm full. That was gorgeous.'

'It certainly was,' said Susan. She looked at her watch. 'Did you know, we've been here for over two hours.'

'That's the only problem with coming to the Grove,' Frieda said. 'You eat way too much and forget about the time.'

'I could do with a nice, lazy stroll,' Susan said. 'There's a path that goes from here, around the hill and back. You can even find a little chapel with a plaque commemorating the night it was bombed during World War Two. What they don't mention is that even then the chapel was falling down, and that the bomb that hit it came from a damaged American plane trying to jettison its load.'

'I don't know if I can stand up, never mind go for a walk,' Gertie sighed. 'Not even to see a bombed-out chapel.'

'A walk sounds like an excellent idea,' Frank said, standing up. 'But first I must pay my compliments to the washroom.'

'You keep your hands off Melanie,' called Gertie after him as he strode towards the pub doors.

Frieda watched him go with a look of concern on her face.

'What's the problem?' asked Susan. 'You look worried.'

'It's probably nothing. Just something that's been nagging me at the back of my mind the whole day. This eighty-five percent business.'

'Leave it behind, Frieda,' Susan advised. 'Percy's looking after it. Relax, enjoy the day.'

'It's not that. It's this list.'

'What about it?'

'The last on the list is the police. I just can't get that out of my mind. What worries me is who might be chosen. I can't help but feel that the obvious target will be someone involved in the case. And Frank is the one who everyone sees. And there's no guarantee this maniac is going to go by the same order as the list.'

'Surely not!' Susan exclaimed. 'Why would anyone want to kill Frank?'

'Apart from us, you mean?' asked Frieda with a thin smile. 'It might not make sense to us, what worries me is that it might make sense to someone not quite sane.'

'That's what Mrs Ziggurat said,' Gertie exclaimed, suddenly remembering.

'Mrs who?' asked Frieda and Susan in unity.

'Clementine Ziggurat. She's a psychic. She came to the station after Nagness was killed. She said that her voices had told her to tell Frank "There will be ten. The list has been made and cannot be unmade". Her precise words. And she was right. There is a list of ten.'

'Pure coincidence,' said Frieda, trying not to scoff.

'And then, when Frank had left the room she told me her voices had a warning for Frank.'

'Go on,' Susan encouraged her.

'"Beware the demon angels three

Beware the twin cycles of the devil machine

Beware the two eyes of green

Beware the fate that sets you free,"' Gertie intoned, 'Those were her exact words. I kept remembering them for the rest of that day.'

There were a few seconds of silence.

'I hope the demon angels don't refer to whom I think they might,' Susan said grimly.

'It's all nonsense,' Frieda pointed out. 'Just fairground nonsense, the sort you can make anything out of if you want.'

'I've just realised!' Gertie exclaimed.

'What?' demanded Susan.

'"The twin cycles of the devil machine" – she meant a motorbike!'

'Really, Gertie,' said Frieda, 'you're letting your imagination run away with you.' She paused under the grim looks of the other two. 'However,' she added, 'there is an obvious real risk as far as motorbikes are concerned, so, yes, we'll keep him away from those.' She turned to Gertie. 'And I want you to keep an eye on Frank. And watch out yourself.'

'I could pretend my flat isn't ready when they're finished with it,' Gertie offered with a guilty look in her eyes. 'At least until we get the eighty-five percent killer.'

'No, Gertie, I'm sure that won't be necessary. We can take turns at his flat when that happens. I'm sure we can find excuses to stay over.'

They were interrupted by the return of a cheerful Frank, unaware that he had obtained a bodyguard, nor that he might need one. He had taken the opportunity on his return, as they sat with their heads close together, of taking a photograph of the three of them. He was pretty sure it was the first photograph of the three in which they weren't ready to sink their claws into each other.

That evening Frank and Gertie sat on the couch in his flat watching television. Or, to be more accurate, Frank was trying to keep his eyes open, while Gertie was trying to read a textbook which she found herself continually having to go back a page or two, finding that she could not remember what she had just read. After lunch the lazy stroll around University Hill had taken a good three hours. The obvious thing to do in such a situation was to recover by having tea at Ethel's, which they had done. In Frank's case, two cups of tea, three scones with cream and jam, one chocolate éclair, and a custard tart, just to taste.

Finally Gertie put her book down, picked up a cushion, dropped it in Frank's lap and curled up on the couch with her head on the cushion.

'Just five minutes,' she said, 'don't let me fall asleep, now.'

Frank put his elbow on the arm of the couch, leaned his head against his hand, and stroked Gertie's hair gently.

'Mmmm, that's nice,' she said sleepily.

It is, rather, thought Frank as his eyes slowly closed. He dozed off, his hand on Gertie's shoulder.

Outside, in a dark shop doorway opposite Frank's flat

someone watched the lounge window behind which lay Frank and his sleeping bodyguard.

Week Two: The Whirlwind

Monday: A lawyer

'We've checked all telephone records,' Percy told a crowded ops room. 'The estate agents, Wayne Kegglon's mobile and his landline. We've also gone over the calls made to Damien Hellman's mobile – his landline was disconnected a year ago because of non-payment. One thing stands out: both victims received a call from a public call box a short time before we believe they were killed. One call was made from the railway station, the other from the Old Town.'

He paused.

'For the benefit of the younger officers, those who sometimes appear to have been born with a mobile phone stitched into their ears, a public call box is a phrase used to refer to an old-fashioned telephone for use by the general public after suitable coinage has been inserted into a slot provided. It means that we have no means of identifying the caller, unless we can trace anyone who can remember seeing who was in the said call boxes at the time.'

'What about fingerprints?' asked Frank. 'Is it worth checking for those?'

'We had a look at them yesterday afternoon.' Percy replied. 'The one in the Old Town was clean as a whistle. The one in the railway station – you might not believe this, but it gets cleaned every day. Not that I suppose it matters much, I can't see anyone having the nous to use a public call box to avoid being traced and then being stupid enough to leave fingerprints lying around.'

'What about the coins themselves?' asked Frank. 'The ones in the machines.'

Percy frowned in irritation.

'Da – dash!' he said. 'I should have thought about that. Make a note, Pete.'

'Probably a waste of time,' Frank said. 'But you never know, we might get lucky. What about our main suspects?'

'Ah, yes, our main suspects,' Percy said with a grimace. 'I'm sure you will all be happy to know that not one of them has an alibi for Saturday night. Robert Bagley swears blind he was sitting quietly at home reading his bible. The vicar, ditto, preparing for Sunday service, apart from a call-out to a seriously ill parishioner; that checks out but still leaves him plenty of time. Mrs Blower ditto, watching television while sorting out clothes for a coming fete and writing the parish newsletter all at the same time, an interesting feat which only Mrs Blower would be capable of. Tom Sampson, also watching television. Phil Walters admits he was out, but claims he was merely driving around on the off-chance of getting some pictures of Saturday night violence for an article he's working on.'

'What about the nutty professor?' asked Gertie. Percy gave her a bitter smile.

'Oh, he's the best of the lot. Says he went for a walk at about eight o'clock, to clear his head after a long thinking session. He can't remember where he went, or what time he got back, but for some reason he found he was carrying an empty hamburger box. His conclusion was that he had either been hungry and had bought a hamburger, or had seen some litter and decided to pick it up, but he can't remember which. Asked us to let him know if we found out.'

Frieda stood up.

'So, there you have it. Whoever it is is remarkably clever or incredibly lucky. Probably a mixture of the two. Today we are going to start pushing that luck of theirs. Re-interview the main suspects. Grill Hellman's girlfriend, the killer obviously knew his or her victim. Yes, Frank, something you wanted to say?'

'This list,' Frank said, 'it's been nagging me. On the theoretical side, what is it about the list that's caused the killer to choose the victims? Is it someone who has lost touch with reality? Or is the list actually a blind, something done deliberately to confuse us? On the practical side, the killer has access to a number of copies of that issue of the Herald. I'd like to have another word with Phil Walthers about who might have more than one copy, apart from himself. I think we should also keep an eye out for things like recycling groups. Possibly visit as many newsagents as possible to see how many recall selling one of our suspects a copy. And I'd like to find out how Phil Walthers came up with that list.'

'Aye,' said Pete Phillips, 'I wouldn't mind having a cosy chat with him about putting us in – and at number ten. If we're going to be in we should have made a better score.'

There was a ripple of smiles.

'Precisely,' said Frank. 'We might not be everyone's favourite visitor, but I wouldn't have expected us to make the top ten of Wellbury's major dislikes.'

'Okay, Frank, you and Gertie have a word with Phil Walthers this morning. I'll give the rest of you your assignments. Percy, I presume you and your crowd would like to get a bit of rest?'

'Aye,' said Percy, standing up and stretching, 'it was a long weekend. Let's hope we catch this burgher before the next one.'

He smiled grimly at the swear box.

'Shop!' shouted Gertie happily in the Herald's office reception giving the counter bell a good smack.

She was rewarded with silence. No receptionist, no Phil Walthers, just the dying echo of a brass bell.

'Shades of the Mary Celeste,' murmured Frank.

'Mary who?' asked Gertie. 'Not another one of your ex-girlfriends?'

'Not quite, Gertie. The Mary Celeste was a ship, a sailing ship. She was found floating the seas back in 1872, if I remember correctly, without any crew. No damage, tables laid as if for a meal, just the entire crew vanished, and were never seen again.'

'What,' asked Gertie, giggling softly, 'you think maybe Phil Walthers has run off with young Sheila? Maybe they've eloped together? Or been snatched by aliens?'

'Not quite, no, Gertie. For a start we don't even know if this young Sheila exists. Possibly Phil Walthers once had a young assistant called Sheila and has never got around to replacing her, but likes to pretend he normally has someone on reception. However,' he continued, walking around the reception desk, 'it could be argued that it is our duty as police officers to ensure that this property is secure. Phil Walthers might be lost in developing, or possibly suffered a heart attack and is lying helpless in his office.'

'Sounds like having a look around might be a good thing, Sarge,' Gertie agreed, following him.

Frank had just put his hand on the door handle when the front door opened.

'And just what the hell do you think you're doing?' asked a girl's voice. They turned around to find a red-headed young woman who looked about sixteen with a faceful of anger of someone much older.

'And you would be?' asked Frank mildly.

'Yes, I bloody well am. And I'm the one who is going to call the police right now.'

'We are the police,' Frank replied with an easy smile. He showed her his warrant card. 'Detective Sergeant Frank Summers, this is Constable Gregson. Anything interesting in that bag?' he asked, nodding at a white paper bag the girl was holding.

'My breakfast, if it's any of your business.'

'That definitely sounds interesting. What's for breakfast?'

'Are you sure you're a policeman?' the girl asked suspiciously.

'Quite sure,' Gertie said, not overly happy with the chatty way that Frank was approaching things. 'Let's start with your name.'

The girl looked her up and down while appearing to hold her nose. Her nose wrinkled at Gertie's bosom with the word "tart" hanging over it.

'I wasn't aware that we had actually reached the era where the police were running the country,' she said with condescension that washed around the room like a heavy layer of hydrogen looking for an open flame to curl up next to, 'even though I know some of you would prefer things that way.'

'I'll give you running the country, little Miss Muck,' Gertie began.

'Now, now, children,' Frank said, unruffled. 'Let's all be good girls and boys and play nicely.'

The two women looked at each other considering the option when an agitated Phil Walthers came in through the front door.

'Sergeant Summers!' he said excitedly, not even noticing the other two. 'I've just come from your police station, I was looking for you, there's something we need to discuss. Please, come through.'

He swept past them, opened the door and went through. Frank looked at the young woman, raised his eyebrows, smiled, shrugged, and followed Walthers. Gertie did the same, after giving the other woman a final threatening scowl.

The first thing that Frank noticed was that the passageway was clean and clear. All the boxes and other litter had been removed, and the floor polished, or at least cleaned. Phil Walthers' office had also been giving a going-over. The coffee mugs on the sideboard were new, unadorned stoneware from one of Wellbury's Arts and Crafts shops.

'Please, sit down,' Walthers said, sitting behind his desk. His fingers tapped the desk nervously as Frank took a seat. Suddenly Walthers jumped up and rushed to the door.

'Sheila?' he called.

'Yes, Mr Walthers?' came a voice from the front.

'Coffee, please, coffee for three.'

'Yes, Mr Walthers.'

Phil Walthers returned to his desk and drummed his heels on the floor. He looked at Frank with bright, worried eyes.

'I know there was another eighty-five percent murder yesterday, and I know who the victim is,' he said. He held up a hand to stop Frank denying it, a wasted gesture as Frank had not intended to say anything. 'I know you won't admit it, so we won't say anything further on the subject. But, you see, I know who the next victim is going to be.'

He paused to let this sink in. Two faces looked back that should have been surprised, but weren't.

'You don't believe me, I can see. I'll show you something.'

He jumped up and hurried to a filing cabinet, taking out a copy of the Herald. As he was doing so Sheila entered with a tray of coffee things.

'Yes, yes, thank you Sheila, just put them on the sideboard, thank you.'

The girl looked at him in puzzlement, did as she was bidden and turned to go. She looked at Frank. He smiled and winked.

Sheila blushed and left.

Gertie frowned and stayed.

'Last week's Herald,' Walthers announced, handing the newspaper to Frank. 'Have a look at page eleven.'

Frank flicked through the pages slowly.

'Good sale on at this furniture place,' he noted on page five. 'Is their stuff any good? I find furniture always looks good in the photograph but falls to pieces after a month or so.'

'Page eleven, Sergeant, please do concentrate.'

'Page eleven,' Frank announced, reaching the promised page. 'Mayor Awards Most Improved Prize For Wellbury Gardeners. You know, I love the way everyone in Wellbury is so dedicated to their gardens, hanging baskets and that sort of thing. It really does make the place almost idyllic.'

'No, no Sergeant, not that. Lower down. The list of Wellbury's top dislikes.'

'Wellbury has dislikes?' asked Frank in a surprised voice as Gertie smothered a giggle. 'My goodness. Who would have thought it?' He paused. 'Well, well, I see the police force are at number ten. This is definitely something we shall have to investigate. Quite thoroughly. Very thoroughly, in fact. I'm glad you brought it to our attention.'

'Ah, yes, that was unfortunate,' Walthers said in a deeply embarrassed voice. 'Just the way the figures came out. But look at the top four. Look at the top four!'

'Nosey neighbours,' Frank said in a tone of mild interest. 'Understandable, I suppose, though I can't say that's something I've ever thought to be a major problem in Wellbury. Still, you never know. Let's see – traffic wardens? Ah, yes, that will be the national media making a bandwagon to jump on. Number three, estate agents, well I never. Number four, ah, another media creation, the famous White Van Man. Number five – '

'No, stop!' cried Walthers. 'Don't you see? There's a pattern. There's a pattern.'

'What, sort of like plaid?' asked Frank innocently. 'You have another article I should look at? The Women's Institute annual knitting sale?'

'Sergeant Summers,' Phil Walthers said in agony, 'the first four victims, think of it, I beg of you!'

Frank paused in thought.

'I don't think I would have put nosey neighbours at number one,' he said, as if trying to be helpful.

'Sergeant Summers!' Walthers almost shrieked and came flying around the desk. He jabbed at the newspaper.

'Nosey neighbour Nagness, number one! This Chiffon woman, a traffic warden, number two! Kegglon, an estate agent, number three! Hellman, your original White Van Man, number four! Oh, I know all about them, you can say "No comment" as much as you like. But you can't deny that this killer is following my list exactly!'

'Well, well, fancy that,' Frank said, 'what say, Gertie? Think Mr Walthers might have stumbled across an important clue here?'

'Sounds a bit dubious to me, Sarge,' Gertie replied, poker-faced.

Walthers looked from one to the other as if they were mad.

Then suddenly he closed his eyes and shook his head violently.

He walked back to his seat, sat down, opened a drawer, took out a bottle of whiskey and a glass.

'You won't join me, I presume?' he asked. Frank shook his head.

Walthers poured out two fingers, took a sip and grimaced at the taste. He looked at Frank and raised his glass.

'I used to keep a bottle of sherry, for appearances' sake. Horrible stuff. But I salute you, Sergeant Summers – and you, Constable Gregson. In over twenty years of running a newspaper in which I gradually took more and more of what is commonly known as the Mickey out of people, I have never once been bested. Twenty years. Until today.' He gave Frank a sour smile. 'You knew all along, did you not, Sergeant Frank Summers?'

'I could not possibly comment,' Frank replied, a smile twitching about his lips.

'Eric Johns said you were one to watch,' Walthers said. 'The one time I should have listened to him, and I didn't.' He sighed, took another sip of whisky, and smoothed back his hair. 'So, how can I be of assistance, Sergeant Frank Summers?' He looked at Gertie. 'Might as well help yourself to a cup of coffee, dear, it's really quite good, and it's just getting cold.'

'Sarge?' asked Gertie.

'Go ahead, Gertie, I won't have one.'

'Sarge prefers tea,' Gertie informed Walthers as she happily poured herself some coffee.

'Er, right,' Frank said, his thoughts momentarily derailed. 'Now, Mr Walthers, we'd like to know where this list of yours came from.'

'Ah, yes, well, it's what's called a filler in the business,' Walthers began, the embarrassed tone returning to his voice. 'Very popular these days, for some reason, lists. Favourite books, you know the sort of thing. Pure rubbish as far as I'm concerned, but the readers adore them. Anyway, I can't afford to hire a company to do that sort of poll, so whenever I'm interviewing someone – that is to say, whenever I remember – I ask them for their opinions on the best films, worst films, that sort of thing. You'd be surprised at how many letters I get on the subject. I could almost print the entire newspaper consisting of nothing but correspondence. I'm not sure it wouldn't sell better.'

'Not quite a professional questionnaire, then?'

'No. I would say sadly not. Anyway, it accounts for why the

police are in the list. You see, I normally interview people after something newsworthy has happened, which quite often involves a visit from the police.' He smiled. 'Which also accounts, no doubt, for the reason journalists are at number nine. I'm rather surprised we didn't make number one. Nosey neighbours made number one, I rather think, because a lot of curtain twitching goes on when someone's apparently in trouble.'

'Tell me something, Mr Walthers, I notice you seem to have had a clear-out. Somewhat of a tidy up. Any reason for that?'

'I'm afraid that's rather your fault, Sergeant.'

'My fault?'

'After your last visit I had a closer look at those mugs that were on the sideboard. I hadn't realised how filthy they actually were. The result of being a bachelor, and being more interested in the newspaper and people, I'm afraid. I have a housecleaner who comes in twice a week to do my house, so that is looked after. Here, I am afraid a cleaner would only get in the way. Anyway, I called Sheila in and pointed out that a little tidy up might be in order. Apparently she'd been suggesting just such a thing for some months. Before I knew it we had carried out everything short of a complete re-decoration. I'm afraid some of these young girls become motherly to an old bachelor like me. I have no doubt their own mothers would be completely amazed if they knew.'

'So any old copies of the Herald would have been thrown away? Such as copies of this issue?'

'Thrown away? Oh, no Sergeant, older issues, yes, but I always keep five or ten copies of recent issues to give away to prospective advertisers. Not that that happens very often, those who advertise in the Herald are all well established and have been doing so for years.'

'You still have them? The recent issues?'

'Yes, of course, they're in reception.'

'Does anyone, apart from newsagents, receive a number of copies?'

Walthers looked surprised.

'Not that I'm aware of. You'd need to speak to the printing company, they also carry out distribution, but I very much doubt that anyone would want more than one, or two, at most. Possibly the hospital, care homes, perhaps. Why do you ask?'

Frank smiled. Phil Walthers' journalist nose was twitching.

'Let's just say I'm indulging in a little lateral thinking,' he said, standing up.

'I rather suspect your thinking is often more convoluted than lateral, Sergeant,' Walthers said, a disbelieving look on his face, 'if not downright devious at times. However, there is one favour I need to ask. Would it be in order if I printed this? About the list, I mean. If I hurry I could get a special edition out first thing tomorrow morning. It would be such a joy to beat that rather snide and revolting creature on the radio. If it won't hamper your investigation, naturally.'

Frank thought about this.

'The official police comment is no comment,' he said. 'However, unofficially, just between us, I would be more than happy to see it come out. It would be a way of alerting potential victims without panicking all of them over the edge. Number five is a lawyer. We wouldn't want an alarmist article causing a sudden rush of panic-stricken barristers heading for the hills, now would we?'

'I take your point, Sergeant. Naturally the Herald does not need to indulge in such gutter tactics for its sales. But there is another thing,' he continued, one hand reaching for a file while the other took a camera from a drawer, 'a little picture of our brave Sergeant who rescues little girls' kittens before arresting dangerous burglars. I couldn't have dreamed up a better story if I tried.'

Frank held up a finger which had all the appearance of being a large club.

'Don't even think of pointing that thing at me, Mr Walthers,' he said in a firm voice which seemed to include the phrase "or I will thump the merry shit out of you".

Walthers sighed and put the camera down.

'Somehow I thought you might say that,' he said, standing up. 'Could you see yourselves out? I have so much to do if I'm to get a special edition out.'

He rubbed his hands and looked at them with bright eyes.

'I fear I might be getting a little enthusiastic. Not a good thing for an old cynic like me.'

'Bit of a coincidence, isn't it, him cleaning up that place just at this time,' said Gertie as they walked back to the station.

They had paused only long enough in the Herald's reception for Frank to look at the retained copies of the current issue to make sure there were no little snippets cut out. He had then inquired as to whether Sheila had enjoyed breakfast. She had indeed, two Danish pastries from a local cake shop. Gertie mentally wished that the young redhead had choked on them, and then suggested it was time to get back to the station.

'Not necessarily,' he now replied to her question about Walthers' sudden urge for hygiene. 'I've known a few bachelors who get so used to living on their own they no longer see what's around them – until someone pops in for a visit and they suddenly realise that maybe it's time to get the vacuum cleaner out, if they can find it under the rest of the rubbish.'

'But that Sheila had already told him it needed a good clearout.'

'If what he says is true he's probably used to it. Every time he gets a new Sheila they would have suggested something like that.'

'So you don't think Phil Walthers is our man? He doesn't come across as a cold-blooded killer.'

'Oh, I didn't say that. I just said that there wasn't that much of a coincidence about him having a tidy-up. If it is him behind the murders he would hardly use his office to compose the notes. Too much chance of Sheila walking in on him. No, I wouldn't mind a quiet look around his house. While he was somewhere else, of course.'

'You mean organise another report of a burglary, Sarge?' asked Gertie, giggling at the idea.

'Trouble is, we didn't organise the last one, not as it turned out. No, for the moment we'll just have to wait and watch, bide our moment.'

'Still, you'd never let your place get into a mess like that. Your flat's always – well, almost sparkling.'

'Ah, that, my dear Gertie, is because I myself was once one of those bachelors who never noticed the dust level, or the fact that the curtains weren't closing properly, or got used to the coffee table being propped up by a pile of books. When I realised the state everything was in I vowed never to make the same mistake again.'

'What happened? Did you bring a girlfriend home? Did she walk out on you?'

'Worse, Gertie, worse. My mother made a surprise visit.'

He sighed.

'I've never been subjected to so much tutting in my life,' he said sadly.

The time left before lunch they went through all the statements again. Then they had lunch and continued with the statements. Frank ended up feeling like throwing something.

'Nothing!' he said in disgust. 'Our main suspects are either definitely at the scene, or don't have an alibi so they could have been. No-one remembers anybody using the public call boxes at the time stated, or they remember an entire queue, none of whom match any of the suspects, and most of whom the witnesses probably imagined. No evidence, apart from a morgue quickly filling up with bodies. And cells permanently full of previously staid citizens who need some sense knocked into their heads.'

'The forensic report did say that they recovered fibres from Hellman's van, Sarge,' Gertie pointed out.

'Yes, any number of fibres, which could have matched his girlfriend's clothes, which, as we speak, they are going through in order to cross them off the list – unless it was the girlfriend who did him in in the first place, a conclusion, from what I have read of his behaviour, would seem an entirely likely possibility. It would be – ironic – if that turned out to be the case, and Hellman wasn't killed according to the list. Extremely unlikely, however, considering the notes.'

He had been about to say "just our luck", but his luck was normally good, and he disliked the suggestion that it might be otherwise. That sort of thing could put a jinx on it.

'We're going in circles, Sarge,' Gertie pointed out. 'If you start wondering whether this one wasn't our eighty-five percent murder, but the others were ... where do you stop?'

'Precisely, Gertie, precisely. You end up playing the numbers game like a crypto-analyst. What if numbers one, three and four are linked, but not number two?'

'Or even number five,' suggested Frieda in the doorway, coat on, looking grim.

Frank took only a second before jumping up and putting on his jacket. Gertie was a second behind him.

'Who, how, where and when?' asked Frank as they followed a swiftly-moving Frieda out to the rear car-park.

'All I can tell you at the moment is that a note was left with the body,' Frieda said as she got into the Range Rover and started the ignition. 'It sounds just like the others.'

She turned to Gertie in the back.

'One thing, Gertie, something I meant to mention to you the other day. There's no need to over-rev the engine on this car. Or leave tyre tracks on the road. It's a very nice car, and she responds well to gentle treatment, okay?'

She didn't allow Gertie a chance to reply before over-revving the engine and leaving tyre-tracks in the car-park. And her passengers holding on for dear life.

'Cedric Oldfield,' Frank said, reading the gold letters on a window of an office in Old Merrick. 'Solicitor.'

This time the pavement in front of the office had been cordoned off, and two uniformed police officers were there to keep any passing interest moving. Five others were interviewing staff from the adjoining businesses. Inside Oldfield's office Susan and Tracey were busy. Frank, Frieda and Gertie were not allowed in at that moment. But this time Frieda was going to hit it with all they had. Percy had already been alerted to attend a briefing session at four-thirty. Shifts might change, but the investigation would continue, throughout the night if necessary.

'A solicitor,' said Frieda. 'And what was number five on the list? Lawyers. A solicitor would be close enough as to make no difference.'

'I wonder,' murmured Frank.

'You disagree, Sergeant Summers?'

'No, but I do wonder,' Frank answered, rubbing his chin.

'That means you do,' Frieda said, taking his hand from his jaw. 'You always do that when you don't agree with me. Stop it.'

'Not necessarily,' he replied, folding his arms. 'I'm just not sure about something. I don't know what. It'll come to me sooner or later.'

'Make sure it's sooner, Frank,' she said, squeezing his arm. 'We seem to be running out of time on this one.'

He paused at the thought.

'That's it,' he said.

'What's what, Frank?' Frieda asked impatiently.

'I don't know. I wish I knew, but I don't. But there's something there ... '

Frieda turned in a circle, her eyes rolling, her face suggesting that Frank Summers might not last long enough to make it into the tenth position. He was saved by the appearance of Susan coming out of the solicitor's office, carrying two plastic folders.

'We aren't anywhere near finished,' she said, 'but I thought you might like to see these. The first is the note left behind. Tracey's instinct is that it's a match with the others. I agree, but we'll need to do tests to confirm that, of course.'

They looked at the note. "8","5", "%", "-5".

'Then there's this,' Susan said, producing the second folder and handing it to Frank.

He skimmed it and then read aloud.

'To Name,' he read, 'As you know I will be retiring shortly. I have thoroughly enjoyed my time in Wellbury, and, as I am sure you will understand, hope to accumulate sufficient capital to acquire a generous retirement in one of the more salubrious French or Spanish resorts. Naturally I will not reveal any of the many financial and other secrets which have come to my attention during my service to you, providing that you agree to a little final contribution.'

He stopped.

'That's it? Where did you find this?' he asked.

'In the waste-paper basket. It looked sufficiently important to show you as soon as I could.'

'It certainly is, Susan,' Frieda said, taking the folder from

Frank. 'It looks like the draft of a blackmail note.'

'Strange way to begin a blackmail note,' Frank remarked. 'It starts with "To Name", as if it were going to be sent to a number of people.'

'Presumably he had a number of people in mind,' Frieda replied. 'It's very nicely suggestive, without giving any facts. Typical of someone chancing their arm, I would say. It reminds me of the story about the man who sent telegrams to all his friends saying something like "Get out, all is discovered" – according to the story a number of them did, without waiting to find out what it was that had been found out.'

She looked at Susan.

'I presume our Mr Oldfield has filing cabinets containing details of his clients and the work he did for them?'

Susan nodded.

'We should be finished in about half an hour or so. You can take them then.'

'How was he killed?' asked Frank.

'From the looks of it someone stood behind him as he sat at his desk,' Susan replied. 'Whoever it was hit him over the head with a bust of Cicero, several times.'

'Cicero? Several times?'

'That is what I said, Frank.'

'Any idea of the time?' asked Frieda.

'Early this morning, I would say, between five and nine o'clock, as a first guess. I'd better get back.'

Frieda took her radio out of her handbag as Susan returned to Oldfield's office.

'As soon as they're finished in there I want all those files taken to the station,' she said. 'We're going to go through them with a fine tooth comb. The killer obviously knew enough about Cedric Oldfield to know that he was the type to resort to blackmail. And who knows what else he might have got up to, if that were the case. Yet again the victim is hardly a shining light of innocence and purity.'

Frank looked around as Frieda radioed instructions to have a van sent around to pick the filing cabinets up. He noticed Ken Edgars and Steve Right making their way back from interviewing the people in the other offices.

'Afternoon, Sarge,' Ken said with a grin, holding up his notebook, 'I think you'll like this. The newsagent down there was opening up shop this morning. Guess who he saw leaving here at six-thirty?'

'From the smile on your face it was either the tooth fairy or some bloke holding a sign saying "I've just popped in to murder a lawyer",' Frank said. 'Which one?'

'Not quite with a sign,' Ken replied. 'But it was one of our main suspects, Mr Robert Bagley. And there was someone else around.'

'Let me guess, someone wearing an illegally loud waist-coat and bow-tie who goes by the name of Phil Walthers?'

'How did you know?' asked Ken, surprised.

'I'm clairvoyant,' Frank replied, smiling.

'On the other hand,' Frieda said, putting her radio back in her handbag, 'it could be because Phil Walthers told our Sergeant Summers here that he had been tailing Bagley, looking for a story. Even Frank can put two and two together without too much effort.'

'There is also that possibility,' admitted Frank. 'Did the newsagent see what Bagley and Walthers were doing?'

'Sorry, Sarge, he only saw Bagley leaving. He said Walthers looked like he was following Bagley, but by the sounds of it it wasn't far from Detective Clouseau.'

'Nothing else, such as Bagley having blood stains down the front of his jacket or shirt?'

'Sorry, Sarge, the newsagent didn't take much notice. He was sorting out the morning newspapers, noticed Bagley and Walthers, and went on with his work.'

'Frank, you and Gertie get onto Bagley right away,' said Frieda. 'I'll sort out this end.'

'What about Phil Walthers?'

'From the sounds of it you might be able to do them both at more or less the same time. But, just in case, Ken, Steve, you two get off to Walther's office. I want to know exactly where he was every minute of the day. If he's not there, let me know immediately.'

'Come on, Gertie, fast driving time,' Frank said. 'You can play our theme tune. If nothing else it might make Wellbury think we're actually doing something.'

They found Robert Bagley in his office at the Blue Bliss. It was a room sealed off from all natural light, chrome and light wood looking as if it had once been smart but was slowly losing its sheen. Bagley was sitting at his desk going through a number of computer printouts when they were shown in.

'You two again,' he noted, looking over delicate half-moon spectacles which clashed with his burly forearms showing out from half rolled-up shirtsleeves.

'Apologies for the intrusion, Mr Bagley,' Frank said politely, 'but there are some questions we need to ask you.'

'Ask away,' Bagley said, taking off the spectacles. 'I could do with a break. I've been here since first thing this morning, trying to find out where these accounts have been fiddled.'

'Your accounts have been fiddled?' asked Frank, taking a seat.

Bagley grimaced and rubbed his eyes.

'I can't say as to whether they've been fiddled by an expert, or it's just your usual cockup by people who don't understand that everything has to be accounted for. John Mandon – my manager here – is extremely good at managing the place, making people comfortable, getting them to enjoy themselves and spend as much as they can afford, or more, but he's bloody useless at putting the right figures in the right columns.'

'What's first thing in the morning for you?'

'Eh? How d'you mean?'

'You said you'd been here since first thing this morning.'

'Oh, aye, seven-thirty, near as I can remember.'

'You're an early starter, then?'

'No, lad, I'm a late starter. I don't normally get to bed before midnight or one in the morning, and I like to get my sleep. No, I had to be up early, my solicitor wanted to see me. Only when I get there there's no answer. So I decided, since I was already in a bad mood, I might as well come over here, sort out these figures, and give John Mandon the bollocking he so richly deserves. And I will do, as soon as I work out what half these figures mean.'

'Your solicitor called you? What time was that?'

Bagley scowled at him suspiciously. He picked up a pack of cigarettes, offered them to Frank who shook his head, lit one and lit it.

'Gave up for ten years,' he noted. 'Took it up again when the wife left. It's the one weakness of the flesh I have yet to conquer.'

He paused and exhaled smoke.

'Care to tell me why you're asking some very strange questions?' he asked softly.

'I'm afraid not, Mr Bagley. What time did your solicitor call you?'

'He didn't,' Bagley replied slowly, keeping his eyes on Frank. 'There was a note pushed through the letterbox when I got home last night. I thought it odd at the time, but Cedric – my solicitor, Cedric Oldfield – was coming up for retirement, and he seemed to have become something of a little boy again. Almost as if he were sloughing off the image of a proper, upright and restrained solicitor. I presumed the note was in a similar vein.'

'You still have the note?'

'No, I threw it away in a litter-bin when I walked back to my car. I was irritated. To be honest, I wondered if someone wasn't playing a practical joke on me.' He gave Frank an open stare. 'I don't have a sense of humour, Sergeant. I'm quite happy to admit that. I believe that it's a waste of the time the good Lord gave us.'

'But the accounts aren't?'

Bagley smiled a thin smile.

'Give to Rome what belongs to Rome,' he said. 'I don't need

the extra hassle of having the tax people on my back, they're suspicious enough as it is. Don't seem to believe a man can run an honest business without trying to fiddle the accounts, not one like this.'

'You don't employ an accountant?'

'Oh, aye. I make sure all the figures are in all the right boxes, he comes in, signs his name, and then charges me a fortune for it. I can't afford to pay him for sorting out this mess at the same time.'

'What is your relationship with Mr Oldfield?' Frank asked.

'How d'you mean?'

'Do you get on? Is it purely professional?'

Bagley looked at him in amazement.

'Don't tell me you're investigating Cedric Oldfield,' he said in some surprise. 'What's he supposed to have done? Overcharged someone? Fiddled some wills? Not the Cedric I know. He's as straight as they come. Wouldn't hold on to a penny if he thought it didn't belong to him. And I'm a good judge of character.'

Not your wife's, thought Frank. Which could mean that Bagley was one of the many who wasn't very good at what he claimed to be good at.

'What is the main business of your relationship with Mr Oldfield?' he asked.

'Property. I used to own a lot of property. Cedric helped me when I was buying, then he helped me when I decided to sell it all.'

He leaned forward and tapped the desk with a stubby finger.

'It shows you what sort of a man he is, Sergeant. He advised me not to sell. Told me the time wasn't right, suggested waiting a month or two. He made a tidy few bob out of the sales and it made no difference to him, so he was going against his own self-interest. Shows you what an honest bloke he is. He might not share the faith as much as I would like, but he's an example to us all. The good are not all to be found in church, nor are all those to be found in church the good. I don't know what your business is, Sergeant, but I promise you you won't hear me say a bad word about Cedric Oldfield.'

He stubbed his cigarette out, looking at it angrily at it if it were a temptation he should not have succumbed to.

'Now, if you haven't any further questions, I'd like to get this mess sorted out,' he said, putting his spectacles back on in an unmistakable signal of dismissal.

Frank stayed seated.

'Did you enter the office – Mr Oldfield's office – this morning when you got there?' he asked.

'No. It was locked,' Bagley said, resuming his perusal of his accounts.

'You tried the handle?'

'Of course I tried the bloody handle, Sergeant. You don't think I turned up first thing in the morning, rang the bell a few times, shrugged my shoulders and walked away, do you? I gave the door handle a good trying, just in case it was jammed. If the locks weren't so solid I would have rammed it open.'

'Did you see anyone else around at the time?'

Bagley sighed and took his glasses off again.

'Get to the point, Sergeant, you're wasting my time.'

'Did you see anyone else around at the time?'

Bagley sighed again.

'A newsagent opening up, sorting out his newspapers, or whatever they do. And our fearless journalist, Phil Walthers, who desperately needs some lessons in the art of stalking someone. Apart from that, no-one I remember. Can I go now?'

'Go?'

'Well, lad, this is my office, I know that, but I'm quite happy to take this little lot somewhere else while you sit here and carry on asking questions – have a look in my filing cabinets, go through my desk, do what you like. But – stop – wasting – my – bloody – time! Understand?'

Frank regarded him imperturbably.

'Would you say Mr Oldfield is a friend of yours, Mr Bagley?' he asked.

'Out!' said Bagley, standing up, his face going red. 'If you want to carry on this nonsense we can do it down your station, with my lawyer present. Send me an official invite, I'll be there. Otherwise, much as I disapprove of strong language, you, Sergeant, can bugger off and leave me in peace. Understand? Out, now!'

Frank sat in his chair, one leg crossed over the other, looking at Bagley as if he were a rather uninteresting specimen in an academic exercise.

'Let me explain something to you, Sergeant,' Bagley continued, leaning on his desk with his fists, 'I am a Councillor, I have a number of friends, and of enemies, who owe me a favour. If you value your stripes I'd advise you to leave now.'

Frank slowly uncrossed his legs and stood up.

'Very well, Mr Bagley,' he said.

He turned as if to go, paused, and turned back.

'Out!' said Bagley, pointing a threatening finger towards the door.

'Just one thing, Mr Bagley,' Frank said calmly. 'You'll hear the news soon enough, so I might as well let you know now. Cedric Oldfield was murdered early this morning. Around about the time you were knocking on his door.'

Bagley froze, his finger still pointing. His eyes slowly grew wide in disbelief.

He sat down slowly, looking at the desk in front of him.

'Not Cedric,' he murmured. 'Not Cedric, he wasn't supposed to die.'

'Care to explain that statement, Mr Bagley?' Frank asked. 'If Cedric wasn't supposed to die, who was?'

Bagley shook his head.

'Not Cedric,' he repeated.

'Answer the question, Mr Bagley,' Frank said, leaning over the desk. 'Who should have died? Who had you decided should die? Who was the unworthy person who had no right to live? Who murdered Cedric Oldfield by mistake?'

'You don't understand,' whispered Bagley.

'Oh, I understand perfectly,' Frank replied, grinding the words out. 'You and another obsessed maniac decided it was your duty to bring the Second Coming forward by a few days, didn't you? Only this time your partner got it wrong, didn't he? He murdered the wrong man.'

He paused.

'What's the name of your fellow murderer, Bagley?' he asked softly. 'The game is up. There isn't going to be a Second Coming. You and your friend in crime are just that – criminals. You see, your biggest crime, in your book, is that you sent people to hell without allowing them time to repent and atone for their sins. Think about that, Robert Bagley, had you not intervened they might have seen the error of their ways. It was up to God to decide their fate, not you. Now, the name of your fellow murderer.'

Bagley smiled bitterly and looked up at Frank. He took a cigarette and lit it.

'You really don't understand, do you Sergeant?' he asked rhetorically. 'I haven't killed anyone. I don't have a partner, as you put it, who has killed anyone. The whole idea, Sergeant, is that these killings – these purifications – are the natural result of a decadent society, a society which has turned its face from God. Purely natural. The righteous need not lift a finger against sinners, the sinners will do it themselves.'

He stubbed the cigarette out violently, and immediately lit another.

'I can't believe it,' he said, shaking his head, 'To kill Cedric – what purpose is there in that? What logic? What reason? Cedric had no firm beliefs, but he was one of the good. It doesn't make sense.'

Frank stood upright, realising that the moment for pressurising Robert Bagley had passed.

'Good luck with your accounts,' he said as he turned to go.

'Fuck the accounts,' Bagley said, looking blankly at his desk.

'Blimey, Sarge, what was that all about?' asked Gertie as they walked from the entrance doors of the Bliss to their car.

'I will tell you, Gertie,' he replied grimly, 'when I understand it myself.'

They got into the car and he snapped his seatbelt home.

'Bagley, if we are to believe him, has been revelling in these killings, seeing them as a sign that the end of the world is nigh. Never mind that the plagues, World Wars One and Two killed one or two more, and despite that the world has yet to come to an end, we'll ignore that particular flaw in his thinking. But up pops Cedric, and down goes Cedric, a man who to Robert Bagley – again, if we are to believe him – was a gentle, thoroughly warm-hearted old duffer. Except that we know that he was apparently engaged in a little bout of blackmail. It would be truly ironic if Bagley, who believes we are all sinners, got Cedric Oldfield totally wrong.'

'Property,' said Gertie. 'They were both involved in buying and selling property. One of the main ways of money laundering. You don't suppose that Kegglon was also involved – they had some sort of scam going on? He was an estate agent. Perhaps Kegglon fell afoul of them and had to be dealt with, but Cedric Oldfield wasn't supposed to cop it?'

'An interesting thought, Gertie. That presumes a direct interest in the victims. The problem is, where does Chiffon Brady fit in? Nagness, yes, maybe that was a spur of the moment thing, a sudden loss of temper. Possibly totally unrelated to the others. But Chiffon Brady doesn't fit the pattern. Nor, I would say, Damien Hellman. If there was some sort of group involved in dubious property sales Hellman might have been on the fringe, but no way would Bagley have trusted him with even the slightest details. Not enough to require his permanent removal.'

He grimaced.

'Back to the station, Gertie. Let's see if they've found anything in Cedric Oldfield's files that might tell us who he was planning to blackmail and why.'

'Nothing, so far,' Frieda said. She, Frank and Gertie were sitting in the nearly-empty canteen having a cup of coffee in the late afternoon after a long and fruitless day. Frieda had suggested it. She was hardly ever seen in the canteen – Frank couldn't remember it ever having happened. He suspected that it had been her method of keeping a distance from the troops when she had first arrived at a station wary of a new, female inspector. Now that she had established her own rules, she wanted to remove some of the distance. Whether it would work or not was another question.

'We've only just started,' she continued, 'but it looks as if someone has gone through the files recently and removed quite a lot. There were half a dozen bin-bags of papers in the back of Oldfield's office. Matching them up with the right files could take weeks.'

'Makes sense, if he was about to retire,' Frank said. 'Cleaning out years of accumulated junk.'

'True. An alternative reading is that either he or someone was getting rid of the evidence.'

'No paper-shredder in the office?'

'There is one. What looks like three pages in the bin. Bobby Stang is busy putting them back together at the moment. I felt a bit sorry for him. He was so bright-eyed and ready to go when he came on shift. Instead of a night spent strolling the streets he's sitting at a table in the ops room trying to match up thin strips of paper.'

'Sounds like it's likely to be a wasted effort. Six bin-bags and only three pages shredded? Oldfield probably shredded them for some purely technical detail. And whatever he had on whoever he was planning to blackmail, I can't see him keeping it in his office. Not unless he was singularly stupid.'

'Has to be done, Frank, you know that. Anyway, it won't quite be a wasted effort. It will improve Bobby's jig-saw solving no end. If he does jig-saws. And we've got a team going through Oldfield's house at the moment.'

She stood up.

'You might as well get off for the day, Gertie. Get some study in. Take Frank's car, I'll drive him back. Frank, my office in half an hour.'

It was going to be a long night, Frank thought as he and Gertie returned to their office. He had been looking forward to the concert, but that was obviously out now. The eighty-five percent case was getting out of control, and there was no way Frieda was going to take her eyes off it for a moment. It would be more than embarrassing if something went wrong while the Inspector in charge was indulging in a concert – especially of American music. Wellburians were a tolerant lot as a rule, but they did have a hang-up about anything to do with America.

Up until now they had been a tolerant lot, anyway.

He sat down at this desk and looked moodily at the top as Gertie slipped her jacket on. She came around to his side of the desk and gave him a kiss on the cheek.

'Enjoy the concert, Frank,' she said, and then left.

He watched her receding back in a great deal of surprise.

Gobsmacked surprise. How had Gertie known that he was supposed to be going to a concert? He had not mentioned the fact, hoping to be able to drop it into the conversation at some point as if entirely trivial, perfectly normal that he should accompany Frieda to a concert, nothing in it, merely a couple of colleagues who happened to have a shared love of music, just as two coppers might have a pint together with no suggestion of any further involvement.

How he was going to say all that in one throw-away line he wasn't sure, but it no longer mattered. The nearest he was going to get to music that evening would be if he went out, sat in a patrol car and switched the siren on.

This was ridiculous, he thought. He had evolved a very strong philosophy of life, one of the enjoyment thereof. You didn't get too involved in a case. You took the ups and downs of life with equanimity. You did not become fixated. Life was a hurly-burly which often made no sense. Try to pin it down and you ended up like people such as Robert Bagley, all your golden rules gone in an instant.

No, Frieda could continue with her obsession and her relentless march towards promotion, but he, Frank, would engineer an escape.

Pick up a video on the way home.

Something Gertie would enjoy.

They could order a pizza take-away.

With garlic bread. He liked garlic bread. Even when the butter dribbled down his chin.

He imagined Gertie wiping it away with a napkin.

What the hell was the problem with Robert Bagley? Why had he seemed so cut-up on the news of Cedric Oldfield's murder? What the hell was Phil Walthers doing in the vicinity at the time? Were he and Bagley playing a double-game? Each giving the other a kind of alibi, while, in reality, they were co-murderers?

He decided to pay the ops room a visit. If he was going to get more involved than he should, he might as well make a good go of it.

The ops room was deserted apart from a forlorn Bobby Stang trying to piece together strips of paper.

'Get yourself a tea, Bobby,' Frank said. 'I'll take over for a few minutes or so.'

'Cheers, Sarge,' Bobby Stang said in relief. 'This is doing my head in. I ain't bin trained for this. Don't see how anyone could.'

'Off you go, Bobby,' Frank said, settling down at the desk.

There has to be a scientific way to approach this, he thought to himself, looking at the lump of shredded paper. A logical way. A way of method.

Slowly he began to pull errant strands out in an entirely unscientific way. In a short while he was lost in the task, oblivious to time.

'Blimey, Sarge, you've almost got a page there!' Bobby Stang's voice cut into his concentration.

Frank took a few seconds to get used to the interruption. Lost within himself, his first reaction was to tell Bobby to go forth and multiply. It would have been unfair to the young constable.

'It's a question of how you look, I think,' he replied instead, mildly. 'Stop thinking of it as a page of words, and look at it as a question of matching patterns – a jig-saw, if you want – and things slip into place.'

'Here, Sarge, I think I might have got you into trouble with Fabulous,' Bobby Stang said, putting down his mug of tea, still entranced with the progress Frank had made.

'Oh? How so?' Frank asked, absent-mindedly, a part of his brain inviting him to consider who "Fabulous" might mean.

'She was asking where you were, the Inspector was.'

Frank consulted his watch. Of course. Frieda equals Fabulous. It had been a long time since anyone had used her original nickname, Frigid.

'Still got a few minutes to bollocking time,' he noted.

'I think maybe you better get up there soonest, Sarge,' Bobby said. 'I think I'd rather top myself than have to face Fabulous when she's angry.'

'Ah, she's not that bad, Bobby, you just have to know how to handle her,' Frank said with nonchalance, standing up. 'I find the best way of doing that is running like hell.'

Bobby Stang watched Frank leave the ops room with some awe and admiration. The sort of awe and admiration one would have for somebody strolling into a cage of tigers which have just had rocks thrown at them.

Frank tripped up the stairs, whistling to himself. He was wondering how long it would take for him to think up a reason for giving up for the evening. His personal best was two minutes and twenty-three seconds, but he doubted if he would better that this time.

Mary, Frieda's secretary, had left for the day. He walked

through her deserted office, knocked at Frieda's door and entered at the order. He stopped suddenly, the door and his mouth open.

'Come in, Frank. Shut the door behind you.'

He shut the door carefully and turned to look at Frieda. She was putting an earring on, looking into the mirror on the back of an opened cupboard door. She was wearing a strapless evening gown, shimmering blue velvet cascading down to a pair of navy-blue high-heeled shoes. Her hair was up, her neck bare apart from a pearl necklace.

'Well, what do you think?' she asked, finishing with the earring, smoothing down the dress, checking her appearance critically in the mirror.

'I think you'd better not go out in public,' Frank said, sitting down. 'You're likely to cause poor innocent men to crash their cars.'

She smiled and blushed slightly.

'It isn't often I get a chance to dress up for a night out,' she said. 'The concert is just the excuse I need.'

'We're still going?' he asked.

'Of course we're going, Frank.' She turned and walked elegantly over to where he was sitting. 'I've decided to adopt your philosophy for a change,' she said, stroking his cheek, 'enjoy life when you get the chance.'

Whee-ha! thought his mind, or the part of him where his mind normally resided, his mind itself having decided to take a temporary holiday.

Or possibly even a permanent one.

She picked up a matching blue velvet shawl and walked back

to the mirror, checking to see it was on properly.

'If I'd known I would have dressed up specially,' he said, standing up to see whether his legs were still working.

'You look fine, Frank, you always dress smartly anyway.'

She came back towards him, dusted the shoulder of his jacket of imaginary specks, checked his tie was straight, and pulled his jacket together. Finally she was satisfied with his appearance.

'You can drive, Frank,' she said, handing her keys over. 'These shoes aren't the best for driving.'

Not having ever worn high heels while driving, nor at any other time, Frank could only presume that she was right.

But he rather regretted not having an evening suit to wear, bowtie, cummerbund and the rest. The way Frieda looked it was called for.

They arrived early enough to relax with a couple of glasses of wine and review the programme, which surprised Frank, pleasantly. Frieda had forbidden talk about the case, a distinction he found interesting – not "shoptalk", but "talk about the case". He presumed that meant salacious gossip was permitted, though he had no intention of going down that route. He suspected that there was quite a bit of that going around with himself as the central protagonist.

He and Frieda received a number of looks, Frieda the most, from men looks of obvious admiration; from women the looks ranged from admiration to envy. He himself was the recipient of looks from men, mainly of the "lucky bastard" variety. Frieda did not seem to notice. Had he been silly enough to imagine it, he would have said that she only had eyes for him. He was well aware that Frieda could look straight ahead and see things behind her back. He knew that from experience.

'Nuisance,' commented Frieda at one point, 'Mary has applied for early retirement. Her husband's not well, and she needs time to look after him.'

'That's a pity,' Frank remarked. 'It'll be hard to find someone as efficient as her. And as pleasant.'

'I know.' She chuckled. 'And someone who can lie to the Chief Constable about where I am with the straightest face I've seen.'

'I can see the job advert now,' Frank said, smiling. 'Wanted, poker-faced liar. Also needs to be good at typing and filing.'

'A dying breed, these days, secretaries. In the modern computer world you're expected to do your own typing, and everything's held on disk. Call me old-fashioned, but I prefer someone human to take calls and meet people, rather than having an electronic voice asking you to press fifteen different buttons and then leave a message, or telling you that you're third in the queue. Our system of police force relies on help from the public. We can't afford to create a distance.'

Frank chuckled.

'I'd love to see the Chief Constable's face if he phoned you and heard this recording assuring him that his call was important to us, and could he please wait while listening to some relaxing music. Edith Piaf for preference.'

'That would make it almost worthwhile,' Frieda said, smiling at the thought. She sighed. 'Ah, well, I suppose I shall have to start interviewing people soon. I have this horrible feeling that the applicants will be one of two kinds: either middle-aged women set in their ways who refuse to change, or youngsters who think it's perfectly acceptable to turn up to an interview with chewing gum in their mouths. I'll probably end up taking on someone young and hoping that I can train them up into something vaguely useful.'

Frank snapped his fingers as a thought occurred to him.

'Tricia!' he exclaimed.

'Tricia?' asked Frieda suspiciously.

'The girl working at the estate agents. She claims to be good at office work, and she's desperate to get out of that place.'

'Good looking, is she?'

Frank considered the point.

'I don't know,' he said, 'I haven't really thought about it. She comes across as a bit of an artful dodger. Did I tell you how she slipped into the station behind Eric Johns without him realising it? I think she'd be well suited to lying to the Chief Constable and anyone else you wanted her to. And I think she's the loyal type. Give her a job and she'll fight your corner like a terrier.'

'Really? She sounds a bit too good to be true.'

'Worth having a word with her, anyway.'

'I'll consider it, Frank. Now enough of young Tricia, it's time to go in and enjoy ourselves.'

When they went in he discovered that they seemed to have some of the best seats in the house. He leaned back in his chair as the music began, preparing to lose himself for an hour or so. To his initial surprise he found that Frieda had taken his hand.

What the hell, he thought, these seats were too close together anyway. Holding hands was a good way of sitting comfortably.

Frank liked comfortable. He found he liked holding Frieda's hand. The music was superb. At the end of each piece they would sit up and clap enthusiastically, and then lean back and intertwine hands again.

To Frank this was one of his heavens. Good music, a beautiful partner who whispered in his ear during the breaks for applause, to whom he also whispered, noting the softness of her neck and the subtle but sultriness of her perfume. He would be happy if it never ended.

But end it did, on a high, with the orchestra playing a spirited rendition of the Battle Hymn of the Republic, the end of which resulted in the entire audience demanding an encore. It felt to Frank like the last night at the Proms. Silly, jingoistic music, but stirring in a very British way, an excess of emotion being blown away, and a return to tea cosies and dead-heading the roses the next day, humming the music of the night before. The orchestra obliged with the one encore, the conductor inviting the audience to sing along, which they did, Frank and Frieda lustily bawling out the words.

And then it was over. The orchestra members cheerfully packing up, while the members of the audience turned to each other in a somewhat embarrassed manner, sheepishly saying things like "That was rather jolly, wasn't it? What say we really go to town and have a mug of Horlicks when we get home?" Frieda and Frank looked at each other. Part of her hair had come loose, and he had this overwhelming urge to brush it back.

'I think we could do with something to eat,' Frieda said, interrupting an embarrassed silence between them. 'There's a

Greek taverna around the corner from here. They keep themselves very low-key, but it's probably the best Greek food you could find outside of Greece. Possibly even inside Greece.'

'I'm famished,' said Frank. 'A meal in a taverna which echoes the great beliefs of earliest democracy, art and philosophy, and, needless to say, which revered the beauty of women, with a woman who could easily beat Helen of Troy, well, what man could resist?'

'That's enough, Frank,' Frieda said, blushing, 'I think the wine might have been too much for you.'

'It's the music,' said Frank, 'I can't resist it. I can't imagine what life would be like without music.' He sighed. 'I keep on thinking of buying myself a small piano to play. Trouble is not even the smallest would fit in my flat. And seeing as how I hardly ever take out my guitar these days, what chance I would spend the time you need to to play a piano properly?'

'Maybe one day, Frank. Come on, let's see if we can get out without being crushed by the crowds.'

He put a hand around Frieda's waist to ensure they did not get separated in the throng leaving. To his surprise she did not object. If anything she leant in towards him.

And then she put a hand over his, keeping it there.

'Though I must admit,' he said, his mind racing through a few gears, all of them wrong, 'I could do with a visit to the little boys' room.'

He attended the little boys' room while Frieda went to the powder room. He took his time, knowing that women needed longer over these things. To his surprise she was waiting for him, across from the door, standing in the exact spot he would have done had he been waiting for someone and expecting trouble, scanning the passing throng with professional eyes.

They went on to the taverna, where Frieda was instantly recognised. The first drink was "on the house". Nothing was too good for the Inspector and her fine young man. The proprietor's nephew was inveigled into playing a lament of love on his violin, just for them.

At some point Frank decided to buy Frieda a rose. It was perhaps cheesy, but it seemed the right thing to do. While Frieda was attending to the powder room he discussed the matter with the proprietor's wife. She understood immediately.

'You no buy,' she said. 'I get you. Buying a rose is bad. Giving is good.'

He didn't quite understand that, but it seemed to make a strange sort of sense, especially the look Frieda gave him when he handed her the rose the proprietress had slipped into his hand.

Frank didn't pause to think of its provenance. Some things a police officer did not want to know.

And then there was the dancing in-between courses. It seemed obligatory to get up with other diners and dance every so often. Frieda's hair had long unwound, and they were thoroughly enjoying themselves in trying to get the steps right, and probably failing miserably. But it didn't matter.

'I don't think I've had this much fun ever,' Frank said as they returned to their table after yet another course and another dance.

'No reason it shouldn't continue,' Frieda said, sitting down, giving him a sultry look that would have his heart going one way and his brain another, had not the latter organ long decamped.

He took her hand gently. Unfortunately it was the one to which was attached the wrist that held her watch.

'Bloody hell,' he said, 'is that the time?'

'Oh, Frank, forget the time. Epicurus would never have bothered with time, would he?'

'Well, no, but old Epi wasn't a police officer. We still have to go to work tomorrow. Or today, to be more accurate.'

She sighed and looked at him.

'I suppose you're right,' she said. 'We'll have to get a taxi home, though, I don't think either of us would pass a breathalyser test.'

Frank called the proprietor over and asked if he could arrange a taxi.

'No, problem, Mr Frank,' replied the proprietor, George, 'my little cousin Francesca drives a taxi. Very good record, five years, only one crash.'

'His cousin's only been driving for five years?' asked Frank in surprise when the proprietor had left to arrange the taxi. 'Must be a lot younger than our George.'

'I think "cousin" means someone vaguely related – as to "little", let's hope he's tall enough to see over the steering wheel.'

It turned out that "little" did not refer to the taxi-driver's size, but rather to age. And Francesca wasn't a "he". She was about twenty-five, with long black hair, wearing skin-tight jeans and a t-shirt which was a size or two too small. Frank's eyes nearly popped out in surprise. Frieda noticed.

They left the taverna with everyone's best wishes ringing in their ears. They got into the back of the taxi and Frieda cuddled up to him.

'I suppose you'll have to be dropped off first,' she said. 'Probably the easiest for Francesca.'

When they arrived outside his flat Frieda held him long enough to give him a kiss of heroic proportions, one that quite unequivocally stated that she was not, at that moment, his boss. At least not in the work sense.

'Right, go on, get inside, let Gertie take care of you,' she said when they surfaced for air. He gave her a quick final kiss, and got out, waving the taxi goodbye, floating in euphoria.

Inside he tiptoed up to his flat, opened the door quietly, and walked softly to the kitchen for a glass of water. He was drinking it when a sleepy-eyed Gertie came in.

'Gertie, I didn't wake you did I?'

'Not really,' she said, 'I was sort of half awake anyway. Just came in to make sure you were okay.'

She came up to him, put her arms around him and lay her head on his chest.

'Mmm,' she sighed. She gave him a hug, a kiss and let him go.

'So long as you're okay,' she said, walking sleepily back to the lounge.

Frank watched her go in puzzlement.

Why shouldn't he be okay?

'Good evening?' asked Francesca in the taxi.

'Very good,' said Frieda, 'almost perfect. Almost.'

She was a little irritated with herself. She had had it all planned out. The concert, a quiet meal, Frank would drive her home – she hadn't quite worked out how to arrange that, but there would be some excuse – she would invite him in for a coffee, perhaps they would have a glass of wine rather than a coffee, and then, who knows?

Instead they had been caught up in a thoroughly enjoyable evening, which she could not regret. Frank had joined in the goodnight kiss with some passion.

She could have told Francesca to take them to her house first, but she couldn't take the chance of Frank deciding not to come in for a cup of coffee. She had no intention of leaving him alone with the young woman, there was enough competition as it was.

Gertie tomorrow, Susan on Wednesday. She wondered what she could do to sabotage those two days.

More important was the question of what she would do on Thursday. Sooner or later one of them would get Frank. Time was running out. It was all or nothing now.

Thursday, Frank Summers, is going to be your lucky day, she thought, smiling to herself. Or unlucky, depending on which way you wanted to look at it. Either way Frank Summers would not have a say in it.

In the sofa bed in Frank's lounge Gertie rolled over, a smile on her face. Today's my day, she thought happily.

In her cottage Susan dreamed of Wednesday. She was going to pull out all the stops on Wednesday. No prisoners. No rules.

A blissfully ignorant Frank Summers slowly fell into slumber, wondering who the next victim would be, and what he could do to protect them.

Tuesday: Bad manners

Gertie was in a good mood as she drove them into work, humming to herself and tapping the steering wheel. Frank was in a more pensive frame of mind.

'Cheer up, Sarge,' Gertie said. 'It's a lovely day, the sun is shining, it's a wonderful morning. Isn't it great to be alive?'

'If you say so, Gertie.'

He had thoroughly enjoyed the previous evening. It was when he woke up and remembered that goodnight kiss that he began to have reservations. He was supposed to be going out with Susan, not enjoying passionate clinches with his boss, or overly affectionate hugs from Gertie in her nightie.

But was he actually going out with Susan, he wondered.

If he was why hadn't she called, if only to say hello? Admittedly he should have called her, but work was hectic, she knew that.

And if he wasn't actually going out with Susan, was there really a problem with going out with Frieda? Admittedly it was entirely against his solemn vow never to have a relationship with someone at the station, but surely there's always one exception?

And, logically, given that there had to be one exception, surely there was an argument that Gertie herself could be a second exception.

Admittedly that sounded perhaps a weak argument, but it was an argument.

Admittedly, he thought to himself, you are like a blind man playing pat-a-cake with piranhas.

He decided to take the one way out that he could see. He

would lose himself in this eighty-five percent case. He wouldn't go out with anyone until it was over. Hopefully by the time he surfaced on the other side things would have sorted themselves out.

'They should have finished going through Cedric Oldfield's files,' he said. 'If we're lucky we'll be able to eliminate some of the suspects. Not all of them could have known Oldfield.'

Gertie made a moue. Frank was getting obsessed with a case again. Whenever he did that he forgot that women existed.

Well there was one woman he wasn't going to forget. She fully intended to see to that.

'Morning, Gertie,' Eric Johns said as they walked into reception, 'morning double-oh-seven.'

'Double-oh-seven?' asked Frank, puzzled. 'You haven't gone and put funny-tablets in your tea by mistake again, have you Eric?'

Eric Johns grinned.

'You know, even in a world gone mad there is something to cheer you up. The cells are full, there were so many call-outs overnight they had to replace the tyres on most of the cars, Wellbury has gone crazy and we're thinking of pulling everyone back to the station to defend it as a last stand. And then there's this.'

He held up an issue of the Herald.

'Phil Walthers has done us proud,' he said. 'Special edition dedicated to Wellbury police force. How we're right on the tail of the eighty-five percent murderer, and while we might say no comment, nothing slips by our steely gaze.'

'Oooh, let's have a look,' Gertie said, taking the paper.

'There's a stack on them in the canteen, courtesy of our Phil,' Eric continued. 'But you might want to read the article on page two, at the top.'

Gertie opened the newspaper. She scanned the article quickly, and then giggled.

'Here, Sarge, listen to this. "Casually, almost James Bond like, elegantly clad in a three piece charcoal suit, Detective Sergeant Frank Summers of Wellbury Police paused nonchalantly in his mission to detain a nefarious burglar just long enough to save a little girl's treasured kitten caught helpless in a tree, before going on to single-handedly deal with the desperado hiding from the long arm of Wellbury's finest". Sounds like you're a hero, Sarge.'

'Sounds like Phil Walters is working too hard. For a start there were three of us, and secondly Vic Brown could hardly be described as a desperado. And we just gave him a ticking off. And it was a two-piece light grey suit. And he didn't mention my tie. Something I'm going to give Phil Walthers, along with a kick up the backside for good measure.'

'I wouldn't do that, Frank,' Eric said. 'Phil is only trying to help, which is extremely rare, and I hear the Chief Constable intends to have this special edition framed in his office.' He leaned forward and whispered. 'I bet you can even say bugger in front of Fabulous and get away with it.'

'No, he won't' came Frieda's angry voice from the internal doorway. 'Ops room now, you two. I'll deal with you later, Sergeant Johns.'

Frank and Gertie followed Frieda's angry back, while Eric Johns behind the reception desk tried to be as small as possible.

Inside the ops room a weary group awaited them, Percy, Pete Phillips, Sid Feeler and Harry Wheatley.

'Inspector Hanson has some news for you,' Frieda said grimly. 'While we were safely tucked up in our beds our friend appears to have struck again. Percy, the floor is yours.'

'Eral Jackson,' Percy said gloomily. 'Twenty three years old, found in the same alley as Chiffon Brady. Same MO as the first ones, hit over the head with a lump of iron or something. Same note, same letters taken from the Herald.'

'Number six was Bad Manners,' Frank noted. Percy nodded.

'Oh, Eral Jackson – I think maybe they meant Earl when they christened him, but got the spelling wrong – qualified for a bad manners award alright. We've done him for drunk and disorderly five times in as many months. He's been thrown out of more pubs than I've had hot dinners. God knows where he gets the money from, seeing as how he's on the dole. Or was on the dole. No doubt the dole office will throw a party. According to Jackson's record he was known to be particularly abusive even when sober, I don't think he would be likely to have responded well to any suggestion that he should get a job. Added to that is the problem that apparently he was as thick as a plank. Can't see anyone wanting to take him on.'

'What time did it happen?' asked Frank.

'Around one o'clock in the morning. We know he'd been drinking at the Stag a few streets away. The landlord insisted that they had closed at eleven thirty as legally required, until I pointed out that this was a murder enquiry, and he could be done for aiding and abetting. He finally admitted that they hadn't closed until much later – claimed they were having a private party, but I can't see anyone inviting Jackson to a private party. He was slung out about half-twelve. Just our luck the restaurant alongside the alley closed at midnight, or they might have seen something.'

'What was he doing in the alley?'

Percy smiled bitterly.

'You're going to love this. He was attending to the call of nature. Normally, by all accounts, he would have done so wherever he felt like it. The one time he chooses not to make a public display of himself, he gets the final call. The young couple who discovered him thought initially that he was a pervert playing with himself, until they realised he wasn't moving. Their story is that they popped into the alley for a kiss and a cuddle. I don't think the sight did anything for their romance, if that was what it was. They called us at just after two. A bit late for a kiss and a cuddle in my books.'

'And our suspects?' asked Frank, not looking anywhere near Frieda, who seemed to be absorbed in her fingernails and not thinking anything about kisses and cuddles in the early morning.

'Oh, we hit their houses within fifteen minutes of finding out that it was an eighty-five percenter. Every single one of them safely tucked up in the land of nod, or so they claim. If it was one of them they would have had enough time to get home and into pyjamas before we came calling. We even quietly checked their car bonnets for heat. Nowt. Cold as the night air.' He yawned and stretched. 'Could do with a bit of shut-eye myself.'

'You get off, Percy,' Frieda said. 'We'll carry on from here.'

Percy and the others left gratefully.

'How are we doing on the Cedric Oldfield front?' asked Frank.

'Oh, just fine,' replied Frieda sarcastically. 'It turns out that our Cedric did work for all our suspects, so we can't eliminate even one.'

'Not even Tom Sampson? What would he want with a solicitor?'

'Oldfield helped him when he bought his house a number of years ago. More recently Tom Sampson decided that he needed to have a proper will drawn up. Frank,' she said, going to her handbag, taking a fifty-pence coin from her purse and dropping it into the swear box, 'this is really beginning to piss me off. I want whoever it is caught and caught soon. I cannot believe there have been six murders and we are no further than we were before. It's bloody ridiculous.'

She added another coin to the swear box.

Frank walked to the whiteboard, to which the photograph of an unsmiling and quite ugly face of Eral Jackson had been added.

'We could get search warrants for all their houses. If they're going to continue to use that issue of the Herald for their notes they must have a supply somewhere. If we're lucky they won't have disposed of the ones they've already used.'

'Percy applied for search warrants this morning. The answer was no. The judge decided we didn't have sufficient evidence. And apparently he wasn't at all pleased at being woken up at three in the morning.'

'That's another point. Whoever it is is now relying on night-time to get away without being seen. I think we should have them tailed over the next few days. They seem to be in a hurry to get to the end of the list. I wouldn't be surprised if they don't have another go tonight.'

'We don't have the resources, Frank, you know that.'

'We could choose two or three of the most likely. Alternatively, we could come at it from the other side. Who's next on the list – door-to-door salesmen, isn't it? See if we can find someone who sells door-to-door, someone known to our suspects, someone with a bad reputation.'

'And put a tail on them, you mean? Frank, I've heard of long shots, but that's not pushing the envelope, more like taking a hockey stick to it.'

'I don't think so. We could pop around to each suspect for some routine, mundane excuse – apologising for waking them up, quite possibly. While we're there we just happen to mention the subject of door-to-door salesmen. See how they react. Whether or not they mention any names.'

'You think the murderer will know their next victim? Frank, all they have to do is wait somewhere until someone comes along with a large suitcase, knocking on doors. A bit of a dead give-away.'

'Two things. Firstly, all the victims have, you could argue, been of the type that few people will miss. It would go against the flow for some harmless charity worker to be found with their head smashed in. Secondly, I can't imagine door-to-door salesmen would work very late, you're hardly going to get a favourable reception much after seven or eight in the evening. It would be one hell of a chance for our maniac to take, attacking someone in a built-up area in the evening when people are about. Whoever it is knows that, they've taken to running around in the early hours of the morning. That means they have to know the victim in advance, or at least know of whoever it might be. They have to be certain the victim won't be missed – the victim has to appear to be in the eighty-five percent.'

Frieda tapped a pen against a table, thinking.

'Very well, Frank, you can try it out. But don't waste too much time on it.' She paused. 'And if – I say if – we can get one or two teams together for tonight, which of our suspects would you put as top billing for a tail?'

Frank rubbed his jaw.

'You don't ask for much, do you?' he asked rhetorically. 'It could be any of them. But, if pushed, I suppose I would go for the vicar, if only to eliminate him from the list. We've got too many unlikely suspects.'

'The vicar? Not my first choice, but there you are. Gertie, who would be top of your list?'

'Robert Bagley,' said Gertie. 'There's definitely something wrong with his eyes.'

'He would have been my first choice as well,' Frieda commented. 'Instead I'll go for Tom Sampson. I know he's an ex-copper, but that doesn't mean he hasn't gone round the bend.'

'You're going for three teams?' asked Frank.

'If possible. I'm going to see how many people I can scrounge from neighbouring divisions. We should have two cars and four people per team, but if we limit it to two in one car we might even manage three teams.'

'A little risky,' suggested Frank. 'A tail of two in the middle of the night and only one car? Even if they did manage to keep the target in sight they'd be lucky if they weren't spotted. More than lucky.'

'I know, Frank, I know. It depends on how many people we can get. Like I say, I'm going to ask the Chief Constable if we can borrow some bodies from elsewhere. I'll do that now. I'm going back to my office, you get on with your interviews.'

'Fancy a tea first, Sarge?' asked Gertie as Frieda left the room.

'Make that a coffee, Gertie. I could do with a strong cup.'

He turned back to the whiteboard while she went off to get two coffees. Mentally he began dividing the pictures into two groups, those who could have been chance victims, and those who the killer must have either known or known of.

Nagness the nosey neighbour could have been either. Perhaps the killer had dropped some litter, and been given a talking to by Agnes, the woman who complained about everything. The killer snaps, hits her over the head, and then comes up with the idea of leaving the note. Possibly a random occurrence which sparked off some brainstorm in the killer's head and resulted in the later attacks.

Chiffon Brady. Quite possibly a chance killing. The murderer waits in the alley, attracts her attention, Brady walks deep into the alley and the deed is done. Had Brady been a living saint in her spare time, the words "traffic warden" would have damned her for the vast majority of drivers. Any tabloid newspaper that suggested traffic wardens might have a human side seriously risked losing sales.

Wayne Kegglon. All the suspects had met him or must have known about him. None had been fooled into thinking that Kegglon was anything but grasping, devious and none too intelligent.

Damien Hellman. He was the one victim that made Frank so sure that the killer was aware of the identity of his or her victims. You couldn't kill someone just because they drove a white van. The chances of a van driver being less adorable than the rest of the human race were just as good as those that he was a loving father with three adopted children who ran a dog sanctuary in his spare time.

Well, maybe not just as good, but enough not to take a chance.

Cedric Oldfield. Again, known to all the suspects. A would-be blackmailer. Yet Bagley thought him one of the upright and good. Unless Bagley had been one of his blackmail victims, and he was throwing off smoke.

There was something wrong with Cedric Oldfield as a victim, he thought. Something gnawed at the idea.

Eral Jackson. If ever there was a chance victim it would be Jackson. All the killer had to do was hide in the alley and wait for some drunken yob to stagger by, it didn't matter which. Anyone wandering around drunk at one o'clock on a Tuesday morning was unlikely to qualify for the best-behaved award of the year.

He turned around at the sound of the door opening. To his surprise it wasn't Gertie, but Susan. She looked surprised to see him.

'Hello, Frank, I was looking for Frieda. Doctor Wood asked me to pop in and drop off his initial findings on this morning's victim. I was told she was in here.'

'Oh, good, let me have a quick look,' he said, holding out his hand.

She came into the room reluctantly and handed the file over.

'Anything interesting?' he asked.

'Nothing, I'm afraid. A re-run of the Brady case, more or less down to the footprints.'

'Maybe we should install a camera in that alley,' Frank mused, flipping through the pages. 'You doing anything tonight? Fancy a movie or something?'

'Er, I'm busy tonight, I'm afraid.'

'Oh, okay, no problem.'

'How about tomorrow night,' she said quickly. 'I was going to play badminton at the club, but I can give it a miss for once. Or you could come along, if you fancy a game. We could go for drinks or a meal afterwards.'

'No, I wouldn't want to get in the way of your friends.'

'It's a social club, Frank, not a close-knit group of friends. Come, on, say yes, it seems like ages since we last went out.'

He looked at her in surprise. There was a mixture of nervousness and pleading in her voice. She kept glancing to the doorway as if worried that someone might burst in on them.

'Well, okay, if you're sure it won't be a problem.'

'Don't be silly, Frank,' she said, her voice now relieved. 'I must get that file to Frieda, and then I've got about three days backlog of work to get through.'

Gertie came through the doorway. She stopped at the sight of Susan. She looked very unhappy.

'Dropped in for a chat, Doctor Pleadle?' she asked in a tone of controlled anger.

'Hello Gertie, no, I was looking for Frieda, actually. I was told she was in here.'

'She's gone to her office,' Frank said, puzzled at Gertie's attitude and Susan's almost meekness.

'I'll be off then,' Susan said, disappearing like a scalded cat.

'Bloody trespassing,' Gertie muttered, handing Frank his coffee.

'Trespassing?' asked Frank in surprise. 'How do you mean?'

'Oh, er, nothing, Sarge, I was thinking of something someone was telling me at the coffee machine.'

'Oh? What was that?'

'Can't remember, Sarge,' Gertie replied. 'Who are we going to see first? What about Phil Walthers?'

Frank shook his head as if to clear it. There were times he really didn't understand women.

Sheila was manning the reception desk when they arrived at the Herald.

'Hello, Sergeant Summers,' she said, giving him the benefit of a warm smile, 'nice to see you again.' She glanced down, and then back up with a demure look that could have won the heart of a block of ice. 'I thought it was terribly brave of you to rescue that little girl's kitten,' she said. 'I'm sure anyone else would have left her there crying, and gone after the burglar instead.'

'You shouldn't believe everything you read in the newspapers,' Frank said with a smile.

'Is that your car parked out there?' asked Gertie. 'The one without a tax disk?'

'I don't have a car,' Sheila said, without bothering to look at her. 'But there was a little girl? And a kitten? And a burglar? And you did rescue the kitten before going after the burglar? I'm sure Mr Walthers wouldn't make it up, he would never do that sort of a thing. Besides, there's the picture of the girl with her kitten in the special edition.'

'Well, yes, in a way,' admitted Frank. 'But as you can see from the photograph, it's a little larger than a kitten. Vicious little thing, too, it almost had my hand off. And I didn't know the burglar was in the house at that stage.'

'But I thought that's why you were there in the first place.'

'Ah, yes, well, that is true, I suppose. I, er, thought it was a false alarm.'

'I don't care, you're still my hero.'

'Is Mr Walthers in?' asked Gertie. 'Only we don't have all day.'

'Yes, good point, Gertie,' said Frank, anxious to get away from the hero-worship.

'I'm sure Mr Walthers will always be in for you, Sergeant,' said Sheila, pressing a button on an intercom box. 'Mr Walthers? Sergeant Summers is here to see you.'

'Send him right in,' came Phil Walthers' expansive voice.

Sheila opened the connecting door to allow them through. As Gertie passed, walking behind Frank, Sheila stuck her tongue out at her. Gertie froze for a second, before showing Sheila two fingers. Sheila responded with one. Gertie's reply was a finger on each hand, and she turned and followed Frank before Sheila could reciprocate.

Frank marched on to Phil Walthers' office, oblivious to the sign-language going on behind him.

'Cometh the hour, cometh the hero,' Walthers said, standing up as they walked in. 'A tea or coffee, Sergeant, or perhaps something more suitable for a celebration?'

'Celebration?'

'My little special issue, Sergeant, or should I say Sheila's and my special issue. A veritable success, both in journalistic and commercial senses. The telephone has hardly stopped ringing. The national papers are begging to use my copy, television companies are pleading to pay me for an interview, and my advertisers can hardly thank me enough for including their adverts, even though I hadn't troubled myself to ask if they were willing to pay for the privilege. Which they will, of course.'

'So long as the national papers don't reprint that rubbish about little girls with kittens up trees,' Frank said, sitting down. 'We'll forego the tea, Mr Walthers, if you don't mind.'

'Not at all,' Walthers said, sitting down and replenishing a coffee mug from a whiskey bottle in his drawer. He smiled. 'I'm afraid I need something to keep me awake. Sheila and I were busy until midnight, and then your colleagues awoke me about half past two. A very exciting night, I must say.'

'Yes, apologies for that,' Frank said, taking out a pad and pen. 'A rather over-excitable sergeant got carried away.'

'Now, Sergeant Summers, please. Please do not treat me as a simple minded member of the public, I beg of you. I know there was another eighty-five percent murder last night, and I know I'm a suspect.'

'Well, that is true, unofficially,' said Frank, 'but we like to keep up a pretence of politeness. You went straight home after finishing up here?'

'Straight home, Sergeant – or, to be more precise, straight home after I'd dropped Sheila off at her parents' house. Not good for a young girl to be wandering on her own in the early hours of the morning. When I got home I had a night-cap and collapsed into my bed, to dream dreams of success, of a wonderful world in which the public were rushing to buy their own copy of the Wellbury Herald.'

'What time did you get home?'

'Twelve twenty-five precisely, Sergeant, as your colleagues should have told you.'

'Ah, yes, unfortunately I just missed the shift handover. You're very sure about the time?'

'Very sure, Sergeant. I have an old grandfather clock which is twenty five minutes slow. It was ringing in midnight when I opened the door. I really should correct it, but I'm afraid I might damage it.'

'Well, that more or less covers everything,' Frank said, standing up and putting his pad back into his pocket. 'To be honest, Inspector Garold just wanted us to pop in and make sure the others hadn't been too heavy-handed last night – or this morning, rather. It often happens when people are tired, and we don't like making enemies of the press unnecessarily.' He paused and patted his pockets. 'What did I do with my pen? Ah, it slipped onto the chair.'

He leaned over and picked up the pen, holding it up for Walthers' inspection.

'Silly, really, I bought it off some charity last night, young bloke with a speech impediment, selling door-to-door. Doesn't even work properly. Felt a bit sorry for him, really. I suppose you get them as well?'

Phil Walthers looked at him sadly.

'I am most disappointed in you, Sergeant Summers,' he said. 'Speaking as a former would-be thespian I can honestly say I have probably never seen a worse performance.'

'Performance?' asked Frank innocently.

Walthers sighed.

'Number seven on the list is door-to-door salesmen. You were about as subtle as an unclad stripper in a monastery. Let me show you.' He picked up a pen and pad and pretended to write something on it. He looked at the pen suspiciously, shook it, and tried again. For all he world he looked like a man struggling to get a pen working. 'I knew I shouldn't have spent good money on this,' he said. 'Some charity called the other night, thought I might as well buy something. You don't have a pen that works, do you?' he asked, holding out his hand.

Without thinking Frank handed over his pen.

'The other thing to remember, Sergeant, is to make sure the pen doesn't work. This one appears to be in perfect condition.'

He handed the pen back with a smile.

'I was that bad, was I?' asked Frank with a wry grimace.

Walthers smiled.

'Not really, Sergeant. Your biggest mistake was in saying that you bought it last night.' He opened another drawer and took out two A4 size envelopes. 'Two copies, one for yourself and one for that incredibly charming Inspector of yours. Your presence at the concert made my twenty minutes there all the more worthwhile. I had to be there to take at least one or two photographs. Had it not been for the special issue I would have been there from start to finish. I do so love music.'

Frank opened one of the envelopes and took out a black and white photograph. It showed Frieda in her evening dress, shawl dropped to her elbows, a strand of hair hanging loose. Next to her was Frank, firm-jawed, his arm protectively around waist. Her hand was firmly on his.

Walthers must have taken it as they were leaving. Frank didn't even remember a flash going off.

'Oh, wow,' whispered Gertie, leaning over him. 'She looks absolutely gorgeous.'

'Yes, well, thank you Mr Walthers, Frank said, hastily putting the photograph back into the envelope. 'We'll be in touch if there's anything more we need to know.'

'No, come on, give,' said Gertie, snapping her fingers at the envelopes. 'I want a proper look.'

Reluctantly Frank handed the envelopes over. Walthers smiled at him.

'Don't worry, Sergeant Frank Summers,' he said, 'it's not for publication. I like to think it's rather a good photograph, even if I say it myself. And I get much more satisfaction from giving people personal photographs than I do those which end up in the paper.'

'Very kind of you,' Frank said. 'I'm sure Inspector Garold will be most appreciative.'

He left, with Gertie trailing behind, still studying the photograph. Sheila received a curt nod as he walked out, surprising her. Gertie paused next to the young girl and showed her the photograph.

'Wow!' said Sheila. 'She looks smashing. Who is she? Some sort of film star? Was Frank her bodyguard?'

'No, that's Detective Inspector Frieda Garold,' Gertie replied. 'Frank's boss. And the competition. You don't even come into it, my girl, you haven't got a chance.'

'Strikes me you haven't much of a chance either, with her looking like that.'

'It does make things a little harder,' admitted Gertie. 'But I intend to make up for it in other ways. A car might look shiny and bright, but what's more important is how it drives. Inspector Garold can take the moral high ground. I intend to take the immoral low ground, as low as I can go.'

Sheila giggled and looked at Gertie in admiration.

'Good luck then. I suppose I'll have to settle on Mr Walthers. He's such a sweetie. Maybe he likes the immoral low ground from time to time.' She sighed. 'I always fall for older men,' she said.

And he's about two hundred years too old for you, thought Gertie as she hurried out after Frank. On their walk back to the station they went into a newsagents where Frank spent fifteen minutes trying all the pens in the shop before finding one that didn't work. They left behind a bemused old newsagent wondering if he had just witnessed the beginning of a new trend.

Searching for – and paying for – a pen that didn't work? Youngsters these days.

'I know Frieda doesn't think much of the idea,' Frank said as they drove to have a word with Tom Sampson, 'but I'm convinced that there's a good chance of identifying the next victim if we play our cards right. If we can do that we should be able to prevent another murder and nail the murderer at the same time.'

Frank didn't need to do his pen trick for Tom Sampson.

'For a moment I thought you were Jehovah's Witnesses or double-glazing salesmen, I rarely get visitors,' Sampson said as he led them into his kitchen.

'Get a lot of them around here, that sort of visitor?' asked Frank.

'Not normally, no. One a month, usually, if that. I've often wondered whether they put a mark on the gate, like they say Gypsies used to do, something small which other people would miss, but another Gypsy would be able to read, telling them whether it was a good household or not. I think mine would read "don't bother".'

'I've had a few myself, recently,' said Frank, inventing quickly. 'One was a Korean, I think, couldn't speak English very well, but he wanted to discuss the state of the world for some reason.'

'State of the world?' asked Sampson scornfully. 'I'd give him state of the world. State of his pants after a quick boot up the backside, more like.'

'He's been here as well?'

'No, can't say I've had any Koreans. Mostly youngsters straight out of school who haven't a clue. Had one selling double glazing who didn't know what a sash-window was. Bloody modern world. Replace everything with PVC or whatever it's called, that's what they want to do.'

'Recognise any of them? The salesmen, I mean.'

'No, should I?'

'I was just wondering if any of them were young offenders on one of these rehabilitation schemes. Sending them out to knock on doors instead of breaking into them.'

'No, the ones I get are mostly new at the job, terrified, mainly. I feel sorry for them sometimes. I doubt whether they last long.'

'Well, that wasn't much use, was it?' asked Frank as they drove away. 'If Sampson is our man he's giving us a brilliant act. But then, whoever it is, they've played a blinder so far. Either that or beginner's luck.'

'I can't see it, Sarge,' Gertie said. 'I admit Tom Sampson might have done Nagness, but to carry on like this? He'd have given up long ago.'

'You might be right, Gertie, you might be very right. Let's go have a word with Councillor Bagley. See what he has to say about people who come knocking on his door uninvited.'

Robert Bagley positively welcomed uninvited door-knockers.

'I believe that God sends them to me to show them the way of the light and the truth,' he said, sitting in his council office. 'Whether they come as salesmen or those who have strayed from the true path into abhorrent beliefs, I make sure none go away without hearing the word as it is.'

Probably the most effective way of getting rid of the buggers, thought Frank.

'Have you converted many?' he asked. 'Any of them join your church?'

Bagley gave a wry grimace.

'One, once, almost. She attended services for a few weeks, and then disappeared. I later found out that she had joined a commune in Cyprus. Some Indian cult, I believe. In general they don't tend to return. I can only presume the fault lies with me. No doubt God will show me the way to convert the unbelievers when He is ready.'

'I'm surprised,' Frank said. 'I would have thought that that sort of thing would come naturally to you as a councillor.'

'For some reason people believe me when I say I will lower their council tax, which we haven't ever been able to do, but not when I bring them the obvious truth.'

'Do you ever see any of them again? In the street, shopping, that sort of thing? I've always wondered if they come from out of town. They never seem to be locals.'

'Yes, I've often had that impression, Sergeant. Apart from the young lady I've never seen one of them twice. You may well be right. Maybe they are travellers, going from town to town.'

'Scratch two,' said Frank. 'So far my brilliant idea has been less than wonderful.'

'Perhaps it means they're innocent,' suggested Gertie.

'Possible. But there's always the other option. That they're bloody lying.'

Frank was sitting in his office after lunch, drawing little diagrams of nothing much while waiting for Gertie when Frieda appeared in the doorway.

'Any progress yet, Frank?' she asked.

'Nothing,' he said, screwing up the piece of paper and throwing it at the waste-paper bin. 'Sampson and Bagley have the entirely normal reaction to door-knockers. Or at least Sampson does. Bagley claims he tries to convert them, which I can well believe. I have this terrible feeling that we might be wasting our time.'

'Don't give up yet, Frank, it's worth a shot. And we have almost nothing else to go on at the moment. At least you're putting pressure on them. Whoever our killer is, they'll slip up sooner or later. Though sooner would be better, of course. Yesterday or last week would have been ideal, as far as the Chief Constable is concerned.'

'And it won't be long before the media start shouting in earnest,' Frank noted.

'No, it won't,' Frieda agreed. 'I'm surprised Kerouac is the only one shouting the odds at the moment. Let me know how you get on with the others.'

'By the way,' Frank said as she turned to go, 'here's a little present from Phil Walthers.'

He held out one of the envelopes Walthers had given him. Frieda came forward and took it with a surprised look. She opened it and looked at the photograph. A slight smile played on her lips.

'He is a very good photographer, isn't he?' she asked.

'Couldn't really go wrong, considering the subject matter,' Frank said.

'Meaning?'

'Meaning that you are very photogenic,' Frank said, resisting the urge to add "and you bloody know it".

Frieda blushed slightly.

'You're not too bad yourself,' she said. 'But I think next time you will have to wear evening dress.'

Gertie entered. Her face assumed a glower as she saw Frieda standing next to Frank, looking at the photograph.

'Forensic evidence?' she asked.

'Er, no,' Frieda said, slipping the photograph back into the envelope. 'Er, right, I'll let you two get on with it.'

She disappeared out the doorway quickly. Frank watched in puzzlement. It was almost as if Gertie had frightened Frieda off.

Impossible, he thought.

Though he believed that, if you saw a pink tiger walking down the street, either you were hallucinating or there really was a pink tiger walking down the street. And hallucination is unusual unless preceded by the ingestion of severely psychedelic foodstuffs.

He wondered what he had eaten recently to induce hallucination.

He shook his head to clear it.

'You okay, Sarge?' Gertie asked.

'Um? Oh, yes, fine. Just fine. Come on, let's go pay the vicar a visit. See how he handles unwanted guests.'

There was no response to their knock on the vicarage door. They were about to leave when the unmistakeable sound of an epithet came from the direction of the garage, one worth about three pound fifty had Frieda heard it. They walked over and Frank opened the slightly ajar door. The vicar looked up in surprise and guilt.

'Oh, it's you,' he said with some relief. He was nursing a finger. He wore a pair of jeans and an old t-shirt, both covered liberally with grease stains. In front of him stood a pale-blue motorbike, largely stripped down. Frank noted that the t-shirt revealed a surprisingly muscular torso and arms, something the vicar's normal garb kept hidden.

'Finally got around to taking the old girl out?' he asked.

'Yes, indeed,' the vicar replied with a shy smile. 'For a moment I thought you might be Mrs Blower. I don't think she would approve. I'm hoping to get everything back together and under cover before she turns up. You don't mind if I carry on, do you?'

'Not at all,' Frank said, perching himself on the edge of an old desk, watching Parsons return to his work.

'She's in excellent condition considering she hasn't been looked after for five years,' the vicar said. 'Just needs a bit of oil and grease in the right parts. Some of the bolts are a little stiff. I caught my finger just before you arrived, I hope I didn't say anything too rude, or at least, too loud.'

'Not that we overhead,' Frank assured him. 'We only heard a noise, and came to investigate.'

'And caught me red-handed,' smiled the vicar, tightening a bolt, and patting the machine. 'Caught me red-handed with my secret love. You won't tell any of my parishioners, will you?'

'I wouldn't be surprised if some of your parishioners rather liked the idea.'

'You may well be right, Sergeant. However I'm afraid Mrs Blower would not. So I think a fait accompli is called for.' He picked up the fuel tank and began to fix it to the bike. 'But I presume you are not here to discuss the finer points of propriety of a country vicar's mode of transport? Your visit is to do with these terrible murders?'

'We just popped in to make sure our colleagues' early morning call wasn't too upsetting. Our Inspector is worried that the night shift were a little too zealous. Some of the younger ones watch too many American movies. They forget that we do things differently here.'

'Not at all, Sergeant, your colleagues were most respectful. Though I do agree with your Inspector. Sadly the world seems to be losing the good elements of tradition.' He sighed. 'Perhaps I'm becoming an old fogey. Perhaps it was ever so.'

'Fortunately Wellbury seems to be resisting the notion,' Frank said, standing up. 'Oh, while I remember, there is one old-fashioned tradition still alive. Hawkers flogging duff goods. I bought a pen off one of them the other day, some charity selling door-to-door. It didn't work. I mentioned it at the station, which got a good laugh. Apparently it isn't a charity at all, just a gang of travelling salesmen selling cheap rubbish at expensive prices. You haven't had any of that, have you?'

'Door-to-door salesmen?' asked the vicar, standing up and looking at the motorbike doubtfully. 'No, I don't think I've ever had one of those. I suppose they avoid vicarages. There's a reason for the saying "as poor as a church mouse". Hmmm, I think I'd better get this covered up. I can finish off this evening, after Mrs Blower's gone home.'

'Looks almost finished,' Frank said as the vicar dragged a tarpaulin across and began covering the sight from Mrs Blower's potential gaze.

'Oh, indeed, very close. If I'm lucky I might even get a spin out of her this evening.'

'I feel jealous,' Frank said, smiling. As he turned to go he stopped suddenly. The tarpaulin had been covering neat stacks of newspapers and magazines. One was a pile of issues of the Herald.

'You seem to have collected quite a few newspapers,' he commented.

'Eh?' asked the vicar absent-mindedly. He turned to follow Frank's gaze. 'Oh, those. That's one of Mrs Blower's pet projects, recycling. No doubt a good cause, and it allows her to organise the youngsters and keep in touch with the parishioners, but not something I can get excited about, I'm afraid. Everyone has their own recycling bin these days, so no doubt it will eventually stop.'

'No doubt,' echoed Frank. 'Well, thank you for your time, vicar.'

'Not at all, my boy. Come back in a few days, I should have the old girl ticking over like a Swiss sewing machine.'

'Well, well, now that is interesting,' Frank said when they got back into the car.

'Suspicious, more like it,' noted Gertie. 'Whoever heard of a church collecting newspapers for recycling?'

'No, Gertie, that used to happen a lot before councils got involved and started giving every household a recycling bin. A local group like the scouts would collect newspapers and bottles and the rest. Even used to make a couple of pence out of it at one time. Not surprising that it's still going on in Wellbury. As the vicar said, it'll die out one of these days.'

'We could have had a quick look through them,' suggested Gertie.

'It did cross my mind, but I doubt that the killer would have left the evidence there. The question is, who knows about those newspapers? Who has access to the garage? I think we should have a word with Mrs Blower.'

Gertie gave him a look before starting the car.

'Just one thing, Frank,' she said. 'No motorbikes. No taking a spin. They're far too dangerous. Okay?'

'Of course not,' Frank said, wondering if he could get away from Gertie for a few hours over the weekend and see if the vicar would let him have a little spin.

'I mean it, Frank.'

'Absolutely. Let's get on to Mrs Blower. There are more important things than motorbikes to worry about.'

Saturday, he thought. Saturday afternoon. The vicar wasn't likely to be doing anything on a Saturday afternoon. And he should have the bike ready by then.

'You again!' Mrs Blower said incredulously when she opened the door to find them on the doorstep. 'Aren't you satisfied with waking me up at some ungodly hour, banging on the door loud enough to wake the dead? I will be writing to the Chief Constable to demand an explanation. Never mind the state of the Tombola list.'

'Well, that's why we're here, Mrs Blower,' Frank said, giving her the benefit of a charming smile. 'Our Inspector sent us here to make sure you weren't unduly imposed upon. Could we come in?'

Mrs Blower hesitated before opening the door to let them enter.

'Unduly imposed upon?' she asked with scorn. 'How else would you describe being woken up by the police at two in the morning? I've had dreams about that shirt, you know. I totally fail to understand why on earth someone thought it necessary. Waking me up to ask me if I'd been out at all. What ridiculous nonsense! A perfectly good pair of walking boots, but will anyone look at them? Come through to the kitchen, the sitting room is still full of items for the jumble sale. As if I would go wandering around at a time like that. Preposterous. Would you like some tea?'

'Tea would be marvellous,' Frank said, feeling once again the sense of bemusement at the way Mrs Blower could hold two or three conversations at once. 'How's everything going? The jumble sale and so on?'

'The fete. You're trying to divert me from my complaint,' Mrs Blower said, switching the kettle on. 'Sit down. Don't try that with me, young Sergeant Summers. I have every intention of making sure that I receive a full apology. As it happens, I think it will be the best sale we've had. People have been very generous this year. Three o'clock in the morning? Preposterous. I've decided that the shirt and the flared trousers aren't a match after all.'

'In that case, I apologise on behalf of Wellbury police force, Mrs Blower,' Frank replied, taking a seat. 'I'm sure that peoples' generosity has been a response to your arduous efforts.'

She turned and gave him a frown.

'I know what you're doing, Sergeant Summers, and it won't

work. You can stop that charming-boy smile. Very well, as it's you, I shall accept the apology. But you can forget the flimflam. What you mean is that people are too scared of me not to donate as much as they can. I am well aware of that fact. So be it. I hope you will be attending the fete. Would you like some lemon cake? I was trying out a new recipe this morning. Have you ever helped out in a Tombola stall?'

'Just a very small slice, Mrs Blower. I have every intention of being at the fete, work permitting. I look forward to it.'

'I doubt it,' Mrs Blower said, pouring hot water into a teapot before turning to take out the cake. 'You young people prefer more modern pastimes these days. Sit down young lady, you can hardly eat while standing, it is very bad for the digestion. Those trousers would look good on you at a fancy-dress. Computer games, or whatever the latest craze is.'

'I try to avoid computer games,' Frank said as Gertie sat down obediently. 'They can be very addictive.'

'Can they?' asked Mrs Blower, passing them tea and cake. Frank noticed that he received a relatively small slice as requested, whereas Gertie got a wedge close to a quarter of the whole cake. 'I shall have to try them out, then,' she noted, sitting down.

'Oh, wow, this is yummy,' Gertie said, tucking in.

Mrs Blower's face softened as she watched Gertie with her head down, intent on the lemon cake. She looked at Frank. A sense of sad understanding seemed to pass through her eyes.

'Always make the most of your opportunities, Sergeant,' she said softly, 'you don't want to find yourself looking back and regretting what might have been.'

Frank guessed that she wasn't referring to a slice of lemon

cake.

'That's very much part of my philosophy, Mrs Blower.'

'I have no doubt about that, Sergeant. Whether you practice that philosophy, that I do wonder about. I wonder whether flared trousers will ever come back into fashion.'

'Ah, yes,' Frank said, thinking that this was not where the conversation was supposed to be going. 'Er, I noticed that you collect newspapers for recycling. There was a stack in the garage at the vicarage.'

'Yes, indeed, Sergeant. I presume you have just come from there? Apologising to the vicar for his early visit? Ridiculous nonsense, I can only presume someone suffered a brainstorm of some fashion. This will be the last collection. It's something the previous vicar, kindly man, instituted many years ago. But the world has moved on. In many ways it is a pity, as it gave the children a sense of purpose, collecting goods for recycling. We need to find something else for them to do. It is all very well for the wealthier children to sit in darkened rooms playing Space Invaders, or whatever it's called, but it is not only unhealthy, it leaves the less wealthy with nothing to do but roam the streets causing mischief.'

'A good point, Mrs Blower. How are the newspapers collected? Do people just leave them on the doorstep, or in the garage?'

'The youngsters put them in the garage. It's almost always open. There's nothing there to be stolen apart from the vicar's old motorcycle, which he has trying to get working for the past few weeks, though he thinks I don't know it. He will not go about riding a motorcycle, not so long as I am alive. Terribly unsafe machines. Not on their own, as far as I understand it, but because they are more or less invisible to a car driver. Probably just as well, they are a fire hazard, I think an insurance company might refuse to pay due compensation should a fire break out. I almost knocked one over myself the other day.'

Frank thought he was following Mrs Blower. The newspapers were a fire hazard, the rest referred to motorbikes.

But from the sounds of it the vicar would have a struggle ahead of him. Which meant that he, Frank, might lose out on an occasional jaunt on a motorbike along the country roads.

'I had someone on my doorstep a couple of weeks ago trying to sell me one,' he said conversationally. 'I was quite surprised. I'm used to people from charities, or double glazing salesmen, that sort of thing, but I've never had anyone on my doorstep trying to sell me a motorbike before.'

'I would say I presume you sent him away with a flea in his ear, but I rather imagine you invited him in and discussed his catalogue over a beer or two.'

Frank smiled.

'Yes we did, I must confess. I presume you must have more than your fair share of itinerant tradesmen, living in a house like this?'

'On the contrary, Sergeant. It is precisely because I have such a large house that I do not suffer from such intrusions. You would have to be a very simple or overly optimistic salesman to look at a house such as this and think for one moment that the occupants would even consider purchasing anything on the doorstep. The greater likelihood is that an extremely large dog would intercept you before you were half way up the drive.'

'Good point, Mrs Blower,' Frank said, standing up. 'Well, thank you for the tea and cake, it was delicious.'

'I'll say,' said Gertie. 'I'll definitely be coming to the fete. I'll drag this one along as well, if I can.'

Mrs Blower smiled.

'You take care of him. Make sure he doesn't go anywhere near a motorcycle.'

'Oh, don't worry about that, Mrs Blower, he won't ever so much as sit on one, I'll make sure of that.'

Frank wondered if Gertie needed a quiet word about discipline, and respect for a senior officer. Or at least how to pretend she respected her senior officer.

'In other words, nothing,' Frieda said in the ops room after Frank had related their day. The new shift looked awake and ready for work. The old shift lounged in their chairs, their weary faces speaking of much footwork, many interviews and no results.

'That's what it boils down to,' Frank admitted. 'The only one we couldn't find was Professor Humphries. If any of the others had a specific door-to-door salesman in mind they meant to remove they didn't show it.'

'Not to worry, lad,' said Percy. 'It was a good idea as they go. We'll have a tail on Professor Humphries within the hour. If he's our man we'll know soon enough.'

Not with only two men and one car you won't, thought Frank. Not unless you're bloody lucky.

He dropped a mental fifty pence piece into the swear box.

'I've asked the Chief Constable for support from

neighbouring divisions,' Frieda said, as if reading his mind. 'Unfortunately this eighty-five percent nonsense is spreading to other towns. Everyone is spread thin as it is. If things do develop, and we need more officers, Inspector Hanson will inform me and start calling in members of the day shift. Obviously we don't want to do that, a few false alarms and we'll all be half-asleep on our feet within a few days. But I'm afraid that you'll have to be prepared for the eventuality.'

She paused.

'Any questions?'

There were none.

'Right, day shift get off home. Have an early night, we start again first thing tomorrow. That includes you, Frank and Gertie.'

Gertie had a sour look on her face as they left.

'Come on, Gertie,' Frank said, 'a little detour and then home, I think.'

'She's planning something, I know it,' Gertie muttered to herself.

'Who?'

'Frieda, that's who.'

Frank paused, puzzled.

'Of course she's planning something,' he pointed out. 'The whole operation, as it happens. What on earth are you talking about?'

'Oh, nothing, Sarge. What's this detour you're on about?'

'That's Phil Walthers' house, three doors up,' Frank said as Gertie pulled into the pavement under a tree. 'I wonder what the chances are he might be out and have left his door unlocked.'

'Not much chance of that, Sarge.'

'No, sadly not. Anyway, let's see if he's in and will offer us a cup of tea. I might need to go to the little boys' room while I'm there.'

'You mean snoop around while I keep his attention, Sarge? Wouldn't it be better if I did the snooping and you kept him occupied?'

Frank had to admit that she had a point. Walthers wasn't stupid. He probably used the do-you-mind-if-I-use-your-bathroom-and-snoop-around trick himself on the odd occasion. Gertie as the semi-invisible subordinate might just get away with it, Frank wouldn't stand a chance.

Walthers would probably call out helpful suggestions as he left the room.

'Let's see if he's in first,' he said.

There was no answer to the ringing of the doorbell. Frank surreptitiously tried the door. It was firmly locked. He turned and looked around the front garden.

'Looks like we're out of luck, Gertie,' he said. 'Might as well call it a day.'

'Seems like the lock's a little dodgy, Sarge,' said Gertie. 'Door's just sort of opened.'

Frank turned around to find the door ajar. He noticed Gertie slipping something back into her handbag.

'Gertie how did you – '

She winked.

'A little trick I picked up somewhere,' she said, smiling

happily.

'Along with your university studies, no doubt. Talking of which, have you done the section on breaking and entering? Or at least illegal entry?'

'Isn't really illegal, Sarge. We find the door ajar, it looks suspicious, we pop in to make sure no nefarious deeds are afoot. It's our duty. Come on.'

'Yes,' Frank noted bitterly as he followed her inside, making sure the door was again locked behind them. 'If we're really, really lucky we might come up against a judge who hasn't heard that one more than ten times.' He sighed. 'Still, in for a penny, in for a pound. Let's start with upstairs.'

It took them an hour. If Phil Walthers was hiding something he had done so extremely well.

'Our last hope,' Frank said. 'Cupboard under the stairs. Most people think it an ideal place to hide something. God knows why.'

As he opened the door to the cupboard a noise came from the front door, the noise of a key being inserted into the lock.

'Quick,' said Gertie, bundling Frank into the cupboard and following him in, closing the door behind them, with her back to him. The cupboard was cramped, full of dusty old boxes, with the stairs above making a low ceiling, forcing Frank to crouch over Gertie's back, his hands around her waist. He felt Gertie fold her arms, holding her hands tightly over his.

The last time I had a woman holding my hands to her waist like this, thought Frank, someone took a picture.

'Put the box down there, my dear,' came Phil Walthers' voice. 'I'll sort it out later.'

The same person who is now standing three feet away from us, thought Frank.

'Are you sure, Mr Walters?' came the voice of Sheila. 'I'm more than happy to give you a hand.'

Sheila? What's she doing here, Frank wondered.

'Quite sure, Sheila, quite sure.'

'Is there anything else you want me to do, Mr Walthers? I'm not doing anything tonight.'

'No, Sheila, no. I need to get something from the sitting room and I'll drive you home.'

'Are you going on a stake-out again tonight? I could come with,' Sheila's voice said, moving away, presumably following Walthers.

'Sheila, really, I am not going on a stake-out tonight, and I haven't done that sort of thing for years.'

You lying little tinker, thought Frank. That meant Sheila didn't know about Walthers tailing Bagley. Why was that, he wondered.

'I know you're doing something. It's not fair. I'll do anything for you. Please let me help. You know I'm falling in love with you.'

'The little minx!' said Gertie forcefully.

Frank rescued one hand and clamped it over Gertie's mouth.

'What was that?' asked Walthers 'I thought I heard someone.'

'I'm sorry, I've embarrassed you,' said Sheila. 'But it's the truth. You don't have to change the subject.'

'I'm not changing the subject, I definitely heard something.'

Phil Walthers' voice was coming closer. He would be in the

passage now.

Frank could feel Gertie trying to repress a giggle. He held her more firmly. She might think it funny, but if Phil Walthers discovered them the newspaper headlines would not be "Police Enter House Illegally" but rather "Closet Affair Between Kitty Sergeant and His Constable".

If he were lucky. There were other ways of phrasing things.

'It came from somewhere near here,' Phil Walthers said, right outside the door.

Frank was trying to resist two physical urges. The first was to sneeze, and the second, for some strange reason, was a sudden need to go to the bathroom.

'Please, Mr Walthers, I know I'm young, and you probably think me immature, but I'll make up for it. I learn very quickly, you know that.'

Frank's eyebrows raised in the darkness. It was not Sheila's declaration that had surprised him. Gertie was licking the palm of his hand. It tickled.

He clamped his hand further over her mouth. Gertie had the right sense of mischief, but her timing was diabolical.

To Frank's immense relief the doorbell rang.

'What now?' asked Phil Walthers in irritation. They could hear him walk to the door and open it.

'Good evening, sir, are you the owner of this property?' asked a voice Frank thought he recognised.

'Yes, officer, I am the owner of this property. What, precisely, can I do for you?' By the sound of his voice Walthers was becoming less happy with life every second.

'We've had a report of two shady characters hanging around

your front door, sir. One of your neighbours rang up. Is everything secure?'

'Ah, the good old shady characters story. I would have thought you might have been a little more creative than that. Sergeant Summers sent you, I presume? Asked you to have a look around, pretending to check for signs of forced entry? Well, go ahead, Constable, look all you like, but please be quick about it, I'm in somewhat of a hurry.'

'I'm sorry, sir, I don't understand.'

'Please do not treat me like an idiot, Constable. I shall have words with Sergeant Summers about this. Now, are you going to search my house or not?'

'Er, I'm sorry, sir. Could I clear up what appears to be some confusion? Have you or have you not had a break-in?'

'No, Constable, I have not had a break-in. Now what do you say to that?'

'Well, in that case, sorry for disturbing you, sir. Have a pleasant evening.'

Frank could hear two pairs of footsteps receding down the path.

'Sheila, come,' said Walthers imperiously. 'I will take you home and we will say no more about this nonsense.'

'But Mr Walthers – '

'Enough. One more word out of you and you're fired. Really, if it isn't bad enough with the police paying me visits every five seconds. As for that Sergeant Summers, I must admit I thought he was far more subtle.' He paused. 'Though they didn't come in. That's strange. Perhaps I am maligning Sergeant Summers unfairly. Never mind, come on, Sheila.'

The door closed and footsteps could be heard walking down the path, Walthers' firm, Sheila's dragging.

Frank waited until they had definitely gone before releasing Gertie and taking a deep breath. Gertie opened the door and they emerged back into the passage, Gertie giggling furiously. She looked at him.

'Do I look as bad as you?' she asked.

Worse, I would imagine, he wanted to say. They were covered with the accumulated dust of months, if not years. Gertie's mouth was streaked where Frank had held his hand, making her look as if she had been eating some strange ice-cream, badly. His own suit would need dry-cleaning.

'Well, I would say that proves that nothing was hidden in there. It probably hasn't been opened in months. Let's get out of here before Walthers gets back,' he said. 'One close call is enough for the day.'

He opened the front door a crack to check whether the coast was clear. Then they were out, scuttling down the front path. Just as they came out of the gate a firm voice stopped them.

'I wonder if I could have a moment of your time, sir?'

Frank stopped and turned. Harry Wheatley looked back at him in astonishment. Behind him was Ed Watts. It was Harry's voice he had recognised.

'Blimey, Sarge, what the hell? Don't tell me you were in there the whole time?'

'You never saw us, Harry. It was three other blokes with a dog, and you didn't get his name either.'

'Sure, Sarge,' Harry replied, his mouth still half open as Frank and Gertie made quickly for their car.

'You've got to admire the bugger,' Ed Watts said. 'She's living with him, but they break into someone else's house for a quick hows-your-father. And he's getting off with Fabulous. And Doctor Pleadle. Talk about living as if it was the last day of your life.'

'If he carries on like that,' Harry said mournfully, 'it will be the last bleeding day of his life.'

'Home, Gertie,' Frank said. 'I think a shower, followed by a bottle of wine, a pizza and a movie from the rental shop sounds good. Shut the world out for the evening. Above all, I never want to hear about cupboards under stairs for the rest of my life.'

'Sounds good to me,' said Gertie, who intended to remember that moment for the rest of her life.

It had been great fun.

They picked up the wine and movie on the way home. Gertie showered after Frank. While he had opted for jeans and a t-shirt, she had put on her nightdress and a thin dressing gown. He presumed he would get used to the sight eventually.

They sat eating pizza and drinking wine, watching Four Weddings and a Funeral. When the pizza was finished Gertie wiped her hands and cuddled up next to him.

This is the life, he thought as she rested against him. He was going to miss Gertie when she went back to her flat. Never before had he realised how much he had missed in not having a sister when he grew up. It was fortunate the builders were living up to their reputation.

Out in Old Merrick Detective Sergeant Pete Phillips and

Constable Bobby Stang sat in an unmarked car watching Professor Humphries' house.

'Notice that Audi three cars behind on the other side of the road?' asked Pete Phillips.

'Yes, Sarge. Bloke apparently asleep. A bit suspicious.'

'That's our friend Phil Walthers,' said Pete Phillips. 'Why do you suppose he's staking out the Professor's house? I thought he was supposed to be after Bagley.'

When the movie ends I am going to give him a kiss he will never forget, thought Gertie. He'll turn his head slightly towards me, and whammo! Passionate won't even come close to describing it. A slow start, though, as if I didn't mean to, but couldn't resist him. Let the dressing gown slip slightly. Show a bit of flesh.

'Control to Sergeant Peters, come in Pete.'

Pete Phillips recognised Percy's voice.

'I'm here, Inspector,' he answered softly.

'Reports of a tearaway motorcyclist in your area, Pete, we need someone to check it out. What's it look like at your end?'

'Dead quiet, Inspector,' Pete said, keeping his voice down. 'We also have Phil Walthers on post. God knows what he's doing here.'

'Well, at least that leaves one pair of eyes. I need you to do a circuit of your area. Just to show the flag, as it were, just for the record. We've had six complaints about this motorcyclist so far. Just drive around the block and return to position.

Understood?'

'But Inspector – '

'But me no buts, Sergeant, just do it.'

Frank put his feet on the coffee table. Gertie stretched hers out on top of his.

A good night's kip, thought Frank, trying not to look at Gertie's legs, her gown having slipped off them, and her nightdress being a little short for his comfort.

Sleep wasn't the first thing on Gertie's agenda.

'Sarge, do you have that awful feeling we're about to make a mistake?' asked Bobby Stang.

'Aye, lad,' Pete Phillips said as he started the engine as quietly as possible. 'We're about to make a mistake big-time. And I wish I were Sergeant bloody Summers, he would know how to disobey a direct order and get away with it. But I'm not, so let's get on with this mistake and make right as soon as we can, eh, lad?'

Before he could pull out a motorcycle roared past them.

'Right, lad, you're nicked,' said Pete Phillips.

He could do something about people who broke the speed limit.

The credits began to roll. Frank yawned pleasurably.

'That was nice, wasn't it,' he said, turning to Gertie. She looked up at him through dreamy eyes, smiling with slightly moist lips. An angel could hardly have looked sweeter.

He felt his head coming down towards hers, irresistibly. Slowly, gently, towards a face that glowed, towards lips which had to be kissed.

Gertie put her hand behind his neck and pulled him down softly.

Which is when the telephone rang.

They both started and looked towards the telephone.

'Ask not for whom the bell tolls, Gertie,' said Frank, standing up. 'I think duty calls.'

'Don't answer it, Frank!' Gertie said, grabbing hold of his jeans leg.

'Now, Gertie, don't be silly, I – '

He paused as his answering machine kicked in. They heard his metallic voice cheerfully informing the caller that he was unavailable, but if they would care to leave their name, a message, and the time, he would get back to them as soon as fate and karma would permit. Gertie let go of his jeans, a wistful look on her face.

'Frank? Frieda here. It's bad news, I'm afraid. They've found number seven. Forensics are on the scene. Percy doesn't think anything else will happen tonight, and I tend to agree. Get a good night's sleep, I don't think we need worry about being called again. See you first thing in the morning. Love, Frieda.'

The last two words sounded as if a tired Frieda thought she was writing a note.

Gertie was torn between hatred for Frieda and sympathy. She had sounded worn out. At the same time there was no reason to phone up like that.

'Well, that's that,' said Frank. 'Might as well get a good night's kip. We might not have too many of those in the next few days.'

He leaned over Gertie, put a hand on her bare shoulder and gave her a chaste kiss on the forehead.

My lips, you fool, she thought. Give me one on my lips.

'Sleep tight,' he said, giving her a brief kiss on her mouth, surprising her.

He wandered off to brush his teeth before bed. She watched him go. Angrily she began making up the sofa bed.

One second, she thought, slamming down sheets and pillows. She had been one second away from making Frank Summers hers. Indisputably hers. He might hanker after the others afterwards, but he would have been hers, all hers.

She passed his bedroom on the way to the bathroom. The light was out and the door closed.

She could have wept.

That bitch Frieda had done that on purpose, she decided, climbing under the sheets she had hoped she might be sharing with Frank.

Well, two could play at that game. Tomorrow was Susan's day, and then Frieda's. Friday was hers. All she had to do was find a way to sabotage the next couple of days ... Damn. Friday was out. For all of them.

She had been given Saturday instead.

A small accident, she thought. Nothing serious, just enough to ensure Frank Summers was physically out of action until Saturday.

Nothing serious.

In his bedroom the proposed victim looked at the ceiling and wondered what the hell he was doing.

Who number seven had been.

Who number eight might be.

Wednesday: A door-to-door salesman

A rumpled Percy stood in the ops room facing the two teams, one tired, the other fresh, none of whom were smiling.

'As you all know, apart from what seems to have become the standard mayhem and general anarchy of the day, we had number seven last night,' he said. 'What some of you might not know is the identity of the victim. Ironic, really. It was one Professor Jonathon Humphries.'

'Humphries?' asked Frank in surprise. 'That doesn't make sense. Why would – oh, shit.'

He stood up, walked over to the swear box and pushed fifty pence in.

'Damn! Damn! Damn!' he said, forcing more money in. 'Of course! Bloody obvious! I should have guessed. A two year old child could have guessed.'

The others looked at him in bafflement.

'Seeing as we lack a two year old child in the room,' Frieda said, 'perhaps you could explain?'

Frank turned to her.

'It was on Zack the Prat's show. No-one would publish Humphries' book, so he had it printed privately and sold it door-to-door. Humphries announced on the radio to the entire listening world that he had been a door-to-door salesman and we didn't even pick up the connection. I can't believe it. I really, really cannot believe it.'

He walked up to the wall and hit his head against it.

'Now, Frank, calm down,' Frieda said, taking his arm and leading him back to his seat next to Gertie. 'Most of us heard that programme, none of us made the connection.'

'Aye, don't be so hard on yourself, lad,' said Percy. 'None of us made the connection until you pointed it out.'

'It does explain why he was the victim,' Frieda said, leaving Gertie to check for a bump on Frank's forehead. 'Unfortunately it doesn't tell us anything else. Percy?'

Percy gave a wry grimace and rubbed his unshaven cheek wearily.

'It was only due to a rather unexpected and fortuitous set of circumstances that we found him last night. Otherwise he may have laid undiscovered for days. Briefly what happened is this: we had a couple of complaints about a motorbike being ridden at high speed and very noisily through suburban avenues. We were overstretched, so I asked Pete and Bobby Stang to go around the block just to show we had actually done something. As they were about to pull out the motorcyclist raced past them. They put their siren on and chased after. By doing that they woke up another person who had been staking Humphries out, our friend Mr Phil Walters.'

'Phil Walters was staking Humphries out? Not Bagley?' asked Frank.

'Aye, son, but it doesn't end there. Walthers says that, after waking up, he decided to have a look around Humphries' house and call it a night if he didn't see anything worth printing. Claims that he looked through the lounge window and saw Humphries' feet lying on the carpet. When Pete and Bobby returned he was waiting for them, very agitated, jumping from leg to leg apparently. They had a look, tried to wake Humphries up by banging on the window. When that failed they made a forced entry and found him dead. Same MO. Same note. Unfortunately they failed to notice that Phil Walthers had followed them in. He saw the note and recognised the printing immediately. I think he's preparing another special edition as we speak.'

'I'll go around and have a word with him,' Frank said. 'He's pretty reasonable about not publishing anything we don't want him to.'

'You must have a special touch, then,' Pete Phillips said sardonically. 'I told him he couldn't publish anything and he more or less told me to go to hell. Gave me a right earful about the freedom of the press.'

'He was probably tired and irritated, I think we all are,' Frank said diplomatically. 'I would imagine he'll think differently after a good night's sleep.'

'Have a word with him, Frank,' Frieda said. 'But don't worry about him publishing details of the notes. It might as well come out. Someone might have seen something, a strangely cut issue of the Herald thrown away. We'll just have to take the risk of copy-cat murders. Percy?'

'Aye. We're up to number seven now, and no further on. Anyway, back to Professor Humphries. Frank, lad, your idea of tailing the suspects was probably a good one. Unfortunately it appears that Humphries got his call about the time we were having a shift hand-over last night. Yet again, no witnesses, our remaining suspects have no alibis, they could all have done it. A couple of Humphries' neighbours thought they saw someone leaving his house as it was getting dark, but they couldn't tell if it were man or woman. Apparently Humphries has been getting visits from all sorts, journalists, fans, you name it, so a visitor was none too special. He had a delivery by motorbike courier just before that, but that checks out, we've interviewed the rider. Oh, and as for the speedway expert Pete and Bobby pulled up, it turned out to be the vicar, just to add to the general confusion. He claims he was testing his bike out, but it had a problem with the exhaust, muffler not working or summat, which is why it was making such noise.'

'I can vouch for him on the motorbike side,' Frank said. 'When Gertie and I went around yesterday he was working on it.'

'Unfortunately that doesn't get us any further,' Frieda said. 'By the time the racing vicar was waking up the neighbourhood Humphries had already gone to another world. Now Percy's shift didn't manage to interview all the neighbours, some were out, so that's one thing we have to do. Frank, you and Gertie get off and have a word with Phil Walthers straight away, clear up any misunderstandings. I don't want to read any articles about police officers threatening the freedom of the press.'

'And if he won't listen,' Frank said, standing up, smiling, 'we'll hit him over the head with a truncheon until he does.'

'That's enough of your warped sense of humour, Frank,' Frieda snapped. 'I suggest you start taking thing seriously for once.'

Frank looked at her, his smile gone, and walked out.

'Blimey,' said Gertie as they left the station, 'she's in a right temper.'

'Letting this business get to her,' Frank replied grimly. 'But she hasn't any right to take it out on me.'

Gertie said nothing. Frieda obviously wasn't the only getting the hump.

Still, that was one competitor out for the moment. Now all she needed to do was get Susan mad with Frank. That shouldn't be difficult.

'Ah, Sergeant Summers,' Phil Walthers said as they entered the Herald's front office. He was sitting at the reception counter scanning a mock-up of the Herald. 'I was expecting you. Percy might use thugs like Pete Phillips, but I knew Inspector Garold would send around her iron fist in the velvet glove. But I must warn you that your mission will not succeed. I fully intend to publish. I have a duty to my readers, and I refuse to be cowed by threats from an increasingly fascist police force. All that evil needs to succeed is for honest men and women to do nothing.'

Frank smiled.

'Have you finished?' he asked.

'Oh, dear me, no, Sergeant Summers, there is a great deal more I have to say. However I will let you read it in my new special edition which, hopefully, will appear tomorrow. Unfortunately young Sheila is off sick, which does make things a little difficult.'

'You might want to rewrite some of your article,' suggested Frank. 'Adding a bit about how two charming police officers personally popped in to apologise for any misunderstandings that might unfortunately have taken place due to the tiredness of all those involved.'

Phil Walthers looked at him suspiciously.

'I'm still going to print details of that note,' he said defensively. 'The Herald itself being used in the most monstrous crime wave to ever hit Wellbury. I absolutely refuse to miss such an opportunity.'

'Totally understandable,' Frank replied easily. 'I don't blame you. Two special editions in a week. I bet that's never happened before.'

'No, it hasn't,' Walthers replied slowly. 'So, if you aren't here to threaten me with prison, why are you here?'

'Oh, as I said, just to clear up any misunderstandings – and, possibly, to ensure the facts you publish are correct. About the other murders, I mean.'

Walthers eyes opened in surprise. He hopped off the stool.

'Come through to my office,' he said.

'Sheila's off ill, you say?' asked Frank as they followed him.

'Yes,' replied Walthers sadly. 'It always happens this way. First they have a migraine, then they send a letter saying that they've become too emotionally involved with the job and they're moving to London or somewhere. That's why I never let them know about any special enquiries I might be making.'

'Always?' asked Gertie in disbelief. 'All of them?'

'Yes, my dear, all of them. It really is a nuisance.'

Frank sat down as Walthers established himself behind his desk, rubbing his hands in anticipation.

'So, what lovely facts have you got for me?' he asked.

'Not much. Only that almost all the bodies had similar, if not identical, notes on them.'

'Almost all?' asked Walthers in amazement. 'All with cuttings from the Herald?'

'From the very same issue. The list of Wellbury's pet hates issue.'

'But that means ... ' He paused as a thought hit home. 'So that's why you wanted to know how many issues we kept here! Of course!'

'Precisely. Whoever's doing it has access, or had access, to at least six copies so far. If you printed that hopefully someone might remember someone they know buying more than the usual number. Or perhaps they saw someone rummaging in their recycling bins. Or any other possible reason.'

Walthers nodded.

'And the reason you haven't revealed this information until now is that you were concerned about copy-cat murders?' he asked.

'More or less, but we'll have to take that chance now. Any chance of you telling me why you were staking out Professor Humphries place last night?'

Walthers smiled.

'I wasn't staking Professor Humphries' house. I was on my way back from Bagley's residence, nothing having happened, when I spotted your two officers and thought I'd hang around to see if I could find out why they were there. When they took off after that motorbike I thought I'd have a quick look around before giving up for the night. I never expected to find anything, certainly not what I did.'

'Lucky for us that you did – unofficially, anyway. We'll leave you to get on with the special issue.'

'I see I shall have to revise much of what I've written, Sergeant Summers,' Walthers said happily. 'I should have known that Inspector Garold would be much more subtle than to send the rottweilers in. However,' he added, wagging a finger at Frank, 'the article about threats of being arrested under the new terrorism legislation will remain. I might not blame the police force as a whole, but I do have Sergeant Phillips in my sights.'

'Pete Phillips didn't do that, did he?' asked Frank in astonishment. 'Frieda – Inspector Garold will go ballistic when she finds out. Look, Pete Phillips isn't such a bad stick, he's overworked and he has problems at home. Let me have a private word with him, I'll sort it out.'

'Ah, I'm afraid it's too late for that,' Walthers said, embarrassed. 'I posted a letter to the Chief Inspector last night, or perhaps early this morning to be more precise. I'm afraid I was in rather a foul mood.'

'Well, if it was to the Chief Inspector we might have a chance. He's away fishing most of the time. I'll nip into his office and see if I can get hold of it before anyone sees it.'

'I shall rely on you, Sergeant Summers. But only this once. I don't care what they do in London, but Wellbury will not tolerate the erosion of centuries of hard-gained liberal practices and traditions. If you think you have problems now, they will appear minor to what will happen when the little people of Wellbury take to the streets.'

'I'll sort it out,' Frank promised, standing up, appearing more optimistic than he felt. The people of Wellbury were already taking to the streets, and they're weren't practising any liberal traditions.

'Fabulous want to see you,' Eric Johns told Frank when they returned to the station. 'Toute suite, immediately. If I were you I'd put on a fire-proof suit before going in. She's in one hell of a mood. Dragged Percy and Pete Phillips back to the station for some reason. Personally I reckon she's living dangerously, she isn't Chief Inspector yet, and Percy won't forget.'

'Any idea what it's about?'

'None whatsoever,' Eric said, shrugging and turning back to the paper he had been reading. 'And I don't want to know. I intend to keep my head well down. I'm like Switzerland, I don't get involved in other peoples' wars.'

If Eric was avoiding a potential source of gossip, Frank thought as they headed for Frieda's office, it must be bad.

On their way they passed Percy and Pete Phillips. Percy looked furious. Pete Phillips looked shell-shocked.

'Sergeant Summers,' Mary said as they entered, 'you can go straight in. Gertie, you're to wait here until Inspector Garold is ready for you.'

Frank entered Frieda's office in grim mood. If Frieda was looking for a fight she was going to get one, he decided.

'Frank, come in, shut the door behind you,' Frieda said, standing looking out the window.

Frank did as he was bid and stood looking at her back.

'First things first, Frank,' she said, turning around. 'I apologise for snapping at you this morning. It will never happen again. Ever. Understood?'

'Okay,' he shrugged, relaxing, relieved that some form of peace seemed to have broken out.

'I mean it, Frank,' she said, coming towards him. 'I took my frustration out on you, and that should never have happened. It won't ever happen again.'

'Yes, I sort of got the first "never",' he said. 'The job gets to you some times.'

'Forgive me?' she asked.

'Of course. These things happen.'

She smiled, leaned forward and kissed him gently.

'I really shouldn't be doing that today,' she said, 'so don't tell anyone. Promise?'

'Absolutely,' he said, wondering why today should be different, and thinking that he wouldn't object to Frieda kissing him every day.

It would certainly give a whole new meaning to the idea of job satisfaction.

'Right, enough of that. We have work to do,' she said, going to her desk. 'Ask Gertie to come in.'

Frank called Gertie in and sat down in front of Frieda's desk.

'What's wrong with Percy and Pete Phillips?' he asked casually. 'They don't seem to be happy bunnies.'

Frieda smiled thinly and lifted a letter.

'I took a little of my frustration out on someone who did deserve it,' she said. 'This is a letter from Phil Walthers. Pete Phillips threatened Walthers with the terrorism act. I won't have that on my patch.'

'Er, wasn't that addressed to the Chief Inspector?' asked Frank.

'And how would you know that, Frank?' Frieda asked.

'Phil Walthers told us. I think he rather regretted sending it. He's promised to let the thing lie this time.'

Frieda shook her head in amazement.

'Frank, I swear you could walk into a den of angry lions and have them purring within minutes. How did you manage to calm Walthers down?'

'Oh, he's pretty reasonable. I promised to have a quiet word with Pete Phillips. Looks like I'm a little late.'

'Not to worry, Frank. I think both Percy and Pete Phillips now see things my way. Percy was going to laugh it off until I put him right. Pete Phillips is going to personally apologise to Walthers.'

Frank would have dearly loved to have been there when Frieda "put Percy right".

'Percy and Pete aren't essentially bad coppers,' Frieda mused, 'it's just that they don't stop to think of the wider implications, Pete especially. You have to restrain them.' She sighed. 'Ah, well, now that that silliness is out the way, back to the case. Any ideas?'

Frank shook his head irritably, stood up and walked to the window with his hands rammed into his trouser pockets. His automatic response would have been a frustrated "bugger all", but that option wasn't open any more. They had to do something and do it quickly.

There was a buzz on Frieda's intercom.

'Send her through,' she said after Mary had spoken. The door opened and Susan came in.

'Latest report on Humphries,' she said, waving a folder. 'He was hit on the back of his head as he sat in an armchair. Plenty of prints around the place, none of which match anything from the other crime scenes. I hear he recently received quite a few visits from the press and television, plus strange people who wanted to discuss his weird theories, so we haven't much hope of matching them all up, even if our killer was kind enough to leave his own. But we'll do it anyway.'

She paused as she saw something on Frieda's desk.

'Nice photograph,' she noted, picking up the framed

photograph Phil Walters had taken of Frieda and Frank. 'You come out very well.'

There was a chill in her voice which suggested that it was not a totally heart-felt compliment. Gertie moved forward to look. Both she and Susan shot furious looks at Frank's back.

'It is rather good, isn't it?' Frieda said, taking the photograph and placing it on her desk, stroking the frame.

'I wonder if our killer has a sense of irony,' mused Frank, looking out of the window, hands in pockets, oblivious of the optical daggers hitting him between his shoulder blades.

'How so?' asked Susan. 'You mean Humphries being killed by his own theory? Something like that?'

'More or less. His theory is proved by the very fact of him being in the eighty-five percent.'

'I think he was just a fortunate option – fortunate for the killer, anyway,' Frieda said. 'The link between Humphries and door-to-door selling is tenuous, but it might just stand up, and the killer didn't have to wait anonymously in the darkness hoping a salesman would cross their path. That would be too dangerous. Knowing where their victim lived made things much easier. They could plan everything in advance. Don't you agree?'

Frank didn't reply at once. His body stiffened and his hands came out of his pockets.

'Of course!' he said, turning around and looking at them wildly. 'That's it!'

'What, Frank, is what?' asked Frieda impatiently.

'Something Phil Walthers said. He said something about not having a go at the whole of Wellbury police force, but insisted he was going to target Pete Phillips.'

'And that helps us how, Frank? In the context of this slight problem we have with a madman or madwoman wandering around Wellbury, removing examples of the eighty-five percent unwanted, according to a list kindly supplied by Phil Walters.'

'But that's it! It's all wrong. Don't you see?'

'I can see your life is in danger, Frank. Come on, spit it out. Enlighten us lesser beings.'

'Okay,' said Frank, 'where do you hide a tree?'

'In a forest, Frank, in a forest,' replied Frieda. 'Next question.'

'And where do you hide a body?'

'In a cemetery,' said Gertie.

'Correct. And where would you hide a murder?'

There was a pause as the question hit home.

'In a slaughter,' said Susan quietly.

'Precisely,' said Frank. 'This isn't some deranged psychopath cleansing society. One of the murders is the real thing. The others are a smokescreen.'

'Some smokescreen,' said Frieda, standing up. 'Let's get down to the ops room and test this theory out.'

'Nagness,' said Frieda, tapping the photograph of the first victim. 'I can't see anyone going to these lengths to hide her as a target.'

'It's unlikely,' agreed Frank. 'However, it's possible that she saw something that she shouldn't have. Perhaps she told the killer she was going to the police. He or she had to do something immediately. The idea of disguising it might not have occurred to them until just after the deed had been done. But I agree the chances aren't high. The same goes for Chiffon Brady and Wayne Kegglon. They might not have been the best examples of the human species, but I can't see them being a danger to anyone, not unless something unusual happened.'

'That takes us to Damien Hellman. I think he could qualify. He had a record. He was known as a fence. Quite possibly he found out something about one of our suspects that he shouldn't have.'

'Cedric Oldfield was blackmailing someone,' said Gertie. 'Or at least it appears that way.'

'Let's skip Oldfield for a moment,' Frank said. 'Eral Jackson. I think he falls into the same stereotypes as Nagness and Chiffon Brady. Professor Humphries – well, he just looks like a handy victim for the killer. Which leaves us with five possibilities.'

'Five?' asked Susan. 'I count only two – Damien Hellman and Cedric Oldfield.'

'I think that Frank is including the remaining three on the list – politicians, journalists and the police. Not so, Frank?'

'Yes. I don't think we can forget about them. But I tell you who my money would be on.' He tapped a photograph of a shy, elderly man. 'Cedric Oldfield. What I don't understand is why Bagley thought he was such a decent person, whereas it looks like Oldfield was leaning on someone to contribute to his pension fund.'

'Unless that someone was Bagley himself,' suggested Susan.

Frieda checked her watch.

'I have an appointment in five minutes. Frank, you and Gertie get something to eat, then pay Mr Bagley a visit. Have a word with Mrs Blower also, find out what her impression of Oldfield was.'

'If it was Oldfield who was the real target, isn't it likely that the killer won't be in a hurry to finish off the list?' asked Gertie.

'It's a nice thought, Gertie,' said Frank. 'Unfortunately I think the reverse is true. Especially if we're wrong and the real target is one of the last three.'

After lunch Frank sat at his desk, waiting for Gertie to return from the ladies'. He was concentrating on a piece of paper in front of him. He had written the names of the victims on one side and the names of the suspects on the other. Now he was involved in drawing connecting lines between the two, all with question marks against them. Suddenly he had a feeling that he was being watched.

He looked up. A young woman stood in the doorway, hand delicately resting against the frame, blonde hair made up, clear blue eyes, rich red lipsticked lips, a cream skirt-suit with maroon piping, silk blouse, stiletto-heeled maroon shoes, one stockinged-leg cocked slightly in front of the other.

'I'm not disturbing you, am I Frank? You looked totally absorbed there.'

Frank? he asked himself. How does she know my name? How long has she been watching me? Who is she? How could I ever forget a stunner like that?

No doubt someone from the national press who had sneaked by a snoozing Eric Johns.

'Not at all,' he said, standing up. 'I wasn't getting very far anyway. How can I help you, Miss – ?'

'You don't recognise me?' she asked, coming into the office.

'Um, I'm afraid not. I'm sure I would remember such a – um, such a – well, to put it bluntly, such an attractive woman.'

She smiled and blushed.

'I can see my first problem,' she said. 'Frieda said I should keep well away from you. I can see what she meant.'

'Frieda?'

'Your Inspector upstairs. You might remember her. She's rather attractive in her own way. She certainly looks ravishing in that photograph of the two of you.'

'Ah,' said Frank. It was all he could think of saying.

'I owe you a favour, Frank,' said the mystery woman. 'I knew you wouldn't forget. And you didn't. Even though your memory doesn't seem to be working that well at the moment. Does the name Tricia ring a bell?'

'Tricia?' he asked in surprise, looking at her closely. 'From the estate agents? You look totally different.'

'I do, don't I?' she asked, gaily pirouetting and letting her dress fan out for his approval, showing a lovely pair of legs. 'I decided to pull out all the stops to impress Frieda. And it worked. I got the job.'

'Well, that's excellent,' Frank said, rubbing his hands, and then folding his arms, feeling a little of a fool.

'Isn't it just? And I get to see you every day. Won't that be marvellous?'

'Yes, absolutely, marvellous.'

'I must dash,' she said, looking at her watch. 'Like I say, I owe you one. Drinks, sometime?'

'Drinks would be – marvellous,' he said as she came around to his side of the desk and kissed him on his cheek.

'I start next week. I'll see you then,' Tricia said, twirling gaily to the door, almost bumping into Gertie who was just coming in.

'Bye, Frank, see you next week,' Tricia said, waggling her fingers at him before she disappeared.

'Who was that?' asked Gertie suspiciously.

'Didn't you recognise her? Gertie, you should do something about that memory of yours,' Frank said, sitting down and pulling papers towards him as if intent on work.

'Who was she?' demanded Gertie.

'Tricia from the estate agents, of course. Frieda's taken her on to replace Mary when she goes, apparently. She popped in to say thanks for mentioning her name to Frieda. I'd forgotten all about it, to be honest.'

'Frieda's taken that thing on? Is she mad?'

'Mad? In what way?'

Gertie scowled at him. She was about to tell him that he had bright red lipstick on his cheek, but a thought struck her. A smile played around her lips.

'Never mind. She said she wanted to see us before we go.'

'Who wants to see you?' asked Frieda, walking into the office, a smile on her face.

She stopped abruptly at the sight of a smile on Frank's cheek made of bright red lipstick. She looked suspiciously at Gertie. The grim enjoyment on Gertie's face as she looked at Frank, plus the absence of any lipstick on her lips proved that she was not the culprit.

Frieda nodded her head as understanding came.

'Frank, five minutes after I agree to take on a new secretary I find you wandering around with her lipstick all over your face. Allow me to make something very, very clear to you. If you play around with my secretary you will end up wishing you were dead. Capisch?'

'Now hold on a minute,' Frank protested, wiping his cheek with a handkerchief. 'She just popped in to say thank you for recommending her to you. I'd totally forgotten even doing so. You can't blame me because she surprised me and gave me a thank-you kiss on the cheek.'

'Oh, I can, Frank Summers, I can,' Frieda assured him. 'And I will. Gertie, I think you'd better keep a closer eye on Sergeant Summers. Any more of his shenanigans, give him a good slap and bring him to me to finish off the job.'

'Shenanigans?' asked Frank as Frieda made her exit. He looked at Gertie. 'And what are you smirking at?'

'Oh, nothing,' she said, leaning forward to make sure all trace of lipstick had gone. She held his face firmly and gave him a long kiss in the same spot. 'There,' she said, 'that's in its right place now.'

She skipped to the door.

'Come on, Sarge, time to getting talking to Bagley.'

Frank face was a picture of disbelief. Frieda had kissed him. Tricia had kissed him. Now Gertie had given him a good few seconds' worth.

And tonight he was going out with Susan.

He probably wouldn't be entirely truthful with her if she

asked how his day had been.

'Mr Bagley, you said that Mr Oldfield was a very decent man?' Frank asked. They were sitting in Bagley's office at the Blue Bliss.

'Aye, probably the most decent man I've ever come across.'

'Not the sort of person who might indulge in a little blackmail, then?'

'Blackmail? Cedric? You must be joking. Look, I'll show you something.' He rummaged in a drawer and came out with a letter. 'Here, this is his invitation to his retirement do. Read that.'

Frank took the letter and skimmed it quickly. It was very similar to the letter they had found in the waste paper basket. This one read: "In exchange for keeping all the terrible and wicked secrets you have told me over the years, I demand a forfeit, that of suffering my company for an evening on the occasion of my retirement. I hope it will not prove to be an overly onerous payment for services rendered.'

'See?' said Bagley. 'He was the type who was so honest he could joke about it.'

Frank perused the letter once more. What Bagley said could be true. On the other hand exactly the opposite could be read into it. The innocent would see it as humorous. The guilty would understand the true import.

'Mind if I borrow this for a few days?' he asked.

'Aye, if it helps you catch the bastard who killed Cedric. I am not often given to rage. I try to model myself on the forgiveness of the Lord. But for whatever scumbag murdered Cedric I am prepared to make an exception.'

'Would you regard yourself as a consummate politician, Mr Bagley?' Frank asked, standing up.

'If you mean, am I good at it, then yes.'

'You know these murders are following a list published in the Herald a week or so ago?'

'Are they? I never read the newspapers. The bible contains all I need to know.'

'The next on the list is a politician. I suggest you look out for yourself.'

'Ha!' scoffed Bagley. 'I used to be a damn good boxer when I was young. Maybe I use my fists for thumping the bible mostly these days, but I've still got a pretty good left hook. Anyone wants to take me on, they're welcome to try. I shall ask forgiveness of the Lord afterwards.'

'Unfortunately our killer tends to attack people from behind. I'd watch your back if I were you, Mr Bagley.'

'A lovely man,' Mrs Blower said as they sat in her kitchen testing her new recipe for scones with cream and jam.

'A bachelor, wasn't he?' asked Frank.

'Yes, sadly. I'm afraid we women are not always that good in choosing our menfolk. We end up with people like my husband, who was a first class – well, I won't use the word I'm thinking of. And men like Cedric end up on their own. I'm sure he would have made a wonderful husband.'

'Mr Oldfield and the vicar must have got on very well. Being such similar personalities.'

'I don't think they really knew each other, to be honest. The vicar leaves all the paperwork down to me. He dislikes anything to do with paperwork and accountancy, and most of the work Cedric did for us was merely to fulfil legal formalities.'

'Did Mr Oldfield send you an invitation to his retirement do?'

'I haven't received one. I'm sure he would have sent one if it wasn't for ... Well, I'm sure he would have.'

There were tears in her eyes. Frank and Gertie made their excuses and left. Cedric Oldfield must have had something. Mrs Blowers had not wandered from the topic once.

'Could we make a little detour on the way back?' asked Gertie. 'I need to get a photograph for my student card. I've been meaning to do it for ages, and if I don't do it now I'll forget again.'

'Of course. There should be a photo booth on the railway station.'

Indeed there was. Gertie and Frank stood reading the instructions.

'I don't understand this,' Gertie said mournfully. 'Why do they always make these instructions so hard to follow?'

'Seems easy enough to me,' Frank said. 'It says put your money in this slot here.'

'Okay, money in slot,' Gertie said, feeding in pound coins.

'And then you open the curtain and sit on the stool like this,' Frank said, matching actions to the words. 'When you've preened yourself you press the large red button – this one, I presume – and try not to blink as the flash goes off.'

'You always make things seem so easy, Sarge,' Gertie said, climbing in after him and sitting on his lap, closing the curtain.

'Now just a second, Gertie,' Frank said, involuntarily putting his hands around her waist.

'Smile for the birdie,' Gertie sang, pressing the button and leaning back into Frank, holding his hands and pulling them higher.

The first shot was of a happily grinning Gertie and a rather puzzled looking Frank. By the third she had got him to smile the way she wanted. By the fourth she had his hands where she wanted.

It was the sort of photograph which could be easily misconstrued by the more prurient.

Frank didn't notice that the Open University, however tolerant and broad-minded their views, would be extremely unlikely to accept any of the snapshots to grace one of their student cards.

But Gertie was happy. It might not have the sophistication of Frieda's, but she now had a photograph of herself and Frank she could show to their grandchildren. And it would look good next to her bed. And one would look good on her desk at work.

'Frank has come up with a new theory,' Frieda told the two shifts in the ops room. A morose Pete Phillips stood at the back of the room close to the door.

'Not another of the Wellbury Wonder's theories,' groaned someone at the back. There was a ripple of laughter. Frieda frowned.

'This time I believe we're on the right track,' she said. She explained briefly the theory that there was one murder concealed by others. 'We aren't certain whether that murder has taken place or is still due. However, Frank thinks, and both Percy and I agree, that the probability is that the murderer will strike again soon. Percy?'

Percy stood up.

'Next on the list is a politician. Now I know many of you might think that can only be a good thing, but as police officers we need to be impartial. Robert Bagley. He's on our suspects list, but he's also a potential victim, so we'll be keeping a close eye on him over the next few days. We'll have a tail on him, on the editor Phil Walthers – whoever's on that tail, please be very, very circumspect. Mr Walthers already has his blood up, and he'll go for us if we give him the slightest excuse. Finally, Mrs Blower. Any objections, young Frank?'

Frank shrugged.

'Toss a coin time, isn't it?' he asked rhetorically. 'We aren't going to be tailing any other politicians?'

'Too many of the burghers,' Percy noted. 'Bagley's high profile, what with his church and the Blue Bliss. If your guess about Cedric Oldfield is correct, Bagley is a prime choice for blackmail. Any further questions? Right, get off you lazy day-shift. Let the real workers get down to it.'

Pete Phillips stopped Frank as he was leaving.

'I owe you one,' he said softly. 'You dropped me right in it, you bastard, telling everyone I'd threatened that poofter Walthers. Think because you live in Frigid's knickers you can do what you like. You'd better watch out, son, because I will have you. That's a promise.'

At Frank's side Gertie bristled.

'Oh, really, Sergeant Phillips?' she asked loudly. 'The others in the room turned to stare. 'You want to take Frank on? You'll be taking me on too. I'm not like Frank. He's too gentle with shits like you. I'll rip your bloody arms off, and your legs, you —'

'Enough, Gertie, enough,' Frank said, pulling her away. 'I'll see you in our office. Go on, go. Now.'

Gertie left unwillingly. She gave Pete Phillips a foul look as she left, leaving no-one in any doubt that she meant what she had said.

Frank took Pete to one side.

'You've been drinking,' he said. It was a statement of fact rather than an accusation. 'Have you spoken to your wife about a holiday?'

'I was planning it as a surprise,' Pete Phillips mumbled, suddenly aware that he was the centre of attention of the whole room.

'Come on, Pete, let's get some coffee into you,' Frank said, taking his arm. 'I think you might be labouring under a delusion about my telling anyone anything about Phil Walthers.'

'How do you suppose Frank does it?' Frieda asked as she and Gertie stood carefully out of sight, watching Frank and Pete Phillips sitting on the bottom of the stairs at the back of the station, each with a cup of coffee in his hand, exchanging a muted conversation.

'He always understands other peoples' troubles,' Gertie replied. 'It's his own he's not too good at. Not so much his own worst enemy as his own worst friend.'

'Badminton tonight with Susan, I understand,' said Frieda.

'Seems to me that Susan is our biggest problem.'

'Yes,' agreed Gertie bitterly. 'He won't go out with colleagues, and she isn't a colleague. It would make a more level playing field if she was out of the frame.'

'I have every respect for Doctor Death as a professional. However I'm afraid I don't trust her otherwise. I'll bet the only thought in her head is how to bed Frank as quickly as possible. I think we owe it to him to prevent that. A little oil on the soles of her pretty little badminton shoes might do the trick.'

'He's got his sports stuff in the boot of the car. We could do something about that. Nick one of his shoes, maybe?'

'Never look a gift horse in the mouth, Gertie,' Frieda said, smiling evilly.

Frank found Susan waiting for him in his office.

'Have you got your togs with you?' she asked.

'They're in the boot of my car.'

'Why don't we go in my car? That way Gertie can drive home herself.'

'Good idea,' Frank said, thinking how happy it was they all seemed to get on together these days.

'Hello, Susan,' Gertie said cheerfully, walking in.

'Hello, Gertie,' Susan replied. 'We've just agreed that I'll drive Frank to badminton. That way you can have the car to yourself.'

'Oh, goodie,' Gertie replied with enthusiasm. 'That way I can go to Aikido class. I miss too many of them these days. Here, Sarge, give me your keys, I'll put your badminton stuff into

Susan's car.'

They handed their keys over, Frank happily, Susan with a hint of I-don't-like-this in her eye.

'Won't be a tick,' Gertie said.

'Now, Frank,' Susan said, slipping her arms around him. 'A night to ourselves, okay? No shop-talk, no new theories, just you and me, okay?'

'Sorry, I was looking for Gertie,' Frieda said, appearing in the doorway.

'She's shifting my kit to Susan's car,' Frank said.

'Right,' said Frieda, disappearing quickly.

'There's something strange going on,' Susan said.

'Who you gonna call?' asked Frank. Susan looked at him blankly.

'It's from the film Ghostbusters,' he explained.

'I see,' she said, as someone who thought watching Ghostbusters something not normally mentioned in polite company.

'Oh, come on, Sue, lighten up,' Frank said. He slipped his hand beneath her hair onto the nape of her neck, pulled her close and gave her a slow, enjoyable kiss.

'Enough of that, Frank Summers,' she said, drawing away with a smile. 'We'll continue later. Firstly let's not outrage the club by jumping on each other too much.'

Frank sighed and followed her out. The women he didn't want kisses from were more than happy to oblige. The woman he did want a kiss from was worried about propriety.

You just couldn't win.

Unless you betrayed your principles.

But then, as Epicurus would have said, principles are a guideline, not an ideology. If they did not conform to reality they should be discarded.

Or that was, Frank presumed, what Epicurus would have said. Had he thought about it.

'What do you mean, you can't remember which bag is whose?' Frieda asked in frustration.

'I had to repack things to make them fit,' Gertie replied. 'I was in a hurry. I was worried about those two coming out.'

'We'll have to take a quick guess,' Frieda said, unzipping a tog-bag, revealing the underneath of a shoe. She lifted a can and gave it a quick spray. 'Come on, let's get out of here.'

'I know I shouldn't say it,' the woman sitting next to Frank on the bench said, 'but these people being killed – how shall I put it? They aren't the most beneficial to society. Not the sort you would shed a tear over. Not if you were being brutally honest. I know it sounds terrible, and that's how I feel – terrible – about saying it.'

Frank didn't reply immediately. He was watching Susan prepare to receive service in a game of mixed doubles. After each game partners split up to give everyone a chance to play with each other, and with full courts he and two others sat waiting for a game to finish. Susan was wearing one of the smallest skirts he had seen outside of Wimbledon. It should have been erotic, but wasn't. He was watching her calves and thighs, noting how they tensed, thinking that she planned to rush the service. Had he been on the serving side he would have dummied a short serve and whacked it long and high instead, way over her head.

'Sorry,' he said, 'I was miles away. You were saying? About these murders?'

'Ah, of course, you're probably thinking about them all the time. It must be difficult in your job to leave the office behind, I suppose?'

On court Susan's opponent went for the short service only to find Susan smashing the return back at him, the shuttlecock hitting him slap-bang centre of his face.

'It is an occupational hazard,' Frank said, thinking that he would find it much easier to leave work behind if people like the well-intentioned woman alongside didn't bring it up. She called was called Cynthia, a happy mother of three grown-up children.

'Still it's nice to see Susan settling down with someone,' Cynthia said. 'She's always had boyfriend problems, you know.'

'Really?' enquired Frank. It was not the best reference anyone could give. 'What sort of problems?'

'Oh, one doesn't like to gossip, of course, but somehow they never seemed suitable. Too aggressive, if you know what I mean. They didn't really fit in here. We're very much a social club.'

On court Susan's service opponent was trying to staunch the flow of blood from his nose with a small paper handkerchief.

'I can live with that quite easily,' Frank said. 'Obviously you play to win, but the enjoyment is the main thing.'

Inside he was thinking, an early finish, a shower, drinks and then dinner.

'Oh, look,' said Cynthia. 'They're coming off. It looks like Gerald has a nose bleed. He gets them quite often. Still it means we have a court. We're short a lady for mixed doubles. Susan, would you fancy another game?'

'I'd love another game. I feel like I could go on for hours, yet,' Susan said.

Oh, great, thought Frank.

Gertie put her text books to one side. She had done three hours of study, and was feeling ready for a long and peaceful sleep. Except that she knew it wouldn't be peaceful. She felt guilty about trying to sabotage Frank's night out with Susan. Or, to be more precise, she was concerned that, instead of sabotaging Susan, they might have sabotaged Frank.

And if they hadn't managed to sabotage either, Frank and Susan were probably in her cottage right at that minute, canoodling away.

And everyone knew what a bout of canoodling could lead to.

She heard a key inserted into the front door, the door open, and voices come through.

'It's only a ricked ankle,' Frank said. 'It'll be fine by tomorrow.'

'Now, Frank, it could be much worse than that,' Susan said. 'Let's get you into the lounge where I can have a closer look at it.'

Gertie stood up. A limping Frank supported by Susan entered the lounge.

'Frank? Are you okay?' Gertie asked nervously.

'Yes, yes, I'm fine,' Frank replied testily. 'Gertie, there's a tube of muscle rub in one of the drawers in my bedroom. Left hand side, bottom drawer. Could you get it for me?'

'Right away,' said Gertie, who knew precisely where it was, having rifled Frank's bedroom the first chance she had got. Once a copper, always a copper had been her excuse.

When Gertie returned Susan took the tube and began applying the ointment to Frank's ankle.

'What happened?' Gertie asked.

'We were having a game of singles to finish off,' Susan said. 'Frank thought I was going to serve short. Instead I lobbed it over him. And instead of letting it go he tried to turn and follow it. I think he's pulled his ankle.'

'It's only a slight sprain,' Frank insisted. 'It's not even swollen. It'll be fine in the morning.'

'You need something like a whiskey,' Gertie said, relieved that it hadn't been her fault.

'That's the last thing Frank needs,' Susan said emphatically.

'Actually, a whiskey sounds quite nice,' Frank said.

'A beer at most, Frank,' Susan said.

'I can live with that idea,' Frank said.

'One beer coming up,' Gertie said, waltzing out of the lounge.

Susan sighed. She patted Frank's leg.

'I'm sorry. It wasn't supposed to be like this,' she said.

'Accidents happen. Look, you should be getting off home. It's late, and we're all likely to be going to be very busy over the next few days.' A thought struck him. 'What about we have drinks on Friday? Drinks and a meal somewhere?'

She stood up, fumbling with her fingers.

'Um, Friday's out. There's a – a symposium at the university over the weekend. Lots of stuff to get ready before Saturday.'

'A symposium? Anything interesting?'

'Oh, no. Just the usual.'

'The usual?'

'Er, education, I think. Look, what about Monday? I should be free by then.'

'Monday it is, then,' he said, feeling slightly disappointed. It would have been nice to have gone out with Susan on Friday, especially as it was his birthday. He didn't put much store by birthdays generally, but he did like to have someone to go out with when they came around.

'One beer only, Frank,' Susan said as Gertie came in with a glass and bottle. 'Then have something light to eat and get some sleep. And if the ankle doesn't feel right in the morning don't try walking on it.'

'Right you are,' Frank said cheerfully, clearly intending to ignore all her orders.

She sighed, bent down and kissed him.

'You look after yourself, Frank Summers.'

Outside in her car she felt like screaming with frustration. She had had everything carefully planned. At most an hour of badminton. A shower, a declaration that she didn't feel like eating out and why didn't they go back to her place for a bottle of wine which just so happened to be in the fridge. She could throw some food together for dinner, food which also just so happened to be in the fridge waiting to be cooked. And then …

And then she had blown it. She had been on form. She hadn't lost a single game, no matter how dire her partners had occasionally been. Just one more game, she had thought each time, and before she knew it most of the others had left and she was playing Frank at singles. And the idiot couldn't lose gracefully, he had to go for every shot.

Just once, Susan Pleadle, she thought bitterly as she drove off, just once in your life stop thinking of yourself. Just for a few hours.

Back in his flat Frank accepted another beer from Gertie. He never felt hungry after running around. A couple of beers to rehydrate himself, a good night's kip, and he'd feel right as rain in the morning. He knew his ankle. It might be slightly tender when he woke up, but no more than that.

'Gertie,' he said, stretching his back and relaxing happily, 'seeing as how we're likely to be working over the weekend, what say we treat ourselves on Friday evening? Couple of drinks after work and a meal in the most expensive cheap place we can afford? What do you say to that?'

She smiled happily.

'I'd say – Bugger!' she said, her face dropping.

'Bugger?' he asked in surprise. 'Funny sort of a thing to say.'

'No, I mean I can't make it. I've got – er – a double tutorial on Friday night. Probably won't be back until late.'

'Pity. Ah, well, some other time then, eh?'

'Definitely,' she said, cuddling up to him. 'Definitely as soon after Friday as possible.'

So that was Susan out. And Gertie. That simplified thing enormously, Frank thought.

Frieda wouldn't be busy with symposia or double tutorials.

Thursday: The two eyes of green

'The hills are alive, with the sound of music,' Frank sang in the car in the way into work early on Thursday morning.

'Sarge, do you have to do that?' asked Gertie, wincing.

'Ah, my dear Gertie, it's just one of those days it's great to be alive. A wonderful early summer's morning, fresh air, the sun is shining, and I have this strange feeling everything is going to go just right today.'

'Why does that make me think that today is going to turn out to be a very bad day?'

'Now, now, Gertie, no need to be negative.'

'I'm not being negative. I just know that when you get the feeling that everything's going to turn up roses it normally means everything's about to go badly, badly wrong. What about your jacket, for a start?'

During breakfast Gertie had accidentally dropped some jam on his jacket, leaving a stain that meant wearing it to work was out of the question. With two suits already at the dry-cleaners and his other jacket being the comfy sort with the seams going just at the right places – and consequently inappropriate for anything more than a stake-out as a beggar – he had been forced to resort to wearing his black leather jacket.

'Ah, but it's perception, Gertie, perception. I actually like this jacket. It's very comfortable, for a start. I wouldn't normally wear it to work, but now I quite like the idea. So you see, it's turned out well after all. It's just a case of looking on the bright side of life.'

And a tie wouldn't go with the jacket, so he was wearing an

open-necked black shirt that Gertie had encouraged him to put on. With black trousers, Gertie had convinced him it was a good match. It was totally alien to his normal image. It was nice to have a change every so often.

'Just so long as you don't start singing Look On The Bright Side Of Life,' Gertie said, thinking that, the way he was dressed, he would never be allowed into any of the wine-bars or fancy restaurants Frieda preferred. In fact no woman in her right mind would go out with anyone dressed like that. She only wished he had a thick, gold chain to complete the ensemble.

It had taken two attempts to drop that jam in the right place.

'Da-dum, da-dum,' he said, beginning to sing Look On The Bright Side Of Life.

Keith Bute looked up wearily from the reception desk as they walked in.

'All quiet on the Western front, Keith?' Frank asked cheerfully.

'Quiet as the grave, Frank,' Keith replied, blinking at Frank's clothing. He shook his head and checked his watch. 'Cells empty, not a single arrest, not even one stolen car reported.' He sighed. 'Another half an hour and then I'm off duty. Can't come too soon.'

'I thought you liked quiet nights.'

'I do, normally.' He nodded at a hand radio next to him. 'Been listening, waiting for something to go off the whole night. It's like that scene in the Battle of Britain where the pilots are absolutely knackered after fighting the Luftwaffe for weeks, and they're all sitting there in their deckchairs waiting for the next round, but nobody turns up. Worse than something actually happening, it is. Percy and Pete Phillips were prowling around until after midnight. Kept asking Control if anything had happened. Finally they fell asleep in the ops room. Only woke up about an hour ago.'

'I wonder,' Frank said thoughtfully, stroking his chin. Keith gave him a dubious look.

'Not having another idea of yours, are you Frank?'

'Well, I was wondering if this quiet is a response to the news of Humphries getting his turn as an eighty-five percenter. If he's in his own eighty-five percent, the theory starts to look a little strange.'

'I hope you're right, Frank, I certainly hope you're right. It'll be nice to get back to quiet nights.'

'Oh, I don't think we're quite out of the woods yet, Keith. The phrase "the lull before the storm" comes to mind.'

'Cheers, Frank, thanks for the optimistic thought.'

'My pleasure. Come on, Gertie, let's grab a coffee in the canteen before we start.'

'Percy and Pete are in the canteen,' Keith said, 'looking like a pair of refugees who've been tramping through bleak winter nights for months. Wish I'd brought my camera.'

'I think I'll delay the pleasure of seeing their unshaven faces for a short while. A cup from the machine, and then on to the ops room.'

Frank opened the door to the ops room. Inside it was deserted apart from an oblivious Frieda with her back to them. She was poised delicately, a wadded piece of paper in her outstretched hand. She brought her hand back and threw.

The paper flew across the room and landed dead-centre in a waste-paper basket.

'Yes!' she exclaimed softly, punching her fist in the air.

Frank coughed gently. Frieda turned around in embarrassment.

'Ah, Frank, Gertie, um, good morning.'

'Morning, Inspector,' Frank said cheerfully. 'No end to the paperwork, is there?'

Frieda's look of embarrassment turned to one of incredulity as she saw how he was dressed.

'Frank, what on earth are you dressed up as? We'll never get into ...'

'Get into?' he prompted as she fell strangely silent.

'Oh, nothing, I was thinking of something else. But Frank, where's the suit?'

'A little accident at breakfast. Everyone else is at the dry-cleaners. I thought I would adopt a casual pose today. From the sounds of it I might as well have come dressed in shorts and trainers carrying a newspaper to read. Nothing happening?'

'Not quite nothing, Frank. But we don't seem to be short of a politician this morning, as we expected. Bagley didn't move from his house, and no-one else has been found dead.'

'Hardly seems worth turning up to work, doesn't it? Has anyone called on Bagley to make sure he is actually in the land of the living?'

'I'm ahead of you on that one, Frank. Ed Watts and Steve Right are going to pop in on some pretext in the next half an hour.'

She smiled.

'There is some good news, though. Zack the Prat called to ask for police protection – demand would be a better word. He said that number nine was a journalist, and he was obviously the target. I had great satisfaction in declining the request, and suggesting that he should take his own measures if he felt that he was in the eighty-five percent. He announced on radio this morning that he was going into hiding for his own safety.'

Frank grinned.

'Couldn't have happened to a better person,' he said. 'I do so like a bit of irony to start the day. Now that that's sorted, what's our plan of action for today?'

'We are going to review everything we have so far,' Frieda said. 'Every single witness statement, every note taken, every theory. It is entirely possible that our murderer is not one of our main suspects. In fact it is starting to look that way. We won't have a debrief this morning, there's no need. Instead I want you and Gertie to take the Jonathon Humphries case and go through that. I'll be giving different victims to different teams. At eleven we'll get together and go through summaries of each case.'

'Can't we have Oldfield?' Frank asked. 'I'm convinced he's the real victim.'

'That's precisely why you can't have him, Frank,' Frieda said. 'Go on, take the notes to your office.'

On their way back to their office they passed through reception. Eric Johns had taken over from Keith Bute.

'Keith's a lucky sod, got out in the nick of time,' Eric complained, motioning towards the radio Keith had left behind. Voices crackled over.

'Anything exciting?' asked Frank.

'Depends on what you call exciting. This one's a fight in a bus queue. A fight in a bus queue? All my years in the force, and I've never heard of one of those in Wellbury. How can you have a fight in a bus queue? It's unnatural.' He sighed. 'Just my luck.'

'Ed Watts to Control, come in Control,' gasped a voice over the radio.

'Control here, Ed, go ahead.'

'We need a patrol car, quick. Someone's nicked the bus.'

There was a pause.

'Control here. Please repeat your last message, Ed.'

'I told you, someone's nicked the bus. One of the passengers. We're trying to sort out the rest of them, they're trying to have a punch up. We need someone to get after the bus. The driver's having a right go at us.'

'Confirmed, Ed. Can you give a description?'

'It's big, red, looks like a double decker bus, has the number 29 on the front and is being driven all over the place by a bloke in a pin-striped suit with a pink tie. That good enough for you?'

Frank's eyebrows rose.

'Someone has nicked a bus?' he asked. 'Looks like it might be quite an entertaining day.'

An angry looking woman appeared in reception carrying a large leg of lamb.

'I want to see the Chief Superintendent, now,' she demanded.

'Come on Gertie, office, now,' said Frank, hurrying away. Gertie followed, throwing a surprised look behind at the woman.

'Don't you want to know what that's all about, Sarge?' she asked.

'Yes, but from a distance, Gertie, from a distance. It's one of my rules in life. Never get involved with a woman who walks around in public carrying a leg of lamb.'

'Funny sort of a rule,' noted Gertie.

Frank stood with his hands in his pockets, looking out of his office window. They had been poring over the notes from the Humphries case for two hours, and it was time for a break. Gertie had gone to get some coffee and an update on what new misadventures the people of Wellbury were getting themselves into.

'You'll never guess the latest, Sarge,' she said, coming back into the office.

'Constables Allison Hardbury and Harry Wheatley are in love,' Frank replied.

'What? Those two? She can't stand him.'

'Ah, so that's it. I was wondering why she belted him with her handbag.'

'You're joking, Sarge,' she said, coming to the window. Outside an apologetic Allison Hardbury was tending to Harry Wheatley sitting on the ground, holding his head and looking dazed.

'Looks like the excitement is getting to the troops,' Frank commented, sitting down. 'So, what is it I wouldn't guess?'

'You know, I think you might be right, Sarge,' Gertie said, still looking out the window. 'I think she does fancy him.'

She turned and went to sit in the chair in front of Frank's desk.

'They caught the bloke who nicked the bus,' she said. 'He said he was a stockbroker with important business, and he couldn't wait for a bunch of useless old eighty-five percenter pensioners to sort out their argument. He's down in the cells at the moment.'

'A stockbroker catching a bus? What is the world coming to? Anyone else going slightly bonkers out there?'

Gertie began ticking off her fingers.

'A bust-up in Marks and Spencers – in the pastry section. Sid Feeler got a chocolate éclair between the eyes. A dentist has been taken to hospital after his assistant attacked him with a drill. A punch-up in the Hangman, Steve Right almost got hit by a barstool coming through the door as they got there.'

'The Hangman? At this hour? Bit early, isn't it, just after opening time?'

'Apparently it was a barmaid and the landlord's wife. The landlord legged it as soon as they got started. Oh, and apart from that there've been about ten traffic accidents reported so far. From the sounds of it the whole town will be gridlocked in a very short time. Sergeant Johns reckons the whole world has gone mad.'

'Certainly sounds like it,' Frank noted, taking a sip of coffee. 'Under normal conditions I wouldn't mind popping out for a look. Maybe take some photographs for posterity. However, I'm afraid we have work to do. All this nonsense is because of this eighty-five percent rubbish. If we can find out who's behind it maybe the good citizens of Wellbury will wake up and realise they've been conned. Let's take it from when that motorbike courier turned up at Humphries' place. He was still alive then.'

'Six-thirty,' Gertie said. 'Which means that he was probably murdered shortly after then.'

'Hang about, Gertie, it was six-fifteen. Let's be accurate about these things.'

'Six-thirty, Sarge. That's what the notes say.'

'Six-fifteen, Gertie, be a good girl and don't argue with your nice Sergeant, he's beginning to get a headache.'

Gertie scowled at him angrily, stood up, stomped to her desk, rifled through papers until she found the right one, stomped back and slammed it down in front of him. He sighed and read it.

'Well, well,' he said thoughtfully. 'Looks like I owe you an apology, Gertie.'

He rifled through his half of the file and came out with his own piece of paper.

'Ed Watts interviewed the couple living next to Humphries, and they say they saw the courier leaving at six-fifteen. Sid Feeler was talking to the couple opposite. They had just got back from work, noticed the courier, and claim it was six-thirty. So we're both right. You forgive me, Gertie, or do I need to hide from your handbag?'

Gertie blushed and looked down.

'Sorry, Sarge,' she muttered.

'No matter, Gertie, some of this excitement outside is probably getting to us. However, listen to this: Ed's lot describe a motorbike courier wearing leathers, riding what was probably a red bike – though they couldn't be sure, but they did remember the company logo on the back of his jacket, which is why we were able to confirm their story so quickly. Sid's lot, on the other hand, say they saw, and I quote: "Someone on a motorbike delivering a parcel". No logo, just a leather jacket, and they say the bike was white.'

'Two couriers?'

'One courier and A. N. Other,' Frank corrected. 'Very sloppy, Gertie, very sloppy, this should have been picked up at the time. That's what happens when you rush around the whole time, getting tired and achieving nothing. Ed, or Sid, probably told the other that the neighbours had seen a courier. The other replies that that's what they've just been told, they don't stop to compare descriptions, and neither did we. Come on, let's go have a word with the second lot, see if they can remember some small detail, like a number plate or the exact details of our second man's face.'

As he was about to stand up the phone rang.

'Yes, Eric?'

'He what?'

'Look, give him a cup of tea and a sticky bun and tell him I'll see him later, tomorrow or next week.'

'Okay, okay, Eric, I'll be there shortly.'

He put the phone down.

'Our Victor Brown wants to see us,' he told Gertie, standing up and putting up his jacket. 'Something trivial, no doubt, but Eric Johns wants him out as soon as possible. He says the place is already overloaded with people in the process of being brought in, there isn't any space left for the innocent. He's put him into interview room two. Let's give him a quick smile, a pat on the shoulder, and kick him out.'

Victor Brown jumped up when they walked into the interview room.

'Gawd, Mr Summers, I ain't half relieved to see you. I'm in deep trouble. I need some of that police protection, like now.'

'Vic, you're more likely to get a police boot up your backside. What did I tell you about the fake accent?'

'Okay, sorry Mr Summers, really I am. But I mean it, someone's gonna to try to kill me.'

Frank sighed and sat down. Victor Brown followed his example nervously, his eyes locked on Frank's face.

'Okay, Vic, I'm listening. You have one minute.'

'Thank you, Mr Summers, I knew you was a true gent.' Noticing the look on the true gent's face he carried on quickly. 'Look, there's this bloke I knew in London, Sebastian Sykes, only no-one called him that, he hated the name. It was Mr Sykes to his face and Psycho Sykes when he wasn't around. He was a real mean piece, evil, that's what he was, pure evil. I reckon he wanted to be worse than them Kray brothers. People he didn't like ended up dead.'

'I think we've got the picture, Vic,' Frank said. 'One evil psycho named Sebastian Sykes. Why should we be interested in him?'

'I mean it, Mr Summers, bad isn't the word. He had the sort of smile that would freeze hell over, you kept well away from him if you knew what was good for you. Educated, too, kept quoting Shakespeare or someone. Anyway,' he continued hastily as Frank checked his watch, 'And then I seen him this morning, here in Wellbury. Didn't half give me a turn. Petrified I was, shaking in me boots. You see, he seen me too. An' I know he recognised me. Gave me that funny smile of his. "Victor", he says, "what a delightful surprise, we must get together sometime for tea and tiffins". So I say, "yes, we must", and leg it as soon as I could.'

'So what you're saying is that he threatened you with a dangerous cup of tea? Victor, I know we live in an ever changing world, but I don't think they've quite made that an offence, not yet, anyway.'

'No, you don't see, Mr Summers. Before I gets away, with me life, but only just, he tells me not to worry, 'cause he's got religion since we last met. Said something about following the path of the light. Only I know he's lying, see. Last I heard of him he'd been sent down for life. Drugs, prostitution, property scams, you name it, couple of the competition got done, not very nice either. No way they'd let Psycho Sykes out. He must have escaped somehow. Now he's here and I'm here and he knows I knows he's here and I knows he ain't gonna do nothing. You've got to help me, Mr Summers, please, I'll do anything.'

'Just a second, Vic, you say this Sebastian Sykes was into property?'

'Yeah, that's one of the things they got him on, he was laundering money through property. Only he needed a dodgy estate agent to fiddle the paperwork. That's how they got him. They picked up the estate agent and he sang like a canary. Wasn't long before they had most of his mates banged up, them singing as well soon as the coppers told them someone was going to go down for the murders and they'd do quite nicely.'

Frank stood up quickly.

'Thanks, Vic. Come on Gertie, we have someone to see, very

urgently.'

'Here, what about me?' asked Victor Brown plaintively.

'Ask Sergeant Johns to arrest you for aggressive use of a fake cockney accent in a built up area during daylight hours,' Frank replied.

'But there ain't room in your cells,' pleaded Victor.

Frank was just about to open the door when Frieda came marching through.

'Frank. I need you to go around to Bagley's house. None of uniform have been able to make it. They're too busy trying to cope with what appears to be mass hysteria.'

'Just where we were on our way to,' Frank said cheerfully. 'I think we should be able to clear up this mess in a short while.'

'What's he doing here?' asked Frieda belligerently, noticing Victor Brown trying to hide in his seat.

'Helping us with our enquiries,' Frank said.

'Morning, ma'am,' Victor said, standing up and tugging his forelock. 'Always 'appy to be of assistance to the brave men in blue.'

Frieda looked at him as if he were something she wouldn't like to find on her shoe.

'If you ever tug your forelock at me again, Mr Brown, I will rip your head off your shoulders and use it as a football. Get going, Frank.'

'On our way,' Frank said. 'Mr Brown has something to tell you that you might be interested in,' he added as he and Gertie raced off.

'I doubt it,' Frieda said, looking at Victor Brown. She turned and marched out of the room.

'Whole world's gone bleeding crazy,' moaned Victor Brown to himself.

He looked at the open door. Quickly he closed it and locked it. He returned to his chair and began to roll a cigarette.

When the world's been taken over by the nutters the safest place for an honest criminal was inside a police station.

'I've always wondered why Kegglon had that stake hammered into him,' Frank said as they neared Bagley's house. 'Either it was done to confuse us, or there was a reason. Sebastian Sykes was dropped in it by his dodgy estate agent. He escapes, turns up in Wellbury as Robert Bagley, buys the Blue Bliss, gets back into property dealing, becomes a councillor, starts preaching the good word, confuses everyone because he seems a contradiction. No-one would imagine that he's actually a con on the run. Except for Oldfield. He found out something about Sykes, thought he'd try a little blackmail, didn't realise what he was taking on. Bagley, or Sykes rather, has no compulsion about killing. He comes up with this plan to hide Oldfield's murder amongst the list of ten. He just had a bit of added fun with Kegglon.'

'You sure it's Bagley, Sarge?' asked Gertie as she parked a few doors away from Bagley's house.

'Absolutely. Remember what Vic Brown said about Sykes getting religion? And the eyes?'

'But, if Bagley is Sykes, shouldn't we wait until we have some backup? He doesn't sound the type to come quietly.'

'Oh, we aren't going to arrest him, not yet,' Frank said. 'We're just paying a polite visit to make sure he's okay. After all, the next victim is supposed to be a politician, and Bagley hasn't been answering his phone, so we're a little worried. I just want to make sure that he hasn't scarpered, and that he thinks we haven't a clue about him being Sykes. Soon as we've made sure of that we find a nice quiet place to watch his house, radio to the station and organise about eight people, maybe ten. I don't know how we're going to get them with all the nonsense that's going on, but they'll have to be spared somehow. When we take Bagley, or Sykes rather, it's got to be out in the open. While he's walking to his car, something like that. You'd have to be mad to try to take someone like Sykes indoors.'

'Just be careful, Frank, I don't like this.'

'Smile, Constable Gregson, we're two plods having to carry out orders which we think are a waste of time. Let's go give Bagley our best performance. He's probably watching from behind the curtains, trying to work out whether we're after him or just carrying out a routine visit.'

There was no response to the doorbell, nor to the heavy rapping of Frank's knuckles on the door.

'I told you it was a waste of time, Constable,' he said in a voice loud enough to be heard on the other side of the door. 'Mr Bagley is probably at his office or somewhere, or at the Blue Bliss trying to work out those accounts of his. Might as well get back to the station and get on with some real work.'

'But Sergeant, the Inspector told us to make sure Mr Bagley was okay,' Gertie replied in an equally loud and unbelievable voice. 'Maybe he's out in the back garden and can't hear us.'

'I suppose you're right, Constable. We'll check around the back just to make sure.'

The side garden gate was open. They walked around with

heavy footsteps, making sufficient noise to convince anyone listening in the house that they were two heavy-handed plods totally ignorant of any idea that a madman might lie in wait.

There was no-one in the over-grown back garden. They walked up steps to the kitchen door. Frank peered through the glass.

'Hang about, Gertie,' he said softly. He chuckled. 'He's sitting inside with his head on the table. There's a bottle in front of him, looks empty to me. I reckon he got himself totally sozzled last night. His head isn't going to feel too good when we wake him up.'

He tapped lightly on the glass. The door swung open. Frank looked at it, puzzled. He was about to step in when he noticed something. He put out an arm to stop Gertie from stepping inside.

'Something wrong here,' he said. 'See those?'

Gertie looked and nodded. The kitchen floor was tiled. There were muddy footprints criss-crossing the floor, all unmistakeably from a woman's shoes.

'Looks like someone came in from the back garden,' he said. 'Stay here, Gertie.'

'No, Frank,' she said, grabbing his arm. 'He might wake up and have a go at you. I'll go.'

'Stop it, Gertie,' he said, prising her fingers from his jacket. He patted her hand. 'I have an awful feeling that our Mr Bagley isn't going to have a go at anyone, ever.'

'I'm not with you, Sarge.'

'Just stay here.'

He stepped carefully into the kitchen, trying to avoid the

footprints. He took three long strides and looked down at Robert Bagley. Bagley's eyes were open, looking surprised. Dead surprised. There were sickeningly familiar signs of his head having been hit several times with a blunt object. Frank felt for a pulse. There wasn't one.

He patted his pockets, looking for his radio. He swore. He'd left it in his flat, in his jam-flavoured jacket.

'Gertie, call the station. Tell them that Bagley's the killer's latest victim. Tell them we need forensics around here right away. And a uniform to stand outside and look pretty.'

'Just one uniform, Sarge?'

'Just one. One's enough.'

He turned slowly, looking around the kitchen. Something lay half-hidden under the door of a kitchen cabinet. He knelt down to take a closer look.

He smiled to himself.

He stepped out of the kitchen with the same care he had taken in entering.

'They're on their way, Sarge,' Gertie said. She looked at him. 'You're looking pleased with yourself.'

'Am I? I shouldn't be, seeing as I got everything totally wrong. Could I borrow your mobile for a second?'

Gertie handed her mobile over. Frank looked at the tiny thing with a frown.

'How do you dial with these little buttons?' he asked.

Gertie sighed with exasperation and took the mobile back.

'Who do you want, Sarge?'

'Frieda.'

Gertie pushed a few buttons and handed Frank the mobile.

'Frieda? Frank here. Listen, we're at Bagley's place. You've probably heard about Bagley.'

'I've just heard a few seconds ago. What's going on, Frank? I thought you said you were going to sort this mess out, not find another victim.'

'A little misunderstanding. Listen, did you speak to Victor Brown?'

'I don't have time to exchange social chit-chat with petty criminals, Frank.'

'I told you he had something to say to you,' Frank said with irritation. 'Why didn't you listen?'

In her office Frieda looked at her phone in disbelief. Sergeant Frank Summers was daring to criticise her?

'Listen,' Frank carried on, unaware that he was now last on Frieda's most favoured list. 'Victor Brown recognised someone he knew in London, a man called Sebastian Sykes. Apparently he was a pretty nasty character, got sent down for life.'

'I am aware of Mr Syke's reputation, Sergeant Summers. Also that he escaped from a high security mental prison several years ago – an extremely devious and intelligent psychopath. I seem to recall England beat Germany two-one the night he escaped. Otherwise his escape would have been more widely publicised. You're going to tell me that Robert Bagley is Mr Sykes, no doubt.'

'No. That was the first conclusion I jumped to. But now Bagley is lying in his kitchen with his head split open, gone to the great paradise in the sky he was always on about. But you remember how we kept coming across footprints from a woman's shoes at almost every crime scene? There are the same type of footprints in Bagley's kitchen. And half-hidden under a cabinet door is a brooch with a dove on it, one that Mrs Blower usually wears.'

'Mrs Blower? She's our murderer?'

'Oh, no. That's exactly what our murderer wants us to believe. Mrs Blower is in great danger. We have to get to her before the murderer does.'

'And you know who the murderer is, of course. Perhaps you'll deign to let us mere mortals know, when you feel you have a few seconds to spare.'

'I know who it is. If I'd stopped to interview Vic Brown properly as I should have done I wouldn't have jumped to the wrong conclusion. He said that Sykes told him he had got religion. What he would have said, had I asked him what Sykes looked like, is that Sykes was wearing a dog-collar.'

'The vicar?'

'Sykes pretending to be a vicar. How that happened I don't know, but I think we'll find the real vicar's body lying hidden somewhere between here and London. At the moment we've got to arrest the vicar – Sykes – as soon as possible. We're going to check on Mrs Blower. Get a vanload of men off to the vicarage, Sykes isn't going to come meekly.'

There was a pause before the explosion.

'Sergeant Summers, you will never, ever try to give me orders again, understand? You and Gertie will look after Mrs Blower. I will look after Mr Sykes. And when you get back we are going to have words.'

Frank winced as the sound of Frieda's phone crashed down in his ear. He looked at the mobile.

'Yes, Inspector. No, Inspector. Three bags full, Inspector,' he said, and handed the phone back to Gertie.

'Trouble, Sarge?'

'I think I'm dead, Gertie my dear. Frieda wishes to have words with me after we've sorted out this little lot.'

'Oh, dear, that's terrible,' Gertie said, trying not to smile.

They turned at the sound of someone coming around the side of the house. Susan appeared, carrying a metal case. She stopped at the sight of them.

'Is that you, Frank? Or has the Lone Ranger come to town? Or maybe it's Zorro.'

'Very funny, Susan. It seems to be criticise-Summers'-dress-sense day. Come on, Gertie, we'll pick up my radio from my flat on the way.'

Susan watched them go, a sad feeling tugging at her heart. She had only been teasing him, he didn't have to fly off the handle like that.

Frank ran up the steps to his flat. Inside he switched his radio on to make sure it was working.

'We need more men, Control,' Ed Watts was saying.

'Steve to Control, Steve to Control, come in Control.'

'Control to Steve, wait your turn. Ed we haven't anyone to send, you're going to have to deal with it yourself. What's your problem, Steve?'

'They're murdering each other here, Control. Traffic's jammed up for miles and they're having an open-air boxing competition, only with more than just their fists. We need another three cars and a van, at least.'

'Oi, we asked first,' Ed interrupted.

'Ken to Control, Ken to Control, urgent, over.'

'Oh bloody hell,' said Control.

Frank switched the radio off and slipped it into his jacket pocket. He had enough to worry about without that racket. He raced back down the stairs.

Inside reception Eric Johns blew his breath out slowly as he relaxed for the first time that morning. The competing voices on the radio next to him told him that it wouldn't be for long.

'What the hell's going on?' asked Frank as they approached a T-junction. The road ahead was jammed with cars, a single traffic officer desperately trying to sort the mess out, directing people off the main road and into the empty leg of the T, people who refused to listen.

'Hang about, Gertie,' he said, getting out of the car. He strode up to the traffic officer. 'Sergeant Summers,' he said, showing his warrant card. 'What's going on here? We're in a hurry. We need to get to Lords Acres immediately.'

'You'll be lucky,' the traffic officer said bitterly. 'I'm trying to sort this out on me own, none of these bastards will do as I tell them, even though they can see there's no way they're moving if they stay on this road. They won't go down where you've come from even though they can see that's their only chance. Total breakdown of law and order. Never seen anything like this before.'

'We've got to get through,' Frank said. 'It's a matter of life and death, literally.'

'And you are literally not going to get through this way, mate. You'll have to go the long way. Unless you've got a helicopter in the boot of your car.'

Frank had to admit he had a point. The traffic was more than bumper-to-bumper, cars were trying to bump the one in front out the way. Hooters were going, there was much shouting, and there were already two slugging matches under way. Standing on his driver's seat poking out of a sunroof was a young, long-haired man with a bible in his hand, calling on his impromptu congregation to repent. In a horsebox an amused horse was looking out, watching one of the fights with some interest.

Frank jogged back to where Gertie was waiting.

'We aren't going to get through there,' he said, 'we're going to have to ... '

His eyes lit on the traffic officer's motorbike parked at the side.

'You go around the long way, Gertie, I'm going to borrow a motorbike,' he said running towards the machine.

'No, Frank, you can't do it,' Gertie pleaded, struggling out of the driver's seat.

'Needs must when the devil drives, it's the only way to get through,' he called back, starting the engine.

'Frank! Frank! Stop!' she cried running after him.

'I'll return it as soon as I can,' Frank called as he passed the astonished traffic officer.

'Why didn't you stop him?' Gertie asked the traffic officer. Silence fell upon the traffic jam as they watched him steer a path between the cars, revving the engine and lifting the front wheel off the road.. One of the sluggers recovered sufficiently to deal his opponent a surprise and a winning blow.

'Go for it, brother!' called the young man with the bible. 'Jesus loves you!' The horse neighed approval.

'He can't do that,' said the traffic officer.

'He just has,' pointed out Gertie.

'But – that bike's dangerous. I hit a pothole. The front wheel has a wobble. The brakes are dodgy as well. I was taking it back when I got this emergency call.'

'Great, just what I bloody wanted to hear,' Gertie growled as she ran back to her car.

She pulled her radio out of her handbag.

'Gertie to Inspector Garold,' she called, 'Gertie to Inspector Garold, come in Inspector.'

''Ere, you can't do that,' Control said in surprise. 'There are procedures, you know.'

'Inspector Garold to Gertie. Go ahead,' came Frieda's voice.

'Blimey, I suppose she can,' someone else said.

'We got stuck at a traffic jam on the way to Mrs Blower's house,' Gertie said. 'There isn't a way through. Frank's borrowed a traffic officer's motorbike – without his permission. What he doesn't know is that the front wheel's loose. And the brakes don't work. We've got to stop him before he kills himself.'

'He what?' asked Frieda. There was a pause. 'Right, I'm closer than you. You turn around and make as good a time as you can. I'll try to cut him off before he gets to Lords Acres. Go Gertie!'

'I'm going,' Gertie said, wheels spinning as she executed a U-turn on the same spot.

Some drivers stuck in the traffic jam watched. Suddenly one

decided that Gertie had the right idea. Another followed. Then another. The traffic officer watched in amazement as the jam began to untangle without his assistance, Gertie disappearing into the distance, blue light flashing, siren clearing the road ahead.

'Okay, Control, I'm still in charge,' Frieda said over her radio as she ran down the stairs. 'Anything happens you let me know straight away.'

'Er, okay, Inspector,' came back a meek voice. 'Can we start using our radio again, please?'

'Don't try to be clever, Control, or I'll use your testicles for table tennis.'

'Understood,' Control said quietly.

There was a few seconds silence.

'Um, Control, about the extra bodies we asked for,' Ed Watts began.

Control told him where to put his extra bodies.

'Susan?' Frieda asked on her mobile phone as she climbed into her Range Rover, tossing the blue light onto the roof.

'Frieda? What's up?'

'Frank's stolen a traffic officer's motorbike. He and Gertie were on their way to Mrs Blower's. The bike's got something wrong with it. We've got to stop him before he has an accident. I'm coming in from the Old Town. If you come in from the University we should have a better chance of cutting him off.'

'I'm on my way,' Susan said.

Sergeant Eric Johns stood in reception and shook his head. He had followed the latest exchange on the radio. He had never heard anything like it in all his years. He closed his eyes, hoping that he was having a bad dream.

'Any chance of a cuppa tea?' asked a voice in front of him. He opened his eyes to find Victor Brown standing there.

'You still here? I thought you left ages ago.'

'Fell asleep in the interview room, didn't I? Ain't half parched, I am.'

Eric Johns rubbed his eyes wearily. Frank nicking traffic officers' motorbikes. Fabulous taking over the radio. Civilians asleep in the interview rooms. The cells full to bursting. More on their way.

He took some coins from his pocket.

'There's a machine back there that does half reasonable tea,' he said. 'You can bring me one while you're at it. White, two sugars.'

Frank wished he knew where the switch for the light and siren on the bike was. He was going too fast to start playing around with switches to see what they did. At one point he fancied he felt the front wheel wobble, but dismissed the thought. No traffic officer would ever go out with a bike that was less than one hundred percent serviceable.

He hadn't had this much fun in his whole life, he decided.

"'Beware the demon angels three

Beware the twin cycles of the machine

Beware the two eyes of green

Beware the fate that sets you free,"' Gertie repeated to herself.

She took a corner on two wheels. She knew the demon angels. They were named Gertie, Susan and Frieda. She knew the twin cycles of the machine. Frank was sitting on them.

They had to stop him before he came across the eyes of green. Whatever those were.

Doctor Wood's head rose as the sound of a car being over-gunned shattered the academic peace. He looked out of his office window to see Susan's MG reverse, skid, and roar off.

He sighed. Susan had always been a bit of a tomboy, a bit excitable and too ready to run around. He had hoped that the young Frank Summers would be a calming influence. Unfortunately Susan seemed to have lost interest in the young man. Such a pity.

Eyes of green, thought Frieda, eyes of green. What the hell were the eyes of green?

Load of absolute rubbish, she told herself.

Frank was out there racing to disaster.

Unless she could work out what the eyes of green were before he found them.

The fate that sets you free had an all too obvious explanation.

'Used to be a great place, the Smoke,' Victor Brown told Eric Johns. 'Do a job in the afternoon and go to the theatre in the evening. Lovely, it was, 'til they started bringing all these extra laws, coppers with guns everywhere. Downright dangerous, it is.'

'Ed to Control, I was first in the queue,' crackled the radio.

'You went to the theatre?' asked Eric in amazement.

'Your custom is very important to us,' said Control, 'please hold and one of our agents will be with you shortly.'

'Too right. I love the theatre. Course I had to go in disguise, mind, I'd have lost me reputation if any senior coppers saw me there. Most of us grew up together, you know. Thick as thieves we were.'

'Allison to Control,' a weak voice said over the radio.

'Funny thing about Wellbury,' Eric said reminiscently. 'Everybody complains when they get posted here, but after a few months they don't want to leave.'

'Control, it's my turn,' insisted Steve Right.

'Allison to Control,' came the weak voice again. 'Please help ...'

Eric Johns and Victor Brown looked at the radio. A look passed over Eric's face.

'You'll just have to wait your turn, Allison,' said Control.

Eric picked up the radio.

'This is Sergeant Johns,' he said loudly. 'Clear the air. No-one is to say anything unless I say so. Repeat, no-one is to say anything. Come in Allison. Come in Allison. Over.'

You are playing with your pension Sergeant Johns, Frieda thought. She reached for her radio to impose her control.

'Allison to Control ... to Sergeant Johns ... to ... the vicar ... Sykes ... we didn't ... Harry's not moving ... need an ambulance ... '

'Shit!' thought Frieda to herself. She had told Control to send two uniforms to pick up the vicar.

A vanload of men, Frank had said. Instead she had sent just two.

'Control, get an ambulance organised straight away,' she snapped into the radio. 'Allison, report your position.'

'... vicarage ...'

'Okay, Allison, hold tight, the ambulance will be with you shortly. Where's Sykes?'

'... gone ... got away ... sorry ...'

Sorry be damned, thought Frieda. It was her fault. Two uniforms down and now Sykes knew they were on to him.

'All units,' she said into the radio, 'abandon what you're doing now and head for the vicarage. Immediately.'

She tossed the radio aside as she came screaming up to a junction.

She swung the wheel left, cat's eyes in the road giving added traction as the Range Rover began to skid.

She only saw a flash of white before the motorbike ploughed into the side of the Range Rover. It hit it a glancing blow, the front wheel trembled, and the bike and rider shot on, shedding panniers and pieces of metal, heading for the pavement and a brick wall. The bike shuddered momentarily as it hit the raised pavement and both black-clad rider and bike lifted and flew over the wall.

Frieda brought the Range Rover to a juddering halt.

Cat's eyes. Eyes of green.

No, she thought, it couldn't be.

'You heard what the Inspector said,' Control said. 'Everyone to the vicarage. As in now.'

There was a silence as they all waited for someone to point out that the order was perhaps a little too hastily given. And impossible to execute.

Sod that, thought Gertie as she screamed down a narrow street. There was only one thing she was going to do, and that was find that bastard before he killed himself.

'Um, Inspector?' Control asked. 'Um, Inspector?'

Frieda's radio lay on the passenger seat. No-one was listening.

Frieda ran across the road and up a driveway. Beyond bushes to her right she could see an old man bending over the body of someone in black wearing a leather jacket. Beyond lay the mangled ruins of a motorbike. The man looked up as she ran towards him. He stood up and advanced towards her, holding his arms out.

'There's nothing you can do,' he said. 'I'm afraid he's dead.'

'Get out of my way,' Frieda shouted. 'Frank! Frank!'

The old man gripped her and held her firmly.

'I'm a doctor, my dear,' he said gently. 'Retired, now, but I still have all my faculties. There's nothing you can do. He's dead.'

'Let me go!' Frieda screamed. She was looking over the doctor's shoulder at a the body. The crash helmet lay at an angle which left no doubt that the owner would never ride anything again.

'Sorry about this,' the doctor said. He leaned back and brought his hand whipping across Frieda's face. She looked at him in surprise.

'No,' she said. 'No, it can't be.'

'You're in shock,' he said, pulling her away. 'Come up to the house and have a nice cup of tea. I'll call an ambulance and the police. I'm sure it wasn't your fault.'

Frieda pulled her arm away and looked back.

'I am the police,' she said. 'And it was my fault.'

She stood silently for a while, looking at the dead body. Then she began walking back down the driveway, shaking.

The doctor watched her go in puzzlement. With all his experience he never ceased to be amazed at the way people reacted to shock. He hurried to his house.

The police indeed.

Frieda walked drunkenly back to her Range Rover, staggering every so often.

'Control to Inspector Garold,' the radio was saying. 'Come in, Inspector.'

Frieda took the radio from the passenger seat and leaned against the side of the Range Rover. She took a deep breath.

'Frieda to Gertie,' she called softly. 'Come in Gertie.'

Eric Johns' eyes almost fell out. "Frieda"?

'Gertie to ... Gertie here, over.'

'Where are you, Gertie?'

'I'm coming up to the Old Town now. I should be with you in twenty minutes.'

'Pull over, Gertie.'

'Sorry?'

'I said pull over, Gertie. Stop the car.'

'Yes ma'am, if you say so,' said Gertie, applying the brakes. 'Car stopped, ma'am.'

Frieda took another breath.

'It was an accident,' she began, trying to get the words out.

'An accident?' asked Gertie.

Frieda felt the tears coming, swallowed and tried to control her voice.

'Eyes of green,' she said, feeling an urge to laugh hysterically. 'Cat's eyes in the road, Gertie, cat's eyes in the road.'

'Cat's eyes?' asked Gertie.

'Frank's dead, Gertie. He clipped the side of my car. He hit the pavement and went over a wall. He didn't have a chance. He just went over. Just went over.'

All over Wellbury police officers listened to this with disbelief.

In reception Eric Johns and Victor Brown looked at the radio, each with a rollup half way to their mouths.

Control was silent.

Ed Watts looked at his radio. Behind him the fights continued.

Steve Right looked at his radio.

Gertie stared at the windscreen in front of her.

'Control?' asked Frieda, slowly slipping down to the road.

'Control here, Inspector,' Control said softly.

'Tell everyone to sort out what they're doing at the moment. Then we're going after the vicar. His real name's Sebastian Sykes. He's a murderer. He's the reason Frank's dead. The gloves come off now. Use whatever force is necessary.

Unnecessary force is also an option. Anybody hesitating to do what an officer tells them to do is breaking the law. Break any heads if that happens.'

'Yes, ma'am,' replied Control.

Frieda let her hand and the radio slip down on to her lap. She didn't hear Control say "You heard the Inspector, lads". She was beyond caring about anything.

Gertie slumped against the steering wheel. Slowly she forced herself upright. Frieda needed company. She needed company.

Miles apart police officers drew out their truncheons.

'Right, you sons of bitches,' said Ed Watts.

'You asked for this, you bastards,' said Steve Right.

Across Wellbury recalcitrant citizens became vaguely aware of a new threat. Two motorists indulging in a wrestling contest paused, looked around and found a belligerent Ed Watts coming towards them.

'Oh, shit, I'm out of here,' said the one, rapidly disengaging.

'Wife's expecting me,' muttered the other, running for his car.

Susan changed down a gear as she took a bend. She'd be in Lords Acres within three minutes.

'I'll be happy to get out of here,' Victor Brown said to Eric Johns. 'At first I thought it was my idea of heaven. The Old Town, open fields, pretty old houses, the river and canal ... But – well, Mr Summers was a diamond geezer, you know? A diamond geezer.'

'He was that,' agreed Eric Johns. 'Somehow Wellbury won't

ever be the same. I was going to retire here, but now ... Cornwall sounds nice.'

'Give me a few moments alone with this Sykes bloke,' Pete Phillips said, buckling in next to Percy. 'I'll teach him what tough is. He won't need to come to trial. It's his fault Frank's dead. I'm going to sort Sykes out, whatever anyone says.'

'You might find yourself in a queue,' Percy replied. 'Anyway, I thought you hated Frank.'

'Nonsense. Best mate a bloke could ever have. And fuck the queue. I'm going first.'

'You might find three people ahead of you,' said Percy.

Pete Phillips considered this for a moment.

'Yeah, but I'm first after them.'

Frank swore. There was definitely something not right about the bike. The front wheel was playing silly buggers every so often. The brakes were a bit ropy as well. At times it seemed as if the bike bounced and he was floating in open air. Almost amidst the clouds, if he let his fancy run away with him.

Still, he'd be at Mrs Blowers in two minutes. Less, if he really gunned it.

And he really felt like really gunning it.

Gertie saw Frieda's Range Rover. She pulled up behind it. She got out and walked around to where Frieda was sitting, dazed. Gertie sat down next to her and took her hand.

'It's all my fault,' Frieda said listlessly.

'It's all of our faults,' Gertie said. 'You, me, Susan.'

427

'I should phone Sue.'

Gertie thought about this.

'Best leave it for a while,' she said. 'She doesn't need to know yet.'

'I've always hated wearing black.'

'I don't think I will ever wear anything else again.'

The last bend, Frank thought, leaning with the bike. It was a narrow road with no pavements, and tall hedges bordering the tarmac.

He frowned as he saw two eyes suddenly appear a hundred yards ahead, seconds away. Green eyes.

The cat wandering across the road paused at the noise, looking towards him with its head twisted slightly in curiosity at the sight.

Oh, no, he groaned to himself, not another bloody puddy-cat.

One minute, fifty two seconds, thought Susan. So long as I get there before Frank I can save him.

And he'll be eternally grateful to you? asked a caustic voice.

Well, something like that, she admitted, embarrassed.

It was him or the cat.

Tough luck, kitty, was his second thought.

Unfortunately his first was to jettison the bike and roll away. The wobbling front wheel and useless brakes made the question academic. He flung himself away from the sliding motorbike. He knew the drill from experience. Let go, don't let the bike fall on your leg, roll away from it.

Instead he wasn't rolling away but sliding away. The bike passed one side of a curious cat, Frank the other. He could feel the tarmac ripping his leather jacket to pieces.

Concerns for his jacket evaporated as he saw he was headed directly for a hedge. He tucked his head in, made obeisance to the god of four-letter words, and stiffened as he entered a good old-fashioned privet hedge head first.

Susan geared down for the final bend. In less than a minute she would be at Mrs Blowers'.

She came around the bend to watch in disbelief as a delivery van scrunched over the remains of a police motorbike.

Frank? she thought. Oh, please dear God, no, not Frank.

She brought the MG to a screeching halt and ran over to the van. The van driver was alighting in shock.

'I tried to stop,' he said. 'I tried to stop, he went straight under. I couldn't do anything about it!'

'You mother fucking son of a bitch!' Susan cried, bringing her fist back. She swung a wild punch into the van driver's face.

He said something like "Glwow?" and slumped against the van, slowly slipping down.

Susan looked around. A few yards away a cat sat looking at the sight.

A cat with green eyes. Two eyes of green.

'Frank?' she called to the underneath of the van, unable to keep her eyes off the cat. 'Frank, are you okay?'

Brambles. He hated brambles. First the bloody motorbike

going beneath him, then the tarmac taking half his smartest leather jacket, then the hedge ripping his face and hands to pieces. Now it was brambles reaching out and tearing his clothes.

He staggered forward, holding his left arm which no longer appeared to want to work. At least he had arrived at the right address. He stood at the front door and looked at it malevolently after it failed to open in response to his banging. One kick, he thought.

The bright side of his brain kicked in and suggested he try the handle first. He did. The door was open.

'Mrs Blower?' he called softly.

No answer.

'Mrs Blower?' he called again, moving towards the sitting-room door, holding his arm, aware that Sykes could be lurking, probably was lurking, in the shadows. He opened the door quietly. Mrs Blower was slumped in an armchair, one arm trailing over the side. Frank stepped in quickly, checking for anyone hiding behind the door. Apart from Mrs Blower the room seemed empty.

Mrs Blower seemed to be fast asleep. He shook her roughly, but there was no response. A bottle of tablets and a notepad lay on the coffee table. He picked up the notepad and read the first few lines.

"All I have done was to protect the reputation of the church and our parish. I realise now that there can be no forgiveness for my actions in this world."

He checked the bottle of tablets. Sleeping tablets.

So that was your way out, thought Frank. Get Mrs Blower to take down your own confession, slip something into her tea, and everyone would presume it was her own confession. Mrs Blower wouldn't be alive to deny the story.

He checked for a pulse. There was one, but very weak.

'Sorry about this, Mrs Blower, but I'm about to do something a little undignified to you.'

He dragged her out of the sitting room to the downstairs bathroom. He pushed her head into the toilet while holding her waist between his legs. He took a toothbrush from a glass on the windowsill and inserted it carefully into her mouth, forcing her to retch, holding her head gently to prevent her choking.

Then he took his radio out and switched it on.

'Summers to Control, Summers to Control, I'm at Mrs Blower's house and I need an ambulance urgently.'

'Bit late for an ambulance, Frank,' Eric Johns said sadly.

Then he did a double take and looked at the radio intently.

'It can't be,' said Frieda incredulously, looking at the radio in her lap. She picked it up and turned up the volume.

'Control to ... Control here, identify yourself, caller.'

'I've just told you, Control, it's Frank Summers here. Stop pissing around and get an ambulance around here right away. I've got Mrs Blower between my legs here and she's in a bad way.'

Frieda jumped up.

'That has to be Frank. No-one else would admit anything like that over the radio.'

'But you said – ' Gertie started.

'Just a second, Gertie.' She flicked the transmit switch on her radio. 'Control? Inspector Garold here. Stop, as Frank puts it,

431

pissing around and get an ambulance out to Mrs Blower's house.' She switched off transmit. 'Now, Gertie, let's see who the person is who has been pretending to be our Frank.'

They hurried up the drive and around the bushes. Frieda knelt over the body and turned the crash helmet slightly. Sebastian Sykes alias vicar Parsons' unseeing eyes looked back at her.

'Frank wasn't wearing a crash helmet,' Gertie noted.

'It's Sykes!' Frieda exclaimed, jumping up. She looked at the remains of the motorbike. 'That motorbike isn't white,' she said, 'it's pale blue. Gertie, it's Sykes, Frank must be alive.'

They hugged each other deliriously.

'Come on, Gertie,' Frieda said. 'Let's go give that wonderful son of a bitch a hand. I'm not sure whether I'll hug him or hit him. Probably both.'

The retired doctor looked out of his front window and shook his head in disbelief. He had seen many strange things in his time. But he had never seen two women dancing a jig next to a dead body before.

Good thing the police had promised to get there as soon as possible.

Just before Mrs Blower's drive Frieda pulled up as she found Susan peering underneath a van calling 'Frank? Frank?' A bemused looking man sat against a hedge watching her, holding his jaw.

'He's up at the house,' Frieda called.

'At the house? The bastard, I've been killing myself with worry, thinking he'd been run over. I'll murder him when I find him.'

'There's a queue in front of you,' Frieda said as she drove on.

They found Frank sitting on the front steps, nursing his arm, morosely watching two paramedics pushing a stretcher into an ambulance.

'She'll be okay,' the one said, shutting the doors. 'But I reckon you could do with a look at.'

'I'll pop in later,' Frank said.

'Suit yourself, Sergeant.'

The ambulance began to move away as Frieda, Gertie and Susan drove up in a three-car cavalcade. They were out of the cars before the engines had stopped running. Frank found himself at the centre of a scrum.

'Ow! Careful! My arm hurts like bloody hell.'

They stepped back. Susan began to investigate his arm.

'Frank Summers, you have a lot to answer for,' Frieda said.

'I know, I know. I suppose I'll be paying off that motorbike for the rest of my life.'

'Oh, stuff the motorbike. Why didn't you radio in when I told everyone you'd been killed?'

Frank's mouth fell open.

'You did what?' he asked.

'You didn't have your radio on, did you?' accused Gertie. 'How many times have I told you to switch your radio on?'

'Hold still, Frank,' Susan scolded, 'I can't get a proper look at your arm if you keep moving around like that.'

Frank looked at Frieda mournfully.

'Permission to leave the force and become a monk,

Inspector,' he asked.

Frieda laughed and gave him a gentle kiss.

'Permission denied, Sergeant Summers. Susan, you get him off to hospital.'

'Before you do that, my turn,' said Gertie, giving him a kiss. Susan smiled and followed suit.

'Come on, Frank, stop acting like a little boy,' she said, taking his good arm gently.

He shook his head in bewilderment and allowed himself to be dragged away. By rights they should be very, very angry with him. Instead they were treating him as the hero of the hour.

The anger would come later. He intended to be far away by that time.

Friday: The demon angels three: plus one

Frank woke up late, feeling as if his body had been through a mechanical meat-tenderiser. He found a note on the coffee table in the lounge from Gertie saying that she hoped he had had a good night's sleep and reminding him that the doctor had signed him off duty for the next week, to get a good day's rest, and that she'd see him later that evening if he was still up but he really should have an early night and take care of himself.

He could have done with someone to take care of him. A hot bath helped some of the muscles unwind, but there were plenty of others still sulking. Dressing with only one useable arm proved to be an interesting if painful exercise, but he managed it inside an hour.

While he was making coffee his mother phoned to wish him happy birthday and complain that she had phoned the station to do the same only to find out that he'd been involved in a terrible accident and why hadn't he called her himself when he knew she worried about him all the time and was he looking after himself and she was coming down to see that he was looking after himself and eating properly and not surviving on those terrible take-aways she knew he was so fond of.

He only just managed to get a word in edgeways to assure her that it was a very minor accident, only a few cuts and scratches, and she needn't worry, he was eating very well and had a new girlfriend, a trained nurse, who was taking care of his every need, plus she was a great cook, almost as good as her, if such a thing were possible.

His invented new girlfriend served the double purpose of

calming his mother and suggesting that she wouldn't be helping this new relationship by coming all the way to fuss over him. It also reminded him that it was actually his birthday and so far he had no-one to celebrate with.

After his mother had called he sat down to watch television. Within half an hour he was so bored with inane quiz shows and talk shows involving girls whose boyfriends had run off with their mothers or a passing badger he switched the television off and tried to read a book, but found his concentration continually slipping.

About midday the phone rang. It was Frieda.

'Frank, I hope you're resting,' she said.

'Well, I was watching television,' he said, 'but I found myself hitting my head against a wall every so often to feel some pain, just to relieve the tedium. Why is morning television so dire?'

'Probably to keep down the number of sick days, I would imagine. Most people would rather be ill at work than have to endure morning television. Listen, Frank, I know you're supposed to be taking things easy, but I need you to come in and sign a few papers.'

'The motorbike, I suppose. I knew I was going to get into big trouble about that.'

'Er, yes, that's it,' Frieda said hesitantly. 'It's about the motorbike. But don't worry, Frank, I've squared it with the Chief Constable. He agrees that it was a matter of life or death, and it was the best thing to do under the circumstances. He's even talking about a medal.'

'A medal? Blimey, next time maybe I'll nick a riot-control vehicle. I'd get the George Cross.'

'Now, now Frank. Speaking of riots, everything's quiet as the grave here. According to a news report on the radio – prepared by Zack the Prat's assistant Julia, who seems to have taken over from him – the firm action I took in ordering my officers to enforce law and order as strictly as necessary was the determining factor in calming the situation down. I think that's a diplomatic way of saying I told everyone to get out and belt the bloody lights out of anyone who looked as if they were thinking of sneezing the wrong way. Oh, hold on a sec.'

There was the sound of a fifty-pence piece joining a number of its colleagues.

'Where was I? Oh, yes, so I'm also in the Chief Constable's good books. Though personally I think it was the news that the whole thing was perpetrated by Sykes that quietened everything down. I rather think the good citizens of Wellbury are going around looking a little shame-faced now they realise they were taken in by a bogus professor and a psychopath.'

'Speaking of Sykes, how are Allison and Harry?'

'They're fine, Frank, thank god. I think Sykes was in too much of a hurry to get away. He got in a few good punches, jumped on his motorbike and shot off as fast as he could.' She paused. 'I should have listened to you Frank. I'm sorry.'

'I wouldn't worry about it. We were all losing it a little, I think. It happens when you let events take control. How's Mrs Blower?'

Frieda laughed.

'Very, very unhappy. Physically she's fine, she discharged herself from hospital last night – I think Sykes underestimated the number of tablets it would take to kill her. But she's fuming that she let Sykes con her for so long. Apparently, if he were still alive, he would have a fatal accident with a pair of flared jeans and a Hawaiian shirt.'

'Any idea how Sykes managed it?'

'We know there was a real vicar Parsons who was supposed to take over at the vicarage. Our latest guess is that he was on his way when he picked up Sykes – hitchhiking, possibly. Sykes found out that no-one in Wellbury had seen the vicar, and took an incredible chance by taking over his role. He pretended to be a meek and mild old duffer – cutting his hair short and dying it grey. Everyone thought Mrs Blower was in charge, but he was actually using her to avoid meeting anyone who might have known the real vicar Parsons. An incredibly devious, intelligent and dangerous man.'

'Let me guess. Cedric Oldfield did send an invitation to the vicarage, and Sykes found it before Mrs Blower. The problem was that he didn't know Oldfield. He thought it really was a blackmail attempt. That Oldfield had found something out about him, or suspected something. I should have realised. I thought we were looking for someone who knew Oldfield well, we should have been looking for someone who didn't.'

'Well, that's the current theory. The alternative is that he was a murderous psychopath who had had enough of playing the part of being an absent-minded vicar.'

'Pity Vic Brown didn't see him earlier. Ah, well, that's the way things go, I suppose. When do you want me to come in?'

'I'll be busy most of the day. Can you make five o'clock this afternoon?'

'No problem, I'm not doing anything. I was thinking of picking up my dry-cleaning just for a touch of excitement. Hey, I might even walk in this afternoon. The exercise will do me good.'

'No you won't Frank, it's far too far for you to walk in your current condition. I'll send a car for you. I am not going to have you tiring yourself out unnecessarily. Understood?'

'Yes, ma'am!'

'You're obviously not feeling too bad, playing with your life like that, Frank.'

A thought struck him.

'Well, if I'm coming in at five, what do you say to a few drinks afterwards? Maybe dinner?'

'I'd love to Frank, but I've got a meeting this evening. All inspectors in the area, that sort of thing. No doubt I'll spend most of the time trying to stay awake and pretending to be interested in someone else's statistics. You go straight back home afterwards and rest, Frank. That's an order.'

He sighed.

'And I always obey orders,' he said.

'That will be the day!' snorted Frieda. 'See you later, Frank.'

He put the phone down. He would do as Frieda ordered and stay home that evening. But that didn't mean he couldn't have someone drop in for a few drinks and a take-away pizza.

But who? Frieda had a meeting. Gertie had a double tutorial. Susan had a symposium to prepare for.

Sometime between then and five o'clock he would have to come up with an idea. He was not going to spend his birthday watching television by himself. Not if he could help it.

There was a knock on his door at quarter to five exactly. He opened it to find an attractive young woman police officer in uniform.

'Sergeant Summers? I'm Constable Harvey. Inspector Garold sent me to pick you up.'

'Come in Harvey,' Frank said with a smile. 'I was just getting ready. You're new to Wellbury, aren't you? Do you have a first name?'

'Constable Harvey will do, Sergeant. I'm on loan for a week from the neighbouring division. And I'm engaged. I'm getting married in a month. Inspector Garold warned me to keep my eyes on you and not let you sweet talk me or charm me into doing anything I shouldn't. I'm to take you to the station, and then straight back here after you're finished.'

'Your fiancé's a lucky man,' Frank said, leading the way into the lounge.

'That's exactly what the Inspector said you'd say, Sergeant,' Constable Harvey noted.

'Inspector Garold exaggerates a little. You couldn't give me a hand with my jacket, could you? It's a little painful when I try to put it on.'

'And then he'll do the little boy hurt bit and ask you to help him with his jacket, Inspector Garold said.' She looked at him critically. 'However, since it does look like you've taken a bit of a beating, I'll oblige.'

She put his jacket around his shoulders gently. Coming back round to his front she straightened his tie.

'I can see why Inspector Garold is worried about you, Sergeant Summers. I think I should get you to the station as fast as possible. You can sit in the back.'

'I never sit in the back,' Frank protested.

'Inspector Garold's orders.'

Frank was beginning to think that Frieda was getting a little carried away with giving orders. Yesterday must have gone to her head.

'Hello, Eric, still beavering away?' asked Frank as they entered reception. He turned to Constable Harvey standing behind him, making him feel nervous. 'Why don't you get yourself a coffee?'

'I'm to make sure you don't get lost or have an accident,' Constable Harvey replied, not moving.

'Now I know how prisoners feel,' Frank grumbled to Eric Johns. 'I'm thinking of going to the gents and slipping out the window to escape. Except Frieda would probably kill me.'

'Ah, I have a message for you from Fabulous,' Eric Johns said, picking up a note. 'She sends her apologies and says she can't make it. She adds, "Make sure Sergeant Summers goes straight back home. Do not let him wander around. Do not let him talk to any strangers. Do not let him play with any sharp objects. Do not let him slip out for drinks with anyone".' He looked at Frank with a smile. 'Seems to cover most things, I would say.'

'Sounds like she's getting a little carried away. Has anyone mentioned that I'm old enough to tie my own shoelaces these days?'

'She wants to protect the hero of the hour. Here, you didn't half give us a shock yesterday. We all thought you'd copped it. I was about to get a collection going.'

'Sorry to disappoint, Eric. I'll try harder next time.' He turned to Constable Harvey. 'Come on, we'll take the scenic route back. I have a little time to spare this evening.'

She nodded.

'That will assist me in getting to know the area,' she told him.

Great, he thought. I was hoping for a drive with a pretty young woman. Instead it looks like I'm going to be giving instructions on Wellbury's roadmap to a robot.

Constable Harvey dropped him off outside his flat an hour later. To his surprise she did not insist on accompanying him inside. Probably worried I might try to seduce her, he thought bitterly as he walked up the stairs.

He wandered into the lounge, dropping his jacket on the couch, wondering whether he should crack open a beer or not. Some instinct made him turn around suddenly. He almost had a heart attack.

'Happy birthday to you,' Frieda, Susan and Gertie began singing, 'happy birthday to you, happy birthday dear Frank.'

They came forward and he found himself showered with kisses. Gertie took his jacket to hang up in his bedroom cupboard where it wouldn't get creased. Frieda made him sit down. Susan poured him a glass of wine.

'Not too much, now,' she said. 'Alcohol and painkillers don't mix very well.'

'That's okay,' Frank said, 'I haven't had any painkillers since last night.'

Susan frowned at him. Then a smile crept across her lips.

'Okay, I'll let you get away with it Frank, just this once, just because it's your birthday.'

'I think it's time for the birthday boy to open his presents,'

Frieda said.

'Presents?' asked Frank, his eyes open like a ten year old. 'You shouldn't have.'

'I know,' said Frieda. 'We shouldn't have. But we did. Here you go, this was Gertie's idea.'

Frank took a small parcel from her, wrapped in bright paper. He opened it carefully with one hand.

'Oh, wow! This will take pride of place on my mantelpiece,' he said, looking at a book entitled The Coming Wave by Professor Jonathon Higgins.

Frieda and Susan stood up and pulled a large, wrapped box around from the side of the couch.

'We didn't think we'd be able to afford this,' Frieda said. 'But Mrs Blower called up this morning wanting to show her appreciation for your saving her life. When I told her it was your birthday she insisted on contributing. Go on, take the wrapping off.'

Frank began tearing away the wrapping as they held it for him. Gradually it revealed itself.

'Oh, wow and wow again!' he said, looking at a box that informed him it contained an electric piano of the latest and most sophisticated technology.

'We'll set it up for you, Frank,' Frieda said. 'It's far too heavy for you in your current state. Come on, girls.'

Frank stood up and watched the three assembling the small piano and speakers, sipping his wine happily, being told to shush as he tried to add helpful suggestions. The thought crossed his mind that this had to be his happiest birthday ever, even beating the one where he had just turned ten and

Mary-Anne gave him a passionate kiss behind the bushes.

'There you go, Frank, your own piano, just the right size for your flat,' Frieda said. 'Give it a go.'

Frank tried a few keys with his good hand. He played a few bars of Beethoven's Fifth. He turned and looked at each of them.

'I think I must be the luckiest man in the world,' he said.

'Shush, Frank,' Frieda said as they all blushed. 'Come, sit down now, you mustn't get too excited.'

Frank let Frieda and Susan take his arms and gently propel him back to the couch. Gertie replenished his wine.

Then the phone rang.

'Ah, I'd better get that,' Frank said, struggling to rise as Frieda and Susan held him back.

'Nonsense, Frank,' said Susan. 'It's probably a double-glazing salesman at this hour. Let them talk to your answering machine.'

'No, really, I'll just take it quickly and tell them not to disturb us again,' insisted Frank.

'Sit!' ordered Frieda as the sound of his recorded voice told them that he was presently unable to attend to the caller and would the caller be so good as to leave a message and he would return the call as soon as humanly possible.

'Frank?' said a young woman's voice. 'It's Tricia. I'm running a little late. I should be at your place in half an hour. See you then. Love you, byeee!'

Frank looked up as three faces turned back from looking at the telephone to inspect his own face.

'Look, I can explain ... '

End of Book Two

Other novels by Bill Dughaille:

The FFSG series (aka the Wellbury Chronics)

Summers

The first in the FFSG series.

Detective Sergeant Frank Summers is a man on a mission: to keep his head down, stay out of trouble and enjoy the relaxed atmosphere of the easy-going, genteel town of Wellbury, his new posting. It's a town just made for him, where, he believes, even the criminals take bank holidays off. But, while perceptive in his professional life, he tends to miss the subtleties in his private life. In this case he fails to realise that his own tranquillity is being threatened by three women and a philanderer. The fact that the women in question are his boss, his constable and the local pathologist adds just the touch of danger to his life that he had hoped to avoid. The philanderer has been dead several decades. The women are very much alive. And ticking.

Fakes, Fraud and Deception

The third in the FFSG series.

Detective Sergeant Frank Summers is in the doghouse, despite having recently arrested an internationally sought con-artist. And since he is in the doghouse he has no intention of pointing out that there is something very strange about the attractive French police woman who has come to interview the arrested man, not to mention the two detectives claiming to be from Scotland Yard. Oh, no, he is going to stay well out of the way this time. Definitely.

Jokers

The fourth in the FFSG series.

The doctors have pronounced Detective Sergeant Frank Summers physically fit following recovery after his shooting, but his colleagues fear that his sense of humour was extracted along with the bullet. They are, as always, more than willing to interfere in his life in the pursuit of a good cause. If that wasn't enough, a bunch of criminals calling themselves the Joker Gang are laughing at him, the university students are creating mayhem during their rag week, and someone called The Shocker is trying to kill him. The only advantage is that it take his mind off of the ultimatum the three women in his life have given him, one that he has only until the Sunday to resolve. Or leave town.

Prophecies

The fifth in the FFSG series.

Detective Sergeant Summers is under a hex, otherwise known as his colleagues. First they don't want him to get married, then it is imperative it must happen. Then they decide that a prophecy has been made which threatens the wedding. They don't believe in prophecies, but aren't sure that prophecies understand that. So they'll have to Do Something About It. And if their bumbling efforts aren't enough to ensure he never makes it to the altar, he has to cope with visiting aliens and resident ghosts. He does have tiny Squishy to protect him, but what match can even this plucky little kitten be against a prospective mother-in-law?

Loonymoon

The sixth in the FFSG series.

The Inspectors Summers have tied the knot and embarked on their honeymoon in a small family-run hotel in Normandy. She has very definite ideas of what she wants out of a honeymoon: to set a seal on their love, and to form a foundation for life-long devotion. He just wants to nick a French police officer's kepi. He had a Bobby's helmet nicked from him once by a French girl while he was on crowd duty one New Year's Eve in London, and now he intends to return the favour. Neither is about to achieve their aim unless they can solve the mystery of the woman in the bath and the missing heroin. Which means pitting their minds against the French Inspectors Simenon. That's Mr and Mrs Simenon, whose marriage has gone beyond the rocks and is now beating itself to death against humdrum reality. One or either or both or neither could be the guilty crumpet. More importantly, is their marriage a portent of what could become of the Loonymooners? Ultimately the decisive question could well be: which side do the peas go?

Others:

The Window

Jim Allbright, ex-bobby and now easy-going window washer, innocently responds to an advert for window washing placed in the newspaper by the local council. The response is a torrent of paperwork, political correctness and a computer system doing exactly what it was told to do, but not quite what was intended. But if the system cannot be beaten, the interchange of letters can be used to have a little fun and get to know some of the people struggling behind it. There's Sandi, who signs herself as "(pp the Administrator)"; her four-year old little angel Helen; Graham, a shadowy computer programmer who definitely has too much time on his hands, and a slew of Project Managers and Senior Administrators eager to ensure standards are upheld no matter how many problems they create. Against a run of bad luck and circumstances Jim and Sandi aim to meet up one day, eventually. Hopefully. The window might even get washed. Maybe.

Diary of a Sane Man

In a cross between 'Last Of The Summer Wine' and 'One Flew Over The Cuckoo's Nest', set against a backdrop of the brave new world of New Labour's end of honeymoon, Fred is the Last Cynical Optimistic Realist.

Believing that he's found the perfect niche – three square meals a day plus all the newspapers he can read just for occasionally pretending to be mad – he's not going to be the one to rock the apple cart. Oh, no.

Safe from the wiles of women and the woes of the world, he's not going to rock the boat. Oh, no.

No, he's just going to sit and observe, and comment quietly on the insanity of life outside.

Well, maybe just little one tug of the loose strand of wool on life's jersey ...

Did you know they elected a monkey as mayor in Hartlepool?

The Weekend At Longwood

A whodunnit in the classic sense, set against the backdrop of World War II and the trials, tribulations and romances of nine suspects.

A group of friends get together during the last weekend of August 1939 at the rural retreat named Longwood, just a few miles from Portsmouth. They are there to celebrate the last time they will see Georgina Riley, famed American novelist and socialite, for some time, as she is scheduled to leave for her native New York in order to marry her childhood sweetheart. During the afternoon they good-humouredly assign to each other the most suitable names of the nine muses, the daughters of Zeus and Mnemosyne:

Calliope: the muse of epic poetry and rhetoric

Clio: history

Erato: love poems and mimicry

Euterpe: lyric poetry

Melpomene: tragedy

Polymnia: hymns to the gods and heroes

Terpsichore: dance

Thalia: comedy

Urania: astronomy, astrology and prophecy

The following morning Georgina is discovered in her bedroom covered in blood, her throat slit, barely alive. Her American maid is dead. A tiara Georgina had been flaunting the day before has disappeared.

Detective Inspector Rudman arrives to investigate. But with Georgina in a coma and no solid evidence there is little he can do apart from haunt their lives. With Germany's invasion of Poland a week later they disperse across the land, some to the air-force, some to the army, others to reserved civilian jobs.

But Rudman does not give up. Wherever they are he can be found. Whatever other duties he is tasked to, he will find time to keep tabs on them. Whatever the defeats and victories of the Allied cause, he has only one aim: to find the person responsible for the murder done that weekend in Longwood.

The war ends; some of the Muses have survived, some not. Some have prospered, some married, some matured, others have found despair. And then comes invitation to spend another weekend at Longwood. The message is that Rudman has found the evidence he has been looking for.

And so one of the surviving couples motor slowly down to Portsmouth, remembering the original weekend, the trials and the tribulations of the past years, and wonder: what will be revealed during the coming weekend at Longwood?

Firelight

A modern-day tale of an ordinary family gathering at Christmas; the good, the bad, the dysfunctional and the forgotten.

George Browne and his wife Winifred have retired to a large, run-down pile in the country. Rumour has it that it was once the abode of a mad aristocratic family with a penchant for Satanism, and that both they and their victims still haunt the corridors. Other rumours are that it was a lunatic asylum for much of the nineteenth and twentieth century, and bodies of the inhabitants are buried around the large gardens in unmarked graves.

The Brownes are an unremarkable retired couple who, depending on who you might ask, have bought it as an investment, or alternatively as somewhere with enough bedrooms to accommodate their children, grand-children, and the little baby great-grandchildren. Too often in the past excuses have been made at special times, the most common of which has been of the "I don't want to put you to any trouble" variety. That excuse can no longer hold water.

Now it is approaching Christmas. Winter has set in, but the house is snug with oil heaters and real fires. As the various relations arrive, or don't arrive, it becomes clearer why invitations might have been refused in the past. The men of the family believe in having their way. The women of the family are strong-willed in their own different ways, and have various means of getting what they want.

The guests of the family - friends, boyfriends, girlfriends, wives and husbands - discover that their partners have a totally different side to them as the explosive hatreds of long-nurtured fights and feuds simmer to the surface before quickly boiling over.

One evening Winifred Browne encourages them to each tell a story as they sit in the lounge with the large fire warming them, the television off, no access to broadband, computers or mobile connections. Reluctantly at first they begin. As each evening passes: with different members taking turns, they announce in stories the feelings and hopes they cannot voice in public.

Finally it's the turn of Winifred Browne. Her story will be the one that tells them who they are, where they come from, and maybe why they have turned out the way they have.

For further details on these visit:

www.dughaille.info